RO

SKYFALL MOUNTAINS

DRAGON PEAKS

NUSKA

The Great Divide

The Shallows

JAARIN

Dorsal Mountains

RED RIVER

SIORA

Isles

AARAN

YOVAR

THE FOREST

TERRATT

TARYN

THE
STORM
GATHERS

THE STORM GATHERS

MAELAN HOLLADAY

INIMITABLE
BOOKS
UNFORGETTABLE STORIES

Published by Inimitable Books, LLC
www.inimitablebooksllc.com

THE STORM GATHERS. Copyright © 2024 by Maelan Holladay.
Map copyright © 2023 by Grayson Wilde.
All rights reserved. Printed in the United States of America.

Library of Congress Cataloguing-in-Publication Data is available.

First edition, 2024
Cover design by Keylin Rivers

ISBN 978-1-958607-02-2 (hardcover)
10 9 8 7 6 7 6 5 4 3 2 1

To my favorite chess partner.

TRIGGER WARNING

Murder, graphic violence, discussion of genocide, kidnapping, depictions of drowning, mentions of attempted suicide, depictions of choking on air and water

PROLOGUE

E mira Zaya, Queen of Okaro, stood in a graveyard filled with her kin. Her line had ruled this island since Extoir the Great first graced her shores. Not once had Emira believed that she would be the last of the royal Zaya line. She had done everything right. *Everything*.

Arya would have been a perfect queen. Kind and beautiful and strong, she had had the potential to lead Okaro into a new age. Instead, her body lay encased in stone.

Emira looked down at the smooth coffin buried halfway into the ground. It was a black stone, not the white of former kings and queens, and that color alone seemed to mock her. She wanted to rage. She wanted to rip this grave-yard apart and force the twins of Life and Death—Etresyum and Etrim—to return her daughter to her. But they were not gods and they could not hear her, and so she stood in silence and mourned all that never was.

She ran a hand over the grave. It was clean, but it wouldn't remain that way for long. Dust would gather until it was washed away by the frequent storms, only to gather again. It was a cycle, endless and unforgiving.

Emira couldn't stand it. This knowledge of ruin and decay that would fall upon them. Her daughter. Her country. Her. She couldn't stand to think of it. And so, she fled the city of dead.

She made it halfway to the palace before her feet drew her to a halt beside the cliffs. The Western sea was spread before her, dotted with white caps and ships. Slowly, her gaze rose to the horizon—the white line that separated sea and sky. On the other side of that horizon sat Alana. The new

Queen of Jaarin, and Emira's second-born.

Emira clenched her fists and turned her head to the captain of her guard, Victor. "Is it done?" she asked.

The man stepped forward. "I am not certain, Your Majesty. We received a package from councilman Bane. It awaits you at the palace."

Emira frowned. "A package?"

"Yes, Your Majesty."

"Why would he send a package?" A simple letter would be confirmation enough of the woman's death.

"I do not know," he admitted. After a moment's pause, Victor cleared his throat and said, "You know I will always support your decisions, Your Majesty. However, I hope you do not fault me for expressing an opinion…" When she did not stop him, he hesitated a moment longer, then continued, "Perhaps we should have waited until Alana had produced an heir. That way your House would live on."

"And give her the opportunity to make a play for my throne?" She shook her head. "We did the right thing in killing her. If the Zaya line is to end, it will end with me."

Victor bowed his head. "Of course, Your Majesty." He returned to the guards' formation.

Emira kept her eyes on the ocean.

Each time a new leader of Okaro was crowned, a Starreader offered a prophecy foretelling their reign. It was a formality used to appease the elder generation—it wasn't supposed to mean anything. Yet, thirty years later those words still haunted her.

"*I see a coin,*" the Starreader had said, "*a beautiful maiden on one side and a dragon on the other. It spins through the air but has yet to fall. On which side will it land?*"

The crone had smiled at the queen with sharp, white teeth and a tongue painted black. "*One will save the world. One will destroy it. And both will come from inside your womb. No matter which, there will be disaster. I see ships painted in flames. Castles toppling to ash. Armies smothered in darkness. The world consumed. And still, the coin falls, spinning through the air.*"

THE STORM GATHERS

You will try to stop the coin—I see that too—but it will slip through your fingers. The stars foretell it."

Emira had never believed in the fortunetellers before. Never believed that the turnings of the world could be easily mapped out in the heavens... until Alana was born. Each boom of thunder that night had seemed to echo the Starreader's laugh.

The maiden—Arya.

The dragon—Alana.

She prayed to the gods that the latter was dead. In truth, she should have killed her daughter long ago. There was something strange about that girl. Something that reminded Emira of the xygriths that roamed Okaro's coast and the electricity of a coming storm. There was a darkness that lurked in her. Something that did not belong in their world. Something that would destroy it if left to fester for too long.

With one final look at the ocean, Emira turned, continuing her path back to the palace.

Despite the heavy boots entrapping her feet, she made no sound as she walked. Her husband, Madoc, used to call her a ghost. Now it seemed like another one of life's cruel jokes that the ghost was still alive and he, a man so full of life, was entombed beside their daughter.

Ignoring the servants and guards that stumbled out of her way, the queen climbed the warped stone stairs to her office. Sitting atop her desk was a large, circular basket tied with a series of ropes. A note on top addressed it from the Bane estate.

Slowly, Emira untied the knots securing the package and reached for the lid. She hesitated a moment, every instinct she had told her to leave this room. Something was wrong. She considered calling in Victor, then thought better of it. She was a *queen*. She would not be ruled by her fear.

Steeling herself, she tore off the lid and came face-to-face with a pair of glassy brown eyes. For the barest moment, she thought—hoped—that it might be her daughter. But Alana's eyes were gray, and her hair was not this yellow.

No, this was the head of Cedric Bane, Emira's accomplice in the plot to assassinate Alana. Inhaling a shaky breath, she forced herself to look past the severed head. There was no visible note or declaration of war. Still, Emira had to be sure…

"Victor!"

Her captain entered the room a moment later.

Emira gestured to the basket. "Remove the head, please."

Victor took a cautious step forward and cringed at the sight. "This is not Alana—"

"Yes, I am aware. Now, remove the head and tell me if there is a message beneath." She turned her back, not wanting to see the gruesome sight as he followed her orders.

"There is no note, Your Majesty."

There was a meaty thump as the severed head fell back into the basket.

Emira turned to face him. "Thank you, Victor. You may leave."

"Would you like me to remove the package as well?"

"No, that's all right."

Victor hesitated by the door. "This means she knows it was us."

"I am aware of that."

"Still, it is a good news that there is no message. It means that while the princess is angry, she is not willing to take public action."

"*Queen*," Emira corrected. "She is no longer a princess, but a queen. That is my doing. I thought…" She shook her head. "This is *not* good news, Victor. The head is the message. Alana knows she doesn't need to start a war to win my throne. She is a Zaya. The *last* Zaya. She will inherit this country as soon as I am dead."

"Are you suggesting she'll make an attempt on your life?"

"Perhaps," Emira murmured. "Or perhaps she'll do nothing." The queen shook her head bitterly. "She loves to play games."

"I'm putting the guards on alert," the captain of the guard declared. "And I'm having every member aboard that ship from Jaarin questioned."

Emira didn't bother to respond as he swept out of the room.

Looking back at the severed head, she shivered. "What have I done?"

ONE

*O*ne day, my dear daughter, you will destroy the world.

Alana Zaya, Queen of Jaarin, stood in the dining hall, goblet raised as her husband delivered his speech to the two newlyweds. She was certain it was filled with heartfelt sentiments and pretty words for love and the future.

Alana hated every second of it.

She missed her home country. She missed Okaro. It was a land made up of sheer cliffs, endless storms, and crashing waves. Wild and wonderful. Brutal and beautiful. There, the dinners weren't filled with endless formal speeches. People ate and danced around bonfires during celebrations that lasted until dawn.

Compared to Okaro, Jaarin was a prison. A gilded cage. It was little wonder why Emira had sent her daughter here.

"...and by Rion's light, I pray the two of you have a long and happy union!" Erik finished his speech with a flourish and the tables broke into applause.

Alana took a long sip from her goblet and returned to her seat, hoping the alcohol would hit her soon and take the edge off the unpleasantness of the night. There was a reason she avoided these gatherings. She hated the people, the food, and the endless well wishes.

Lords and ladies from all corners of Jaarin had come to see the king's nephew wed. They stared up at her now, silently plotting against her.

They thought they could manipulate her.

They thought that she cared enough to join in their power games.

They were wrong.

Alana stared back, daring them to challenge her.

"Excellent speech," she murmured to her husband, smoothing out the wrinkles in her dress. "Beautiful sentiments."

Erik chuckled low under his breath. "You didn't hear a damn word I said, did you?"

"I caught the end."

The king made a motion to the servants and plates piled high with meat, beans, and an assortment of other foods emerged from shadowed doorways and placed before each guest at the many tables arranged before them.

She sniffed at the food. It smelled normal at least, but...

"Worried about poison?" he asked, a small crease appearing on his forehead. "I could have the taster come again—"

Alana shook her head. "It's not poison I'm worried about." Slowly, she skewered a green bean and popped it in her mouth, instantly cringing. It was sweet. Everything else in the whole damned country was sweet. It was as though the cooks had run out of spices and replaced everything with sugar. She set her fork down on the table and forced her face to look at least halfway pleasant before taking another few sips from her goblet. At least the wine wasn't sugared.

"Just a few more hours, then you can leave," Erik assured her. "Dinner, some dancing, then dessert." He paused, taking a bite of food. "I won't even ask you to dance with me."

"The outcome would have been the same, whether you asked or not," Alana replied. She scanned the faces of the nobles, all well dressed in many layers despite the tropical heat. Their hats and jackets were sewn with jewels and bits of gold.

Alana turned her gaze to the newlywed couple, their heads bent towards each other in conversation. The wife laughed. She looked happy. Alana wondered if she'd ever looked like that. She didn't think so. She'd hardly felt anything in the last five years. Not since she'd been shipped off to Jaarin and Emira had whispered those fateful words in her daughter's ear, her voice so low that they had nearly been drowned out by the crashing waves. Nearly. But Alana had heard. And she remembered. And she wished she could forget.

THE STORM GATHERS

The queen raised her goblet to take another drink, nearly spilling its content when Erik laid a hand on her arm.

"Do you see that man over there?" he asked. "The one wearing green?"

Alana's eyes flicked across the group gathered at the corner table. It wasn't hard to discern whom her husband was referring to. His clothes were far too simple for the Jaarin court and his face was clean of any make-up. Overall, he looked about as excited to be a part of the party as Alana was.

"Who is he?"

"The ambassador from Creft," Erik explained. "He arrived a week early, demanding to speak to me."

Alana's hand tightened around the goblet. This was hardly the time for a serious discussion of foreign politics, but between the ambassador's early arrival and the wedding guests, Alana doubted she would get another chance to speak with her husband regarding her position on the Creft-Nuska situation.

The war had begun less than a year ago, and given recent reports, it wasn't likely to last much longer. If Creft fell, the entire northern half of their continent would be under Nuska's control. It was a sobering possibility.

"You shouldn't have let him in. Bending to his will shows weakness."

"He was going to make a scene at the front gates," Erik explained. "We have a lot of very important people visiting us. I wanted things to go smoothly—"

"Then you should have sent me to speak with him."

"I didn't think your particular brand of…persuasion would be appropriate, given his country's current situation."

"I wouldn't have hurt the man," she snapped. *At least not physically.*

"Alana." Erik's voice smoothed out, becoming gentle and soothing, as though speaking to a wild animal. "This situation was delicate, and you are…not. Besides, I feel for the man's plight. His country is about to be annihilated by the Nuskan army. By the time we wrap up this meeting, he may not even have a home to return to." He sighed. "It's a terrible business. I wish there was something I could do, but there is no army in the world capable of standing against Nuska—even if the countries of Yovar, Aaran, and Siora united alongside us. Which they would never do," he added.

7

Alana watched the Creft ambassador. His eyes kept darting towards the exits as though he were in a room full of enemies. And he was. Coming here was a fool's errand. A last act of desperation from a dying country.

She turned her attention back to her husband. "No one is asking you to start a war against Nuska. Only an idiot would ever consider it. But if you're smart, you will do everything in your power to prevent them from gaining control of the entire north. Give them money. Give them resources. Ally with the northern rebels, if you have to."

Erik took a sip of his wine. "Who would have thought that Alana Zaya, of all people, would believe in fighting for a lost cause?"

"It's called self-preservation. Do you really think Nuska will stop its campaign after they've taken the North? That they will stop at controlling half the world? They will find a way through the Skyfall mountains and then it will be you begging deaf countries for aide."

"It won't come to that," Erik argued.

Alana looked at the high, gilded ceiling and painted marble columns inlaid with precious jewels that snaked upwards in spiraled patterns. It was nothing like the stark stone and wood of the Okaron castle. "Gold is the most malleable of metals, Erik. It does not hold against steel. This castle, these people you care so much about, they will fall. You will fall. And when that day comes, do not expect me to stand with you." With that, she rose to her feet and walked through the table aisles, ignoring the whispers of nobles and their stares as she approached the ambassador.

The man blinked rapidly as she stood before him, his eyes darting around nervously as if looking for aid.

You will get none of that here.

"What is your name, sir?" Alana's voice carried across the room as she spoke, silencing all remaining conversation. In the distance, she could hear the faint murmur of voices coming from the halls—likely from the many servants working the event.

"Quinton Celara, Your Majesty," the ambassador answered, bowing his head. "It is a pleasure to meet you. I have heard tales of your beauty, but they do not do you justice."

THE STORM GATHERS

A faint smile crept its way onto her lips. She was not so vain as to blush or preen at the praise, although it was appreciated. She took after her mother, although she was loath to admit it, with her delicate features and gray eyes the color of the sea in a storm. Their hair was the only difference. Where Emira's was a light brown, Alana's was an orange-blonde shade that cascaded down her shoulders in waves.

"I would like to speak with you, ambassador Celera," she said, not bothering to thank the man for the compliments. "Before your business here is at an end."

He shifted. "I would like that as well, Your Majesty."

"Good," Alana said, dipping her chin ever so slightly in a show of respect. "*Valnuskata*, Quinton."

The man blanched, his eyes darting past her to the rest of the crowd. He swallowed. "*Valnuskata*, Your Majesty. For all the stars."

TWO

"**Y**ou should not have done that."

It had, perhaps, been foolish for Alana to believe that she would escape through the halls before her two overbearing guards caught up to her—regardless of it being their literal jobs. She kept walking.

"And why not, Maria?" Alana asked, keeping her steps casual.

"Because the nobles in there are not fools. Everyone saw the tension gathering between you and Erik. And then, to make matters worse, you strode across the hall like a descending storm and spoke with the Creft ambassador in a foreign language."

Alana smiled at the analogy. "A *dead* language," she argued. "No one speaks the Old Tongue anymore."

"That may be. Still, it does not look good—whispering with outsiders in unknown languages."

"It was a single word."

"And what exactly does *valnuskata* mean?"

"The literal translation is, 'for all the stars,'" Alana said easily. "Saying it means you wish someone victory and prosperity."

"Regardless," Maria pressed. "Your actions tonight make it look as though you and Erik are divided."

"We *are* divided. And you should have told me that Quinton had arrived early," Alana said in a blatant attempt to change the subject.

"I did not know who he was until just before the dinner started," Maria explained. "I was a little busy gathering information about your mother's illness."

THE STORM GATHERS

Alana sniffed and turned her attention to the other guard flanking her. "What about you? Why didn't you tell me?"

The large man lifted his hands in surrender. "Don't pull me into this. I'm your guard, not a spy."

"Fine." She let out a huff of breath. Johnathan had been her guard since she was thirteen. She couldn't be mad at him. Not over this, at least.

"Are we going to your rooms?" Maria asked, gesturing towards the stairway leading to the upper levels of the palace.

"No."

"Care to be a little more descriptive?" The woman's dark eyes glittered with amusement at her queen's withering look. "Do you want me to find a dark corner for you to sulk in?"

"I could have you executed for that tone alone, Mari."

"Then who would you have to complain to?"

Unable to stop herself, Alana let out a low chuckle and gave Maria an appraising look. Her female guard wasn't much taller than her, with jet-black hair that usually drifted in curls around her shoulders but was now tightly braided down her neck. She wore an identical uniform to Johnathan, black leather and seal stamped with the heads of a xygrith—one of the legendary firebirds that traveled across Okaro—and a jungle cat.

The sigil represented the marriage alliance between the naval country of Okaro and the jungle lands of Jaarin. Alana thought it was ugly.

The only difference in her two guards' uniforms was that Maria wore a thick black collar around her neck. It blended in so seamlessly with her attire, Alana doubted anyone noticed it was there, which was likely her guard's intention.

"So," Maria repeated. "Where are we going? The gardens? I am sure I could snag another bottle of that wine you were guzzling from the cook." She winked.

"Honestly, I would rather—" Alana abruptly cut herself off at the sound of metal crashing against stone.

Her guards' hands instantly went to their weapons. Johnathan to his sword and Maria to the two long knives belted at her waist.

"Who goes there?" Johnathan's gruff voice bounced off the polished halls and seemed to silence the steady hum of conversation coming from the dining hall behind them.

When no response was forthcoming, Maria stuck out a hand, pushing Alana behind her. "Show yourself!"

Another moment of silence, then a stumbling figure rounded the corner.

Alana let out a shallow sigh of relief as the drunk page stuck out a hand to keep from falling. She didn't recognize the boy and guessed him to be employed by one of the visiting families. The boy's wide eyes bounced between Alana and her two guards—poised and ready to kill. He opened his mouth to speak and blood began to drip from his lips and onto the floor. The boy's hand slipped on the wall, and he fell onto his stomach on the floor. His head cracked against the stone with a sickening crunch.

Alana stared at the knife protruding from his back. The hilt of the blade was a dark, burnished metal carved to fit someone's hand.

"We need to get you to your rooms," Johnathan growled. "Now."

"No," Alana said, her voice strong despite the shock of the dead boy. "The dining hall is better protected, and we need to alert the king." Without waiting for her two guards to agree, Alana started back down the hall. She hesitated as she reached the door. Something was wrong.

"What is it?" Maria asked.

"It's too quiet."

"We are take you to your rooms," Johnathan said firmly. "We'll seal you in and—" His words were abruptly cut off as shouts erupted from the dining hall. The sounds of tables being turned over and plates crashing to the ground filled the castle.

Alana didn't waste time. She turned and sprinted for the staircase that led up to her rooms, her guards close behind her. She was halfway up the staircase when her shoe slipped on the steps—the heel catching at the corner of the stairs. She let out a loud curse.

"Take them off," Maria growled, offering her shoulder for balance as Alana removed her footwear.

The sounds of fighting swept into the halls, followed by screams and charging footsteps. A moment later, men and women in fine clothes came into view. Some turned to rush up the stairs, others continuing towards the gardens. All of them were slowed down by their heavy layers and bejeweled shoes.

Johnathan's arms were suddenly around her, pulling her up the stairs even as Alana's eyes remained fixed on the scene unfolding below. Searching. Not for Erik or the guards that should have been protecting the nobles, but for the attackers.

She didn't have to wait long. Men dressed in black leather and iron helmets came into view, carrying weapons of the same crude making as the one that had killed the boy.

"Let's go!"

Alana pulled out of Johnathan's grip and ran up the stairs, taking them two at a time until they reached the second-story landing. Her bare feet slapped against the floor as she sprinted for the staircase at the end of the hall that would lead to her wing of the palace.

The sounds of clomping boots echoed behind her as she ran, followed by Maria's cursing.

Alana glanced over her shoulder to see a group of attackers in dark armor charging for them. Beside her, Johnathan skittered to a stop and turned his focus on the intruders. Maria joined him.

"Go!" she urged. "Get to your rooms and bar the door. We'll hold them off."

Alana nodded and resumed her sprint for a staircase that seemed ridiculously far away. As much as she didn't want to leave her guards, she knew that her presence would be a distraction that could put them all in danger.

The sounds of violence followed her as she ran—screams and clashing metal and the smell of blood. She heard Maria shout a warning and Alana glanced over shoulder to see that one man had slipped past her guards and was now barreling for her.

Alana wrapped her hand around the silver banister of the stairway leading to her rooms. She launched herself forward, only to be pulled backwards by her hair. Her body slammed against the ground before once again being yanked in a new direction by her assailant.

"You're coming with me, Your Majesty," the man said. His voice was rougher than Johnathan's, with a slight northern accent that reminded Alana of her father's.

"Wait," she gasped, hating how out of breath she sounded. "You're a mercenary," she reasoned aloud. "Whoever hired you to do this job sent you into a death trap, but if you help me, I can make sure you make it out of this alive."

"I serve only the gods," he declared. "It is by their grace that we entered the castle on this night and it is they who will guide us to safety."

"I see," Alana said dryly. "Well, the gods and I aren't exactly on the best of terms. I suggest kidnapping a different monarch. King Argos of Siora, perhaps? I hear he's as pious as they come."

Still gripping her shoulder, the man pulled her away from the wall. He paused. Maria and Johnathan were still fighting against the rest of the attackers and had been joined by a few other palace guards. The only way out was the stairway leading to the west wing of the castle—*her* side of the castle.

Alana hid her smile as the man pushed her toward the stairs. She waited until they were halfway up before leaping over the loose stone in the seventh step, and sprinting up to the landing. There was a grunt as the mercenary slipped in his race to catch her. Turning, Alana flung her shoes at his face and said a silent apology to the poor things. The heels would be scuffed to pieces by the time she found them again.

Not giving herself the time to mourn, Alana wrenched open the heavy wooden door barring her path and slammed it shut just before her attacker could come charging in after her. She bolted the lock into place and pressed her back against the door, breathing heavily. She surveyed the room—a small welcome chamber furnished with a low sofa, twin chairs, and a carpet. She considered stacking the furniture against the door, but decided against it for no other reason than that she didn't want to wrinkle her dress any further.

Let them come, that tiny voice in her head whispered. *Let them rush in here with their armor and jagged swords. I could destroy them all if I wished. I* will.

No. *No,* she couldn't let that monster take over. She was in control. The world may burn around her, but she would remain in control. After all, fires could be put out.

The door shuddered as the mercenary threw his body against it, attempting to break it down.

Alana settled down on the small sofa and watched the door with a smile on her face.

Where are your gods now?

After a few minutes, the slamming stopped and disjointed voices drifted toward her. A woman with the same northern accent as the man. Slowly, Alana got to her feet and pressed her ear to the wood.

"What's going on?" the female voice demanded.

"The queen, she got away from me," he answered. "Locked herself in here."

"You couldn't handle one unarmed woman? Gods, you're useless. Never mind. We need to leave. Now."

"What about *her*?"

"It's too late. We'll figure something else out."

"But he said there would be others. We need—"

The woman cut him off. "I told you—we don't have time for this. Let's *go*."

Alana kept her ear pressed to the door, waiting, but the voices became inaudible as the pair retreated down the stairs. They would need to fight their way out of the castle and would most likely die. She hoped Erik and his soldiers would have the good sense to leave at least one of the attackers alive for questioning. But somehow, Alana doubted her husband would be so pragmatic. She told herself that didn't matter. From her conversation with the man and the exchange he'd had with the woman, it was clear they were religious fanatics of some sort. She couldn't imagine what they would want with her, of all people, but she had very little interest in finding out.

It was curious, though—their accents. Both of them were clearly from Nuska. It would make sense if they had targeted Quinton, but not her. Were they connected to the war? Or was this something different?

Settling back on the sofa, Alana waited, counting the minutes—twenty-four—until Maria's voice sounded through the wood.

"All clear!"

Alana unbolted the lock and threw it open to reveal her two guards—covered in blood that was not their own. She hid the relief pulsing through her as she looked between them. There were two other guards behind them, also covered in blood, their eyes downcast.

Johnathan took a step forward, his eyes traveling up and down her body, looking for injuries.

Alana recoiled, not from him, but from the smell of blood and gore that was caked to his skin. "Don't you dare take another step forward," she hissed, covering her nose with one hand. "The two of you reek. Go take a bath."

Maria let out a low chuckle. The tight braid she usually kept her hair in was undone, and sweat soaked strands had plastered themselves to her face and neck. "Yeah, okay, you are fine."

"There has just been an attack," Johnathan ground out. "We cannot leave you unprotected."

"Put two other guards on duty and I'll lock myself in my room," Alana said. "But the two of you are not coming anywhere near me until you've washed yourselves."

Before either of them could argue, she slammed the door in Johnathan's face and bolted it before turning on her heel.

She stalked through the many rooms that accompanied her wing of the palace before reaching the largest of them all—the bedroom. It was lined with a carpet so black it seemed to swallow up all the light in the room.

After lighting the lanterns, Alana stepped in front of the full-length mirror and took in the sight of herself. She looked the same. Her hair was perhaps a little unkempt and her dress more wrinkled than it had been, but other than her lack of shoes, nothing about her appearance was unusual. She certainly didn't look like a woman who had been attacked and manhandled less than an hour prior.

Slowly, Alana untied the corset from her body. The simple, repetitive movements calmed the emotions swirling within her. This was not the first time someone had tried to kill her. Although it certainly had been the closest anyone had come in years. Worse, the man could have done it. A single swipe of his blade and she would hear the voice of Death. But he hadn't.

He'd wanted her alive, and somehow, that was even more terrifying.

Alana changed into her nightgown and settled, cross-legged on the black carpet. She leaned back against the cool stone wall behind her and closed her eyes.

It was nearly summer. The spring rains giving way to the heat and humidity that would only intensify as the days grew longer.

Gods, she missed Okaro. The air there was cool and dry, the only wetness coming from the storms that swept in like grim death and devoured their rocky island.

She remembered the rush that busied the castle when the xygriths left the island—a signal of a coming storm. Shutters were closed, the doors reinforced with steel and furniture to keep the rain out. The worst of those storms had come the day Alana was born—or so she'd been told. Winds so strong they had ripped apart entire houses and lightning so bright it had left some men blind.

Okaro. The land of storms.

Too often, Alana questioned whether she would see her homeland again. She didn't belong here in Jaarin. Then again, she'd never felt as though she belonged in Okaro either.

An hour later, a knock sounded on her bedroom door, followed by Maria saying, "I swear I took a bath. Johnathan claims he did, but he stinks as bad as he did before."

Alana smiled. "Come in."

Maria opened the door a crack and slipped in, leaving Johnathan on guard outside.

"Are you sure you are all right?" Maria asked, looking her charge over. "It was a close call today. I saw the man get past and tried to get to you but—" she shook her head, regret and fear coating her words. "I failed today. He could have killed you…"

Alana made a dismissive gesture. "I can take care of myself." Ignoring, Maria's sound of protest, she pressed on. "I need to know how they got into the castle. They never should have been able to make it so far without

17

being detected."

"As far as Johnathan and I can make out, they entered through the eastern gate and used the servant's halls to travel through the castle unnoticed. A few minutes after you left, they swept in, barring the exits to the dining hall."

Alana shook her head. "The guards at the eastern gate should have been able to see them coming. And they certainly would have enough time to raise the alarm."

"Perhaps they had help from someone on the inside?"

Alana drummed her fingers on the carpet. "Maybe." She was missing something, but there was no point in dwelling on it when she had more pressing matters to deal with. "What news do you have of my mother?"

"She is dead," Maria said flatly. "I received word just before the reception that her illness took her in the night a few weeks ago." A pause. "Do you think it is possible she was behind this somehow?"

Alana made a dismissive gesture. "No, Emira would never act so publicly. Still, her death changes things."

"It does," Maria agreed. "You can go home."

Alana hesitated. True, she missed Okaro and hated Jaarin, but the idea of actually returning…

Arya was dead. The only thing that awaited her across the Western sea was a throne that should never have come to her in the first place.

She could feel Maria's eyes on her. "Begin packing your bags," she said, swallowing her apprehension. "We set sail as soon as I can arrange a ship."

Maria removed a small flask from her pocket and handed it to Alana. "A toast, then."

"To my mother's death?"

"To surviving this night," Maria clarified.

"I think the former is more worthy of celebration." Alana took a sip from the flask and then passed it back to her guard.

Maria shook her head. "You certainly live up to your title."

She waved a hand. "Which one? There are so many."

"The Queen of Darkness."

"Ah, that one," Alana said, eyeing the flask. "Yes, I think I've grown into

THE STORM GATHERS

it rather nicely."

Truthfully, she'd never particularly liked the name, but once the rumors started to circulate, there was little she could do but embrace her new title. She suspected it was inspired by her homeland. Okaro was known for cloudy skies and endless storms that cast the country into perpetual gloom. It was only later that the darkness became representative of her actions while on the Jaarin throne.

Not that it mattered.

Whether the perpetrator had known it or not, by giving Alana that name, they had given her protection. Armor. A helm against the swords aimed at her head. Never mind that the steel was actually silk. No one bothered to look that closely, anyway.

Silence swelled as Maria took a long drink. "You know, I used to think that—with enough time—I would be able to move on from what happened in Yovar. But now…" She shook her head. "I guess you cannot move on until you have faced the thing you are running from."

She passed the flask to Alana.

"What if you lose?" Alana murmured, before swallowing down a mouthful. "What if your monsters get the better of you?"

"Maybe," Maria said slowly, "you just have to decide if you would rather live a life in fear or risk dying to find happiness." She took the flask back and tucked it away. "We chose wrong, you and I. Perhaps this new adventure will give us the opportunity to correct those mistakes."

Alana didn't say anything as she slowly turned her attention to the window. Night had fallen, and it was dark enough that she could see her reflection in the glass. She looked tired. But not as tired as she felt.

Perhaps Maria was right—after all, her guard knew masks better than anyone—but Alana couldn't take the chance that she was wrong.

What was happiness to her, anyway?

In all her life, she had only experienced it once and even then, it had been a fleeting thing—appearing only long enough for her to watch the sun set below the horizon. There had been someone next to her, then. Someone who was long gone and who she would never see again. But at that moment, sitting together, she had been happy. Stupidly happy. And no matter what happened, Alana knew she would never feel that way again.

THREE

Rae Toma crouched in the sand, hidden behind one of the many desert dunes that rolled across this section of Siora. The caravan was late, and the men and women behind her shifted uncomfortably. Although they were all dressed for the scorching weather—with light clothes and scarves that wrapped around their heads and concealed their faces—the heat was still unbearable.

A sharp whistle sounded, and she raised her head, eyes flicking across the landscape until she saw the dark shadow of the vehicle coming into view.

She whistled back, hand tightening around the falcata at her waist. It was her preferred weapon. Not the longest sword, but a sharp, single-edged blade, concave near the point and hilt.

"Ready?" Jonah's voice carried from her left.

She turned to see that he had crawled beside her. "Go back to your position," she hissed.

"I thought you might want a few words of reassurance. It's been a while since you've deigned to accompany us on a job."

"You are the career thief," she reminded him. "Not me."

"Thief is such a nasty word. I prefer to be called a procurer of difficult-to-find items." His eyes crinkled at the edges, indicating a smile hid beneath his scarf.

"Get back to your position," Rae repeated, snarling this time. "And remind your men not to open the wagon until it's all clear. I don't feel like having my head blown off today."

Letting out a low huff of agreement, Jonah retreated back down the dune.

Rae returned her eyes to the road. She liked Jonah. She wouldn't have chosen him to be a part of her Val council if she didn't trust him. But the man was infuriating, to say the least. He'd been one of the most notorious thieves in Siora before being captured by the city guard. As punishment, he'd been sent to prison for three years and had both his pinky fingers removed.

After the war broke out, and Rae hunted for people to join her cause, she'd tracked Jonah down in one of the local pubs. Even while drunk and missing two fingers, he'd still managed to steal five wallets from the patrons and snag an extra bottle of ale from behind the bar.

Between him and Cyrus—an ex-mercenary who now waited with another group of bandits on the other side of the road—Rae had found the perfect team to help her rob the military caravans that brought supplies to soldiers at the front.

It won't be long now, she thought as she watched the wagon meander down the road, kicking up dust and sand that flew directly into the eyes of the four soldiers riding alongside it.

It was strange that it wasn't more heavily guarded, but Rae knew there were two good reasons for that. One, the substance inside the wagon was highly volatile, meaning that anyone hoping to rob it would have to be insane—which maybe she was—and two, the king had already sent a heavily-protected decoy three hours ago.

Their target ambled forward slowly, the driver clearly cautious, given the nature of the contents he was transporting.

Rae waited, her heart pounding as the caravan came closer and closer to the road marker.

Jonah was right. It had been nearly eight months since she'd accompanied them on a job. With the Val growing in numbers and notoriety, it had become too dangerous for her to join. Maintaining the secrecy of their commanding members' identities was of utmost importance—especially hers—and to risk exposure on missions she wasn't needed on was foolish. But this was different. And so, Rae was here, crouching in the middle of the desert, sweating her ass off.

After what felt like an eternity, the caravan—pulled by two large, hoofed animals known as ceprra—reached the travel marker. It halted when the

22

right, front wheel became caught in a divot in the road. The beasts pulled furiously against the cracking of the whip, but the carriage refused to budge. Grumbling, two of the soldiers riding ceprra dismounted and made their way to the front of the wagon.

Rae waited for them to disappear from sight, then gave two sharp whistles. When the same call was returned from the other team, she unsheathed her falcata and glanced back at Jonah. With a nod, he and the rest of the men and women behind him started climbing up the dune with surprising speed. Rae waited for them to move alongside her, then she too, began to climb, cresting the dune with swift precision before quickening her pace down the sand to the road.

Across the way, Cyrus's unit came down, breaking into a run as soon as they hit solid ground.

The king's soldiers who had been guarding the caravan let out a cry and drew their weapons. The two remaining on the ceprra charged for Rae and Jonah while the driver and men who'd been helping with the wagon wheel faced off against Cyrus's team.

One of the ceprra riders barreled straight for her, sword raised to strike at her head. Rae rolled out of the way just fast enough to avoid decapitation.

She leaped to her feet, readying herself as the beast and soldier came charging for her once more. Ignoring the enormous animal attempting to trample her, Rae instead focused her attack on the man. She moved out of the way of his strike, then launched her own.

She ran alongside the ceprra for a moment, before leaping into the air. Using the soldier as a handhold, Rae swung onto the animal, tangling herself with the rider, who was now fumbling for his weapon. She flexed her hand, and a blade slid from the gold cuff at her wrist and into her palm. She sliced open the man's throat before he had a chance to cry out, then pushed him off the royal mount, who was now galloping at full speed away from the caravan.

Rae readjusted her position in the saddle. She was too short to get her feet into the stirrups, so she grabbed the reins and yanked them hard, forcing the animal's neck to turn to the left. It moved in a circle, barely slowing down as it charged back the way they had come.

Jonah—who was currently dueling a soldier who'd apparently been knocked off his ceprra—grinned as she approached.

"That was a neat trick you just performed back there," he called.

Rae pulled her newly-acquired steed to a halt. "Thank you." She watched as Jonah dodged a near lethal strike by his opponent. "Need help?"

"Of course not. I have the situation under control." He swung his sword in an arc for emphasis.

Rae rolled her eyes.

To her left, Cyrus and his team finished off the driver and set about freeing the wagon wheel from where it was caught in the road.

"Hurry up," Rae said, returning her attention to Jonah. "We've got shit to do."

The thief shot her an offended look. "This type of duel cannot be—"

The king's soldier let out a short cry, then collapsed onto the sand beside Jonah's feet. Rae dismounted her ceprra, then retrieved the throwing knife protruding from the dead man's back. Jonah sniffed. "That was rude."

"You were taking too long." She jerked her head. "Come on."

Cyrus and the rest of the men gathered at the back of the newly repossessed vehicle.

The mercenary winked at her as she approached—the scar across his forehead crinkling—before motioning to the wagon doors. "The honor is all yours."

Rae reached forward and undid the latch holding the two doors in place. They swung open to reveal crates packed with jars of black liquid. Rae grimaced. She'd hoped the rumors and king Argos's bolstering claims hadn't been true, but there was no mistaking what lay in those jars—Shadow Fire.

Cyrus blew out a breath. "Damn."

Wrinkling her nose and taking one last look at the jars, Rae closed and latched the door.

Shadow Fire had been concocted in Yovar, presumably to be used in one of their many—seemingly endless—festivals, but the substance became highly volatile upon contact with anything flammable. It would consume anything and everything in its path for a few minutes before dying out completely. The black infernos couldn't be smothered or put out with water. The only saving grace was that they naturally dissipated within a matter of minutes, regardless of the amount of fuel they had.

Rae turned to Cyrus. "You know what to do?"

He nodded. "There's a fork in the road about a mile up that leads to the coast. We have a ship arranged to meet us there. We'll load this up, then sink the ship."

Rae nodded, fisting her hands in her tunic to hide her unease.

"Why don't we give it to the Tiskona?" A voice from the crowd asked—a woman by the sounds of it.

"It's Shadow Fire," another snapped. "That much could burn down half the Forest."

That was an exaggeration. But given the lack of argument, it got the point across.

She turned to Jonah. "Your unit will take care of the bodies. I don't want there to be any sign we were here, got it?"

The thief nodded his understanding. Rae stepped to the side as everyone got to work. Part of her missed doing this, getting her hands dirty and fighting alongside people who shared her cause.

She observed the rebel's movements with mild curiosity. They were efficient, but the sense of camaraderie among them was what stood out. They laughed and jostled with each other as they worked, making plans and telling stories.

"You should accompany us more often," Jonah said, sidling up to her.

"Perhaps I will. It's obvious your men are in desperate need of competent leadership."

"They're having fun," he argued. "You may have forgotten the feeling, but the rest of us haven't."

"I have fun."

"You *pretend* to have fun," he countered. "It's not the same."

Rae glowered at the man. Then, resisting the urge to stab him, stalked away.

A quick glance at the sun told her it was nearly midday. She needed to get back to the city.

Eying the crowd of rebels, Rae spotted the ceprra she'd taken from the dead rider. She didn't particularly like the animal and, judging from the way it shuffled as she approached, it hadn't forgotten her antics with its former rider. Rae made a soothing noise with her mouth and stroked the creature's furry face. Slowly, it calmed, and she could adjust its saddle.

"Leaving so soon?"

Rae glanced back at Cyrus. "I have a meeting to attend."

"I hear the prince is set to the return to the Capital," he said casually.

"That's just a rumor."

"Maybe," Cyrus conceded. "But if that rumor proves true, you'll need to leave the city."

"He won't be able to see through me."

"You sure about that?"

"I am." Rae climbed onto the back of the ceprra. "Worry about yourself, Cyrus, and I'll do the same."

She kicked her ride into a trot before the mercenary could respond.

As she started down the desert road, her mind drifted into memory. The war had started when she was just seventeen. For years Rae had witnessed the tension between the Sioran government and the people of the Tiskona forest grow, but she hadn't believed it would come to anything.

Then, the crown passed from father to son and Argos Vedros took the throne. Four years later, there was war. Thousands upon thousands marched from the Citadel and into battle, and just as many fled into the night.

Rae's mother, Hesta Toma, had been in the latter group. She had been Tiskona, from the dense forest kingdom that stretched across the southeast corner of the continent. To this day, Rae wasn't certain if her mother was alive or dead.

She ran a hand over her face, careful not to displace the scarf covering her nose and mouth. She had lost so much to this war.

Her mother.

Her friendships.

Her security.

But worst of all, Rae had lost herself.

THE STORM GATHERS

AN HOUR LATER, RAE RODE into the Capital of Siora. The city itself was enormous, a mixture of ancient architecture made of carved and painted stone mixed with newer buildings decked out in silver, gold, and stained glass.

Rae didn't particularly mind either style. There was a simple beauty to the ancient buildings that reminded her of days long past, ancient heroes, and grand adventures on the backs of dragons. But Rae also liked the newer buildings whose opulence made them shine like gems in the sun's heated gaze.

Yet, the city itself was nothing compared to the palace that shadowed it. The grand building was made of painted glass domes and glittering minarets topped with crushed tile, gold, and jewels shipped all the way from Jaarin. It sat atop an enormous cliff that overlooked the city and the ocean beyond it. Mountains arced around both, protecting both the citizens and nobles from the dangers of the outside world while creating a paradise inside that had never been breached by outside armies.

The only way up to the cliff was through one of the three sky gondolas manned by the city guard. Each soldier religiously checked everyone's paperwork to ensure they had the authorization to venture to and from the castle. Those carriages were the first line of defense for the Sioran king. Any assassin hoping to kill him would never make it past the security measures. There was simply no other way in.

At least, that's what most of the world believed.

The streets were packed with people whose stomping feet kicked up clouds of dust that choked the air.

Rae tied the ceprra to the nearest post, then melted into the crowd. After a few blocks, she turned down a side street and used a downspout drain to climb onto the roof of a building. From there, she made her slow way across the city, hopping from roof to roof in an effort to avoid the crowd of shoppers and merchants going about their day as she made her way to the northwest corner of the Capital.

This part of the city was mostly made up of poorly maintained ancient structures that had a tendency to collapse without warning. It was a project the old king had promised to rectify for years, but had never gotten around to.

Not wanting to risk a building falling beneath her, Rae landed in the street and picked her way through the rubble and makeshift houses until she reached an old sewer grate.

After a quick look around to make sure no one was watching, she bent down and pried open the metal lid. Sucking in a breath of fresh air, she dropped into the tunnel. She was eternally grateful that the city had stopped using the old sewer system fifty years ago in favor of more modern technology. The place still smelled faintly of human waste and mold, but it wasn't unbearable, and certainly not with the scarf still wrapped around her nose and mouth.

Slowly, Rae made her way through the old sewer. Eventually, the tunnel became vertical, and she was forced to shimmy upwards for about twenty feet before it branched out into a more horizontal slope. The pattern continued six more times, vertical, horizontal, vertical, horizontal and so on, until her head bumped against another iron cover.

Cursing quietly at the pain, Rae pushed the lid off and let the afternoon light shine in. She emerged in a small rock outcropping on the outer edges of the castle grounds. There were rarely any patrols this far from the center of the palace, but Rae still tried to be quiet.

Blinking away the spots in her vision, she stripped off her scarf and desert clothes before tossing them back into the ancient tunnels and replacing the sewer cover. Then she silently dressed in the simple tunic and pants she'd stashed earlier.

Sweat coated her skin from the fight, heavy ceprra ride, and effort of climbing through the tunnels, but she didn't have the time or luxury to rest. She had an hour before Argos met with his council and Rae knew better than to keep the king waiting.

FOUR

Alana watched Erik roll a coin across his knuckles as she lounged on her throne.

It had been four days since the attack on the palace, and most of the visiting nobles had fled to their corners of Jaarin. The ambassador from Creft had left as well, without offering either an explanation or a goodbye. Not that she blamed the man. If she were to die in a violent attack, she'd rather it be in her home country than in a foreign land.

Alana looked around lazily. The temple was circular, as were all those in Jaarin. Its walls of crushed quartz and gemstones glittered in the sunlight coming through the marbled glass windows. Statues and tapestries depicting each of the four gods hung or rested throughout the room. Each one was nearly identical to the last, as though the artists were afraid to differ from the predetermined mold of what those in Jaarin believed the deities to look like.

Alana plucked the golden coin from Erik's fingers and held it in her fist—letting the metal dig into her skin as she watched Priest Malik Henderson enter the temple.

He strode towards the raised dais at the front of the room, his black robes billowing behind him in a phantom wind.

"I thought he was busy overseeing burials," she grumbled as the priest removed a large, leather-bound book from his robe and set it on the podium before him.

"He insisted on performing today's ceremony," Erik said. "Something about providing hope in these dark days."

Alana observed the king sitting on the throne beside her. "He's a nuisance and a fanatic. It's time you got rid of him."

Erik rolled his eyes. "You're from Okaro. You think every priest is a fanatic. As for Henderson, I cannot fire him without cause. If I did, his entire congregation would rise against me and denounce my rule."

Alana very much doubted that. She couldn't imagine that Malik was exceedingly popular.

"A hundred men dressed in black whose greatest weapon is an old book…" She raised an eyebrow. "Forgive me, but I believe our guards *might* be able to hold them off." Erik narrowed his eyes and Alana continued. "Besides, we don't have to fire him. Let me arrange an accident, I—"

The king looked pointedly at the images of the deities surrounding them. "I would appreciate it if we didn't speak of murdering an innocent man inside the house of the gods."

That wasn't technically a no. She would discuss the subject with him later. Or perhaps not. It might be better for his conscience if she simply took matters into her own hands. It certainly wouldn't be the first time.

From the dais, Henderson cleared his throat and placed a hand on either side of the stone podium before him. He closed his eyes briefly, as if summoning his strength.

The man couldn't be much older than fifty, with white strands peppering the black of his hair and beard. His eyes and cheekbones were sunken and his lips were pale. Alana couldn't tell if his haggard appearance was from sleepless nights, makeup, or some strange, religious fasting ritual.

"This has been a difficult time for us all," Henderson began. "With so much death coloring our world, I believe we should take this time to remember life. To remember the gods who created all we see before us. Who gifted the lands of Jaarin with wealth and strength. Let us remember the glory of the gods by telling their story."

"Etresyum spare me," Alana muttered.

"Once," Henderson continued, "long ago, our world, Tayrn, was a spread of barren land. Unworthy of notice or note. Even the stars did not bother shining light upon us. That is, until four gods, each made of starlight and shaped through constellations, found their homes above our planet. They saw Tayrn not for its desolate state, but for its potential.

"Eriysha, goddess of the elements and guardian of the natural order, was the first to come to our world. The great serpent pulled herself from the skies. As she descended, water erupted from her scales and spread across the world, creating the oceans. And from those oceans rose two great continents of land. One that we stand on now and one that no longer exists as it once did.

"After seeing the power his sister brought, Orik, god of beasts and guardian of the earth, joined Eriysha on our planet. He created the creatures we live alongside today. The birds and serpents. Fish and insects. He created it all and set them loose to find their place in our world.

"Then came Seoka, goddess of knowledge and guardian of prophecy. She flew down from her perch in the stars to grant wisdom and thought to the life Orik had created.

"Finally, they called to the fourth and final god, Rion to offer his power to their creation. He was the strongest of them, you see—god of darkness and guardian of the light. Without him, the world would not be complete.

"Rion answered his siblings' call and leaped down from the stars." Henderson paused his story to look out upon the crowd, his eyes blazing. "But when the god landed upon the second continent Eriysha had created, he destroyed it for so great was his power. He broke the land into the thousands of islands we now call the Shatter. Islands that, after millennia, still hum with the god's power. Compasses do not work there, and none who have ventured inside have ever returned.

"Still, such destruction was a small price to pay for the protection Rion granted us. He used his power to bind the world together and shield us from the dangers of the cosmos." The priest looked into the crowd, tears gathering in his eyes. "But such acts of power are not without consequence. Rion was too powerful to remain on Tayrn, but neither did he have the strength to return to the stars. So, he offered himself to Etrim—to Death—so that the world he and his siblings had made could endure." Alana wondered how many times Malik had practiced this part of his speech in the mirror. "Do not forget Rion's sacrifice. Remember him and honor his memory by following the words of his brethren." Henderson bowed his head. "Let us pray."

The nobles in the temple bowed their heads, hands resting in their laps as they made wishes to gods that could not hear them.

Alana did not join them.

It had always struck her as odd that Rion, the dead god, was the one everyone worshiped. According to the stories, the others were just sleeping. But Rion—he died creating this world. Sure, his supposed sacrifice deserved to be honored, but it was ridiculous to place prayers in one that no longer existed.

Alana looked over at her husband. His head was down and hands clasped, but his eyes were open, staring at the floor. For the first time, she wondered how the king had fared the last few days. She hadn't bothered trying to visit him after the attack. In truth, the idea hadn't even crossed her mind. How close to death had he come that night?

"Erik…" she spoke his name so quietly she wasn't even sure he had heard.

"Yeah?" he asked after a moment.

Gods, she was no good at this. No good at comfort or talking about feelings and truths. She preferred lies, weaving stories out of nonsense and watching them spread like wheat in a field. Lies were a mantel, an armor she wrapped around herself. They kept her safe, and she could not—would not—let that armor down. Not even for her husband. Especially not for her king. "I need to talk to you. Once we're finished here."

As if on cue, Henderson raised his head. His eyes met hers and he scowled as he noted her crossed arms and raised head. She met his gaze without shame and hid a smile when he was the first to look away.

"Rise, friends," the priest said, his frown replaced with a smile. "I hope you all find peace in the gods during this difficult time. Please know you can always come to me if you need reassurance in your faith."

The sounds of rustling fabric and whispered words filled the room as nobles abandoned the temple to go about their daily tasks.

After a moment, Erik rose from his throne and offered a hand to Alana. She took it, allowing him to lead her toward the dais and the supposedly holy man.

"Priest Henderson," Erik began, "it was kind of you to join us today. I'm sure everyone appreciated it."

"I do what I can. It is a relief to know that my presence is welcome."

"It *is* most welcome," Alana said smoothly. "And I'm sure you would be welcomed across all of Jaarin. Perhaps we should organize a tour so that you may educate and enlighten the masses."

The priest's lips curled. "I think I am still needed here, Your Majesty. There are obviously those who have not yet found the right path."

Fighting the urge to roll her eyes, Alana walked away, not waiting as Erik hurried to catch up. She paused at the door, glancing over her shoulder at the priest. "Be careful tonight, Malik. This castle is obviously not as well protected as we once believed. I would feel terrible if something were to happen to you."

Alana swept out of the room before the irksome man could snap a reply.

"WHAT WERE YOU THINKING?" ERIK demanded when they were alone again. He'd stayed quiet until they had reached his study, but had nearly yanked her arm out of her socket while pulling her inside. "You can't threaten the priest. And you certainly can't kill him. The court is already in a panic after the attack. I cannot have—"

Alana made a calming motion. "I'm not going to kill Malik." Relief washed over the king's features, and she added, "at least not tonight." His expression darkened once more, and she lifted one shoulder in a shrug. "You know me, husband. I like to play with my food before I eat it."

"Usually, you just complain."

Crossing her arms, Alana leaned against the door. "I need to visit Okaro."

Any amusement still left died on her husband's face at the mention of his wife's homeland. "Why?"

"My mother is dead. I must claim my country before anyone else can challenge me."

"You could just let someone else take the throne," Erik suggested.

Alana's jaw tightened. "No."

"Why not? We both know you have no interest in ruling."

"If I were to give up my claim, Okaro would split into civil war as different Houses vie for the crown. I will not put my country through that."

Erik let out a long breath. "I suppose I couldn't have chosen a worse time to bring this up, but," he inhaled sharply, as though the words pained him, "I need your help. The attack has gotten my councilors riled up. They're using it as an opportunity to push their agendas, and I don't know if I can fight them off on my own."

"I don't have any governing power in Jaarin," she reminded him. "I am a queen in title only." Emira had made sure of that.

"I'm not asking you to rule by my side, Alana. I'm asking you to rule the shadows. It's what you do already. I'm simply proposing a unified partnership." He paused. "But it can wait until you return. I believe I can hold them off until then."

"You don't need me," she told him. "If you were willing to get your hands dirty, you could rule on your own. Stop trying to appease everyone and start being a king."

A muscle moved in Erik's jaw. "You don't plan to return to Jaarin, do you?"

Alana met his gaze. "It's for the best that I don't."

FIVE

Nur of the Storm stood outside the doors to the building that used to be her classroom. But, as of yesterday, it had become a place of memory.

"Look!"

She glanced to her left to see Eva pointing at the crack of light beneath the twin doors.

"Someone just walked past."

"You've been saying that for the past twenty minutes," Nur grumbled. "Everyone knows Sylvie's in there. We're waiting for her to come out."

"If she's at the *door*, it could mean she's about to *exit*," her friend said, putting emphasis on two of the words as if explaining something to a very dimwitted child.

Nur crossed her arms. "All I'm saying is that she's passed by about a dozen times, and not once has it opened."

"Don't take that tone too personally," Kaleo said, marching to stand between the girls. "Nur's just pissy because she's stressed."

"Shut up."

He gestured towards Nur, speaking to Eva. "You see what I'm saying?"

Eva chuckled lightly and glanced back at the classroom. "It's unfair that they make us wait like this. You know they must have finished the line-ups last night."

"The Masters have perfected the art of torture," Kaleo said, in a voice that was probably meant to be wise but was undercut by his boyish grin. He brushed aside a lock of hair that had fallen in front of his face to reveal emerald green eyes.

Nur supposed that in another world, those eyes would be striking. But on their islands, he blended in seamlessly with everyone else. Everyone here had green eyes. It was the mark of the Shatter.

Everyone except Nur, whose sea blue irises revealed her eastern blood.

She scoffed at Kaleo. "As if you have anything to worry about. You're top of the class. Some of us," she motioned towards herself, "have real reasons to be afraid."

"You'll do fine," Eva said, laying a hand on her shoulder. "You're underestimating your abilities."

"I'm the only one in the class without an Amulet," Nur reminded her. "That means I can only channel a third of Eriysha's power compared to the rest of you." She tilted her head back with a sigh. "I'm doomed."

"Don't feel too bad, Del Sue. Some people just aren't meant for greatness."

Nur snapped her head toward the new voice. Her hands curled into fists at her sides—so tight that her nails dug into her palm.

"Just walk away, Bird." Kaleo's words came from somewhere behind her, but Nur's gaze was locked on the boy in front of her.

No, her gaze was locked solely on the boy in front of her.

Bird of the Sea crossed his arms, smirking at the trio. "I was only agreeing with Nur's assessment of her abilities. It's a shame, really. Stormborns are rare, and here we are stuck with one who can't even create an Amulet."

He took a step forward. Instinctively, Nur began to draw on her power. She could sense the clouds above—slowly gathering water that would soon pour down onto the world. She could sense the negative and positive charges that ran through the earth and sky that, in a storm, would cause lightning. She saw the wind—the air rushing in and out of Bird's lungs.

"It's your eastern blood. You know that, right?" he continued. "Maybe if your mother hadn't insisted on fucking a foreigner—"

Nur ripped the breath from Bird's lungs. He fell to the ground, mouth opening and closing like a fish as he tried to suck in air that wasn't there. His eyes widened, then darkened with anger and fear as Nur stepped forward. She gathered what power she could around her, pulling it from an unseen Current that ran through the world.

THE STORM GATHERS

But there was only so much magic her body could take. The raw energy that allowed her to command the storms was beginning to take its toll. Numbness spread from her fingertips up her arms. She knew from experience that if she let it reach her chest, she would pass out.

Still, Nur held on, delighting in the way Bird thrashed—all his hateful words trapped in his throat.

"*Nur!*" A face appeared in front of her, one that was not Bird's but Eva's. "Nur, stop!" Was she screaming? "He's not worth it, all right? If you kill him, the Masters will never let you into the Academy. You'll be banished from the islands. They'll send you into the Shatter."

That finally got her attention. Nur released her grasp on the power and Bird finally managed to gasp in a lungful of air.

Swearing, he climbed to his feet and charged for her. Kaleo stepped into his path. "You already got your ass handed to you once today," flames sprouted from his fingers and danced up his arm, "do you really want it to happen twice?"

A muscle worked in Bird's jaw. The two young men stood in a standoff, a cocky grin still playing across Kaleo's face as he silently dared Bird to act just so that he would have an excuse to use his powers.

One minute passed. Two.

Nur could sense everyone's attention sharpening on the four of them, but no one was willing to intervene.

Finally, Eva let out a long, exasperated sigh. "The three of you are acting ridiculous. Surely, there are more important things to focus on than trying to murder one another?" She gestured towards the closed doors. "There will be plenty of time for that tomorrow."

Nur grimaced at the truth laced within those words. She unclenched her fists, wincing as pain exploded through her palms. She glanced down, noting the half-moon cuts in her skin now filling with blood, and swept her hands against her pants.

Conversation began to swell across the students for a moment before being once again silence by the click of a lock.

Nur spun around to see the crushed shell and sea glass doors slide open enough for their instructor, Sylvie, to slip out.

The older woman gazed out at the crowd of students and cleared her throat. "Good morning. Tomorrow, each of you will duel another. Your performance during this test will determine whether you begin the next stage of your education. Let me remind you that entrance to the Academy is not based on strength, but contingent on your control over your magic. There are sixteen of you, and only six spots are currently open for our island. If you do not pass this test, your Amulet will be destroyed."

That means I have nothing to lose, Nur thought grimly.

Amulets were used as a conduit between the goddess's power and their human bodies. They acted as a vessel and allowed Elemental witches to draw more magic than their bodies could typically handle. However, creating one required a degree of control that Nur—apparently—did not have.

Sylvie removed a scroll from her pocket, holding it tightly in her hands. "The listings were decided by the Masters based on each of your affinities and performance rankings. Your opponent cannot be changed. Good luck." Unrolling the scroll, the woman took a deep breath and read. "Gina of the Sea against Eva of the Sea. Siiri of the Flame against Kaleo of the Flame. Dermot of the Sea against Gwen of the Flame."

Nur counted the names off. Six so far.

Sylvie continued. "Bailey of the Storm against Sasha of the Flame. Nur of the Storm against Bird of the Sea."

The world stopped. The sun that hung permanently above them seemed to dim as though night had fallen.

To her left, Bird let out an exaggerated sigh of relief. "Well, I suppose I won't be giving up my Amulet anytime soon."

Sylvie shot him a look, then read off the remaining names.

The crowd around Nur buzzed with conversation as people either bemoaned or applauded their listings for the duels tomorrow. She had the vague impression that Eva was speaking to her, but she couldn't make out the words through the buzzing in her ear.

Nur ranked fourteenth in their class. Bird was sixth. Their pairing made no sense.

"Nur," Sylvie motioned her forward, her eyes full of concern. "I would like a moment with you. To explain. I'm sure you are confused."

Shouldering her way through the crowd, Nur followed her teacher inside.

"I don't understand," she said, once they were alone. "I don't have an Amulet. Shouldn't I be going against Brent and Gwen?"

Sylvie leaned back against her desk at the corner of the room. "The Masters learned of you and Bird's...rivalry. Such things are not uncommon, although the students are usually more evenly matched." She waved a hand dismissively. "Either way, the Masters paired the two of you together because while competition is encouraged on your home islands, it can be dangerous in the Academy. You must remember it is the jewel of our islands. The witches inside protect our archipelago from eastern invaders."

"They're worried that we'll destroy the Academy if we enter together?"

"It's a concern," Sylvie said. "I don't agree with it, but I cannot change their minds." She offered a small smile. "Don't despair. There's always a chance one of the Masters will sponsor your entry. It's happened before. It's how I got in. And it's how both Master Branson and Hettie of the Flame were admitted."

"Branson and Hettie had been sponsored because they are powerful and because one of the Masters wanted to train them personally." Nur crossed her arms. "I don't have an Amulet and am ranked fourteenth in the class."

"Hettie of the Flame didn't have one, either," Sylvie argued.

"But she's *Hettie of the Flame*. She single-handedly destroyed a hoard of eastern pirates while she was still in her island school." Nur shook her head. "I know you're trying to be nice, but we both know I'm not Hettie." She looked down at her hands. "It's my father's blood, isn't it? Why I can't create an Amulet?"

"It's possible. But here," Sylvie circled her desk and pulled out a small pouch from a drawer. "I had this made for you from the last vial of blood you gave me. Let's try."

She handed the pouch to Nur, who took it and pulled out a short glass cylinder framed in an iron ring. A small hoop was attached at the end so that it could be worn as a necklace, or perhaps a bracelet.

Nur turned the piece over. She knew the glass was freshly-blown from sand dipped in her own blood. It was how all Amulets were made and tied to their wearer. But the blood itself wasn't enough.

Nur closed her eyes and concentrated. She didn't have the surge of emotions she'd used when fighting Bird, so it took her longer to draw from the Current of Eriysha's power.

She focused, her fingers tightening around the Amulet as she pushed the raw power of a storm into the glass. Lightning—white, blue, and purple—flickered inside as a cloud grew inside the Amulet. Tiny bits of rain slammed against the glass. Nur inhaled as wind blew through the small cloud, shifting it about even as the lightning continued to strike. She released her hold on Eriysha's Current and took another breath. She could feel the rising power of the Amulet and its connection to her. It remained whole.

She had done it.

The Amulet lay in her palm, lightning and wind and rain—the essence of the power she commanded thrumming through her fingertips. A million thoughts rolled through her mind as she stared at the tiny storm inside the glass. She had a chance now. To beat Bird and to claim her place in the Academy. She needed to start training. She needed to get used to this new type of power. She had—*CRACK*.

Like the sound of metal pinging against metal, the Amulet shattered. Bits of iron and glass scattered across the floor and embedded in her palm.

"Nur!" Sylvie rushed forward, a scrap of cloth in her hand. "Here, let me."

The Stormwitch spun out of the way, tears pricking her eyes. She'd been so close. Nur had *felt* the connection forming, but it wasn't enough. She didn't know what she'd done wrong—couldn't understand why each Amulet she tried to make broke.

It's because of your father. His weak, eastern blood is ruining yours.

On instinct, her finger curled inwards, and she had to bite her tongue to keep from crying out in pain as the shards of glass and metal dug deeper into her skin.

"Let me see," Sylvie said, reaching forward once more. "We need to remove the glass."

Nur shoved her instructor aside and stormed out the classroom door. In the next instant, Eva and Kaleo were there, surrounding her on either side.

"What happened?" Eva demanded, taking her friend's bloodied hand in hers. "What did you do?"

Nur pulled her hand back. "It's nothing."

"It's *not* nothing," Eva snapped. She reached for her hand again, but Nur danced out of the way.

"I just need to think," she said, unable to keep the desperation out of her voice. "Just…give me a minute to think."

"You can think *after* I remove the broken glass from your hand."

Kaleo's voice was calm as he said, "Eva, leave her be."

"Fine," their friend snapped. "If she wants to bleed to death, then that's fine by me." She spun on Nur. "I'm tired of this brooding, self-destructive streak of yours. Don't think I haven't noticed the cuts on your palms from when you clench your fist or the fact that there are dark rings under your eyes from staying up all night training."

Nur fought against the tears threatening to run loose across her face. "I need to get into the Academy, Eva. You know that. If that means a few sleepless nights, then so be it." She took a breath, calming herself. "We all want to get in. We all want to prove ourselves. I don't have an Amulet. That means I have to work twice as hard as the rest of you to even have a *chance* of getting in."

"Not all of us want to get into the Academy." Eva's voice was soft.

Nur blinked. "What?" She hadn't even considered the possibility that not everyone wanted to go. It's what they'd been working towards since each of their powers had first manifested. "What do you mean? You don't want to go?"

"I have responsibilities here," Eva explained. "I have four younger siblings who all need me and…" she sucked in a breath, "none of us ever had a choice in this. Once they found out we were witches, they stuck us in classrooms and…" She trailed off, shaking her head. "You're not your father, Nur. Would it really be so bad to stay on this island? To have a normal life?"

Yes. She sucked in a breath, shaking her head. "People look at me and see an outsider. Bird isn't the only one who thinks me unworthy of my gifts. He's just the most vocal about it." She looked to Kaleo, whose mouth was pressed in a grim line. "I need to show them that I *am* worthy. I need to prove myself."

"To who?" There was a desperation in Eva's voice that Nur had never heard. "Who do you need to prove yourself to?"

"Everyone."

SIX

Eva had stormed off after their argument, leaving Nur and Kaleo standing alone outside the classroom. The humid air pressed against them, offering a stillness that was only interrupted by the occasional chitter of songbirds. Was the Academy like this? Stagnant. As if waiting for something—anything—to interrupt the monotony of daily life.

Kaleo nodded towards her hand, still sprouting bits of glass and metal. "We should probably do something about that, right?"

Grimacing, she said, "I have bandages at my house. It'll be fine." She lifted her chin in the direction Eva had gone. "Don't you want to go after her, make sure she's all right?"

He shook his head. "She'd bite my head off if I tried to talk to her now, and my face is too pretty to not be attached to the rest of my body."

Nur snorted at that. "Keep pining from afar if you wish, but it won't do you much good."

"I'm not pining," he snapped.

"Sure, you're not."

"Don't say it like that."

"Like what?"

"Like you don't believe it."

She waved her injured hand in front of his face. "Hey, remember that I'm hurt. We can talk about your unrequited love after the glass is out of my palm."

"I am *not* in love with Eva."

Nur rolled her eyes. "Whatever." She started down the dirt path that led from their classroom through the small port town.

Kaleo chased after her. "I have plenty of other women who are actually interested in me."

Nur snorted. "I know. You're not exactly subtle about it."

The Flamewitch nodded, spreading his hands wide. "Exactly. And if I were to fall in love, I would choose to do it with someone who actually liked me back."

"We don't get to choose who we love," Nur replied.

"I imagine we should get some say in the matter."

"I imagine a world where this conversation ended five minutes ago."

"We weren't even discussing this five minutes ago," he shot back. "And you're the one who brought it up."

Nur held up her hand. "I obviously have terrible judgment and no impulse control."

Kaleo chuckled. "Isn't that the truth?"

Striking out with her good hand, Nur gripped her friend's arm and shot a few sparks of electricity through him.

Kaleo yelped and furiously rubbed the space where she'd shocked him. "You're going to regret that."

She smirked at him. "You wouldn't harm an injured girl, would you?"

In answer, his arms burst into flames. The sudden show of power was shocking, and Nur couldn't help but marvel at what sorts of things she might be able to do if she had an Amulet to magnify her abilities.

Kaleo grinned wickedly. "Want to test your luck?"

Nur's lip curled, her natural stupidity compelling her to enter a fight she knew she couldn't win.

Plenty of time for that tomorrow.

"I'd prefer not."

The flames winked out in an instant. "Good choice."

They walked through the quiet streets of the fishing village before turning onto a winding road that led inland.

"Does it hurt?" Kaleo asked, nodding to her palm.

Nur looked down at her hand. The glass and metal were holding most of the blood in, but crimson still ran down her fingers to drip onto the dirt path. "When I think about it."

The lane widened slightly as they entered a clearing filled with six houses packed closely together. None had the luxurious glass windows that were used in the shops in town or in the fancier homes. No, these had wooden shutters and doors that didn't quite fit the walls, meaning that during storm season, the families who inhabited them had to get creative.

They stopped before the house at the end. It was slightly less maintained than the others. The paint that had once decorated the door was chipped and peeling, but Nur could still make out the little flowers and clouds she'd painted at the bottom when she was young. She looked away, willing the memories of her father not to surface.

"Is your mom home?" Kaleo asked.

"Probably not."

Truthfully, she had no idea. She'd stopped keeping track of Emma a long time ago. Her mother worked in the Med House some days and spent the rest of her time on the bluffs by the hand-print rock on the far side of the island. It was the place where Nur's father had washed up.

Nur didn't waste her breath in reminding Emma that the man she'd loved was never coming back. She let her mother live with that hope, mostly because she didn't have the energy to get into that particular argument.

Let her waste her future on the past.

It protected Emma from hearing the comments everyone whispered.

But Nur heard them all. Heard and locked them away, letting the hatred fuel her. Her friend didn't understand. Eva's mother was an Elemental witch. Born of the sea, she was a captain of one of the ferries that brought people across the islands. Eva and her four siblings lived in a house with glass windows by the coast, where they could watch their mother sail in and out. They didn't need Eva to win her duel tomorrow. They already had the wealth and prestige the Academy gave.

Looking at her house now, Nur was more certain than ever that she couldn't stay here.

She took the short stairs up to the front door two at a time, Kaleo on her heels. He reached the door first and pulled it open.

The inside of the house was cramped. A table took up most of the space, with a sink and kitchen occupying the back. Two doorways lay across from each other on either side of the room—one led to Nur's bedroom and the other led to her mother's room and the washroom.

Nur quickly peeked inside. Emma wasn't home. It made things easier.

"Where are the medical supplies?" Kaleo asked.

"Under the kitchen sink."

She took a seat and braced her hand palm up on the kitchen table as Kaleo returned with the supplies. He rummaged around until he pulled out a pair of tweezers.

"This is probably going to hurt," he said with a grimace.

"Just get on with it."

Nur clenched her teeth together as her friend started pulling out the Amulet's glass and iron shards. The painful part wasn't removing the large pieces, but the smaller ones that were buried under her skin and had to be dug out. It took nearly half an hour to get it all. And by that time, she had stopped bothering to hide her winces.

"Okay," Kaleo said, turning her hand over in his. "I think that's it. You're going to need to clean your palm before I bandage it."

Nur nodded, then disappeared into the washroom. She leaned over the sink and turned on the faucet, letting the water run for a bit before placing her hand beneath. As she lathered the soap and cleaned her injuries, Nur glimpsed herself in the mirror. Somewhere throughout the day, the band that she usually used to tie back her curls had come undone, allowing stray strands to run loose. But what was more distressing were the blue eyes staring back at her. Her father's eyes. It had been over ten years since he'd left, but his mark remained—his blood corrupting hers.

Refusing to look anymore, Nur turned off the faucet and shook her hands dry.

She returned to her kitchen a moment later where Kaleo was waiting with strips of cloth neatly spread out in front of him.

THE STORM GATHERS

"All clean?"

"I don't need you to baby me."

"Ouch. Someone's in a bad mood."

Nur slumped back into her chair and held out her hand.

Kaleo wrapped up her cuts, his touch surprisingly gentle. "Do you want to talk about it? The duel tomorrow? Bird?" He tied off the first strip of cloth and then added another. "I have a few thoughts—if you're interested."

Nur was tempted to snap that she wasn't, but she managed a deep inhale and said, "Fine. Speak."

Kaleo opened his mouth, the glitter in his eyes revealing a snide remark coming. She gave him a warning look that said she'd roast him alive, fire powers be damned, if he said anything. Wisely, he took the hint and went back to winding the bandage around her palm.

"Bird is like you. He reacts without thinking. That's not a judgment," Kaleo added quickly. "It's just you tend to strike first and ask questions later. He's probably going to try to bait you. Mention your father or something." He finished tying her bandage and met Nur's eyes. "You need to be calm. You can't let his words get to you. He has more power than you do, so you need to learn not to waste yours." He leaned back in his chair. "It's all about control."

"And you don't think I have control over my emotions?"

"You most *certainly* do not." He gave her a wink before rising to his feet. "I've got to go, Nur. I'll see you and Eva tomorrow."

"Try not to drool too much when you see her. It's a bit gross."

Kaleo gave her a vulgar gesture as he left, closing the door behind him.

ALTHOUGH SHE KNEW SHE SHOULD, Nur didn't practice magic for the rest of the day. Instead, she distracted herself by preparing dinner. She collected the ezbi meat that had been delivered earlier from the icebox and set about slicing it into manageable cubes. As she worked, Nur turned on the stove and began to heat the water.

The sun's light had all but faded from the sky by the time her mother returned. She wore an all-black uniform with red embroidery at the hem of her sleeves. Med House then. It was better than pining on the cliffs all day.

47

"Smells good," Emma said, giving her daughter a smile before retreating to her bedroom to change.

Nur added the ezbi meat to the boiling water along with some vegetables and spices for their meal. She let the stew cook as Emma changed, stirring it occasionally. When her mother returned, Nur pulled the pot from the fire and ladled out two bowls.

"I heard the listings were posted today," Emma said. "Why didn't you tell me?"

Nur shrugged. "You didn't ask."

Her mother fiddled with a loose strand in her sleeve. "Do you want me to come tomorrow? To see you? I know parents are allowed…"

"You don't need to come, mama," Nur said evenly. "My duel…it won't be very impressive, I'm afraid."

"I'm sure you'll do fine."

Nur forced a smile and lied through her teeth. "Yeah, you're right. I'm just stressed."

Emma took a seat and motioned for her daughter to do the same. "Please. This may be the last dinner we have together for a while."

"I will visit," Nur assured her. "Whenever I can."

Her mother smiled. "I know you will, Nunu."

It seemed strange to speak of leaving when Nur was confident she'd be sent right back to this island. To this house. To be forever stuck in the past.

No. You can't think like that. She had waited her entire life for this day—to prove herself to the Academy Masters. *Bright side. Focus on the bright side.* Tomorrow she would finally get the chance to pummel Bird without consequences.

"Mama," Nur said, drawing Emma's attention back to her. "If you ever need help with anything, you can ask the neighbors. Dahlia next door offered to bring you fresh produce from her store every week for half the price. Her little boy will do the delivery. She says it will help him learn some discipline."

"You don't need to worry about me. I'll be all right."

If only that were true. Nur was the one who bought the groceries and maintained the house as best she could. She wasn't sure if her mother even knew how to turn off the house water during the storm or where they kept the extra batteries supplied by the Academy. She'd been meaning to teach her everything—and had tried on a few occasions—but Emma's mind seemed to wander to distant places every few minutes.

"You'll need help during storm season," Nur insisted. "You're not strong enough to move all the furniture yourself. And they'll be repairs, after. Marvis usually helps us, but his back is getting worse, so you may need to find someone else this year."

Her mother waved a dismissive hand. "I know all of this."

"Of course." She looked down at her soup and took a bite. "But you've never lived in this house alone. It might be difficult at first, but remember that I am coming back." *Unlike my father.* She didn't say the last, but judging from her mother's flinch, the implication was not lost on her.

"Focus on the task you have ahead of you, Nunu," Emma advised. "I can take care of myself. I did it long before you were born, and I can do it after you leave. All right?"

"All right."

Nur wanted desperately to believe that what her mother said was true. But wanting something didn't make it so. She downed the last of her soup, washed the bowl, and set it to dry.

She hesitated before the door to her room and turned to catch a final glimpse of Emma.

Her mother looked lost, as she always did, but today the sadness seemed more profound somehow. Had it been the reminder of her dead husband? Or the imminent departure of her daughter? Nur guessed it was the former.

Eastern travelers weren't uncommon. They washed up on their island's shores every few years. Although some tried to harm the island, most were just desperate souls lost to the Shatter.

Nur's father had been one of those souls.

Nanook Del Sue.

He had been an explorer from the kingdom of Teratt, journeying to find the mythical compass of the goddess Eriysha which—legend said—was the only thing that could help a person navigate the Shatter. Instead, he'd found

Nur's mother and sired Nur. And then he'd disappeared—stolen a ship from the dock one night and never returned, leaving Nur behind to pick up the pieces of her mother's shattered heart.

SEVEN

Rae got undressed quickly, stripping down until she was wearing nothing but the gold cuffs on her wrists. With a precise wrist motion, she could trigger the blades inside to slide into her palm for easy access. The design was inspired by the ancient, northern warriors of Vetta, whose weapons and fighting style was legend.

She had become fascinated by their technique after learning about Tamar Oshel, who had fought alongside Empress Oriane Asha in her campaign to unite the South from a collection of warring countries into one great nation called Tala. The empire had remained unified for over five hundred years before rising tensions saw the country break into three separate ones—Yovar, Aaran, and Siora.

Rae ran a hand over her cuffs lovingly before crossing to her dresser and taking out her guard uniform. She pulled on the blue, sleeveless tunic and gray pants that were the principal components of her uniform. It looked simple on the outside but, in truth, was meticulously crafted with Sioran steel that was plated like dragon scales in the fabric, turning the simple clothing into impenetrable armor. *Near* impenetrable. Just as long as she wasn't too attached to her arms.

The clock on the bedside table encouraged her to hurry. She pulled on her boots, then started decorating herself in blades.

In addition to the falcata at her waist and her golden cuffs, Rae added three pairs of knives to each of her boots, along with two daggers in her thigh sheathes. She removed a short and slender sword from beneath her bed, slid it into the sheath strapped to her back where it was hidden from detection by her shirt. Finally, she began twisting her dark brown hair into two braids, fastened close to her head by sharpened hairpins.

She strutted to the full-length mirror in her bathroom and looked herself over. All good. There was barely a trace of the desert on her. She looked as she was supposed to. A royal guard loyal to her king.

Except for her eyes.

Golden irises shone back at her in the mirror, complimenting the long, sharp angles of her face. It was rare that she ever got to see them—this piece of her mother's people that was reflected in herself. In all other aspects, Rae took after her father, Edgar Toma. Most of the time, she considered it a blessing that his genes hid the visual reminder of her Tiskona blood, allowing her to blend in with the general populous. But looking at herself now, all Rae saw were the parts she had to hide.

Biting her lip, she pulled a small, brown vial from her cabinet. She tipped her head back and, using the bottle's accompanying pipette, released two drops of the liquid into each of her eyes. Looking back at the mirror, she saw the gold of her irises fade to brown.

Rae put the vial back in the cabinet and adjusted her clothes once more before stepping outside and heading down the hall. As she walked, she passed rows of identical doors, all belonging to the king's royal guard.

"You're late." Rae didn't turn at the sound of Daro, another of the king's royal guard, coming up behind her. "And there's sand in your hair."

She tensed slightly, even though she knew there were a thousand other conclusions he would come to before accusing her of being one of the Val. He didn't even know there had been an attack on the caravan yet.

No one did.

"I take it you had another one of your dalliances with a nobleman's son?"

"Son *and* daughter, actually," Rae replied smoothly.

Daro was taller than her, although not by much. His cheeks were round despite his strong jaw and the shadow of a beard growing across his face. Lean muscles rippled across his arms, visible thanks to his sleeveless tunic.

"What's the matter, Daro?" she teased. "Jealous? You know you're always welcome to join. I'm curious about what's under that uniform…"

"Shut up."

"I have a running bet with Emry. She says there's another uniform beneath that, but I suspect it's something far more scandalous. Red lace, perhaps?"

"I said, shut up."

Rae sighed in disappointment. "You know, I'm just teasing you? It's what friends do."

"We aren't friends."

"We could be."

"We aren't friends because I don't like you."

Rae snorted. "We both know that's not true." She flashed him a winning smile. "Everyone either loves me or hates me. And I suspect that the ones who hate me secretly love me. They just hate themselves because they can't have me."

"As usual, your arrogance is astounding, Toma."

"Every inch of me is astounding, Daro."

He huffed a sound of annoyance. Or perhaps it was a laugh.

Rae grinned at him, and he pointedly ignored her as they rounded a bend into the royal part of the castle.

A thick, blue carpet, threaded with gold and silver designs, covered the floors. High walls and long windows adorned one side of the hall, letting in the afternoon light. Stained glass sconces not yet lit lined the other side of the wall. Tapestries embroidered with mythic creatures, public figures, and depictions of ancient battles hung from the ceiling.

Rae and Daro made their way up a winding set of stairs crowned with a hammered silver banister. Beyond the landing was a short hallway lined with guards wearing traditional armor.

Finally, the pair reached a painted black door with two guards dressed in blue on either side. The guards gave a quick nod to their replacements before starting back down the hall the way Rae and Daro had come.

Daro took up his station while Rae gave a light, patterned knock on the door before stepping aside. A few moments later, the door swung open to reveal a middle-aged man with straight black hair shining with grease. He was taller than Rae but far less muscled, despite the heavy sword hanging at his hip.

"King Argos," she said, giving the man a slight bow.

"Warrior Toma," the king replied before his gaze shifted to Daro. "Warrior Glassen."

"Where are Warriors Ellis and Emry?" Daro asked, referring to the other two guards on duty.

"I sent them ahead to secure the council chamber," Argos said smoothly.

A muscle worked in Daro's jaw. He was technically the commander of the king's royal guard, although no one ever referred to him using that title—aside from Rae when she wanted to tease him. Still, to send soldiers to a new location without informing him ahead of time was both dangerous and against procedure.

A vein began to pulse in Daro's forehead.

"Excellent," Rae said, cutting in before Argos could notice the other guard's irritation. "Shall we escort you to your council chambers, Your Grace?"

"Yes, perhaps if I arrive early, it will cause my councilors to sweat a bit. It may even prompt them to give me some halfway decent advice."

Rae allowed herself a genuine smile, then turned to stand at attention behind the king, matching her pace with him as he walked through the castle.

In the three years since she had started the Val and been promoted to one of the king's personal guards, she'd carefully pruned his council—eliminating the most competent of them either through deception or more violent means. Most of the councilmen and women she'd removed had been advisors to the Argos's father before his death. The replacements his son had brought in were less than useful. Most were religious fanatics, like their king, or were more suited to drinking games and gambling than to actually running a country. The largest problem Rae had yet to find a way to deal with was the king's general and Varim, who served as the military's second-in-command.

Eventually, they reached the gilded double doors of the council chamber. Ellis and Emry were stationed outside, looking profoundly bored. The brother and sister pair were both excellent fighters, especially when facing opponents together, as she had found out during one embarrassing sparring session a few years back.

Rae had a fondness for the sister, Emry, who was much more relaxed than her brother. When she wasn't busy with the Val or on duty, the two of them would play card games with some of the other guards. Neither Ellis nor Daro ever joined them.

Argos motioned to the twins. "The two of you will stay outside. Toma, Glassen, you'll enter with me."

They all nodded once before Ellis and Emry pulled open the double doors, giving the three of them room to step inside. Rae winked at Emry as they passed, and the other guard waggled her eyebrows in return.

The council chamber was enormous. High walls and a vaulted ceiling rested above a long glass table lined with chairs. At the head was a throne cushioned with purple velvet.

Argos took his seat, flanked by Rae and Daro.

The king drummed his fingers on the wooden armrest in a steady rhythm until his councilors started arriving, each one flanked by a single guard and a servant carrying stacks of paper. The king's general and his right hand were the last to appear, each taking seats on either side of Argos.

"Excellent," the king said, his fingers stilling on the throne. "Now we can begin." He gave a vague wave toward everyone at the table. "What are your reports?"

"Tax season will begin soon," councilman Raymond said. The short, rat-faced man sat at the end of the table. He ruffled through some papers with fingers stained black from ink. "I would request that we add more guards to each unit of tax collectors. There have been increasing reports of unrest, and with the Val rebels still at large…"

"Yes, yes," Argos said impatiently. "Take the men from the latest batch of Citadel graduates."

Raymond made a few notes in his notebook, muttering slightly to himself.

"I want to know of our Shadow Fire shipment," Argos pressed. "What news is there?"

"None yet, Your Grace," Varim said. "We expect to get a report tonight when the true shipment reaches the checkpoint. The decoy has already arrived without incident."

"Good. Good." Argos nodded to himself. "That's very good to hear. With the Shadow Fire, we will finally be able to penetrate that damned forest and root out the Tiskona heathens."

"Very true, Your Grace," the general said, his dark eyes darting toward Rae for a moment. "Your son is ready to receive the shipment?"

"Prince Illian is in position," Argos confirmed.

"Excellent. And once we use the Shadow Fire to infiltrate the Forest and command the Tiskona's surrender, what will we do?"

"We should kill them all," a woman suggested.

Rae had not bothered to learn her name, although she was fairly sure she was one of Argos's latest lovers.

"They possess dark magics—powers drawn from the gods themselves," the woman continued, "that steal from Tayrn, leaving our planet weak. They do not deserve our mercy."

"No, no, Mareth," Argos said, an amused glint in his eye. He liked it when people spouted hate toward the Tiskona. It gave him the opportunity to sound like the benevolent leader. "The Tiskona have been led down the wrong path. For those who are willing to end their evil ways, we will give them a road to salvation. Show them the better path. I believe it to be possible." He motioned to Rae. "Warrior Toma is half Tiskona, is she not? And yet you can all see her loyalty to the crown. She attends temple each week—as do we all—and prays to the one true god, Rion."

A few councilmen nodded, their eyes turning to her while she stared straight ahead. The Tiskona did not practice any form of dark magic. They were devoted to the earth and its god, Orik, but their isolation and secrecy allowed for the spread of misinformation that was becoming their downfall. There were even some who claimed that the Tiskona cast dark spells in order to converse with Death. It was nonsense. But the king believed it.

"You did well, Edgar," Argos continued, returning his attention to his trusted general—completely unaware of Rae's growing ire. "Truly, your daughter has proved her loyalty to me time and time again. You should be proud of her."

Edgar Toma bowed his head. "Thank you, Your Grace."

"With all due respect," Varim interjected. "Warrior Toma is only half Tiskona and was raised by her father and I since she was born. Is it truly possible for people, who have only been taught in the ways of the Forest, to change?"

Rae's gaze shot to him. As her father's right hand, he had been responsible for most of her training at the Citadel. He'd been her handler for years and, of all the people in the room, was the most skeptical of her allegiance.

"That is a good question," the king admitted, a cruel smile tilting his lips. "I suppose we will find that out soon enough."

THE COUNCIL MEETING LASTED NEARLY three hours. Most of it was spent arguing over the war and what tactical strategies would be best for penetrating the Forest. In the end, nothing was decided.

There was little talk of the Val rebels, which was both a blessing and insulting. Rae didn't like the idea of her group being high on Argos's list of things to exterminate, but she felt they should warrant more than two mentions in a three-hour session. Indeed, usually there was far more talk of the Val, led by either Varim or Councilman Jeros, who was Argos's spymaster and leader of the Revry.

After the meeting, Rae spent another two hours on guard duty outside of the king's bedchamber before she and Daro were relieved.

Rae half-walked, half-stumbled through the castle to her rooms. She'd barely gotten any sleep the night before, most of it spent preparing for her mission to intercept the Shadow Fire. Now, she regretted not catching some sleep on the ride there or back. She'd slept while riding ceprra before, not that it would have been an entirely restful sleep…

"Warrior Toma!"

Rae had just reached her bedroom door when the sound of her name caught her attention.

Varim, dressed in a dark gray long-sleeved shirt and silver embroidered vest, came striding up to her, carrying something wrapped in brown fabric.

He was shorter than Rae by a few inches, giving her a clear view of the bald spot on his head.

"I'm glad to have caught you." He stopped a few feet from her and frowned, examining her. "By Rion, you look tired. Did you get enough sleep last night?"

"It's a wonder you don't bed more women with compliments like that," Rae replied, her hand drifting instinctively toward her falcata.

"Apologies, it is natural for me to worry. It won't do for you to be guarding the king half-asleep."

"I assure you, when I left King Argos, he was alive and well." She crossed her arms, drawing up to her full height. "Tell me what you want, Varim. I don't have the patience for your antics today."

The man's mouth pressed into a thin line. "I wanted to apologize, Rae. What the king said this afternoon spoke to my soul." He pressed a hand to his heart for emphasis. "You truly have shown your loyalty to the crown, and I have been unfair to doubt you."

"I sense a *but* coming."

"No," he shook his head emphatically. "I am being serious. I discussed it with your father, and he has permitted me to give you this." Varim balanced the bundle in one hand and pulled away the brown cloth with the other to reveal a sword. It was longer than her falcata, thinner too, curving slightly at the end. The hilt was wrapped in black leather and stamped with ancient runes. Rae reached forward and took the blade from him. She pulled the sword from its sheath to reveal shining steel. Down the side of the blade was another set of runes etched into the metal. *Vettan* runes.

△□ ⊰⅄⅃ △□ ⊰⅃ᴄ⅄⊰ △□ ⟨ᴄ▷⅄

"Whose was this?" she asked. The sword of made of Sioran steel. It was the strongest metal, created in Siora and used almost exclusively for making weapons as blades forged from it were impossible to break.

Gripping the hilt, Rae knew the sword had never been wielded before, but to have Vettan runes…it would need to be hundreds of years old.

"That sword and its twin were commissioned by Tamar Oshel and wielded only once during the Desfour raid."

"That's not possible," Rae said, re-sheathing the blade. "When Tamar died, her body and weapons were burned with dragon fire. The ashes scattered to the wind."

"True," Varim admitted.

"But this sword was kept by Oriane Asha and Erenahl Terr. The other, named *Desmiil*, was given to their acquaintance, Mileson, and is currently kept by the Empress of Aaran." He nodded to the sword. "This one is named *Teruth*."

It meant *daughter of life* in Old Suhryn. *Desmiil* meant *son of death*.

Rae gripped the sword tightly. "What do the runes say?"

"I don't know. I am not sure anyone does. Even if you were to find someone to translate it, it's likely the Vettan runes have changed in the hundreds of years since Tala rose."

"And...you're giving this to me?" Rae asked, her voice quieter than she'd ever heard it.

He nodded. "You've earned it, Warrior Toma."

"Thank you." She offered a quick bow before ducking into her room, Tamar's sword clutched tightly to her chest.

Varim was wrong. She hadn't earned this sword. Not yet. Not until the war was over and her mother's people were safe.

A tapping on her window drew her attention and Rae opened it to find a black bird perched on the ledge outside. She recognized it as a corvim, a species native to the Forest. She smiled at it and it turned its head to the side, peering at her with startlingly bright orange eyes. It cawed at her twice, then flew away. She watched it disappear into the night with a faint smile. Its appearance was a reminder from Mirella, a member of her Val council, that they had a meeting tomorrow.

Excitement bubbled through her. Rae always enjoyed trips into the city.

EIGHT

Rae took the gondola down the cliffs the next morning. It wasn't unusual for guards to come and go from the city, so she wasn't worried about drawing suspicion.

She ambled her way through the crowds towards the Capital's center, allowing herself to get lost in the mass of bodies.

After a few blocks, she slipped down an alley to where she'd stashed an over-sized parka that covered her blue uniform and hung to her knees. She pulled the hood over her braided hair and slipped back into the crowd.

Rae continued down the main boulevard for another three blocks before stopping at a fruit stand at the corner of two cross streets.

"Hello, Sahira." She greeted the shopkeeper warmly, pulling back her hood just enough so the older woman could see her face.

"You, again," the old woman snapped, her thin lips becoming thinner as she frowned. "I thought I told you not to come back. You owe me money for destroying my stand and ruining half my produce!"

"That wasn't my fault," Rae pointed out. "Besides, it's been years and I've paid double for your fruit ever since. Even though it's worth a quarter of that."

Sahira's face scrunched up into a frown. "Is this you trying to get on my good side?"

"We both know you don't have a good side." Rae gave the woman a wink and picked up two fresh peaches from her stand. She dusted them off on her sleeve, giving each one a careful inspection, conscious of the woman staring daggers into her chest. "I'll take both," she announced.

THE STORM GATHERS

"You'd better, after rubbing them all over your disgusting rags," the shopkeeper snapped.

Slipping a hand into her pocket, Rae pulled out two gold coins and handed them to the merchant.

Sahira's eyes went wide. "How did you get this money, girl? I don't take stolen coin."

Rae snorted. "Sure you do. And for the record, it's not stolen."

Sahira huffed, and pocketed the money, then she made a shooing motion. "Leave. You're scaring my customers."

Biting back her retort, Rae turned away and headed down a cross street. As she walked, she tossed a peach into the air, catching it as she went. She continued down the road to a corner where three neighborhoods collided.

A mix of buildings, old, new, and some in between, spread before her. At its center was a circular building crowned with a domed roof. Twin metal doors, flanked by three-foot-tall doorstops, waited in front of her. On the closed doors were Vettan runes—like the ones stamped into *Teruth*.

Rae had once asked Herba, the bookkeeper, what they meant. He'd joked that they were meant to bring him protection, but all they'd brought was trouble.

She pulled open one of the doors, slipped inside, and was greeted by the smell of old paper and fresh ink.

Books lay in rows before her, their covers made of a mixture of metal, animal skin, and wood. Rae breathed it all in, closing her eyes slightly.

"Enough," a scratchy voice said. "You know that disturbs my customers."

She cracked an eye open and stared at the old bookkeeper at the back of the store. "You're closed right now, Herba," she reminded him. "You have no customers."

"Well, it disturbs *me*."

Rae chuckled. "Fair enough."

She started down the row of shelves to Herba's desk. It was crowded with books, loose papers, and inkwells. "I see you've finally organized."

Herba wagged a finger at her. "I'm in no mood for your sarcasm today, Toma. Your posse is waiting for you inside. Better get in."

Rae pulled another peach from her pocket and set it on his desk. "I got this for you."

He frowned at the fruit. "Did you steal it?"

Rae let out a long sigh. "Why does everyone assume I'm a thief?"

"Probably because you are."

"No, I did not steal the peach. I bought it from Sahira."

Herba shuddered slightly. "Horrible woman."

"She's prickly." Rae cocked her head to the side. "A bit like you."

The bookkeeper frowned. "Get your ass inside before I call the city guard."

Laughing, Rae walked around the desk to a door built seamlessly into the back wall. She pressed on it until she heard a click, then slid the panel open to reveal a small room taken up by a round table. Seated at the table were two men and two women. A final chair waited for her.

Rae took her seat, her humor from a moment before gone. She was no longer Rae Toma. Now, she was the leader of the Val, and this was her war council.

She nodded towards Mirella, seated to her left. The Tiskona woman had been visiting the Capital at the behest of her queen when the war had begun, trapping her in Siora. After learning about the Val, she'd joined and soon became the middleman between Rae and the Tiskona queen.

"The Forest is well stocked with provisions for the summer," Mirella said. Her voice was crisp, with hardly any hint of her accent remaining. "No new weapons are needed, but I will keep in contact."

Rae nodded and turned to her spymaster, Zarah, who sat beside the Tiskona ambassador. The young woman's hair sat in a tight bun, accentuating her cheekbones. She had been two years ahead of Rae at the citadel before being recruited into the spy guild known as the Revry. Her skin bore the marks of her time there with a trail of tattoos that snaked up her arms and disappeared into her shirt. What those tattoos meant, Rae had never asked. She'd learned that the Revry, and Zarah's departure from it, were not safe topics of conversation.

"Nothing of note to report," the woman said. "I've been tracking the Yovar ambassador, as you requested. He's been growing more and more agitated ever since the Shadow Fire disappeared. I suspect the Yovar government doesn't have as much of the substance as they have led the world to believe."

"What makes you think that?" Mirella asked.

"Just a hunch." Zarah turned back to Rae. "It's unclear if they will send another shipment. Since the destruction of House Kitza, the rest of the Royal Houses have been trying to monopolize on the fallen family's Sioran connections. This is the first lucrative deal they've made. I doubt they will want to pack it in, but if my suspicions are correct, they may have no choice. Either way, I'll keep you updated."

"Thank you."

Rae turned her attention to Cyrus. "The Shadow Fire has been sunk," he said simply. "Nothing to worry about."

"There's always something to worry about," Mirella replied evenly, giving Rae a small nod. She returned the gesture and glanced at Jonah, whose face was grim.

"There are new Citadel graduates on the streets," he said gruffly. "Pups snapping at our heels, desperate to prove themselves by finding information on the Val."

"They're early this year," Zarah commented.

"It's because of the war," Rae said. "I expected this. We'll suspend all operations for two weeks, as per usual, then reconvene."

Jonah, Zarah, and Mirella nodded in agreement, but Cyrus held up a hand. "What about the food we have coming into the city in two days? People on the streets are starving. They need this. We've already arranged for passage into the city and bribed the guards…"

"We bribed the *old* guards," Rae replied. "A shipment into the city is too risky right now."

Cyrus's face darkened. "The people are starving."

"You think I don't know that? But if we get caught, we won't be able to help them in the future. It's the long game."

"We've been playing the long game for years," Cyrus snapped.

She raised an eyebrow. "You do understand what 'the long game' means, don't you?"

"I'll see to it personally," Cyrus insisted. "The food will spoil if we don't get it into the city. It's a waste."

Rae ground her teeth. "No. Not you." She turned to Jonah. "Can you do it? Work in small groups. If anything feels off, you abandon the operation and scatter, understand?"

Jonah nodded. "Will do, boss."

"Why not me?" Cyrus demanded. "I know this city better."

"You're also reckless," Zarah said, her voice hard. "And easily noticed."

Cyrus's hands tightened around the arm of his chair. "I've never been caught before. Unlike you."

Zarah stiffened, her mouth curved to reply, but Rae cut her off. "Either Jonah heads the mission, or there will be no food entering the city this week. Which will it be, Cyrus?"

"He can do it," Cyrus snapped. "But—"

"Excellent," Rae said, rising to her feet. "Jonah will bring the food shipment into the city. We will cease all contact for the next two weeks and I'll send word when it's time to meet again."

They all nodded this time and rose from their chairs as well.

Holding up five fingers, Rae reopened the paneled door and slipped into the bookshop, giving Herba a wink before slipping back onto the street. She turned the corner, heading into the older neighborhood that clung close to the bottom of the cliffs.

As she walked, Rae took in the painted white and gray stone. Most of the color had faded from the murals through the centuries, but some artists had come in a few decades ago to touch up the more prominent pieces. Still, even the faded works were beautiful, the muted colors complimenting the texture of the stone. She drank it all in like a tourist. Tamar's sword at her hip gave her a new appreciation for the ancient architecture as she passed a wall depicting Oriane Asha and her white dragon, Kubriel.

Distracted, it took Rae nearly five minutes to notice that she had someone tailing her. She didn't let her shoulders tense or her breath become unsteady. She continued on as she had before, keeping her pace slow and leisurely. Her hood was still up, covering most of her face. It was likely that whoever was after her was just some citizen looking to steal her purse. Still, they were good—Rae wouldn't have been able to detect them if she hadn't been the top of her class at the Citadel.

She made it to the end of the block, then slipped down a side street and pressed herself into the shadow of a doorway. Her pursuer came around the bend, hesitated for a moment, then turned her way. Rae held her breath, counting their footsteps until…

She kicked out with one leg, knocking the man's feet out from under him. Before he had a chance to recover, she sprang forward. With one hand, she caught him by the collar of his shirt and raised to strike.

She froze, eyes going wide as she took in the identity of her stalker.

"Took you five minutes to notice me following you," the man said, a boyish grin spreading across his face. "Your father would be disappointed."

She released his collar with a shove. The man stumbled backward, trying to find his balance.

Rae crossed her arms, surveying him. "What are you doing here, Aram?"

NINE

Alana hadn't been on a ship since the day she'd set foot in Jaarin. Now, looking at the sea spread out in front of her, she felt her body hesitate. It had been five years since she'd last seen her homeland and, in that time, she'd become an entirely new person. She had no doubt her countrymen had heard of her reputation. Would they hate her for it? Fear her? Alana found herself more bothered by the possibility than she wanted to admit.

"Are you ready?" Maria's voice was irritatingly soft.

"I'm always ready," Alana lied. She turned to walk past her two guards but stopped in front of Johnathan, frowning. She glanced at Maria. "What's wrong with him?"

"The captain says that there are icebergs in the north. We are going to take the southern route around the Shallows. He," she made a motion at her fellow guard, "is afraid."

Alana snorted. "I forgot how superstitious you are, Johnathan."

"I'm *practical*," he snapped. "The Shallows aren't natural."

"The Shallows are *very* natural," Alana argued. "They're just rock formations that formed beneath the water when the sea level was higher."

"They say poisonous mist surrounds them," Johnathan pressed. "That dark spirits lurk in the shadows of the spires."

"They also say that the mountains in the Skyfall range move," Alana said. "Do you believe that, too?"

"That's different."

"Is it? It's just another made-up story told to frighten gullible people."

THE STORM GATHERS

Johnathan let out an annoyed huff, arms crossing over his chest. Alana sauntered past him and headed down the wooden ramp to the docks, the sounds of her two guards arguing floating behind her as she went.

The Shallows were an area of the Western Sea between Okaro and Jaarin where ancient rock formations sprouted from the water in great spires that climbed towards the clouds. Before being properly mapped, the rocks had sunk countless ships, leading to the folk myths surrounding that area of the sea. She had never seen the Shallows. They were too far from Okaro to be worth visiting. And on her journey to Jaarin, they had taken the northern route specifically to avoid the area.

Alana made her way up the gangplank of the ship. The rocking of waves against the hull was like a song she hadn't heard in years. It brought back distant memories of journeys along the coast with her father and sister—those few hours when she'd been free from her mother's oppressive presence.

A man appeared in front of her, wearing the tricorne hat that marked him as captain. "Welcome, Alana, I am Captain Abin Ressin, and it is an honor to welcome you aboard my ship."

"The honor is mine," Alana replied, giving the man a small smile that felt wrong on her lips. "This is a beautiful ship. You should be proud."

"I am," the captain said, his hands going to his chest in a gesture of love as he observed the deck. "Make yourself at home here."

"I will do my best. But I admit, it has been a long time since I last set sail."

"I'm certain you'll get your sea legs before the day is out," Abin assured her. "But, perhaps a trip into the scout's nest will serve as a reminder to the princess you once were."

Alana met the captain's gaze and gave him a small nod. Leaving him behind, she weaved around crates and sailors as she made her slow way to the main mast of the ship. For the journey, she'd elected to wear simple brown pants and a black shirt that was covered by an intricately embroidered red coat that hung to the backs of her knees. Alana preferred dresses, but the garments simply weren't practical at sea.

"Excuse me!" the sound of a man's voice came from behind her, and Alana barely had time to jump out of the way before the crate the sailor was

67

carrying dropped to the floor. The man cursed, his face turning red. "I'm so sorry! I slipped and—oh gods, you're…" He got down on one knee. "Queen Alana Zaya."

She raised an amused eyebrow. "You may stand."

He did so, a hand running through his loose, blond hair.

"What is your name?"

"Wren, Your Majesty."

"Be careful, Wren. I'd prefer that none of my sailors break their necks on this journey."

"I'll take steps to avoid that, Your Majesty." He gave her a low bow, then ran back down the deck to help his fellow sailors load up the ship.

Alana returned her attention to the mast and began to climb. Although it had been years since she'd been on a ship, her body adjusted quickly to its movement. There was a time, long ago, when there was no surface she couldn't scale. Her father used to challenge her to climb the tallest trees on the palace grounds or reach the top of the largest ship in the harbor. Alana made it to the lip of the lookout's nest and pulled herself over the edge, startling the boy standing there. He stumbled back, nearly tripping over the edge before she caught his wrist, pulling him to safety.

"Your Majesty!" the sailor exclaimed. He couldn't have been older than fifteen, with light gray eyes and curly brown hair. "You shouldn't be up here. It's dangerous."

Alana's eyes ran over the boy. There was something so familiar—and yet so foreign—about him. Finally, her attention flickered out to the ocean. "You needn't worry over my safety. I have an army of people who do that already. What's your name?"

"Penn, Your Majesty."

A small smile graced Alana's lips. "Tell me, Penn, how did you come to sail with Captain Abin?"

"He came to my orphanage a few years ago," he said, frowning at the memory. "He needed someone who was a fast climber to keep watch at night."

"Fortunate then, that he chose you. You get to sail the world. Such a life must be exciting."

THE STORM GATHERS

Something sparked in the boy's gaze. "It is. You wouldn't believe the things I've seen, Your Majesty."

"Tell me."

"Really?" he asked, clearly surprised.

Alana shrugged. "I always enjoy a good story."

He eyed her. "Are you sure you're Alana Zaya? The Queen of Darkness? The woman who executed a man during her first months as queen? Who burned the Seacrest estate? Who they say even the sea fears?"

Alana fought a laugh. "The very same."

"Pardon me, Your Majesty, but you aren't what I imagined."

"And what did you imagine?"

"Someone far more..." Penn trailed off as he searched for the right word, "terrifying."

"Sometimes the people you should fear the most are the ones who are the least assuming. People don't whisper my name in dark corners because I'm some brute with a knife in an alley."

"Then...why do they?"

"I told you, I like stories." A gull cawed in the distance. "Hold on."

Alana gripped the railing tighter as the last of the docking ropes were undone. They pushed away from land, and the boat lurched beneath them, rocking against the waves that carried it away from the shore. Riggers climbed the masts, unfurling the sails and securing them before the wind picked up, pushing the boat through the water.

Towards Okaro.

Towards home.

TEN

N ur woke early the next morning. She dressed in simple loose clothes in patterns of gray and white that she tightly secured to her body with scraps of colored cloth. Looking at herself in the mirror, she couldn't help but smile. She'd always known this day would come. Known, but hadn't really believed. Some part of her had assumed that the Masters would learn of her father's blood and dismiss out of hand. Now, wearing the traditional dueling clothes that molded seamlessly to her body's curves…it felt like a dream.

She tugged on her soft boots and tied her hair back away from her face. *Focus on the duel. The rest of the world does not matter.*

After a quick check to confirm her mother was still asleep, Nur slipped out the door. She was too nervous to eat breakfast, but set out some leftover stew on the table for when Emma woke up.

The sun hung above her in the sky, in the same place it always was, shining a dim light on the world. In the East, they told stories of a sun and stars that made a grand journey across the sky each morning—arcing from one horizon to the next. They spoke of constellations that could be tracked through the seasons and used to tell direction.

But none of that existed in the Shatter.

The sun never moved from its spot in the sky, its light fading in and out to brighten the world. The stars that surrounded it shifted places each night. Some spent years tracking their movements, looking for patterns that didn't exist. Others set their sites on uncovering the location to the mythical Compass of Eriysha. It was all in vain. The Shatter was simply a puzzle that no one could solve.

Nur made her slow way down the path that led to the harbor. As she grew closer, she could see the white sails of Academy ships as they approached the shore. People pushed past each other and climbed onto one another's shoulders—trying to get a better look. Despite the chaos, the crowd parted for Nur as she passed, recognizing that the clothes she wore marked her as a contestant in the upcoming duels.

Most of her classmates were already at the docks. Kaleo and Eva stood together in conversation.

Slowly, Nur made her way up to her friends. "Hey," she said when she reached them.

Kaleo gave her an exaggerated smile. "Nice of you to join us."

Ignoring him, she turned to look at Eva, whose eyes were on the horizon, tracking the progression of the incoming ships. "How are you?" Nur dared ask.

Her friend was silent for a moment, then let out a long sigh. She turned, hesitated, then tackled Nur in a hug. "You're a reckless idiot," she murmured. "But I've known that since the day I met you."

"And you're stubborn and overbearing," Nur replied, squeezing Eva's body with affection. "But I've known that since the day I met you, too."

"Awe," Kaleo said, stepping between them. "Do I get a hug?"

Eva slammed her palm against Kaleo's shoulder. "Hush!"

"Ouch!" Kaleo laughed, rubbing where he'd just been struck. "That's not very nice. I expect that behavior from Nur…"

"Watch it," Nur snapped.

"Sorry."

"Look!" Eva bounced forward, her hand wrapping around Kaleo's bicep. "The ships are coming in."

Nur took a small step away, not missing the smile that spread across her male friend's face at Eva's touch.

There were three ships—long canoes with an added cabin at the back and a large triangular sail sprouting from the middle. The railings and masts were decked out in flowers, twisting pieces of driftwood and threaded sea glass. One person stood on top of each cabin, their arms raised as they pushed the ship forward with a steady stream of wind. At the bow of the ship was another who monitored and controlled the tides to ensure a straight journey. A few more members of the Academy decorated each ship—professors and students who'd agreed to make the trip.

Each island in their archipelago was carefully marked with signs pointing to the other islands. Nur had no idea how long it had taken to chart their lands—or what deadly mistakes had been made—but she was grateful that some soul had had the initiative. Still, travel between the islands was discouraged. At sea, there was no means for telling which direction you were going, only to face forward and hope that the tides and wind didn't lead you astray. That uncertainty was why only those at the Academy who were blessed by the Storm or Sea could ferry people between islands. Their gifts could keep a boat on course, assuming no storms interrupted the journey. If Nur got into the Academy, it was possible that this was the role she would be tasked with once her training was complete.

The ships pulled into the harbor and were quickly tied to the deck by attendants waiting on the docks. A single person stepped from each boat, a scroll in their hands. One by one, they read off the list of people allowed on each ship. The organization seemed random, but everyone knew the Masters had carefully decided who would sit with whom.

Nur was with Kaleo, along with Gwen, Bailey, and Brent.

No one spoke as they boarded and took their seats. The man who'd read off their names disappeared into the cabin at the back of the ship. There were three others from the Academy on board. The Stormwitch and Seawitch both rested at their stations, rebuilding their strength for the journey back. The final member on board was a red-haired woman. She couldn't have been much older than Nur, with dark green eyes and skin spotted with freckles. Her hair was tied back from her face in a neat bun.

The woman caught Nur staring and winked.

"See something you like?" Kaleo murmured.

"Shut up."

He chuckled softly. "I didn't know redheads were your type."

"I will burn you alive." Forget that she wasn't a Flamewitch. She'd find a way.

Kaleo wisely kept his mouth shut, but laughter danced in his eyes.

Nur didn't dare another glance at the red-haired woman.

It was a tense trip. The Sea and Stormwitch bent in concentration as they brought them out of the harbor and into open water. Overall, the crossing was surprisingly quick, with only a few minutes spent in absolute silence before the island of the Academy appeared in the distance. It was smaller than Nur had imagined and unexpectedly flat, with a single raised mountain peeking out from the far-right side of the island. Its dark slope and jagged top made her suspect it had once been a volcano before becoming hollow and dormant.

As they drew closer, the buildings of the Academy came into view. They were low to the ground and most appeared to be carved from the same dark, pocked stone as the volcano, but Nur could see wooden supports plus a mixture of other materials, likely used to repair the structure after storms. Jungle trees and other plants prevented her from taking it all in, but from the brief glimpse as their ship skated past, she knew it was magnificent.

They sailed past the main buildings of the Academy and around the bend to a cove where a small harbor was set up. Attendants waited at each dock, and more members stood behind them to give directions to each student.

Nur felt her fingers clench into fists, nails digging into the still injured skin of her palm. She bit back a hiss of pain and settled for rolling her shoulders as their ship slid into the docks.

Once everything was secure, the man who had read their names earlier called each person individually off the ship. They were then escorted up the paths toward the amphitheater.

Kaleo and Bailey were called first, followed by her.

Nur got to her feet as the ship swayed beneath her and took the hand offered as she descended onto the deck. As her feet met solid ground, she came face-to-face with the red-haired woman. The stranger winked again at her before turning back to the ship to help another student disembark.

Swallowing down her apprehension, Nur hurried away.

HALF AN HOUR LATER, NUR was in a windowless room with stone walls. The only furniture was the padded wood bench she now sat on. Fuel-free lamps flickered at each corner, the warm glow of fire heating her face as she listened for her name to be called.

Both Eva and Kaleo had had their duels, although she didn't know the outcomes. She wanted Eva to come to the Academy with her, but after their conversation the day before, she wasn't certain her friend shared that desire. If Nur somehow got in and Eva didn't, would that mean never seeing her again?

"Nur of the Storm and Bird of the Sea, please enter the arena," a distant voice called. The message repeated three times, spurring her to action. She knew that if she didn't do it herself, an attendant would come for her, so she stood on shaking legs and stepped through the door.

The arena was enormous. A raised platform of seating encompassed one side. Faces of people she didn't recognize from the Academy—and those she did from her island—flashed by in a haze. Nur walked across the gravelly terrain, stopping outside a large, chalk oval drawn into the ground with an "X" resting in its center. Planters and troughs of water for them to use in their duels circled the perimeter of the arena. Across from her, Bird waited outside the outer ring. He met her eyes and smiled. Nur wanted to strangle him.

Control.

That's what Kaleo had told her to do. Control her anger. Control her power. And knock Bird on his ass.

Nur allowed her eyes to wander away from her opponent and towards the stands. It wasn't hard to find the Masters. They sat apart from the rest of the crowd, dressed in white and gray robes. Standing a few feet away from them was a woman in her late forties. She had dark red hair and green eyes so deep that they were nearly black. She wore no robes to mark her as being a part of the Academy, but Nur knew instantly who she was—Hettie of the Flame.

There were rumors that Hettie had been offered a seat as one of the Masters, but had refused. She wasn't a teacher either. Nur had no idea what her role at the Academy was other than being a living legend.

THE STORM GATHERS

"Witches!" A man seated on a small box set apart from the rest of the crowd rose to his feet. He wore a painted mask designed to amplify his voice. "When you hear the bell, you may step into the circle. Once both of you have entered, the duel will begin. It will not end until one or both of you has exited the circle, has yielded, or is otherwise incapacitated. Understand?"

They both nodded.

Nur flexed her fingers at her sides, already opening her senses to the Current of Eriysha's power. Across from her, dressed in nearly identical white clothes wrapped in colorful fabric, Bird was doing the same. She could tell by the way his eyes unfocused slightly.

From somewhere to her left, a bell clanged. Taking a deep breath, she stepped over the chalk line and entered the circle.

Her entire body entered a state of awareness as she and Bird circled each other. She had no Amulet, which meant she only had a third of the power he did. She needed to be in control…whatever that meant.

Bird readied an attack. She sensed the surge of power before the wall of water—drawn from both the troughs and the moisture in the humid air—launched towards her. Nur rolled out of the way as the wave Bird had summoned crashed to her left. He hissed out a breath, his power already gathering around him again. This time with much more force. She was tempted to call upon Eriysha's power. To use her wind to create a shield against whatever Bird attempted next, but she knew that amount of magic would ruin her body and drain her energy. She needed to wait for an opening.

Another wall of water rose. This time, it arched towards her on either side like it was trying to corral her. Nur took a small step back, then stopped. Looking down, she saw her boot heel pressed against the chalk line. If she moved another inch, she would concede victory to Bird. Pulling a fraction of Eriysha's power from the Current, Nur wrapped her mouth and nose in a bubble of air before racing into the wall of water hurtling for her.

The wave, too thin to wash her away, instead wrapped around her. The water pushed at her air bubble. It wanted to get in. It wanted to drown her under Bird's command. But his plan hadn't been to kill her. It had been to force her out of the circle. Through the rippling veil, Nur could see

75

him making the calculations. How much more of this could she take? How much more could he? With each minute she hung onto air, his power was failing. It was only a matter of time before he had to give up. To reset.

Finally, she felt the pressure decrease. Slowly, as though Bird still wasn't sure of his decision. Or he was using the gradual release to buy him time to rebuild his energy, she realized.

Shit.

Screw control. She needed to strike and strike now, before Bird had regained his full strength. It would have to be precise and merciless. A blow like that would take all her energy. A lightning bolt, perhaps? No, as tempting as it was, killing him would only get her sent into the Shatter. She could steal his breath again, as she'd done before. But he would fight her and it would take more than a minute to drag him into unconsciousness. In that time, who knew what sort of horror he might unleash?

Drawing all the strength she could muster, Nur focused her energy on Bird, on the wind and air that entered and left his mouth. It took her a moment to gain the necessary concentration, which was not helped by the punishing force of the water surrounding her, tearing at her clothes and hair. Her ears hurt, the pressure inside them steadily building.

Now.

Nur struck—her storm magic ripping the air from Bird's lungs. His eyes went wide, one hand going to his throat. With his focus split, she felt the pressure of the wave decrease.

Yes. This was what she had wanted. Divided concentration was the downfall of their magic.

She redoubled her efforts. She let go of the magic supporting the air bubble around her and focused all her will on denying Bird air. Water pressed at her mouth, but she held on, relishing the way her opponent's cheeks were turning red. He went to one knee, his mouth opening and closing as he tried desperately to find oxygen that wasn't there.

Yes. The word was a chant against Nur's skin as she saw victory. A few more moments. All she had to do was last for a few more moments…

His eyes snapped to hers. They were rimmed with red and tears.

THE STORM GATHERS

Yield, she urged him. *Yield.*

Instead, Bird did the unthinkable. The water pressure redoubled, knocking Nur over, onto her side. Her concentration shattered with her as she fell. She tried to pull herself together, but her arms were already numb. Water pounded against her head. She felt something in her ears pop. And that final, terrible sound pushed her over the edge.

Nur didn't care if she passed out. If she ruined her body. She was going to destroy Bird.

She could only see him out of the corner of her eye, but that was enough. She reached for Eriysha's magic again, ignoring the mixture of numbness and searing pain that spread through her as she took and took and took.

Then, instead of stealing his breath. She gave it to him. Forced air down his throat the same way he was trying to force water into hers. She heard him stumble back and fall. Gasping and choking. But if she'd hoped it would be enough to stop his magic, she was wrong.

Bird was just as hateful and determined as she, and the force of his attack only grew, finally prying her mouth open. Water washed into her, filling her nose and throat. She gagged against it, blindly searching for even the tiniest scrap of oxygen. To make matters worse, the numbness was spreading. In a few seconds, it would reach her chest—her heart.

Spots danced before her eyes. Which would kill her first? Bird's reckless use of magic or her own? In the end, she didn't know which it was.

All Nur knew was the blackness in her vision as it swept her into oblivion.

ELEVEN

Alana spent most of her time aboard Abin's ship in the scout's nest with Penn. As strange as it was, she didn't mind the boy's company.

The ship she'd chosen was usually used for transporting spices from Yovar and Aaran to Okaro, but occasionally also picked up old artifacts unearthed in the desert. As a result, Penn had a hundred stories to tell of his travels.

"We've passed by Teratt, too," Penn said one day. "But we couldn't stop. They don't let you into the harbors without proper papers."

"How close did you get?"

"Pretty close. I could see the white walls of the city and the shadow of the volcano." His eyes went wide suddenly. "We saw a dragon, too. It was smaller than I thought it'd be. It flew over the city and out to sea."

"Really?" She leaned forward, intrigued. "What did it look like?"

It was rare that dragons left the Shatter, although there were occasional reports of their brief visits to Teratt. Supposedly, the island country had once been a prime breeding ground for the creatures.

"It was a dark gray, I think. But its wings looked blueish. It didn't breathe fire or anything, just flew past us." He sighed. "It's a shame Teratt is so closed off."

"It is," she agreed. "As a child, I always wanted to visit. But until my marriage to Erik, I was never allowed to leave Okaro." She hesitated a moment, then added. "I did think about running away once—leaving behind my family and title and traveling the world."

"Why didn't you?" Penn asked.

THE STORM GATHERS

"I didn't want to leave my sister. But now, after everything that's happened, I can't help but wonder if I should have left when I had the chance." She looked out to sea. "I think it would have been better for everyone if I had."

They stood together in silence for a few minutes. Ahead, a hazy landscape appeared. They'd passed by a few islands—there were many up north—but this seemed...different. Her companion squinted into the distance.

Alana handed him the spyglass without a word.

"The Shallows!" Penn called to the rest of the ship. "Straight ahead. Turn twenty-five degrees south!"

Shouts sounded as sailors hurried to follow orders.

Some, Alana noticed, went below deck. Penn saw where her eyes had gone and explained, "There are those who think it's bad luck to look at them."

Alana let out a sigh as her eyes found Johnathan shifting uncomfortably from foot to foot. "I'd better go. One of my guards is superstitious."

"The big one? Johnathan?"

Alana nodded, then glanced back at the boy, noting the unease in his tone. "Do you believe the Shallows are bad luck too, Penn?"

He swallowed. "I mean...I just...I don't like to tempt fate, you know?"

Shaking her head, Alana started down the netting. "Come on, boy. You can play cards with us until we've passed."

Penn hurried after her. "Really?"

"Yes, you and Johnathan can bond over your poor lying abilities and gullibility."

"I don't lie!"

"Everyone lies."

"You're going into your cabin, too," Penn pointed out.

"I'm going because I know Johnathan won't go below decks without me. And if I were to stay up in the scout's nest, he'd be pissy for weeks."

They reached the deck, and Alana made a sharp motion at her guards. Together, the four of them headed into her cabin opposite the captain's quarters.

The room was small, half of it taken up by a four-poster bed nailed to the floor. She'd had the table and nightstand removed to give the room more space, but it was still cramped with the four of them standing inside. She pulled a deck of cards from the trunk at the end of the bed and motioned for everyone to take a seat on the floor.

They sat, Penn across from Johnathan and Maria across from her. Alana dealt out the deck.

"What are we playing?" the young sailor asked.

"Tal," Maria replied, her dark eyes sifting over her cards. "Gods, Zaya, you sure these were shuffled?"

"They're shuffled," Alana snapped.

Johnathan arranged the cards in his hand. "Badly."

"Penn," Alana said, turning to the boy. "What do you think? Are they shuffled badly, or are these two just looking for something to complain about?"

"Do not answer that," Maria said, shooting Penn a look. "Are we playing doubles?"

"Obviously," Johnathan said, his fingers drumming restlessly on the wood floor.

"If I didn't know better, I'd say you were nervous," Maria crooned.

He glowered. "Shut up, Mari." He turned to Alana. "And I'm watching you, so don't even think of cheating."

She gasped. "I would never!"

Jonathan narrowed his eyes. "If your last name wasn't Zaya…"

"You still wouldn't be able to prove anything," Alana cut in. "Besides, cheating is an integral part of Tal." She smiled at her companions. "Let's begin."

AN HOUR LATER, ALANA AND Maria were comfortably five hands ahead of Johnathan and Penn.

"Damn it, boy," the male guard growled, slamming his last card onto the floor. "Why would you play the ten when you had the king?"

"I thought you had the ace."

"The ace was already played!"

"I forgot!"

"Don't let him intimidate you, Penn," Alana said, placatingly. "I think you played great."

"You're only saying that because you won," the boy grumbled.

80

"True," she admitted. "But I wouldn't feel too bad. I've never lost at cards."

Johnathan snorted. "That's not true. You used to lose to your mother all the time."

"I was fourteen," Alana sniffed. "That doesn't count."

"Feels like it should."

She shoved the cards into his hands with more force than was necessary. "It's your turn to deal."

He took the cards and shuffled, his eyes narrowing in concentration as his large hands attempted to control the small bits of paper.

"Do you think we have passed the Shallows yet?" Maria asked, glancing towards the porthole currently covered by a dark blanket.

"They'll alert us when we've passed," Penn said. "But it shouldn't be too much longer."

Johnathan grunted. "I'm not leaving this cabin until that cursed place is far in the distance."

Maria raised an eyebrow. "And what exactly do you think will happen if you catch a glimpse of the Shallows?"

Johnathan opened his mouth to respond but a shout outside the door interrupted him.

Alana frowned. "Is that the signal?"

"No…" Penn stood slowly and pressed his ear against the cabin. Alana got to her feet after him, legs braced evenly apart to steady herself against the rocking of the ship.

The sailor straightened and turned back to them. "I think—"

Whatever he had been about to say was cut off as the boat lurched violently backward.

Alana was thrown against the wall as the sound of wood splintering and metal crashing filled the air.

Fuck. Fuckfuckfuckfuckfuck.

"We're being attacked!" she shouted.

Maria scrambled to her feet, hands going to her knives.

"Stop." Johnathan laid a hand on her shoulder. "The room is too small."

"Then we need to leave!"

"And go where?" he demanded. "We're in the middle of the ocean."

"Drowning is preferable to being hacked apart by a group of pirates."

Alana couldn't argue with that.

"We have lifeboats," Penn said. "It's part of my job to stock them with supplies in case of emergency."

"How many?"

"Just two. Usually, we have a smaller crew, but Abin hired a few extra hands to speed up your journey."

"The queen is our priority," Maria stated. "We need to get her to safety."

Before anyone could move, the door to the cabin slammed open. Maria drew her knives and poised to strike.

Penn threw up his hands before anyone could move. "Wren!"

The golden-haired sailor came charging into the cabin, slamming the door shut behind him. "We're under attack," he announced.

"I noticed," Alana said dryly, leaning against the wall.

"We were just headed for the lifeboats," Johnathan explained.

Wren shook his head. "Damned pirates slammed their ship right into ours. Crushed one lifeboat, and the other was cut loose in the fighting. I'm guessing on purpose." He took a deep breath, fists clenching at his sides. His knuckles were torn, and blood splattered his shirt and sleeves. "Abin is dead."

Penn let out a weak sound, tears welling in his eyes. "Are you sure?"

Wren's eyes flicked to the queen. "They wanted her, and he refused. That's when the fighting started."

Alana didn't react to the news. Instead, she pulled back the blanket covering the porthole, letting sunlight spill into the room. Trapped on a boat with nowhere to go. She'd lived the nightmare before, except death awaited her now, not a loveless marriage. She wasn't sure which was worse.

"We should go out fighting," Johnathan said, tipping his chin up.

"Aye," Wren said, his hand moving to the sword at his waist.

"You will do no such thing," Alana cut in. She would have no one else die for her today.

"Do you have a better idea?" her guard challenged.

"We wait," she said simply.

"For?"

"For the killing to stop. At that point, I will do everything in my power to negotiate for our lives."

Stepping past the men, Alana took a seat on the bed. She lay with her legs stretched out and her head against the wall as the sounds of dying sailors floating to her.

You could help them.

Alana pushed that thought aside. She couldn't. If she tried, it would only end in more death. She felt Maria's eyes on her. Not for the first time, she wondered exactly what her guard knew of that night in the castle gardens—when Emira's assassin had come for her and lost his life instead.

Outside, the sounds of fighting dissipated. "Pass me the cards, Johnathan," Alana said, extending a hand.

The guard looked at her like she was crazy but he did as she asked, scooping them up from the floor.

Shuffling the deck, she looked up at the four survivors standing before her. "Anyone up for a quick hand?"

"Are you insane?" Wren hissed. "There are men dying right outside!"

Alana shrugged and turned back to her cards. Spreading them out on the bed before her, she sifted through the deck with expert fingers. The echo of footsteps sounded outside her cabin door. Alana ignored it and flicked a few cards to the floor on the opposite side of the bed. She gestured to Penn. "Pick those up for me, would you?"

Penn glanced at Wren, then back to her. Tears stained his cheeks, but he gave Alana a small nod before bending down.

BANG!

The cabin door burst open again, flooding the small room with light. A man stepped from the slash of sunlight and into the room.

He was a little taller than Wren, with a mess of black hair atop his head that was short at the sides. High cheekbones cut his face, accenting a pair of dark eyes that met Alana's instantly. She held his gaze.

Swearing, Maria drew two knives from her belt and positioned herself in front of the bed, ready to defend her queen.

The man cocked his head to the side, a smirk curling his lips that snapped Alana into focus. "Enough of that, Mari."

She scooped the cards into her hand and slid to the edge of the bed beside Maria.

"She's in here," the pirate called. His voice surprised her—smooth and deep, with just the barest hint of a northern accent.

"Hand me your knife, Maria," Alana said, not taking her eyes off the man. Her guard did so without hesitation.

"Now, *what* are you planning to do with that, Your Majesty?" the intruder asked. He leaned against the wall, seemingly unafraid of the two trained guards staring at him.

"Alana, please," she said. "I see no need for formalities given our current situation."

"Flirting with me already." The pirate *tsked*. "You don't waste a moment, do you?"

"I don't," she said simply. Alana twirled the knife in her hand absently. She may not know how to use it in a fight, but her fingers were as nimble with cards as they were with blades. She patted the bed. "Why don't you come a little closer?"

The pirate raised an eyebrow. "Normally, I would be intrigued, but I have a sneaking suspicion that your intentions are less than honorable."

"And what would you know about honor, pirate?"

"More than you, Your Majesty."

Before she could snap a response, the door to her cabin was thrown open once again and two more pirates entered the room. The largest was a man, nearly as tall as Johnathan, with a bald head and a strong jaw. Beside him stood a woman with a muscular build and jet-black hair. The bald man turned towards the dark-eyed pirate, his earrings glinting in the sunlight coming in from the porthole. "You're sure it's her?"

"Positive."

The bald pirate turned to Alana. "Your Majesty, my name is Sarasin. I am captain of the *Fe Ressu*. This," he gestured to the dark-eyed man, "is my first mate, Kaius. And my quartermaster, Layla."

The woman gave Alana a mocking bow. She had a piercing through her bottom lip that gleamed gold.

"How polite for a murderous gang of pirates," Wren grumbled.

"We can be far less pleasant, I assure you," Sarasin said. "I've elected for diplomacy. Something I am sure the queen appreciates."

"Give me a few minutes with her," Kaius suggested. "She's already tried to seduce me."

Alana rolled her eyes. "I was trying to stab you."

The first mate made a dismissive gesture. "Foreplay."

Layla snorted, arms crossing over her chest. "Let's get on with this, shall we?" She nodded to Alana. "You're coming with us."

"And the rest of them?"

She shrugged. "A death by the sword is better than drowning at sea."

Wren's hand went to his rapier. "Why don't you come closer and say that?"

Layla's expression turned vicious, her hand slipping to her own sword. "Try me, pretty boy."

"That's enough," Alana snapped. "My crew lives. You can either leave them here or take them aboard. But no more will die today."

"You're not in a position to be making demands, Your Majesty," the captain said.

Alana twirled the knife through her fingers. "Tell me, do you intend to take me alive?"

"Yes…"

"Then I would say I am in an excellent position to bargain." She nodded to her crew. "They remain unharmed, and I'll cooperate."

Beside his captain, Kaius snorted. Alana fixed him with a glare, eyes blazing. The pirate grinned in response, a mixture of surprise and delight on his face. She wanted to rip out his throat with her bare hands.

"You expect us to believe you would die for your crew?" Layla asked, her skepticism clear.

Alana tore her eyes from Kaius and fixed them on the quartermaster. "I expect you to believe that I would rather take my chances with Etrim than board your ship alone and vulnerable."

She could feel Sarasin's gaze on the side if her face.

"Fine," the captain said after a moment. "There is certainly no reason for this to get uglier than it already is. If your crew surrenders their weapons, they're free to live."

Alana handed the knife back to Maria and offered her crew a nod.

Reluctantly, Maria, Wren, and Johnathan tossed their many weapons onto the floor, taking up what little space was left in the small cabin. Bringing out a length of rope, Layla stepped forward, tying together Wren's hands while Kaius tied Maria's, and Sarasin tied Johnathan's. Layla gave a sharp whistle out the door. A moment later, two more pirates appeared and escorted the hostages onto the deck, leaving Alana unprotected amidst the orchestrators of her current nightmare. Fear threatened to grip her heart, but she pushed it down and met their stares.

Penn was still crouched behind the bed, hidden from view. She held her position in the room. If Layla took another step forward, she would be within sight of the young sailor, and Alana would not allow him to be dragged into this.

She lifted her chin. "You are not tying my hands."

"Gods, you're feisty." Kaius crossed his arms. "Like a little dragon. A *kiydra*," he said, using the Vettan word for dragon.

"Don't call me that."

"Why not? Half the world knows you only as the Queen of Darkness. How is this different?" At her stony stare, Kaius continued. "You know, I've always wondered if you gave yourself that name or if someone else chose it for you."

Alana's jaw clenched. "What do you think?"

"I think…" the pirate's gaze swept up and down her body "…that you've forgotten which it was. Lies become our truths if we pretend for long enough and you, *Kiydra*, have been pretending for a very long time." He cocked his head to the side. "Just as we've been pretending that there are only four of us in this room." Kaius nodded towards the bed. "You can come out now, kid."

Slowly, Penn got to his feet. He kept his gaze on the floor, shame coloring his face. Alana gestured the boy forward, but kept him tucked behind her.

She glared up at Kaius. "Leave him out of this."

THE STORM GATHERS

"I'm afraid I can't do that," the pirate replied. "He either dies, or comes with us. Believe me, Your Majesty, it will be better for everyone if the world believes you are dead."

Layla let out a snort. "It would be better if she were dead."

"Enough of that," Sarasin snapped. He nodded to his quartermaster. "Bind the boy's hands and put him with the others."

The woman nodded and made quick work with her rope.

Before long, the five of them were leaving the cabin. Momentarily blinded by the sun, it took Alana a moment to take in the sight before her. Blood and bodies lay everywhere. Alana had seen death before, but nothing quite like this. It was disgusting. The stench climbed into her nose, forcing vomit up her throat. She pushed it down, her eyes ignoring the many pirates staring at her until she found Maria. Her guard was hunched over, bound hands clutched to her stomach as a brutish-looking pirate with tattoos covering his face, stared down at her, one hand wrapped in chains. A fresh wave of anger wrapped around her. Without thinking, she charged towards the man who had just struck Maria.

"Don't you dare—"

Before she could finish the threat, an arm wrapped around her waist, yanking her into the air and away from the tattooed pirate. All the air left her lungs in a whoosh as Alana struggled against the grip of her unknown assailant. Panic washed over her as her hands were pinned against her by a second arm.

"Breathe." Kaius's voice whispered in her ear. "Do you really think it's a good idea to be picking fights right now, *Kiydra*?"

"Let. Me. Go." She bucked against him once more, and he released her. Alana just managed to find her balance before she could slip on the bloodied deck.

"What was that about her trying to seduce you earlier?" Layla asked, suddenly appearing beside Kaius.

"She's obviously not thinking clearly," he replied, gesturing to the queen.

Before either Layla or Alana could reply, Sarasin spoke. "No harm is to come to the prisoners. Put them in the brig. I'll decide what to do with them later."

There was some grumbling from the crew before Maria was hoisted back to her feet and escorted onto the pirate ship via a gangplank. Alana watched them go, her chest still heaving and her arms shaking at her sides. She felt the pirates' stares on her and fought the urge to close her eyes against the attention.

"Not so scary now, is she?" one man said, daring a few steps toward her. Alana fixed him with a glare, and the pirate paled slightly, taking a few steps back. His fingers moved over his heart in a gesture against evil. "Rion save us…"

"Get back to work," Sarasin snapped, pulling his crew to attention. They hurried about their work, leaving Alana alone with the captain, first mate, and quartermaster.

After a moment, she forced herself to speak. "Whatever you ask for my ransom, Erik will pay it."

"True love?" Layla asked, her tone dry.

Alana snorted. "Hardly. But he'll pay it, nonetheless."

"I'll keep that in mind if I ever need the money," Sarasin replied. "In the meantime, the two of us are going to have a little chat."

TWELVE

"What are you doing here, Aram?"

"What?" he challenged. "I can't say hello to an old friend?"

Rae couldn't help but grin at the man standing across from her. Aram Brayvare, her training companion at the Citadel, and her oldest friend. His curly hair was a little longer than the last time she'd seen him, as though he hadn't had it cut in a while—but other than that, he looked the same as he had three years ago. Gods…it had been three years since she'd last seen this man.

"Seriously," she pressed. "Why were you following me?"

"Curiosity." He gestured to the ratty parka she still had on. "I saw you a few blocks back, wearing that ridiculous outfit."

With a grunt, Rae pulled the thing over her head and tossed it to the ground. "I wear that so the street rats don't try to pickpocket me." That was, at least, somewhat true.

She looked back and found him staring, his mouth partly open. Rae glanced down, wondering if she had accidentally ripped her shirt off too.

"I didn't really believe it," Aram murmured with a gesture at her blue tunic. "They said you joined the king's personal guard, but—" His eyes snapped back up to hers. "We have so much we need to talk about."

Rae made an overly dramatic motion for him to follow and started walking. He fell into an easy step beside her. The casualness reminded her of years long past, when they'd explored the city together—slipping through allies and running across rooftops.

Rae eyed him as they walked. Aram wasn't wearing a city guard's uniform. Was he off-duty?

"I take it you've graduated?" She had been recruited into Argos's service two years before most of their classmates had been expected to leave. After the war broke out, most of their training ended early, but she hadn't heard anything about Aram or his progress.

"Not long after you left, actually," he admitted. "I was sent outside the city, along with a few others, to do some missions in the northern part of the country." Vague, but at least he hadn't been stationed in the south, where the war was.

"When did you return?"

"Four days ago," Aram said. "I've been busy with my family. Otherwise, I would have visited you sooner."

Rae made a dismissive gesture. "That's not what I meant I—" she shook her head, shame creeping up her throat. "I'm the one that left you. I broke my promise. You don't owe me anything."

Aram was silent for a long moment, then he asked, "What happened while I was gone? How did you go from," he made a wild motion with one hand, "to this." He gestured at her clothes.

She shrugged. "It was survival."

Aram looked ready to argue, but hung his head instead. "I'm leaving again. They want to send me and my team on another mission. This time to the south. To the war."

Rae stiffened. "You can't go."

"I thought you were the dutiful little soldier now?" A hint of bitterness laced his tone. "One of Argos's most loyal."

She resisted the urge to bite back. To tell him the truth. To tell him about the Val. But it was too dangerous. She hadn't seen him in three years. There was no telling how corrupted he might have become since then.

So instead, she said, "That doesn't mean I want you marching into a war zone."

Something akin to disappointment flickered across her friend's face. "Don't worry. I'm not going."

"But you said you were leaving? Aram, if you desert, they will hunt you to the ends of the earth."

"It's a good thing that's exactly where I'm going, then." He flashed her a brutal smile. "I've secured passage on a ship heading into the Shatter."

"What? Are you insane?"

He snorted. "Coming from you, that really means something."

She punched him. Hard. "You can't go into the Shatter. You'll die."

"You don't know that. None of us know what's inside for sure. It could be something beautiful."

"Or it could be something that gets you killed!" She stopped, crossing her arms. "You can't go. I won't let you."

"You can't stop me."

"I beg to differ."

Aram looked around. "Can we talk about this somewhere more private?"

"Fine," she grabbed his arm and pulled him through the city towards the gondola. "We'll go to my rooms. They're secure. And then we'll discuss how stupid you're being and how you are most definitely not going into the Shatter."

"And here I thought you might have gotten *less* crazy after three years in the king's employ."

"You're one to talk, Brayvare."

They made it to the easternmost gondola, the one closest to the sea, and Rae's living quarters atop the cliff. There was a short line of other guards and a few nobles waiting to board. Rae kept her grip on Aram's arm as they got in line. Usually, she opted to ignore the line altogether and cut ahead via a series of threats, but somehow, she felt that the man beside her might object to that.

"You know I'm not your prisoner, right?" Aram grumbled. "You can let go of me."

She did so reluctantly, then turned to eye him, idly wondering how hard she would have to hit him to make him see sense.

"And don't punch me either."

She blinked. Had he read her mind?

"I can't read your mind, Rae," he said, making her question the denial. "I just know your first solution to everything is violence."

"Hasn't steered me wrong before."

"Can't you just accept my decision?" he asked. "It's my life. My choice to make. You, of all people, should understand that."

"We can't talk here," Rae said quietly, giving a pointed look to the nobles and guards surrounding them.

Aram crossed his arms and took a step forward as two nobles boarded an oncoming carriage. "This is going to take forever."

Rae shrugged. "I can speed it up. But you won't like it."

Aram narrowed his eyes. "No violence."

She held up both hands. "I promise."

"Or *threatening* violence."

She hesitated. "…Fine."

Aram motioned toward the guards running the gondola. "Go ahead."

Rae gave him a wink before sauntering forward. The man currently operating the machinery was named Greyson.

"What do you want, Warrior Toma?" the guard asked.

"This is taking forever," Rae said, motioning towards the gondola and the slow-moving carriages. "I'm getting bored."

"I can't make it go any faster, I'm afraid."

"I understand that, but I'm in a rush. I have business with the king."

"The king is currently in a meeting with the ambassador from Yovar," Greyson said mildly. "I sent the man up less than half an hour ago."

"Did I say king? I meant the general."

Greyson rolled his eyes. "Get back in line, Rae. You can suffer like the rest of us for a few minutes."

She crossed her arms, widening her stance. "It's like I said, soldier, I'm getting bored. And when I get bored, I tend to say and do things that some people don't like. For example," she nodded to a man and a woman waiting in line together, "Lady Peris is currently being courted by Duke Terrfrul, but his father has already promised him to Lady Marigold. See? If I were to wait in line, I might accidentally spill that very destructive information for everyone to hear…and maybe while everyone's reeling, I'll imply that you're the one who told me."

Greyson's eyes narrowed. "You really want to cut in line so badly?"

"I'm in a rush."

"Fine." The word came out like a growl as he motioned Rae forward. "You're next, Warrior Toma."

She gestured to Aram to follow her.

He did, giving the stone-faced Greyson a weak, apologetic smile.

They stood on a painted white line, as the carriage rounded the great machinery of the gondola and scooped them into their seats.

"I thought you said you weren't going to threaten him," Aram hissed.

"You said threaten *violence*. Social threats don't count." She shot him a smile as they sailed into the air. "Admit it. You missed me."

Her friend rolled his eyes. "I hope you know you can't change my mind. I'd rather go into the Shatter than fight in Argos's war."

Tell him! That tiny voice inside of her screamed.

She'd gotten people out of the city before, resisters and Tiskona alike. But they went to the Forest, and she knew Aram would not be happy there. Still, she might be able to find him passage to somewhere else. Okaro, maybe. They took in travelers, criminals, and refugees from all around the world.

Aram stared at the ground as it gradually grew farther and farther away. "There's something I need to tell you, Rae. Something more important than the Shatter. I—" He hesitated, looking back. The carriage behind them carried two guards, both deep in conversation. It was unlikely they could hear, but…

"Let's wait until we're in my rooms," Rae said. "It can wait until then, can't it?"

Aram gave a weak nod and fidgeted with the rings on his fingers.

A LITTLE WHILE LATER, THEIR carriage crested the cliff. A large wheel, identical to the one beneath them, spun slowly, turning the carriages and sending them back down to the city.

Rae scooted to the edge of her seat and braced her arms against the back of the bench, getting ready to push off. She jumped onto the ground, feet catching her momentum and guiding her forward easily. She'd expected Aram to have a harder time of it—the last time she'd taken the gondola with him, he'd nearly broken his neck getting off—but the man surprised her, escaping the carriage with unexpected grace.

They nodded to the soldiers as they passed and headed towards the wall of buildings that made up the guard's quarters.

After making their way down a short additional hallway that led to her rooms, Rae removed a silver key from her pocket. She fitted it into the lock and turned it, only to find that the door was already open.

"Get behind me."

"Maybe you just forgot to lock it?" Aram suggested, but she saw the way his own hand slid into his pocket to retrieve a weapon hidden there. He had three blades on him. She'd made a note of them when they'd first met. A sword at his side, one in a thigh sheath—the one he was retrieving now—and another small blade strapped to his right bicep.

"Be quiet."

Rae flexed her wrists, her knives sliding easily into her hands as she kicked the door open. She advanced slowly into her room. Nothing was out of place, but she caught the scent of tobacco and spice. The smell was both familiar and unwelcome. Rolling her shoulders, Rae kept the knives out but relaxed her position slightly.

"You can come out, Edgar."

The king's general stepped into view, carrying a dagger that Rae's mother had given to her. She'd never wielded it. It was too beautiful to be used for killing.

The bone hilt was delicately carved in an intricate pattern and painted in light shades of green, pink, and blue. The pommel was gold, as was the guard, but the dagger itself was a burnished gray metal—made from a substance only found in the Tiskona forest. It wasn't as strong as Sioran steel, but it could hold an edge without ever having to be resharpened.

Rae kept her focus on the general. He was dressed simply, in a plain

94

white shirt with a blue sash hanging over it and brown pants. His hair was nearly black, like Rae's, with white growing near the temples.

"I forgot you had this," he said, turning the blade over in his hands, seemingly unfazed by the two trained soldiers in front of him.

"Why are you here?" Rae demanded. "I—"

Edgar finally glanced up, noting Aram. "What is he doing here?"

"Isn't it obvious? We're plotting the assassination of Lady Marigold. I asked her to pass me the salt during the spring solstice celebrating last month and she pretended as though she didn't hear me. Now, if that isn't a reason to kill someone, I don't know what is. Right, Brayvare?"

Behind her, Aram stiffened, and she could practically feel the panic rolling off him. "No. It's not! I—we weren't—Rae!"

She bit back a laugh at his exclamation.

"Do not worry, soldier," Edgar said, his sharp eyes returning to his daughter. "Warrior Toma likes to play games with people. Both socially and in battle. Would you mind giving the two of us a moment? There are private matters that must be discussed."

Aram hesitated, and Rae finally turned to look at him, one eye still marking her father's movements. "Wait outside. This won't take long."

Again, he seemed to hesitate before bowing to the general and hurrying out the door, leaving Rae alone with her father.

"Well?" She crossed to him, snatching the dagger from his hand and putting it on her dresser. "Why are you here? Shouldn't you be with Argos?"

"The king is currently in a meeting with the Yovar ambassador," Edgar said smoothly. "Once he is finished, I will return to bear witness to fresh news regarding the Val rebel group." Rae's heart picked up at that, but she forced her expression to remain neutral as her father continued. "A few months ago, we managed to get a spy into their ranks. A man by the name of Joshua."

Rae bit back a snort at that. She'd let the boy in specifically just to feed him false information.

"Most of what he brought back was useless, but he did manage to note that one of the Val members has an unusual scar across his forehead."

Rae stilled.

"After some digging, we deduced one of the Val leaders is Cyrus Waymond, an ex-mercenary. A few days ago, we assigned two members of the Revry to follow him."

Shit. Shitshitshitshitshit.

"I'm guessing they found something?" Rae fought to keep her voice neutral, but she already sensed where this might be heading.

"Cyrus entered the city last night, and this morning, I received word that he was on the move. One of the Revry sent to track him returned to the castle today via the central gondola. He informed me that he had identified a few members of what he believes to be the Val council, but wouldn't say more until he was in the presence of the king." Edgar smiled, clapping a hand on one of her shoulders. "This is good news, Warrior Toma. If we can track down those rebel bastards, we'll be one step closer to ending this war."

Gods, if she had been identified…Rae had to get out of the city. If she was discovered, she wouldn't get a trial, only a slow, likely very painful, death.

"It is good news, general," she said carefully. "Thank you for telling me."

"Of course." Edgar stepped around her to reach the door.

"That's it?" Rae forced out. That couldn't be all he came to say. She would get a briefing of the events in a few hours. News like this, however significant, wasn't worth a visit from the king's general, even if he did happen to be her father.

"That's it," Edgar confirmed, offering her a smile. "Have a good day, Rae."

"You too, father."

They nodded to each other once before he swept out the door.

Rae wasn't sure why she had said it. *Father.* She hadn't called him that in years.

And Edgar had used her first name. He'd stopped doing that the day she became Argos's guard.

But…it had been a goodbye, she realized.

There was no way she could stay in this city and wait to be hunted down. If she was to have any chance of escape, she needed to leave. Now.

Rae sprang forward, pulled out the leather bag she used on missions, and began stuffing it with clothes and weapons. She had minutes, maybe an hour. She couldn't risk taking the gondola down to the city, so she would have to use the sewers. Quickly, Rae changed out of her guard uniform and pulled on a simple gray tunic and brown pants.

She was re-lacing her boots when Aram entered, his eyes growing wide at the messy room. "Sorry, I was talking to one of our old classmates… um…what's happening?"

Rae finished her boots and began arranging the weapons on her person. "You said you had a boat taking you into the Shatter?"

"Yeah…"

"When does it leave?"

"Tomorrow."

"Any chance it could be ready today?"

"Maybe but—Rae, what's going on?"

Well, there was no point in hiding it now…

Rae stopped what she was doing and stood before Aram. "I am the leader of the Val rebel group. A Revry spy tracked one of my councilors when he entered the city, leading him to me. The king might be learning of this as we speak. I need a way out of the city. Will you help me?"

Aram opened his mouth, closed it, then opened it again. "Fantastic." His tone was nothing short of exasperated. "Yes, I think I can get you a spot on this ship, but you'll have to be the one to convince Ydric and Qasim to set sail early."

Rae nodded, shouldering her pack. "I can do that."

"I'm sure you can." His mouth pressed into a grim line. "Why didn't you tell me, Rae? I could have helped. I would have joined."

"And that's exactly why I didn't tell you. It would have been too dangerous." She gestured to her chaotic room. "Look what's happening now! I made a promise to you twelve years ago that I would keep you safe. How could I honor that and willingly lead you into a world of death and betrayal?"

"I'm not the same little boy you found in the hall, Rae. Protecting me shouldn't come at the cost of lying. You should have told me."

Rae bit back all the excuses bubbling up in her throat. Aram had been her friend since they were eight years old. They had fought their way through the Citadel together, and she had abandoned him. It hadn't been an accident. After starting the Val, she had realized that it would be easier—and safer— if she left her old life behind.

Unable to meet Aram's eyes, she walked out the door, leaving her mother's knife behind.

He chased after her as they wove through the palace halls. "Rae—"

"We can talk about this later," she said, heading for a rock outcropping that concealed the sewer grate. "For now, we need to focus on getting to the docks—I'm assuming that's where the ship is?"

Aram nodded. "It's called *The Wave Finder*."

She rolled her eyes at the name before hunching down in the bushes and pushing aside the foliage and dirt she'd used to cover the metal grate.

He blinked at her. "You can't be serious."

"Don't worry. No one uses it anymore."

"It's disgusting."

"It was disgusting fifty years ago. Now it's just a little icky."

"'A little icky,'" Aram repeated, his lips curling in distaste. "Stars above, Rae, you are going to owe me so big for this."

"Put it on the tab." She opened the sewer and gestured for him to go first.

"No way."

Snorting, Rae lowered herself and her bag over the edge and dropped the short distance into the horizontal tunnel. Crawling forward, she called back that it was clear for Aram. He landed a moment later, letting out a curse that brought her back to days of running laps at the Citadel.

"There will be a vertical drop in about twenty feet," she explained. "It's narrow, so you can use your feet and hands to slow your descent."

"Did I mention how much I hate you?"

"I missed you, too."

"That is not what I said."

Rae reached the lip of the drop, readjusted the pack on her shoulder, then lowering herself down. Although the stone tunnel wasn't slick, it wasn't exactly easy to climb down. Her hands were scraped raw by the time she made it to the bottom. Judging from Aram's foul language, he wasn't faring much better.

THE STORM GATHERS

They continued through the sewer, descending and crawling, descending and crawling, until they reached the city. Rae continued to lead them forward until she spotted the faintest trickle of light filtering in from the world above.

Rae blinked. She didn't know how long they'd been in the dark—at least an hour, but probably more.

Pushing open the grate, she threw her pack out first, then climbed up, offering her friend a hand as they entered the city. They both blinked in the afternoon sun as Aram took in where the tunnels had deposited them.

He gestured to their left. "The docks are that way."

"I know," Rae said. "But I need to do one thing first."

"And what, exactly, is more important than getting you out of the city?"

She grimaced. "I have to alert my council. Get them into hiding."

"We don't have time," Aram argued. "They probably already have guards searching the city. We need to go. Now!"

She shook her head. "I'm sorry. You can head to the ship. Alert the captain. But I need to do this. I owe them that much."

Aram swore, feet shifting between her and the direction of the docks. "Fine," he snapped. "Where do you need to go?"

"Bookshop. It's not too far from here. I have a contact that can alert the rest of my team."

Aram nodded, and they started through the city, keeping their heads down. They took roofs and back allies, occasionally cutting through buildings using open windows until they were just two blocks from Herba's shop.

Instantly, she knew that something was wrong. The street was too packed for this quarter of the city. And the smell...smoke.

Rae sprinted through the crowd, dodging through bodies until...

Oh, gods.

Herba's bookshop was on fire. Flames had burst through the windows, fueled by the thousands of books hidden within the building's walls. Black plumes of smoke curled upwards, choking the air. A few of the city guards were trying to hold people back as they gathered around the sight.

"We need to hide!" Aram hissed, pulling her into an empty alley.

"They burned it," Rae whispered. "Gods, Herba…What if he was in there? What about the others?"

Maybe the fire would be enough to warn them that something was wrong, but…

"Zarah and the rest of your council will be fine," Aram said. "They're smart. They'll get themselves out of the city. We need to—"

Rae triggered the knives at her wrist and slammed into him, pinning him against the alley wall.

"What are you doing?" he gasped.

"I didn't tell you that Zarah was on my council," Rae said.

"What? Yes, you did! Rae, let me go."

She shook her head. "I didn't. And there's only one way you could know." She leveled him with a glare. "You're the second Revry agent sent to spy on Cyrus, weren't you?"

"Rae—"

"Answer me!" Her blade dug into his throat. Any more pressure, and she would draw blood.

The denial died in his eyes. "Yes."

"Is there really a ship into the Shatter, or was that a lie, too?"

"Nothing I told you was a lie," he insisted. "There's really a ship."

"You just left out the fact you were spying on me?"

"I was going to tell you. I swear. That's what I wanted to talk to you about in your rooms. But then the general was there and…"

Rae released her friend. He went to his knees, sucking in a breath. "I'm sorry, Rae. About everything. That's why I went to find you. I wanted to warn you. I was supposed to keep tracking Cyrus, but I knew I had to get to you. I tried to convince Derek to stay, to wait until we had more information, but as soon as he recognized you, he bolted before I could do anything."

"Derek!" Rae exclaimed. "You were partnered with Derek?"

Aram grimaced. "He was recruited into the Revry with me."

"Are the two of you *friends* now?"

"What? No! Really, Rae, that's what you're focusing on? He's an asshole, same as he always was." He glanced to the entrance of the alley. "We need to get out of here. Now."

"You're really with me?"

"Yes."

"I'll kill you if you're lying." She wouldn't, but Aram seemed to believe it.

"I know."

They walked toward the closest intersection, checking either direction for city guards before turning down a side street.

"They'll be patrolling the docks," Aram said. "We can try to sneak in…"

"Or we can use the cliff," Rae finished.

"What?" She pointed to their left. There was a small outcropping off of the larger cliff overlooking the water. It was a ways from the docks, but the path was concealed enough that they might make it there undiscovered.

"For fuck's sake, Rae," Aram muttered. "You want me to jump off a cliff?"

"Into water."

"One day with you and I've crawled through a sewer—"

"Abandoned sewer."

"Been hunted by city guards—"

"That's a little dramatic."

"And now you want me to jump off a cliff?"

"Once again, it'll be into *water*!"

"Fine," Aram said, throwing up his hands. "At least it's on the side closest to *The Wave Finder*."

Grabbing his arm, Rae pulled him forward.

They tried to take the side alleys, but no street in the Capital was truly empty, and they quickly grabbed the attention of merchants and shoppers as they ran. Likely, they just assumed the pair were nothing more than thieves running from the law, but too much attention would draw the guards.

Finally, they made it to another crumbling part of the city that was mostly occupied by the homeless. Ducking through the dilapidated buildings, they reached the edge of the city and the hidden dirt path that led up the cliff.

Before long, they were peering over the precipice and into the swirling sea below. Rae checked the straps of the bag still hung over her shoulder, then moved to the edge. Aram followed her, eyes shifting uncertainty.

"I don't know about this."

"We don't have another option."

"You said the same thing the night we stole the ceprra from Duchess Adam's stables. As I recall, that ended in us being on toilet duty for six months."

"You're a part of the Revry," she reminded him. "Aren't you supposed to be one of the most elite and brave spies in the nation?"

"And you're one of the king's personal guards," Aram countered. "Aren't you supposed to be loyal to the crown?"

She glanced back to the city, her eyes landing on the cloud of black smoke coming from Herba's shop. Her heart clenched. Three years of work… gone, in an instant.

Well, she supposed there was no turning back now.

"Let's go." Rae wrapped her arm around Aram's. "Together."

"I hate you."

"No, you don't."

Before he could say another word, she jumped, pulling him down with her.

Recalling her training, Rae kept her back straight, and her toes pointed towards the water. Letting go of her arm, Aram did the same. They hit the water. The force of the fall, along with the sharp cold of the water, knocked the breath out of her. Rae frantically kicked her way to the surface, breaking the water at the same time as her friend. Aram's hair was plastered to his forehead. The wild, frenzied look in his eyes told Rae that she would never hear the end of this—assuming they survived.

"The ship," she managed, nodding towards the docks that seemed impossibly far. "Come on."

"You pushed me—"

"Pulled."

"Off a cliff!"

She made a dismissive gesture that was hidden by the water. "You're fine."

Grumbling, Aram swam towards the docks, Rae following after him.

The first ship in line wasn't *The Wave Finder*, but the relief of finally being able to touch wood was palpable.

THE STORM GATHERS

Two rows down, and mercifully set apart from the rest, was an unpainted vessel with blue sails that marked it as once being used for commercial fishing. Using the small grip provided by the connecting wood planks that made up the hull, she and Aram braced themselves against the ship.

Rae closed her eyes in relief, ignoring the burn of saltwater in her throat. Her clothes billowed around her in the water and what hair has escaped her braids was now plastered to her face, obscuring her vision. With one hand still steadying her against the ship, she wiped the offending strands away.

Thankfully, her friend didn't look much better.

Aram took a deep breath and called up to the ship. "Ydric! Captain!"

Nothing.

"You have to be louder."

"Thanks," Aram muttered, then called again. "*Ydric!* It's Aram! Throw us a rope!"

Nothing.

Rae and her friend swore in tandem. She was just about to suggest they try to climb up, when a face appeared over the edge.

"Aram?" The man was in his late sixties, gray hair overtaking the brown that was mostly concealed by a black bandana over his head. "What are you doing down there?" He looked at Rae. "Who's that?"

She flashed the man a smile. "I'm his best friend."

The man's eyes went to Aram, widening in disbelief. "Is she serious?"

"Throw us a rope," her friend gasped. "I'll explain."

A moment later, a rope lowered for them.

They climbed over the edge of the railing, then promptly collapsed onto the deck of *The Wave Finder*.

"All right," Ydric said, standing over them with hands braced on either of his hips. "The two of you have exactly sixty seconds to explain what's going on before I throw you back overboard. Or better yet, hand you over to the city guard, given that I'm fairly sure you're who they're searching for."

Rae and Aram exchanged a glance. She couldn't imagine how they looked, the both of them soaked, hair a tangled mess with eyes as wild as

103

the sea in a storm.

She grinned at him, and he mirrored the expression back at her before they both burst out laughing.

THIRTEEN

As it turned out, Alana's *chat* with Sarasin was postponed while he arranged for the remnants of Abin's ship to be sunk. Instead, Alana was ushered down in the brig, where she and the rest of her companions were locked in a large cell that took up nearly half the hull.

"Well, isn't this just fantastic," Wren groused. "We might as well have gone down fighting. They'll kill us all before the week is out."

"They will not," Maria argued. "Alana bargained for our lives."

"They're pirates," Wren said. "They don't have honor."

"Are they?" Alana murmured.

She hadn't expected the captain to accommodate her request. The fact that he had troubled her. Why give in to her demands?

Maria and Wren continued to argue. "They'll ransom her to Erik," the sailor said. "But do you really think he'll cough up any more money to free the rest of us?"

"Erik is a good man," Johnathan cut in. "If there's a way to save everyone, he'll do it."

Alana rolled her eyes. This arguing was pointless, and she certainly wasn't going to rely on her husband to come to her rescue. It was evident Sarasin meant to make it look as though she'd disappeared at sea, but his reasoning for doing still eluded her. *We need to escape.*

The room quieted.

Had she said that out loud?

"And how—exactly—are we going to manage that?" Wren demanded.

Alana looked up at the bars of their cell, each secured to the ceiling with four bolts. The wood was soft from moisture and the smell of rot hung heavy in the air, but it would take too long to push the entire cell off its supports…no, their best option was to get the key. But not until they had a way off the ship.

When she didn't voice her thoughts out loud, Maria and Wren returned to their sniping, occasionally interrupted by Johnathan's attempts to mediate.

Rubbing her temples, Alana walked to the corner of the cell where Penn was curled, and sat down beside him.

"I am sorry for Abin's death," she whispered.

Penn sucked in a breath. "He was family to me. The only real family I ever had. Aside from my brother, but he disappeared when I was a child…" He trailed off. "I just wish I could have saved him."

The boy looked away from her, shivering as tears filling his eyes. He tried to wipe them away but only succeeded in letting them loose across his cheeks.

She couldn't think of anything to say. At least not anything comforting.

After a moment, Alana shrugged out of her red coat and wrapped it around the boy's shoulders as he cried.

Two DAYS LATER, ALANA WAS leaning against the cell bars as she picked at her nails with a splinter of wood.

Johnathan and Maria stood by the door, griping at each other while Wren sat in a corner with Penn. He was telling the young sailor the story of when he'd sung in a Yovari music festival.

Above them, the thumping of pirates echoed through the deck as they went about their business, accompanied by the occasional heavy *thunk*. The sounds blended into each other after a while, as did her guards' arguing, leaving only the light buzz of noise Alana could easily ignore as she day-dreamed about how best to kill their captors. Kaius she would stab—it was only fitting. Sarasin she'd poison. Layla, she would drown. The rest of the crew, she would set on fire.

Alana paused. Actually, that wasn't a bad idea…

There came the whine of hinges as that hatch to the brig opened and someone descended the stairs.

"Nice to see you're all awake," Kaius said, stepping from the gloom into the light of the one lantern they'd been provided. He nodded toward Alana, who pointedly ignored him. "You look good for a woman who just spent her night sleeping on the floor."

"Do not speak to Her Majesty like that," Maria growled.

"Perhaps *you* should be careful how you speak to *me*," Kaius advised. "I'm the one with the sword, after all." He returned his attention to Alana. "And you should keep better control of your guards."

"And why would I want to do that?"

"Loose tongues get cut out."

"Then maybe you should take your own advice," Alana returned. She pulled her attention away from her nails to observe the pirate. "Why did you come down here, anyway? Are you just here to gawk, or are you on an errand for your master?"

Kaius's lips pulled back into a smile. "Sarasin wants to speak with you."

"She is not going anywhere with you," Maria snapped.

"Now, now," Alana said. "If he wants to open that door and tempt fate, then by all means, why should we try to dissuade him?"

Kaius gave the Yovari woman an appraising look. "Forgive me if I'm not afraid of an unarmed guard in a cage."

Maria's grin was feral. "It is not me you should be afraid of, boy."

Alana stepped forward as the rest of her crew retreated further into the cell.

Kaius fitted the key into the lock, his eyes searching hers. "I'm guessing that means you're the one I should be afraid of?"

She lifted her shoulder in a shrug. "Actually, I think she was talking about Penn."

Kaius's gaze flickered to the boy shoved protectively behind Wren. His lips quirked into the barest hint of a smile as he pulled the cell door open enough for Alana to slip through—locking it behind her.

He reached for her arm and she pulled away with a hiss. "I told you not to touch me, pirate."

Rolling his eyes, Kaius made an expansive gesture toward the stairs. "After you, Queen of Jaarin."

107

Alana emerged onto the deck of the ship. The sun blazed above them, momentarily blinding her as she made her way up the steps of the quarterdeck to where Sarasin stood.

She smirked at the bald man. "I hear you've been dying to speak with me, captain."

"Dying is perhaps a stretch…"

"You killed an entire crew so you could get to me, so no, I do not consider it to be a stretch in the least."

Sarasin's lips pressed together, his eyes flicking behind her to Kaius.

"You wanted her up here," the first mate said. "Have fun dealing with her."

His footfalls retreated down the steps of the quarterdeck, leaving them somewhat alone.

"I hope you slept well," Sarasin said, his eyes going to the horizon. "I know the accommodations aren't what you're used to."

"I've slept in worse places."

The captain gave her a curious look. "Have you?"

"Let's jump ahead to where you explain why I'm here."

"We'll get to that eventually," Sarasin said. "But first, I want to hear about you. About your family. Your father is from Vetta, correct?"

"You could say that."

"That's not a straight answer."

Alana said nothing in response, her eyes drifting out to the endless sea before them.

Sarasin cleared his throat, then continued with the interrogation. "You were sent to marry king Erik when you were twenty. Is that correct?"

"You're asking questions like you don't already know the answer."

"I suggest you make an effort to engage in conversation," Sarasin cautioned. "I can make things considerably more unpleasant for you and your companions if you don't cooperate."

Alana glared at him.

Seeming to take her silence as acquiescence, he continued. "Why did your mother send you away? An arranged marriage is one thing, but to send a princess to a foreign land…it's curious, don't you think?"

"Perhaps to you."

"Was she afraid that you would take the crown from your sister?" he pressed. "Although, I suppose you did, in a way, given that she was killed mere weeks after you were married to Erik. A dagger to the heart, if I remember correctly. How poetic."

"Why don't you ask the question you're dancing around, captain? Unless you want me to ask one of my own?"

"Do you know who killed your sister?"

She observed Sarasin out of the corner of her eye. When she'd first seen him, she'd thought he might be from Jaarin—he certainly had the arrogance of the court nobles—but his accent revealed that he was from one of the Southern countries. Aaran or Siora. She guessed the former based on his attire.

Alana *tsked*. "That's not the question you want to ask."

"Fine. Did you kill your sister? Or arrange for her to be killed?"

"Do you miss the deserts of Aaran?" Alana asked, her gaze drifting out to the horizon. "The sea is a desert in its own right. No drinkable water. You can travel miles without seeing another soul, but be bombarded with storms that tear the skin from your body. The desert is the sister of the sea and vice versa. Both equally vast and endless. Beautiful and brutal. Wouldn't you agree?"

"I would." Sarasin's voice was cold even as he conceded her point. "Now answer the question."

"They say the Empress of Aaran, Kyrin El-Tess, killed her brother in order to take the crown. Cold-hearted woman. Still, she's far better suited to rule." Alana met Sarasin's eye, watching as the captain's throat bobbed. "Arya would have made a good queen. Far better than I could ever be. I loved her. More than you can possibly know. So, no, I did not kill her. And if I ever learn who did, I will rip them apart piece by piece."

"So, the Queen of Darkness has a heart, after all?"

"I did once," Alana replied. "But not anymore." She eyed Sarasin's hands, still placed on the wheel, gently steering their course. "You know, it's strange," she said, "that a man from Aaran would be a pirate. Let alone have his own ship. But then again, you aren't a pirate, are you? And from what I can tell, neither are your first mate or quartermaster."

"I don't know what you're implying."

"You don't have a single scar on those pretty hands of yours. Kaius and Layla look more like soldiers than pirates. The rest of your crew, I can believe. But the three of you," she shook her head, "you're something else. Which leads me to wonder exactly why I've been kidnapped..."

"You're quite perceptive, aren't you?" Layla said, striding up the steps to stand beside Alana.

"So, you are a soldier. Or were. Also, from Aaran, I would guess." She nodded to Kaius walking below them on deck. "Where did you pick him up?"

"I think that's enough questions for today," Sarasin said. He nodded to Layla. "Take her below deck."

"What a shame," Alana said, allowing the quartermaster to lead her away, "things were just starting to get interesting."

FOURTEEN

AGE EIGHT

Rae walked through the halls of the Citadel. It was past midnight, and the building was empty aside from the occasional servant she took care to avoid. She rounded a corner and her fingers tightened around the cloth bag she was holding. Inside, she'd packed an assortment of clothes, leftover lunch she hadn't eaten, and the knife her father had given her the day before. Trainees weren't allowed real weapons until they were older, but Edgar had deemed her ready. But she didn't feel ready. She felt afraid.

What happened yesterday was just the beginning. If she stayed here, it would become her whole life and she couldn't allow that to happen.

Rae had just reached the kitchen doors—which had a back exit out of the Citadel—when the sound of someone crying drew her attention. Without meaning to, she set her bag aside and crept toward the sound.

"I told you to. Stay. Down." The words were punctuated by the crack of a fist against flesh.

Rae turned the corner to find three boys standing over a figure slumped against a wall. Another boy, she realized, with blood running from his nose and bruises blossoming across his cheeks. He was the same age as she was, but Rae didn't recognize him—he must have been new.

The three boys standing over him, however…she knew them. The one on the right was Torrin. On the left was Siv. And the middle boy—the one who'd just spoken—was Derek.

The new boy tried to get up again, one hand pressed against his stomach.

Derek let out a false laugh, turning to his two companions. "This one just doesn't learn, does he?" He looked back at the injured boy. "You need to start doing what you're told." His arm lifted, elbow pulled back to throw another punch.

Rae knew she should walk away, knew that these sorts of initiations happened all the time—she'd endured similar beatings when she first arrived… but she hated Derek. She hated his smug look in training and hated how he delighted in other people's pain.

More importantly, the boy was trying to get back up. He was injured, bloody, and half their size, but he was still trying to fight back.

So Rae did what he couldn't, and fought for him.

Lunging forward, she caught Derek's arm and threw him against the opposite wall. Siv and Torrin turned on her, fists raised, but she was faster, ducking under their blows and sending them both to the ground in a matter of moments.

Before she had time to revel in her victory, Derek was back up and ready to fight. He struck out, faster than she'd expected, and his fist cracked her across the jaw. She stumbled back against the wall as he closed in, hunger lighting in his eyes. He aimed another punch, but this time Rae was ready and caught his arm, twisting it behind his back until he whimpered in pain.

"You don't ever touch him again," she growled.

"You can't tell me what to do."

She twisted his arm harder, and he let out a yelp.

"Fine!" he yelled. "Fine! I won't touch him."

She loosened her grip. Derek thrashed, trying to break her hold and attack her at the same time. Instinct took over, and she yanked his arm upward hard enough that she heard it snap. He screamed and Rae let go of him instantly, taking a few steps back but not daring to let her guard down as Siv and Torrin rushed to his side.

"You broke it!" Siv exclaimed. "You broke his arm!"

"Leave, or I'll break yours, too!" Rae screamed. Her voice was bordering on hysterical. What had she just done?

The boys didn't move—perhaps sensing her unease. She couldn't let them think she was weak. She wasn't.

Rae squared her shoulders and met their eyes. "Leave!"

Helping a whimpering Derek, Torrin and Siv hurried him down the hall and out of sight, leaving her alone with the boy still huddled in the corner. She sat down beside him, and he finally looked up at her, brown eyes shining with tears.

"I thought we were going to play a game," he said. "I thought they wanted to be my friends."

"What's your name?" Rae asked.

"Aram," he told her. "Aram Brayvare."

She grinned. "My name is Rae Toma. Don't worry. They're not going to hurt you again."

His eyes went to the corner the three boys had just retreated down. "How did you do that?"

She brushed away some of the hair that had escaped her braid. "I told you, I'm Rae Toma. I can do anything."

Aram offered a small smile and pressed one hand to his bruised eye. "It hurts."

"I know," Rae said. "But it will be fine in a few days. And if you keep your head up during training tomorrow, you'll show them you're strong and the rest of the students will respect you."

"W-will you be there, too?"

Rae hesitated. She had planned to leave tonight. Leave and never return. But looking at the boy beside her…something about him made her want to stay.

"Of course," she told him. "And I won't let anything else happen to you. We're friends, after all."

"We are?"

"If you want to be."

He nodded. "I do."

"Okay, then." She extended her hand to him, and he took it. "I'll make you a promise, Aram Brayvare. And a warrior never breaks their promise." She took a deep breath. "I promise to protect you, against any evil we may face."

Those words were what her father and his cadre swore to each other. It was the oath of soldiers bound by the blood they spilled. In Siora, the vow was considered as unbreakable as a pact between Life and Death. Etresyum and Etrim. And she had just made it to a boy she hardly knew. Her father would kill her if he ever learned of this. But, somehow, Rae didn't particularly care.

"I promise to protect you too, Rae Toma," Aram vowed, gripping her hand tightly. "Against any evil we may face."

FIFTEEN

Nur woke in a room with dark stone walls and white beds. She felt the press of cool, soft sheets against her bare skin and the gentle sea breeze wafting through an open window to her left. Flowers sprouted from a painted vase in the center of the room, adding a pleasant smell. But all the niceties of this strange place were undercut by the pounding in her head and the ache in her throat.

"Oh, good. You're awake."

Nur's head swiveled toward the voice and came face to face with the red-haired woman from the boat.

She opened her mouth to speak, but all that came out was a rasping noise.

"Here, drink this." The woman produced a vial from her apron and handed it to Nur who downed the concoction in one gulp. Almost instantly, her throat felt better, and the pain in her head reduced considerably.

"Who are you?" she whispered, setting the vial on the table beside her bed.

"I'm the lucky student who got put on med duty." She let out a sigh. "And here I thought I might actually get to enjoy my day off."

"Sorry."

"I forgive you, Stormwitch. With the face like that, how could I not?" She gave Nur a small, mischievous smile before retrieving the empty vial and disappearing back behind the curtain. "My name is Talia, by the way," she called. "Since you didn't ask."

Nur frowned. She was fairly certain that she had.

Talia reappeared from behind the curtain, carrying a bundle of clothes. "These are for you."

"Wait." Nur sat up, doing her best to ignore the pounding in her skull. "What happened?"

"You passed out during your duel," Talia said. "It was actually Headmaster Kadar who carried you here. Apparently, there was some question as to whether or not you were even alive."

Nur collapsed back into the bed. "So that's it? I failed? Bird got in?"

Talia pulled out a piece of paper from her pocket and read. "From your island, Siira of the Flame, Jimson of the Earth, Gina of the Sea, Sasha of the Flame, Bailey of the Storm, and Bird of the Sea."

Nur reined in her shock. Neither Eva nor Kaleo had gotten in. That didn't make any sense, Kaleo was the top of their class. He was a far better Flamewitch than Sasha or Siira.

"Additionally," Talia continued. "Kaleo of the Flame was sponsored by Master Turic of the Flame. And you, Nur of the Storm, were sponsored by Hettie of the Flame." Talia folded the note back up with a flourish. "There, you can wipe that devastated look off your face now, Stormwitch. You got in."

Nur blinked. "I…was sponsored?"

"You were."

"By Hettie of the Flame?" She couldn't contain her enthusiasm. Of all people, all the Elemental witches, she owed her admittance to Hettie of the Flame. The woman was a living legend. She was more famous than Headmaster Kadar or Master Branson.

"I would rein in your excitement until you've actually met the woman," Talia advised. "She's…not what you would expect."

"When do I get to meet here?" Nur pressed. "Will she be my instructor?"

"Normally, sponsored students train with the rest of the class of first-years and get extra lessons from their patron in place of getting a work assignment. But with Hettie," Talia lifted her shoulders in a shrug, "who knows?"

"What do you mean, a work assignment?"

Talia gestured around. "We aren't just students. We're responsible for the care of the island. I work in the Med Suite, but other students work in the library or tend to the gardens and paths. There are a thousand jobs overseen by each of the Masters. But like I said, since you're a sponsored student, you'll probably spend that time working with Hettie. Or at least, that's what you're supposed to do."

Nur narrowed her eyes. "You don't seem to think very highly of her."

"On the contrary, she lives up to her myth. But that doesn't mean I ignore her faults."

"What faults?"

Talia gave Nur a sympathetic look. "You'll understand when you meet her."

"And...when will that be?"

Talia gestured to the clothes she'd set at the end of Nur's bed. "I'll take you to her as soon as you put those on."

NUR DRESSED IN THE GRAY shirt and dark purple pants Talia had given her, then followed the woman out of the Med Suite and into the heart of the Academy. Students roamed around her, each dressed in similar outfits with pants in shades of green, blue, or orange.

As they walked, Talia acted as a tour guide. "The buildings are arranged in a semicircle around the main garden. The Med Suite is on one end, and the library at the other. The rest is split between student dorms and classrooms. The dorms are on the Med Suite side, and the classrooms are on the library side. But, if I'm behind honest, the classrooms are rarely used. Our powers are elemental, so the best lessons are taught in nature."

As they walked, the hallway opened up as archways bridged the divide between the inside and outside—revealing snapshots of a brilliantly colored garden and cobblestone pathways.

"The clothes reveal one's power affiliation at birth. As you might have guessed, purple is for Stormborns, blue for Seaborns, green for Earthborns, and orange for Flameborns."

Nur looked Talia over. She'd left the red apron behind in the Med Suite, but her clothes beneath were in shades of gray.

"What about you? You're not wearing any color?"

"I was originally Earthborn. But I have since learned a second power. Flame. Students with more than one affinity wear white or light gray." She gestured to her light gray pants. "White is for Elementals—those who have mastered all four elements."

Nur looked around. "Is there anyone who wears white?"

"Headmaster Kadar. He was Stormborn, originally, like you."

They stepped from the hallway, into the gardens.

"That's amazing," Nur whispered.

Talia shrugged. "Everything is connected. We all draw our power from the same source. It simply manifests itself in different ways, depending on the person."

"And you can control how it manifests."

"I have *some* control," Talia clarified. "Now, continuing with the tour. The instructor for all first-years is Master Emelia. She's assisted by teachers from each elemental group. Currently, there are eleven Flameborns, nine Seaborns, six Stormborns, and four Earthborns in your year."

They walked around a circular courtyard that had a fountain of two fish spitting in the center. Trails branched off from the center, creating snaking paths through the garden.

Talia led her down the path on the farthest left. It was narrow, and branches of waist-high berry bushes brushed against Nur's thighs as they walked.

"If you have two affinities, who did you duel against?" Nur asked. "There can't be many students like you."

Talia pushed aside a clump of branches blocking their path. "I was admitted last year without a duel."

"What?" Nur couldn't hold back her surprise. Everyone had to duel. Regardless of class rank or elemental power.

Talia chuckled lightly. "It's a long story, Stormwitch. One I do not mean to tell today."

Forcing down her curiosity, Nur kept silent.

"Most of the land is uncultivated," Talia said, as they stepped over a shallow stream. "A few clearly-marked paths will take you to different corners of the island, but the rest is just wilderness. I would advise you to not go exploring on your own. Every decade or so, foolish students journey into the forest and are never seen again."

"Don't explore. Got it."

Talia smiled over her shoulder. "I didn't say *that*, Stormwitch. I just said don't go exploring *alone*. I'd be happy to accompany you. All you need to do is ask." Her eyes sparkled.

The path they walked grew steeper, becoming switchbacks that climbed their way up a hill, then back down a valley.

"I'm getting the sneaking suspicion you're leading me to my death."

Talia chuckled. "There are far easier ways to kill you. Ones that don't involve me having to hike through a serpent-infested jungle."

Nur couldn't help but mutter an agreement. She hadn't seen any of the creatures yet, but she could hear them. There were some on her home island that could grow large enough to prey on people, but they were rare and hunted down if ever seen. But if this island was as wild as Talia claimed... no, Nur would certainly not be venturing out alone.

Eventually, they crested another hill, this one leading to a small plateau before a lake that curved sharply to the left. Ahead was a waterfall that stretched dozens of feet in the air. And, there, standing at the edge of the lake closest to the waterfall, was Hettie of the Flame.

She wore a black dress that hung to her ankles with an orange waist wrap. Her red hair whipped around her face as she stared into the churning water. If she knew they were standing nearby, she didn't make any sign of it.

"Good luck," Talia said and turned to go.

"You're just going to leave?" The words came out more frantic that Nur would have liked. The idea of just...just walking up to Hettie was unthinkable. Even if she was her sponsor.

Talia snorted. "You really think I'm going to get into the middle of whatever she's plotting? No. Heed my warning now, Nur—everyone here has an ulterior motive."

"What is your ulterior motive, then?" Nur demanded. "Why help me?"

"I was ordered by Headmaster Kadar and Master Juric to make sure you were treated for your injuries and properly acclimated to the Academy and its workings. As for my ulterior motive..." She gave Nur a once over, a small smile coming to her lips. "Well, I suppose you'll find that out soon enough, Stormwitch."

And with that, she was gone, trekking back down the trail and leaving Nur to face Hettie alone.

Cautiously, she made her way over to her sponsor. The woman's gaze didn't stray from the water even when Nur was standing right next to her.

"Hello." She cursed herself for the lame greeting. Maybe she should have bowed? "Talia, uh, brought me to you."

Hettie turned towards the trail the redhead had disappeared down. She shook her head. "She should not have brought you here. Not now. Dangerous. Very dangerous. No, no, no. I do not like this."

Nur fought the urge to take a step back at the woman's outburst. "I don't understand—"

"But you must!" Hettie cut in, turning towards her fully. "He wanted you for himself. It's why I had to take you from him. But you need to be careful." She turned her head sharply to one side. "Did you hear that?"

Nur could hardly hear anything over the sound of the waterfall. "No?"

"You never know who might be listening," Hettie hissed, eyes darting around. "Serpents and birds and little ezbis."

Nur's hands clenched into fists. What was this woman talking about? She might have expected Hettie of the Flame to be arrogant or aloof. Rude even, but this...was she insane?

"Do you remember him?" Hettie asked. Her voice suddenly calm, she turned back to the water. "Your father, I mean. You must recall some things." A pause. "I remember his eyes above all. A clear blue, like the pale streaks of the sky at dawn." She looked back at Nur. "Yours are darker, though. Like the sky as it is now. A sky that never changes. Endless, endless, endlessly stretching its claws into the horizon."

Before Nur could question how her mentor knew Nanook Del Sue, the woman let out a laugh and threw her hands into the air. Flame sprouted from her palms and licked down her body before disappearing again. The show of power was gone so fast that Nur wasn't sure if she'd imagined it or not.

THE STORM GATHERS

Beside her, Hettie let out a contented sigh and turned to her. The dark of her eyes seemed to lessen slightly—the green bleeding through the black.

"I don't know what you're talking about," Nur told her. "Why did you sponsor me? How did you know my father?" *Are you insane?*

The older woman hummed. "Such good questions. So like him, you are. But the answers are hidden. Locked away but ready to be found."

"What does that mean?" she demanded. "What do you want me to do?"

Hettie looked at her as though the reason was obvious. "I want you to solve the puzzle, Nur Del Sue. I want to be free."

SIXTEEN

Rae stood on the deck of *The Wave Finder*. Dusk had fallen, casting the sky above them in a golden light that was reflected on the ocean's surface.

Argos had sent two ships chasing after them—a fact that their captain, Ydric, was less than pleased about. The rest of the crew—mostly made up of criminals—didn't appear as bothered, most of them just as eager to escape capture. She had heard, however, that the explorer who had organized the journey, a man by the name of Qasim, shared Ydric's ire. Perhaps she should have been worried, but Rae couldn't find it in herself to care. Not after everything that had already happened.

She pulled out four scraps of cloth from her pocket and she slid open the glass of the lantern she'd carried to the railing. Orange flame flickered back at her.

"Do you want help?" Aram's voice came from behind her.

"This is not something you can help with."

"I can at least hold the lantern steady so you don't set the ship on fire."

Sucking in a breath, Rae made room for him beside her. "I know you're not to blame for all this," she started, "but I'm still pissed at you for spying on me. And for not killing Derek. And for working with him at all in the first place."

Aram grimaced. "I know, and I share the guilt for what happened. For the bookshop and what might befall your companions. Especially Zarah. I always liked her."

THE STORM GATHERS

Rae looked back at the strips of cloth in her hand. Taking another deep breath, she dipped them in the flame, making sure each one caught before pulling them back out.

The wind picked up as if readying itself for what came next. The flames from the cloth heated her hand as she held them above the water.

She let go.

The wind caught the fabric before they could fall into the water, carrying the four burning pieces away from the ship and out to sea.

"No sky," she whispered.

"No stars," Aram answered.

Then together, "No gods to light our way."

It was an old prayer, but a common one among soldiers. It was a reminder to rely on each other, not on the prayers of priests or the tellings of Starreaders. Not even in the gods.

The words had always given Rae comfort. It was what her people said to honor their fallen. So, she said them for the people she'd lost. For Cyrus and Jonah. Mirella and Zarah. For Herba. Because even if they weren't dead, Rae would never see them again. Not where she was going.

"Rae...I—"

"You don't need to say anything, Aram," she murmured. "Apologies won't fix what happened, and regret doesn't change the past. We have to keep moving forward, or we die."

Aram was silent for a long moment, then he offered her a small nod. "Qasim wants to see you. In his words, he 'wants to know what idiot provoked the entire Sioran government to interrupt his nap.'"

Rae's lips twitched up at that, but her eyes flicked back to the sea. How could her life change so suddenly in a matter of hours? How could she go from successfully running the Val to being on a doomed ship heading into the Shatter? It didn't seem possible, and yet, here she was.

Her jaw clenched. She had to keep going. Because stopping meant being swallowed by her grief. And Rae did not bow to such emotions. She didn't bow to anything.

Not even to Death.

Exhaling, she pulled away from the deck and forced aside any unwelcome emotions threatening her resolve. Aram watched her for a moment, then led her towards the cabins at the back of the ship.

Most of the living quarters were below deck—converted from storage areas that still smelled vaguely of fish.

As they moved through the ship's hallway, Rae couldn't help but appreciate the simple luxuries of well-built walls void of any stench.

"Try not to stab him," Aram advised, as they reached the room at the end of the hall.

He rapped twice on the wooden doorjamb, then entered without waiting for an invitation.

Rae held back a snort as she sauntered inside.

A long table strewn with papers, books, and maps stretched across the room. There were no chairs lining the sides, as one would expect. She guessed that they had been removed to accommodate the multitude of boxes spread across the room. Maps were stamped across the walls, illuminated by lanterns that cast haunting light through the room and flickered with every rock of the ship. At the end of the table, was a disheveled-looking man in his mid-sixties. Wild, silver hair framed his face, the curls falling in front of his eyes as he scribbled furious notes on some poor piece of paper.

"Qasim," Aram said, clearing his throat. "You wanted to see Rae?"

"Quiet, boy. I'm almost finished." The man made a few more marks on his paper before finally looking up. His gaze narrowed on her. "So, you're the troublemaker." He wagged an accusatory finger. "You interrupted my rest with the ruckus your arrival caused. It is rare that I find any peace from my thoughts, and you ruined it."

Rae walked around the table, her eyes running over the maps and loose papers. "You should try *reinta*, then."

"This is no joking matter!"

"Sure, it's not."

"I think what Rae means to say is that she's *sorry*," Aram cut in, giving her a pointed look.

THE STORM GATHERS

"No, what I mean to say is that my entire life just got uprooted within a span of hours, forcing me to flee onto this death voyage. *Forgive me* if I find your lack of sleep to be of low importance."

There was more hurt audible in her voice than she liked. She couldn't let the pain take over. She had to keep pretending that she was okay. Eventually, if she pretended enough, she would be. Right?

Qasim's gray eyes stared into hers for a long moment, before he turned his attention back to the table. "What do you make of the Shatter?" he asked. "How do you suggest we navigate it?"

"You can't," she replied. "That's the point."

"Ah, but you can. With the right tool, that is." He held up a scrap of paper. On it, a compass was drawn without the directional points but images of each of the gods. Instead of an *S*, the goddess Eriysha was stamped at the bottom.

"You're looking for the Compass," Rae said impassively. "That's original." She gestured to the table. "I'm guessing you have a theory as to how we're going to find it?"

"Only guesses," Qasim corrected. "I can't have theories until I see for myself what type of magic keeps the Shatter guarded from the outside world."

"I still say we use the stars," Aram said.

"And I've told you a thousand times," Qasim spat, "everyone who's ever gone into the Shatter has expected to use the stars. And yet, none have returned. It must be different in there. Some illusion or magic that keeps the night sky from being used as direction." The explorer looked at Rae. "What do you think, girl? How do we find the Compass?"

"I don't know," Rae said simply. "I guess we'll just need to get lost enough to find our way."

Aram snorted. "Brilliant idea."

"It's better than yours," Qasim snapped. He turned from the former Revry agent and back to Rae, eyes twinkling. "I like you, girl. Much more than this one." He jabbed a thumb at Aram. "As far as I'm concerned, we could throw him overboard."

"I'd rather you didn't," her friend grumbled. "I've had enough of being thrown into water."

At Qasim's quizzical look, Rae explained. "We had to jump off a cliff in order to escape the city guard."

"She *pushed* me off a cliff!"

"*Pulled.*"

"Seems to me," Qasim said, "she saved you from a far worse fate."

"You're both insane." Aram muttered, pinching the bridge of his nose.

She made a dismissive gesture at him. "Sanity is overrated."

The old explorer grinned. "Right you are, Rae."

"Oh, so you're calling her by her real name now?"

"Names are of little consequence to me. People come and go, offering their names as easily as one breathes. I don't bother to remember them unless the person is worth remembering."

"And I'm not," Aram deadpanned.

"Not yet."

Rae opened her mouth to speak, but a voice sounded from the door—the captain's. "I hope you're playing nice, Qasim."

"I like her." The explorer gestured to Rae. "But the boy is a nuisance."

"I asked *one* question," Aram snapped.

"A stupid question."

"Qasim," Ydric's voice was full of warning as he stalked into the room. "What did we talk about yesterday? About being kind to people even if we don't like them?"

"It's a ridiculous notion."

"It's *polite*. Now, be nice, or I'm turning this ship around."

"You can't do that," Qasim argued.

"Or maybe I'll just drop you off on some remote island so you can insult the birds that live there."

"You wouldn't!"

"Apologize. Now."

"I don't want his apology," Aram said. "I don't need it, either. Apologies mean nothing without action behind them, and I don't want Qasim to change. The place we're going is insane, and we're going to need his insanity to match it." He glanced at Rae. "Hers, too."

THE STORM GATHERS

"There may be hope for you yet, Aram," Qasim said, giving the spy an appraising look. "Or, at the very least, you can recognize greatness."

Ydric rubbed his temples. "Gods save us all."

SEVENTEEN

Alana Zaya had had enough of pirates. Every few hours, Kaius, Layla, or one of the others came skulking down to the brig to taunt her and her crew. Still, as much as she hated her current predicament, she didn't miss Jaarin either. Her too-large bed in Erik's palace was only slightly preferable to the floor of the brig. So, despite the dismal circumstances, she had adjusted far quicker and far better to their new living arrangements than any of her other companions had.

"I think the smell is getting worse," Johnathan declared on their fifth morning aboard the ship.

"Five people living in one space will do that," Wren replied.

"It's not that bad." That was Penn. Next to Alana, he seemed the most at ease with the situation. "I mean, it could be worse."

Maria narrowed her eyes at him. "How, exactly, could it be worse?"

Penn shrank back slightly. "Um, well…" The hatch to the brig opened and someone began to descend. The young sailor gestured to the steps, seemingly relieved to have something else on which Maria could focus her displeasure. "That's how."

"Maria, dear," Kaius said, stepping into view. "I'm going to ignore that horrid look on your face and assume that you're pleased to see me."

"How about instead you assume that—"

"Maria," Johnathan cut in. "What did we talk about?"

The woman sniffed. "I do not take orders from you."

"You never listen when I give you orders either," Alana pointed out.

"When have you ever given me a direct order? Other than to pass you the wine bottle? Which I always followed."

"Hardly," Alana scoffed. "I remember more than one occasion when you kept it for yourself."

Maria opened her mouth to respond, but Kaius beat her to it. "As entertaining as this is, I'm here for Her Majesty."

Alana batted her eyelashes. "Really? I'm flattered. How about you unlock the door so we can have some real fun."

"Actually, I rather like you in a cage."

"You're not the first man to say that to me."

"I'm not surprised."

"And I imagine you and him will endure similar fates."

"Let me guess. He's dead? And you killed him."

Alana *tsked*. "How unimaginative. No, I can assure you he's still alive. But his quality of life has severely diminished."

"Are you threatening me, *Kiydra*?"

"I think it would be safe to assume that everything I say to you is a threat, pirate."

Shaking his head, Kaius unlocked the door to the cell. "Against my advice, Sarasin has requested another meeting."

She slipped outside. "I would rather you kill me."

"Believe me, so would I."

He led her up the stairs of the brig, then the quarterdeck to deposit her beside the captain.

"The Queen of Jaarin." He turned on his heel. "She's your problem now."

A flicker of amusement passed across Sarasin's face. "I take the two of you are getting along?"

Alana didn't bother answering as she scanned the ship. It had three masts, each decked in black sails that bore no insignia. She let her gaze pass over the pirates, ignoring their faces as she searched for...*there*.

Unlike on the ship she'd boarded to take her to Okaro, the lifeboats of the *Fe Ressu* were solely on the starboard side of the ship. There were six boats, all covered in white canvas. Whether or not they were stocked with supplies was information she would discover later. More importantly, she needed to figure out where they were on the map and where the ship was heading.

"I hope our previous conversation didn't upset you too much, captain."

"On the contrary, I enjoyed our talk. In fact, as I was mulling over our interaction, I remembered a story I once heard about you. About your original journey from Okaro to Jaarin."

"Sounds like a fascinating tale."

"It is. It tells of a princess who was in love with a boy below her station. When her mother found out, she arranged for her daughter to be married off to the king of another country. The princess was put on a ship to this new and strange place, but she was so distraught over losing her love that halfway through the voyage, she leaped from the decks during a mighty storm and attempted to swim back to Okaro. To the man she'd fallen in love with."

"How poetic."

"And with an equally poetic ending," her captor assured her. "She was rescued from drowning by the crew of the ship and kept away from the railings until she reached her betrothed, where they were married. The princess never again saw her lost love or the shores of her homeland."

"Such a sad story," Alana said. "Shouldn't people entertain themselves with happier ones?"

Sarasin's voice flattened, his eyes burning into hers. "Is it true?"

"There are truths in every story, captain. You should know that. Stories grow from truths—or at least perceived truths—but people so often love to romanticize things…"

"You're evading the question."

"Maybe if you'd let me finish, I would have answered," Alana shot back.

"I apologize," Sarasin said, placing a hand against his heart. "Continue."

"Some of it is true. Some isn't," Alana said simply.

"And what really happened?"

Alana scoffed. "I'm not giving up my secrets that easily. The story you just told suits me well enough. I've never heard the part about my long-lost love before. I suppose we learn new things every day."

"There was never a boy back home you were trying to return to?"

"What man could possibly be worth jumping into the sea for?"

"I take it you've never been in love."

"Love only leads to heartbreak, Sarasin. My father's death destroyed my mother. It broke the last of the goodness inside of her. I have watched nobles and servants alike fall in love, only for their hearts to shatter as they hit the ground. Because that is the inevitability of love—it ends."

"Sometimes it's worth it," the captain said, eyes growing distant. "Even when it ends, the time you spent together is worth the pain."

"Who did you love?" she asked, curious to hear how he would choose to answer the question. Honesty? Deception? Evasion?

Sarasin shook his head. "Why are we speaking of this?"

Evasion.

"You asked about love," Alana said casually.

"I asked about *you*."

"It's hardly my fault you got distracted."

The captain looked as though he couldn't decide between laughing and strangling her. She lifted her eyebrow in a silent challenge.

Do it.

Instead, Sarasin shook his head one last time and motioned for Layla to take Alana back to the brig.

"I HEARD THAT STORY TOO," Penn said after Alana had filled everyone in on her latest conversation with the captain. "So, it's not true? You weren't in love with a boy below your station?"

Alana shrugged in response. She was tired and did not like her memories.

Penn made a dismissive gesture. "I never liked that story, anyway."

"The two of you were with her, weren't you?" Wren asked, gesturing to the two guards.

"We weren't," Johnathan said. "We were sent ahead to ensure it was safe for Her Majesty once she arrived. She had other guards with her."

"So…only you know what really happened," Penn said, sitting up. "Are you going to tell us?"

"She will not," Maria cut in.

The young sailor pouted. "Why not?"

Alana avoided Maria's gaze. "Because the real story is far longer and far more complicated."

"Can you at least tell me if it's true?" Penn pressed. "Did you really jump into the ocean?"

Alana raised a questioning eyebrow. "Do I strike you as someone who would do something so reckless?"

Penn opened his mouth to respond, but was cut off by the sound of the hatch opening. A moment later, a pirate carrying a tray of food appeared, descending the steps two at a time.

"Finally," Maria said. "I am starving."

Alana took one look at the gray-ish food. "I'm not."

"You are so picky," Maria grumbled.

Johnathan passed around the food, setting aside a bowl for Alana despite her protests. "You need to keep your strength up."

"If I eat that, I'll vomit."

Johnathan shrugged. "Suit yourself."

After dinner, the bowls and spoons were pushed aside, allowing enough room for everyone to lie down. Usually, Wren told Penn a few stories before they went to sleep, but tonight everyone seemed exhausted—drifting off without a word.

Restless from her conversation with Sarasin, Alana stayed awake for what felt like hours. She wasn't getting anywhere talking with the captain—he was far too careful. Layla was her best bet of the three. With the right motivation, she might be able to spur the quartermaster into revealing some tidbit of information. But once that bridge was burned, there was no going back.

Exhaustion was just beginning to take over when there came the sound of feet pounding down the stairs. More than one person.

"Are you sure they're asleep?" came a rasping voice.

"I emptied the vial into their food, just like you asked."

"And you have the key?"

Two men came into view, their features were obscured by the darkness, but Alana recognized the shorter man as the one who'd brought them their food earlier. His hand was white-knuckled around the key, his pupils wide as his eyes tried to adjust to the dark.

"Are you sure about this, Dawson?" he asked. "The captain says he'll ransom her. We could be rich."

"The captain hasn't done shit since we got her. We've practically been sailing in circles—"

"That's not true," the shorter pirate snapped back. "We've been heading north. He's probably going to drop her off on one of them islands while he does the negotiations."

"And in the meantime, he's just going to parade her around the ship and have lovely little conversations with her? I don't think so, Chris. We shouldn't be giving up our food for her and her crew. Killing her is best. It's easiest. Not like the bitch doesn't deserve it."

The two pirates drew closer to the bars. The shorter one, Chris, still held the key in his hand. "She's over there." He nodded towards the far-right corner. "Already snuggled up next to one of 'em. I recognize her red coat."

Alana's heart leaped into her throat at that. It was Penn. They were talking about Penn, wrapped up in her coat to keep off the chill.

"All right, let's do this," Dawson said. "We kill her, dump her body over the edge, and the captain will think she escaped."

"And the others?"

"Leave 'em. Captain won't bother to keep her crew alive once she's gone."

Chris nodded and inserted the key into the lock. The door swung open, and the two pirates stepped inside. Alana pulled herself tighter into the shadows. She was still beside the door. If Dawson took one step backwards, his leg would brush hers.

She waited until the two men were farther into the cell before scrambling to her feet and sprinting out the cell door. She took the stairs away from the brig two at a time, and slammed into the hatch with her shoulder, throwing it wide. Alana burst onto the deck, expecting to find more pirates, but it was empty. The ship's anchor was down, but there should have been at least a few people on patrol. Unless…unless Dawson and Chris were the ones keeping watch.

She ran up the steps of the quarterdeck, to the helm of the ship, ignoring the thundering footsteps as her two pursuers made it above deck. Gripping the wheel, she turned it as hard as she could and felt the ship rock violently beneath her.

"Stop!"

Dawson reached the top of the stairs and lunged for her. Alana stumbled back, her feet slipping on the slick deck. She managed to catch herself on the railing. She reached up, grabbing onto the rope netting that led up one of the masts of the ship, and hoisted herself halfway into the air. Before she could place her feet, someone grabbed her ankle and yanked her back down onto the ship.

She kicked out, breaking free, and barely had time to raise her arm in defense as Dawson slashed his sword at her. The blade caught her upper arm, slicing down and sending a spray of blood across the deck. Biting back her cry of pain, Alana tried to duck away as the pirate raised his sword again.

"I've got her!"

Before Alana could register the words, her arms were being pinned behind her back by Chris. As the cut from Dawson ripped open further, pain exploded in her right bicep. She thrashed, trying to kick at the legs of her captor, but the pirate's hold was firm.

"Do it quickly," Chris said, his voice strained.

"Not so queenly now, are you?" Dawson said. He raised his sword and pressed the tip to her chest, right above her heart. "You might be royal, but you'll die the same as the rest of us."

A raw chuckle escaped Alana's throat. "We'll see about that."

Dawson pressed the tip of the sword in harder. "Go on, beg for your life. Maybe I'll be generous and make it painless."

She glared up at the man in silence.

"Fine," the words came out like a growl. "I guess we're doing this slow, then. Cut off little bits of you until—" Dawson's words were cut off abruptly as a sword point emerged through his stomach. Blood filled the pirate's mouth and shock colored his eyes. The sword retracted, and the pirate collapsed onto the deck to reveal a wild-eyed Kaius.

THE STORM GATHERS

Behind her, Chris let out a strangled noise before shoving Alana aside—hard. Her head cracked against the ship's railing, causing dark spots to dance before her. She tried to catch herself, but the wet floor of the deck came out from under her, and she fell.

The blackness dotting her vision spread as her head hit the deck again, drawing her into unconsciousness.

EIGHTEEN

Nur was in a foul mood after meeting with Hettie. She wandered the central garden of the Academy, ignoring the other students as she mulled over her sponsor's words.

I want you to solve the puzzle, Nur Del Sue. I want to be free.

As a child, she'd always loved puzzles. Her parents had, too. They used to leave little clues for each other around the house that led to small treasures hidden throughout the island. The little girl inside her wanted to go back to Hettie and find out what the puzzle was, but the more rational part of her brain knew that the woman was insane.

She should have listened to Talia. Then again, it was Talia who had brought her to meet Hettie, against the insane woman's wishes.

Everyone here has an ulterior motive.

"Hey."

Nur spun to see Kaleo walking towards her. He grinned at the look of shock on her face. "I heard you were sponsored. I've been looking for you everywhere. Someone said they saw you with Talia."

Nur frowned. "You know who Talia is?"

"Not until today. She's some kind of genius, isn't she?"

"Something like that," Nur confirmed. "She's Flame and Earthborn."

Kaleo let out a low whistle. "Impressive. No wonder everyone's afraid of her."

"People here are afraid of her?"

"You're not?"

"She was nice to me. At least…" Nur shook her head and let out a defeated sigh. "I don't know."

"You should probably stay away from her."

Nur forced a smile. "I'll do my best."

They started walking, following the twisting path of the garden.

"I wish Eva was here," Kaleo said. "But I think this is what she wanted. She liked our island. She liked the town and the fish market and, honestly, I don't think she would enjoy the competition of the Academy."

They rounded a corner, and the dorms came into view.

Nur cleared her throat. "I heard Master Turic sponsored you."

"He did. He's a nice man. A bit rough around the edges. He runs the Warehouse. It's where they make Amulets, the fuel-free lamps, that sort of thing. I'm going to be his apprentice."

"That's awesome, K."

He nodded. "It is. I'm excited. I've always wondered how different magical objects are made. It seems impossible, but so does drawing power from a goddess." He let out a little chuckle and turned to Nur. "What about you? I heard you were being sponsored by Hettie of the Flame. Is that true?"

"It is," she said carefully. "I met her today. She's…not what I expected. A bit strange."

Kaleo shrugged. "Who isn't? Hey, did anyone tell you about your dorm assignment?" She shook her head. "They're posted on the front door if you want to take a look. We have orientation with Master Emelia tomorrow in the afternoon, and dinner is at eighteen bells."

"You know so much already."

"I've been talking with the other first-years. A few people besides us were sponsored. Apparently, most of the Masters take it upon themselves to tutor one student each year. That is, everyone besides Master Branson, Master Quill, and Headmaster Kadar."

They reached the circular courtyard outside the main buildings of the Academy. Students were sitting on stone benches and perched on the central fountain.

It looked so…peaceful, like everything Nur had ever imagined it to be. And yet, she couldn't shake the foreboding feeling in her gut.

Solve the puzzle.

"Are you all right?" Kaleo asked, nudging her with his shoulder. "You look upset."

She ran a hand over her face. "Sorry, I'm just tired. I think they gave me something in the Med Suite. It's making me drowsy."

"You should check out your dorm then," he suggested. "Get some sleep and meet me back here at dinner."

Nur forced a small smile to her face. "Sounds good."

He hesitated, his green eyes running over her in apprehension. She was tempted to tell him about her meeting with Hettie, but he was so *happy*, and she didn't want to ruin it. Not now. Not yet. So, Nur turned and strode as casually as she could towards the dorms.

The building's doors were made of driftwood and twisted metal attached to the stone walls with enormous hinges. Posted on the door was a list of names beside their room numbers. Hers was written at the very bottom.

Nur of the Storm—13C.

She committed the number to memory, then pushed open the door of the dormitory. The hallway inside was lit by fuel-free lamps that illuminated doors lining either side of the hall, each engraved with a number and a letter.

A few students passed as she slowly made her way down the line of rooms.

"I'd heard you were sponsored. But I have to say, I didn't really believe it until now."

Nur spun to see Bird. He was halfway out of his dorm, hand still braced against the door's handle. "I'm full of surprises."

"You are." He took a step closer and closed the door. "But we both know you don't deserve your place here. You're a half-breed with no Amulet and barely any power. Soon everyone will see you for what you really are."

"And when will people see you for what you are?" she questioned, forcing her feet to carry her beyond him. "A snobby little boy with a dad who hates him and a mother who's too busy drinking everything in sight to pay him any attention." She reached her door, and looked back at Bird. He was still staring at her. "You claim I have no power," she called to him, "but you barely managed to beat me this morning. I could feel it. You were seconds away from passing out. You should remember that, because if I can do that without an Amulet, what damage do you think I could do with one?"

Before he could answer, she pulled open the door and slipped inside, slamming it shut behind her. She took a deep breath and was surprised to find that she was shaking.

Rubbing at her arms, Nur took in the space around her. Her room was sparse—made up of only a bed, a nightstand, and a dresser. Inside were clothes nearly identical to the ones she was wearing—although in slightly different variations. There were pajamas too and an assortment of shoes for trekking over the different island terrain.

Nur laid down in her bed, remembering Kaleo's advice. She shifted back and forth, trying to get comfortable, but her mind was addled by thoughts of Talia and Hettie and Bird. She let out a frustrated sigh. This should be a day for celebration. Why was she letting others interfere with her happiness?

Releasing a breath, Nur climbed to her feet and stormed out of the room.

Remembering Talia's tour, she made her way to the library.

The building was set slightly apart from the rest and was sealed with a massive iron door. She yanked hard on the ornate metal handle and the door slid open on flawless wheels. She stepped inside.

Scroll-filled shelves were set in rows throughout the massive room, interrupted by the occasional footstool. At the back of the room, a set of metal stairs led up to the second level.

Nur walked past a man seated at a desk, who mumbled a greeting to her. She acknowledged him with a nod and continued on, threading her way through the shelves. After wandering around on the first level, Nur made her way upstairs.

The second level was different from the first. Circular tables filled the space. Only the back wall contained shelves holding a mixture of scrolls and books taken from eastern explorers.

Curious, she made her way past the tables and pulled out a scroll.

"You do look like him."

Startled, Nur spun around, only to come face to face with a man in white Master's robes. Emerald green eyes and high cheekbones made up of the face of Headmaster Kadar. She took a step back and bumped against the shelf.

Kadar offered an apologetic smile. "I'm sorry. I didn't mean to startle you."

Nur bowed her head. "It's okay. I was lost in thought."

"They are magnificent, aren't they?" he said, stepping past her and running a hand over the spine of a few books. "I've spent years curating this collection. Below are words of our past, but here…here is the knowledge that will lead us to our future."

Nur looked up at the shelves. "What are they?"

"These contain our knowledge of the Shatter. Speculations of how to navigate it and the monsters that reside within."

"And Eriysha's Compass," Nur said, showing him the scroll she held which was stamped with the symbol of the mythical artifact.

"Yes."

She hesitated a moment, then asked, "What did you mean when you said I looked like him?"

"Your father, Nanook Del Sue," Kadar clarified. "I knew him."

Nur blinked. First Hettie, now Kadar?

"That's not possible," she said. "He was eastern."

"He was, but he was also a friend of mine." Kadar stepped away from the shelf. "He and I worked together for many years."

"On what?" What could an easterner possibly offer the Headmaster?

Kadar weaved through the tables, and Nur followed. "Nanook originally came to the Shatter in search of Eriysha's Compass. Most of his research was lost when his ship disappeared, but I gave him the opportunity to continue his work here. I think he read every single scroll in this room before…"

"Before he left," Nur finished.

Kadar sighed, running a hand over his face. "I have often wondered what happened that night. I thought perhaps that he discovered something. Something big, and attempted to make the journey here to tell me, but got lost."

THE STORM GATHERS

"Why couldn't he just wait until the morning?"

A faint smile spread across Kadar's face. "When your father had his mind set on something, there was very little that could dissuade him." The Headmaster met Nur's eyes. "But one thing I refuse to believe is that he willingly abandoned you and your mother."

Nur didn't comment on that. She'd heard this sort of speculation before from Emma. Everyone wanted an explanation. Everyone wanted to know *why*. But what did the reason matter compared to the result?

Kadar's shoulders drooped slightly, as if reading her thoughts. "I'm sorry. I know this must be a difficult subject for you. But I just…when I saw your eyes in the arena this morning…I haven't been able to stop thinking about him since."

They reached a door built beside the far-left corner of the second story. Its paneling mimicked the wood of the walls, the only indicator of its true nature coming from a keyhole in the wood.

Kadar hesitated. "I have all of Nanook's journals and research in here. Would you like to see it?"

Nur looked at the door, staring intently as though she might be able to see through to the other side. Part of her wanted nothing more to do with her father. But she couldn't get Hettie's words out of her head.

Solve the puzzle.

Maybe this was it. Maybe behind this door were the answers she'd been denied all her life.

"Yes," she said finally.

Kadar gave her a small nod before fitting the key into the lock and opening the door.

The room was small and windowless. A desk lay at the end and on either side were cubbies crowded with scrolls, journals, and glass jars containing fish skeletons, shelves, driftwood, and more—all of it covered in dust.

Nur stared in awe at the sight before her. Her father had kept journals at their house, but nothing like this. In truth, he'd barely had any belongings other than his clothes. In the years that followed his disappearance, she had combed through his belongings for some explanation of why he'd left them.

But all she'd found were descriptions of the island, the geography and architecture of the buildings, along with the plants and animals that lived there.

She walked over to the desk. Laid atop was a large, leather-bound notebook with the name *Del Sue* stamped in silver across the top. Opening the cover, she began to flip through the pages. Most of it was written in their language—what the easterners called Suhryn—but towards the end, it switched to her father's native tongue. A language they spoke only in Teratt, which Nur couldn't read.

Kadar inhaled deeply. "I must have pored over this place a hundred times in the years since his departure. It seems he was drawing close to an answer, but I haven't been able to figure out what. Who knows? Maybe you'll see something that I cannot."

Nur closed the book. "I wouldn't even know where to start looking."

Kadar gave her a soft, reassuring smile. "This task is not one I place upon you. Here." He handed her the key. "If you wish to come back here, do so. But it is your choice."

Nur slipped it into her pocket. "Thank you," she whispered. "For showing me this. I…I don't know what to say."

Kadar waved her off. "I hoped you would make your way here one day, Nur. I have been wanting to show you this for a long time. That being said, however, I do have one small request. Do not show this room to anyone else. Not even your sponsor, Hettie of the Flame."

Needing no extra encouragement, Nur agreed. "I won't."

Kadar smiled once before disappearing back into the library. Reaching into her pocket, Nur gripped the key tightly, letting it bite into her hand.

"Why were you here?" she whispered softly, looking around the room. "And how could it be worth leaving me for?"

Late that evening, Nur finally left the library. She'd spent the afternoon poring over the scrolls her father had collected. It was nothing more than theories, ones she'd heard a thousand times before in various levels of detail.

Ignoring the sounds of celebration, Nur half-walked, half-stumbled towards her room, stopping only when she saw the red-haired woman leaning against her door.

THE STORM GATHERS

For a moment, she thought it was Hettie, but as the woman turned, Nur saw the truth.

Talia.

NINETEEN

N ur stopped a few feet away from the unexpected visitor and crossed her arms. "What are you doing here?"

"How did your meeting with Hettie go?"

"She's crazy."

"I'm aware."

"You could have warned me."

"I did try to…sort of." Talia made a dismissive gesture. "But it wouldn't have mattered. You needed to see who she was for yourself." A pause. "The people on your islands…they idolize Hettie and Branson and Kadar. All the Masters." She leveled Nur with a glare. "But they're just people, like the rest of us. Flawed, sometimes terrible people."

Brushing aside Talia, Nur entered her room. She was just closing her door when Earthwitch held out a hand, catching it.

"They got to you, didn't they? They warned you to stay away from me."

"Maybe I just don't like your company."

She added more pressure, forcing the door closed. Talia still slipped inside. She wasn't much taller, but she somehow seemed to tower over Nur.

"Everyone thinks you're dangerous."

Talia cocked her head to the side. "And what do you think?"

"I *know* you're dangerous."

"Smart girl. Yes, I am. And people here have good reason to fear me, but they have a better reason to fear you."

Nur took a step back.

THE STORM GATHERS

Talia continued. "A Stormwitch without an Amulet gets into the Academy on a sponsorship? That points to extraordinary power."

"No, what it points to is an insane woman who thinks I'm some sort of puzzle that needs to be solved."

Talia shrugged. "I suppose that's one interpretation of today's events."

Nur narrowed her eyes. "What do you know?"

The other woman grinned, and Nur realized Talia had gotten the exact reaction she'd wanted. "Well, to find that out, you're going to have to trust me."

"I don't."

"Fine, then you'll just have to follow me." When Nur remained pressed against her dorm wall, Talia sighed and said, "If you do, I'll answer any question you ask with complete honesty."

"Three."

"Three?"

"You'll answer any three questions I ask."

A small smile played across the Earthwitch's face. "You have a deal."

Talia took her into the woods outside the Med Suite. There was a small animal trail that twisted in a way that reminded Nur a little too much of a serpent. She focused on Talia's red hair, currently twisted into two braids that hung down the girl's back. Nur swallowed, her throat suddenly dry.

Eventually, they reached a small parting in the trees, complete with an overturned log.

Letting out a dramatic sigh, Talia hopped onto the fallen tree, reached inside a hollowed-out part, and pulled out a glass bottle of dark liquid. "Fruit wine," she explained and uncorked the bottle. "Want some?"

"I'll pass." Nur leaned against a tree and waited as Talia took a few sips. "You promised to answer three questions."

"Indeed, I did. Ask away."

"Why did you bring me to meet Hettie?"

"Because she's your sponsor. And you needed to see for yourself what she's like. Hettie may be crazy, but she's not insane. Her power...I don't know what happened exactly, but now she can't turn it off. It's constantly

145

running through her, clouding her mind. It makes her talk in riddles, but sometimes she's able to purge enough of it, and she gets her mind back—if only for a few moments."

"I've never heard of that happening before," Nur said. "Is anyone else on the island like that?"

"No. At least, not that I know of. I think it has something to do with her Amulet. She doesn't wear it anymore—hasn't in years—but I know it still exists. I think it must have been damaged in some way…" Talia trailed off, blinked, then took another sip from the bottle. "You have one question left, Stormwitch."

Nur cursed. She hadn't meant to ask the second one. "How did you get into the Academy if not through a duel?"

"And here I was, hoping we might steer away from the subject of Hettie of the Flame."

"She got you in?"

Reaching up, Talia tugged at one of her braids. "In a manner of speaking, yes. She's my mother." At Nur's look of surprise, the Earthwitch laughed. "What? The hair didn't tip you off?"

"That doesn't answer my question, though," Nur pressed. "How did you get in?"

Talia held up two fingers. "Two reasons. One, I am the daughter of Hettie of the Flame. She may be half-mad, but behind the riddles and games, she knows what's happening. The Masters wouldn't risk angering her by rejecting my admittance. And two, I am a child of two elements. They couldn't turn me away."

"Still, you should have had a duel."

"Against who? I was raised on this island and trained privately. There was no one for me to fight against. And there was no point. No matter what, I would have gotten in."

Nur shook her head. "I guess."

"You don't approve."

"I think it would be safe to assume that I disapprove of everything you've done so far."

"*Everything*," Talia put a hand to her head in mock offense. "I've done many things. Surely at least one must meet your standards."

"I wouldn't count on it." There was a moment of silence, then Nur said, "I met with Headmaster Kadar today. He claimed he knew my father. Is that possible?"

Talia *tsked*. "You've run out of questions."

"Answer one of mine, and I'll answer one of yours."

Talia considered for a moment, then nodded her agreement. "No, it shouldn't be. Kadar doesn't leave the island, and outsiders aren't allowed here." She thought for a moment. "Unless...when I was a child, there were occasionally scholars from surrounding islands that had permission to come here for research or to work with the Masters on various projects. It's possible he was one of them."

"But he was eastern."

Talia shrugged. "Maybe Kadar didn't care. Did he say what your father was working on?"

"That counts as your question," Nur said.

"I know, now answer."

Sighing, Nur leaned back. "Some stuff about Eriysha's Compass and how to navigate the Shatter. Same thing everyone researches." She frowned. "I've never heard of islanders coming to the Academy."

"The Masters kept it pretty quiet. They didn't want normal people thinking they had a chance at coming here. And they stopped allowing passage about ten—maybe twelve—years ago. I imagine most people have forgotten. I'd forgotten until you brought it up."

"Kadar claims they were friends."

"It's possible." Talia considered. "Still, it is odd, though. You're here for less than a day, and you've already met with both Hettie of the Flame and Headmaster Kadar."

"You took me to meet with Hettie," Nur pointed out. "And I went to the library, which Kadar is in charge of."

"But I didn't convince Hettie to sponsor you. And Kadar rarely interacts with students. If you spoke with him, it's because he wanted to speak with you." Talia took another drink and let out a sigh. "You need to be careful, Nur."

"Around you?"

"Around everyone. Whatever you may have been told, the Academy is a dangerous place. People disappear. People die. No one talks about. Not one wants to acknowledge it, but it happens." She looked up at the sky. "Recently things have been getting worse. Something happening. Something's changed. Or someone wants things to change. And, for some reason, you've gotten yourself caught up in the middle of it."

"I'm not special."

"Perhaps not," Talia conceded. "But maybe your father was."

TWENTY

A lana woke in a bed that smelled clean, which was the first indication that she was most definitely not in the *Fe Ressu*'s brig. But neither was she in her chambers in Jaarin—the gentle rocking of the ship told her that much.

Forcing her breathing to remain normal, she peeked through her eyelashes, allowing a vague idea of the room. There was a man sitting in a chair a few feet from the bed she was lying in. His head was turned away from her, eyes looking out the window.

Kaius.

His dark hair was mussed, and the scruff along his jaw was the only thing she could make out of his facial features. But she remembered those dark eyes. They were the last thing she'd seen before the pirate had thrown her against the ship's railing.

With the knowledge that he wasn't looking at her, Alana opened both her eyes and searched for a weapon. A shelf of books lined one wall. In the center of the stack was a small nook with liquor shining an amber color. There were no visible blades or traditional weapons. The only thing within easy reach was a candlestick beside the bed. Definitely not ideal, but she still relished the idea of hitting him with it. Of just hitting *something*.

She inhaled a few breaths, coiling her legs and ignoring the throbbing pain in her head. Springing forward, her hands closed around the candlestick at the same moment Kaius leaped from his chair. He caught her wrist before she could swing and pinned her arm over the side of the bed, twisting it until she was forced to drop the candlestick.

He hovered over her, one hand still gripping hers while the other braced itself against the bed on her opposite side.

"I was wondering when you were going to wake up. Took you a while." Letting out a frustrated sound, Alana pushed against his hold, to no avail. Kaius raised an amused eyebrow. "I see that hit to the head did nothing to help you see sense."

Alana stopped fighting and glared up at him. "Let. Me. Go."

To her surprise, he did so immediately. "If you try to attack me again, I'll put you in irons."

The queen sat up with exaggerating slowness, trying not to wince at the pain in her head and arm...

Shit.

She looked to where the pirate brute had stabbed her, expecting a bleeding gash, but found the injury stitched and bandaged. She glanced at Kaius, raising an eyebrow.

"I couldn't let our most valuable prisoner bleed out and die. Or get an infection, which was admittedly more likely. It should heal quickly, and I'll be able to take the stitches out in a week, or so." There was a beat of silence, then the first mate made a vague motion at her. "That's quite the collection of scars you have, by the way. Wouldn't have expected that of a queen."

Alana frowned down at herself. "What are you talking about?"

"On your hands."

Alana lifted her hands in front of her face, squinting in the dim light. "Oh...these."

Memories of days long past rose to the surface. Of sailing and fighting with Arya on cliff sides. Of fishing with her father and crashing during storms. The adventures of her childhood mapped in the thin white lines that crossed her hands.

"They're from sailing," she said numbly. "A long time ago."

"What's the big one on your palm from?"

Alana narrowed her eyes at him. "Deep sea gorgous," she said, referring to the large, spine backed fish that dwelled in the darkest depths of the ocean. Scholars speculated they were venomous, although she knew from personal experience that was not the case.

Kaius met her gaze. "I was being serious."

"And here I was thinking you could make it as a court jester."

His eyes flickered to the hand she had crumpled in the bedsheets. "It looks like it was painful."

"No more so than this conversion." She gave him a sweet smile. "Can I go back to the brig now?"

Kaius opened his mouth to respond, but was cut off as the ship rocked violently beneath them. A shout from outside sounded, followed by a chorus of voices.

Alana took a deep breath, inhaling the charged air, and grinned. "There's a storm rolling in." The boom of thunder outside punctuated her words. "If you don't take me back to my cell now, we'll both be trapped here. Something I'm fairly certain neither of us wants."

He grunted his agreement and motioned for her to take the lead.

Rolling her shoulders, Alana stepped in front of him and opened the door.

The smell hit her first. Fresh rain, lightning, and the roiling sea. The wind whipped at her hair and sent the water beneath the ship into a frenzy.

Kaius's hand was at the small of her back, nudging her forward. "Come on, *Kiydra*."

Alana danced away from him. Her fingers wrapped around the railing of the ship as the first raindrops fell. He reached for her again, but she smacked him away. "Do. Not. Touch. Me."

His lip curled. "We need to go."

"No."

"*Alana*." His voice was filled with warning, but she didn't move. Her hands tightened on the railing as she stared into the gathering storm. She needed this. Gods, she needed this.

Thunder boomed overhead, and the wind picked up. Lightning splintered across the sky, and the rain fell harder, churning the ocean beneath them. Waves licked up the side of the ship like flames, spilling over the deck.

She laughed. The sound came out of her with an explosion of joy. Yes. This was where she belonged. This had been what she'd wanted to do as a child. Live in the beginning of each storm. Chasing them across the world—just to experience moments like this one.

A face appeared in front of her. Dark hair was plastered to Kaius's forehead as the rain poured down. He stared at her as though she was some strange creature born of both dreams and nightmares. His lips moved, but whatever words he'd spoken were drowned out by another boom of thunder.

"*What?*" she asked.

Kaius looked up, and he shook his head, a curve of a smile appearing on his own face.

Lightning cut the sky in front of them and arced down towards the ocean. Alana inhaled once more, feeling the electricity of the storm in her lungs before turning towards the hatch that led into the brig. She caught his eye and nodded once.

A moment later, they were back in the semi-dry, terrible-smelling brig.

Everyone was awake, whether from the storm or commotion, Alana didn't know.

"What happened?" Maria demanded. Her eyes narrowed onto the first mate. "What did you do to her?"

Kaius stopped at the last step and leaned against the wall, arms crossed. He smirked at Maria.

"Besides, save her life? It's funny. I was under the impression that was *your* job." He winked at Alana. "Hey, if you ever need someone who can actually—"

"I would rather be impaled on a rusty metal spike."

A low chuckle rumbled through the space, and all eyes shot to Johnathan, who did his best to look innocent.

Kaius pulled a set of keys from his pocket and motioned for everyone to back up. "Go to the corner of the cell."

When they obeyed, he unlocked the door, holding it open dramatically as she stepped inside, pointedly ignoring him.

She was surrounded as soon as he left the brig, everyone demanding to know exactly what happened. It took everything in her power not to tell all of them to shut up. Retreating to the corner of the cell, Alana explained, in as few details as possible, what had happened.

"I can't believe they drugged us," Wren murmured.

"I can." Everyone turned to look at Penn, who just held up his hands. "They're pirates, kidnappers, thieves, and murderers. I don't see why they wouldn't have a problem drugging us, too."

"You're all missing the point," Alana said.

Maria crossed her arms. "Which is?"

"The pirate who attacked me had a key to our cell. Which means…" Alana reached into her pocket and pulled out a ring with a single key on it "…we have a key to the cell. Now, all we need is a way off the ship."

Wren blinked at her. "You stole from a pirate?"

"He was a little busy holding me while his friend tried to drive a sword through my heart—he didn't notice."

Maria's fingers twitched at her sides, as though she couldn't decide whether to be angry or impressed.

Alana pressed on before her guard could make a decision. "The life-boats are kept on the starboard side of the deck and I believe that they are stocked with supplies. The issue facing us now is that—aside from the fact we're heading north—I have no idea where we are." She paused. "I'll try to find out what I can if I speak with Sarasin again. At the very least, I'll steal his compass."

"Assuming all of this goes to plan, how are we going to sneak onto the deck and steal a lifeboat without anyone noticing and coming after us?" Wren demanded.

Alana examined her nails. "We're going to set their ship on fire."

TWENTY-ONE

Rae waited in the hull of *The Wave Finder*, observing her surroundings. In approximately two hours, they would be crossing the boundary into the Shatter. Already, Ydric's compass was becoming unreliable—spinning erratically every few minutes before finding South again.

Perched on one of the massive wooden crates that were secured in place with netting, Rae had just finished sharpening her falcata when Aram climbed down the ladder into the hull.

"Ydric said you were waiting for me down here." He eyed her sword. "Please don't say you're going to kill me."

"I need to train," Rae said, giving her weapon a practice swing. "You're going to be my partner."

Aram motioned to the sword belted at his waist. "I don't have a training blade."

"Neither do I." Rae set her falcata aside and pulled out *Teruth*.

"Rae…" Aram took a step back. "I know you're angry with me. But, as I said before, I would prefer you didn't kill me."

She rolled her eyes. "I'm not going to. But I imagine beating you up will make me feel a lot better."

"That still brings us back to the fact that these swords are sharp."

Rae circled him. "Swordsmanship, like all fighting, is about control. If you can't control your blade to inflict harm or avoid it, then you don't deserve to hold the weapon. Fighting like this is about trust. I trust you not to hurt me. And you trust me not to hurt you."

Aram adjusted his grip on the blade. "Fine, if this is what it will take for you to trust me again. Let's do it."

They circled each other for a few moments before Aram struck. He charged her but didn't make any wide strike—keeping the sword close to his body. Rae spun to the left, aiming a low blow at his thigh and turning her sword away at the last moment, hitting him with the flat of the blade.

Aram cursed and danced back, keeping his sword poised in defense.

Rae grinned. "How was that for control?"

"I guess I should be pleased you're not using your falcata."

"You should be happy you're still alive, given that you spied on and betrayed me."

"And you cut me out of your life for years!" Aram shot back. "All because of some stupid promise we made when we were kids."

He lashed out, and Rae blocked him easily.

"I didn't want to bring you into my world. I walked a line between life and death, betrayal and loyalty for years. And look where it led me."

"I'm on the run too, Rae."

"It's different. You're just a spy that deserted. In a few years, you'll be forgotten among the countless others that did the same, but this—" she gestured around, "—this is my life now. I was the leader of the Val and a member of the king's guard. As long as Argos lives, I will be hunted."

Aram's sword drooped slightly, and Rae struck out. He blocked, stumbling backwards as the force of her blow knocked him off balance. He staggered for a moment, but managed to find his balance in time to block her next attack.

"Be that as it may, Rae, but from now on, I don't want you to protect me. If we're going to survive, we need to make a new promise."

He came for her. Their swords clashed in a fury of blows.

Rae ducked and parried before landing a hit on his side with the flat of her blade. Aram jumped back, sword going wide, and she kicked out, catching his foot and sending him to the ground. She pressed the tip of *Teruth* against her friend's heart. "Which is?"

Aram stared up at her, breathing hard from the exertion of the fight. "We promise to fight alongside each other, against any evil we may face."

Rae sheathed her sword and offered him a hand. "I promise."

Aram got to his feet and gave her a small nod. "As do I."

Rae released him and returned to the box where she'd left her falcata. "Just to be clear, I won our duel."

Aram rolled his eyes. "Unsurprisingly, yes."

A FEW HOURS LATER, RAE and Aram joined the rest of the crew on deck. There was no clear line between the Shatter and the rest of the world, but the air had changed. It hadn't grown heavy exactly, but there was a sense of pressure as their ship sailed forward. Ydric's compass lay abandoned beside the helm, the needle spinning uselessly.

Qasim sat by the bow of the ship. His curly gray hair bounced in the wind as he scribbled furiously in his notebook.

"What's he writing about, anyway?" Aram groused. "Nothing's happened ye—"

Suddenly, a wall of hard, warm air slammed into them. Half the people on deck crumpled to the ground. Rae managed to hold herself up using the ship's rail.

Qasim, however, was sent off his perch and fell to the deck. Ydric helped him to his feet while Aram retrieved the explorer's notebook and pencil.

"Look!" A soft voice sounded to their right, and all eyes turned to the sky. It had been evening when they'd crossed into the Shatter, but now the sun was back in the center of the sky, although the light from its glow had lessened considerably, giving way to stars which had reorganized into unrecognizable patterns.

"It appears we now know what piece of magic prevents us from navigating by the constellations," Rae said. "Brilliant."

Aram raised an eyebrow. "Brilliant?"

"It is," Qasim said, his eyes half fixed on the stars as he spoke. "Can you imagine the power of Eriysha's Compass if it can guide us through this place?"

"Is that what you want, then?" Aram asked. "Power?"

"I'm flattered you think me worthy of the goddess's Compass, boy—"

"Ah, so we're back to that."

THE STORM GATHERS

"But even if we do find the Compass, it cannot be me that takes it." He looked at the crew. "I fear it may not be any of us. Not even you, Rae, I had thought perhaps, but..." he shook his head, "you are bound to the Forest. Yours is the god of beasts and the guardian of life, not Eriysha."

Self-consciously, Rae raised a hand to her face. The drops she put in her eye only lasted a few hours. She hadn't even considered what it would mean for people to see the gold. Warily, she glanced around but saw no hateful looks. No, these people were all criminals and runaways. They had no right to judge her.

"Who, then?" Aram asked.

"Someone who is bound to the goddess. Someone who is worthy."

"And this person is just supposed to, what, magically appear?"

"Well, boy," Qasim said, looking up at the new sky, "we are in the Shatter. So, who are you to say what is and isn't possible?"

TWENTY-TWO

Orientation lasted a full week before elemental instruction under Master Emelia began.

When she wasn't in class or with Kaleo, Nur spent her time at the library. Today, she was sitting at the desk in her father's room, reading through the first entries in his massive journal. Musings and the occasional observation about the islands filled the pages. None of which were particularly useful. She had lived here her entire life. The hidden coves, animal species, and hand-print rocks were nothing new to her. And she had yet to find any clues regarding her father's work.

Exhausted from her day of training, she set aside the notebook after only six pages of reading. She was so tired the letters seemed to blend together, so she rested her head in her hands, moments away from taking a nap, when she heard the sigh of air as the door behind her opened. She looked over her shoulder to see Headmaster Kadar.

"I hope I'm not interrupting. An attendant told me you were here."

Nur got to her feet. "It's no trouble."

"A letter arrived today addressed to you. Normally, it would have been given to you sponsor, but given Hettie's… erratic tendencies, it was given to me."

Nur rose to her feet. "Do you know who it's from?"

"I believe it was sent by one of the students you went to school with. A Seawitch named Eva."

Intrigued, Nur followed the Headmaster out of the small room and down the steps of the library to the first floor.

THE STORM GATHERS

"I must admit," Kadar said as they reached the landing. "I'm surprised you received correspondence so soon. Usually, those who have just lost their Amulet need one or two weeks to recover."

Nur frowned. "What do you mean? Does it hurt them?"

"They go from being able to channel a tremendous amount of power to having almost none. Losing your Amulet also impacts your ability to connect to Eriysha's magic. Afterwards, most Flameborns can barely start a fire."

"That's horrible," Nur said, then immediately cursed herself.

"It's for the best, Nur," Kadar explained. "Those who have just lost their shot at the Academy can be hazardous. Our lives on these islands are fragile enough already. It is safer for everyone if we eliminate that danger in advance."

"Why not just let everyone in?"

The Headmaster sighed. "Competition is the key to our survival. It pushes people to be their best. Can you say you would have worked as hard as you have if you knew you were guaranteed a spot at the Academy?"

Nur wasn't certain. To her, the entrance to the Academy was just a stepping stone. A mechanism for proving people wrong. But this wasn't the end. She wouldn't stop until...well, Nur wasn't entirely sure. Until she was Master? Headmaster? Would that be enough? Would anything?

They walked around the library desk to a stone door carved with the symbol of the goddess Eriysha—a sea serpent wrapped around a compass.

Kadar opened the door, and they entered his office.

A cubby of scrolls lined one wall, and on the opposite side were shelves filled with trinkets—shells, pieces of dead coral, knickknacks from the East, and magical objects made in the Warehouse.

Kadar went to his desk in the far corner of the room and pulled out a letter. He handed it to Nur, and she broke the wax seal.

Nur,

I am so proud of you and Kaleo, and I congratulate you both on your entrance to the Academy. Emma is doing well, and I will visit as often as I can.

It is my fate to stay on this island. It's where I belong. I hope you come to understand that.

Tell K I miss him.

Much love,

Eva

Nur folded the letter and slipped it into her pocket.

"Is everything all right?" Kadar asked.

"It is. Thank you for giving me this."

"It was my pleasure." He touched a hand to his heart in dismissal, and she strolled out of his office.

Enthused by her correspondence from Eva, she decided to return to the hidden room on the second story. She would show the letter to Kaleo at dinner. Until then, she planned to read as much of her father's journal as possible.

She flipped open the book, the sheets of paper settling into place at a spot near the end where a page had been removed. There was no text written on either side of the missing page, but…

Nur squinted down at the ridge of paper that had been left behind when the rest was torn out.

Written in tiny lettering was a string of numbers and letters.

7A, 12D, 13C, 11A, 2C, 8B, 16A, 4D, 22B

Taking Eva's letter, Nur quickly scribbled down the numbers on the back of the paper. It could be some kind of code and Nanook *had* liked riddles, but this was different from the word problems she was accustomed to.

Why change the rules now?

Frustrated, she pocketed the paper and left the room.

A LITTLE WHILE LATER, NUR found herself standing outside the entrance to the arena where she had dueled Bird. The enormous stone wall and arcing entrance loomed over her. Looking back, she could barely make out the dark stone walls of the Academy's main buildings in the distance.

Nur was meant to meet Kaleo for dinner in a few minutes, but she'd somehow wandered far enough that the tolling of the hour no longer carried to her ears.

THE STORM GATHERS

She walked across the dirt floor of the arena, careful not to cross over the white oval painted on the ground.

"Hello, Nur Del Sue."

She froze at the familiar voice and slowly turned her attention towards the stadium, eyes scanning the seats until they landed on Hettie of the Flame.

The woman lay stretched out across the bleachers. Her head was tipped slightly towards Nur, but her eyes stared up at the sky.

Nur climbed over the stone railing and made her way towards her sponsor. "That's not my name."

"Isn't it?"

"Only easterners have last names. And I am not eastern," she said firmly.

"Names, names, names." Hettie let out a dramatic sigh. "Everyone is so obsessed with names. What name is right and what name is wrong, but does it really make a difference? You could call me Trisha of the Whels for all the difference it makes. Does it change who I am? No."

Nur supposed there was some truth to that—in a twisted sort of way. Still, names were important. Names may not define the person, but it could define their life. Her last name had certainly impacted hers.

She frowned, troubled to find that she was putting so much thought into a madwoman's words. Then again, perhaps this was just what Nur needed. The code didn't make sense to her, but she was looking at them from the perspective of someone who was sane.

"Do the numbers *7A*, *12D*, *13C*, *11A*, *2C*, *8B*, *6A*, *4D*, and *22B* mean anything to you?"

Hettie singsonged the code back to her. "Such pretty things," she cooed. "I wonder what they would make it if you put them together."

Nur shook her head. This was pointless. The woman's mind was too scattered to be of any use.

"It's best not to get her started."

Nur spun to see Talia standing behind her. Her red hair was loose around her shoulder and her eyes looked sunken.

"Sorry to interrupt, but one of your friends seems to think I've kidnapped you."

Nur frowned. "Who? Kaleo?"

"Is that the name of the Flameborn boy with the foul mouth?"

Nur grimaced. "Yeah."

"Tell him you're still alive and uncorrupted, because if he attempts to threaten me again, I will demonstrate exactly why this island fears me."

Rolling her eyes, Nur strode away from her sponsor and leaped onto the ground of the arena. She made her way to the exit, but Talia blocked her.

"You've been avoiding me."

Nur tried to side step past her, but the redhead grabbed her arm.

"I assume you have someone else you can bother?" Nur snapped.

Talia cocked her head. "You're…upset."

"I'm frustrated," Nur corrected. "I'm tired. And now," she gave a pointed look at the young woman's hand, "I'm annoyed."

Talia released her grip. "I'm sorry. I—" she shook her head. "When Kaleo found me, I was worried that something might have happened to you."

Nur took a step back and crossed her arms. "Why?"

"I've already told you," Talia said quietly.

"What did you tell me?" Nur challenged. "That this place is dangerous? Which is especially ironic considering that the person everyone has warned me away from is *you*."

Nur walked off before Talia had a chance to respond.

Once again, Hettie's words played through her head.

Solve the puzzle.

NUR WAS LATE FOR HER dinner with Kaleo, a fact that he was definitely not pleased about.

"Where were you?"

"I lost track of time." She frowned. "You know, it's funny—you warn me to stay away from Talia and then go running to her the minute you think something's wrong."

"I thought she might have done something to you. I was worried." Her friend ran a hand through his hair. "You haven't been the same this week. I wish you would tell me what's been going on."

Nur clenched her jaw, then reached into her pocket and pulled out the letter from Eva. She handed it to her friend and waited for him to read it. He did so twice, smiling to himself the entire time. Once finished, he folded the paper back up, but paused when noticed the numbers Nur had recorded on the back.

"What are these?"

She hesitated a moment, then sighed and explained the room Kadar had shown her, Hettie's insanity, and the warnings Talia had given. Finally, she nodded to the string of numbers. "I found this on what was left of a paper torn out of my father's journal. It could be a clue to what happened to him."

Kaleo frowned. "Maybe…or maybe you're seeing what you want to see. You think if you find this missing page, it will lead to answers about your father's disappearance. But to me, this just looks like is a random string of numbers and letters."

"My father and I used to play games all the time while I was growing up. He was always giving me riddles and puzzles to solve." Nur tapped the paper. "This is different from what I'm used to, but the way the sequence is written feels intentional. Nanook was careful in everything he did. If he tore out a page, he would make sure all the text came with it. He wrote this *after*. The question is why."

Kaleo sighed, taking back the paper from her and examining it again. "Well, you could try looking for a mathematical association between the numbers," he suggested.

"Maybe," she said, unconvinced.

"It could also be a word," Kaleo added. "Each number and letter sequences corresponding to a letter of the alphabet. Then again, I'm not sure how a single word would help you find the missing page." He hesitated. "If it were me, these numbers would correspond to a hidden location." He handed the letter back to Nur. "I'm sorry, but that's all I've got."

Nur looked over the numbers again. A hidden location.

"Gods, I'm an idiot." She tapped one of the numbers. "13C is my dorm number. The rest of these could be rooms at the Academy. There might be something hidden there. Another clue."

Kaleo shook his head. "This is turning into a damned treasure hunt." He nodded in the direction of their dorms. "All right, then. Let's go."

TWENTY-THREE

R ae sat with Qasim at the long table in his study. They'd been sailing
through the Shatter for a week and, so far, had encountered no islands.
The only sign of life was the fish that was occasionally caught in their nets.

She flipped the page of the book she was reading. It was an autobiography by Ero Beltane, the Southern explorer. He, too, had ventured into the
Shatter—never to be seen again. But before that, he'd helped Empress Oriane Asha in her campaign to unite the South. His book, *Dos sef Ter lan*—or,
What the World is—was an account of his life, including the war. Most
copies of the book had been destroyed and what little remained had been
heavily edited following his disappearance. Still, most historians regarded
Ero's autobiography as the most reliable account of the First Empress's life
before her ascension to the throne.

Beside her, Qasim was writing all of his observations from the Shatter.
Although, after seven days of seeing nothing, Rae couldn't imagine what
there was left to record.

Gods, what will happen when we actually encounter an island? They
could be there for months just so the man could write everything down.

"Well, this is slightly terrifying," a familiar voice said. Rae looked up
to see Aram and Ydric in the doorway, both looking mildly surprised at the
sight before them.

"I've never seen Qasim silent for more than a few minutes," the captain agreed.

"Maybe I have a calming effect on him," Rae said.

"Don't engage," Qasim murmured beside her. "They'll leave if you don't engage."

"But it's more fun to engage," she whispered back.

"Are you insulting us?" Aram asked, a small smile playing on his face.

"That depends, does comparing you to one of those—" She turned to Qasim. "What are those little creatures who live in Yovar called? The ones with vestigial wings and giant ears?"

"Nye-nyes," the explorer said.

Rae snapped her finger. "That's right. Does comparing you a nye-nye count as an insult?"

Aram rolled his eyes.

Ydric let out a sigh. "Qasim, we're approaching a rock formation. It's not an island, we won't be stopping, but I thought you might want to—"

"Yes." The old explorer leaped to his feet, cradling his notebook in one hand as he hurried for the door, shoving past the captain and Aram.

Ydric shook his head and looked at Rae. "Is he being nice?"

She shrugged. "Not nice, precisely. But we get along fine."

"Are *you* nice to *him*?" Aram questioned.

"I'm nice to everyone."

Her friend snorted. "We both know that's not true."

"Maybe I'm just not nice to you," Rae said sweetly. She nodded to the door. "Now, are we going to see what—"

From above deck, someone screamed.

Instinctively, Rae triggered the knives hidden in her cuffs as more shouts echoed from outside. Not wasting any time, she ran for the door. Aram and Ydric followed close on her heels. They burst onto the deck.

The sky was a crystal blue above them, with fluffy white clouds—like the kind children drew—dotting the horizon. Beneath them, the sea was calm—waves lapping happily against the hull. To put it simply, it was a beautiful day. Or would have been, if not for the nightmarish creatures climbing up the side of the ship.

Rae blinked, trying to make sense of the sight before her. The monsters' bottom halves were finned and serpentine—clearly evolved for a life in water. Their tops, however, had multiple limbs ending in sharp claws. But it was the face of the creatures that made Rae's hair stand on end. It was long and reptilian with curling—almost tusk-like—teeth and white eyes. For a moment, she hoped the creatures might be blind, but the way they moved was too precise to be from scent and sound alone.

"What are they?" Aram huffed.

"Ty'vairrs," Ydric supplied, his eyes scanning the scene before them—looking for Qasim. "They paint images of them on the docks in Yovar. They're supposed to be for protection." He shook his head. "I thought they were fictional."

Rae re-sheathed her knives, exchanging the smaller weapons for her falcata. "Apparently not." She met Aram's eye, and they shared a nod. "Try not to die."

"I'll do my best."

They charged into the fray.

Rae wove through the chaos, hacking at the limb of any ty'vairr that she could reach. The creatures moved surprisingly fast—using their tails like clubs to knock over sailors and rip them apart with their teeth and limbs.

Doing her best to ignore the gruesome sights around her, Rae cut through the snout of one of the ty'vairrs and removed her sword—just in time ward to off another coming from her left. She caught a glance of Aram fighting alongside a female sailor. Ydric was making his way to them.

Rae dodged a strike from a ty'vairr tail and whipped her head around, searching for Qasim. Had he gone back below deck?

Something hard slammed into the back of her knees, sending her to the deck. She triggered the knives in her cuffs and raised her arms.

A large ty'vairr jumped towards her, teeth snapping and limbs poised to rip her apart. It slammed into her, claws digging into her sides as it tried to bite her head off.

Rae jerked her neck out of the way just in time and wrapped her arm around the monster's snout.

It strained against her, unable to open its jaws.

With a growl, Rae drove one of her knives into the beast's eye.

The ty'vairr released its grip, allowing her to climb to her feet. She retrieved her falcata and cleaved the dead creature in two for good measure.

Heart racing, she examined the wounds at her side. Thankfully, her Sioran steel tunic had prevented the claws from causing any external injury—although she suspected the beast's strength had bruised her ribs.

She readjusted her grip on her falcata, readying to rejoin the fight. But before she could take a single step, one of the ty'vairrs released a high-pitched call that was soon joined by the others.

Then, one by one, the monstrous creatures crawled back over the edge of the ship and into water.

Rae released a shaking breath. What in Rion's name had just happened?

After a few seconds of waiting for the creatures to return, Rae sheathed her blade and took in the sight before her.

The carcasses of ty'vairrs mixed with the bodies of sailors in a disturbing array of blood and body parts.

Something caught her eye, and she bent down to pick up Qasim's journal. The bottom was soaked in blood and Rae dropped it reflexively. It landed with a heavy plop besides a bloodied human body…with wild, gray hair.

A cry escaped her lips and Rae dropped to her knees beside the explorer. Her fingers searched for a pulse. To her relief, she found one—it was faint, but present. With a groan, one of the Qasim's eyes slid open and met hers.

"Ydric!" she yelled. "Ydric, help him!"

The captain came running over, a bruise blossoming on his cheek as he pushed Rae aside. Qasim was covered in so much blood that it was difficult to see what damage had been done.

"It's going to be okay," Ydric said, looking over his partner. "We're going to help you." He spun to Rae and Aram. "There's a box of medical supplies in my room."

Aram nodded. "I'll get it."

Rae watched her friend go, letting her eyes wander the deck. Their crew of fourteen had been reduced to half. The survivors of the attack were either treating their injuries, crying, or retching.

THE STORM GATHERS

A shadow fell over the ship and, for a moment, Rae feared the ty'vairrs had returned. Instead, an equally distressing sight greeted her as *The Wave Finder* crashed into the rock formation they'd been sailing towards.

The deck rocked beneath them, and the sound of cracking wood filled the air as their ship's hull was ripped open by the rocks.

Aram appeared from the captain's cabin, a wooden box under one arm.

"Oh, gods..." He took one look at the rocky cliffs looming in front of them, then back to Qasim.

Ydric gestured towards him urgently.

Rae crouched at the explorer's sided, Aram joining her. She pushed aside Qasim's shirt and examined the wound beneath. A trail of puncture marks were ripped across his chest—the wounds oozing with dark blood and a pale green liquid.

"Ydric, I don't know if we can save him," she whispered.

The captain shook his head. "We have to."

"Listen to the girl," Qasim croaked. "She's the only intelligent one of you three."

Rae let loose a laugh that bordered on a sob. "I'm so sorry."

"I am, too," the old explorer said. "I hoped to see more of this place before it killed me."

"You're not going to die!" Ydric exclaimed. He rummaged through the medical kit, looking for what—Rae couldn't imagine.

"You need to leave before the ship sinks," Qasim said. "It's—" he let out a little grunt of pain, "too late for me."

"We're not just going to leave you," Aram said firmly.

"Fool," Qasim spat. "Go. I don't want your deaths on my conscious. Let me die in peace."

"You're not going to die," the captain repeated.

"Ydric..." Qasim swallowed, "please. Don't be a fool. Don't waste your life on someone who's already dead."

"You're the fool, Qasim, if you think for one second that I'm going to leave you behind."

The explorer turned pleading eyes to Rae. "Talk some sense into him!"

She shook her head. "It's his choice. I know if it were Aram, I wouldn't leave. No matter what anyone said. Can you say you'd act any differently if you were in his position?"

Qasim looked back at Ydric, and his expression softened. "I can't." He took a rattling breath. "But you, Rae, you need to go."

She nodded and grabbed Aram's arm.

He held firm. "Thank you both," he said, emotion clawing up his throat. "You saved us. I wish we could do the same to you."

Ydric cradled Qasim's head in his lap. "Go, Aram. Find the Compass, if you can. Do what we could not."

There was only one lifeboat left. The rest of the crew had abandoned the ship already. Aram climbed in and got to work on the ropes, Rae hopping in after him. She couldn't take her eyes off the two men. One dying, the other soon to follow. It wasn't right. But she knew there was nothing she could say or do to save either of them.

Aram lowered their lifeboat into the sea and took up the oars, carrying them away from the sinking ship and into an unknown world filled with monsters and magic.

A world that no one had ever returned from.

TWENTY-FOUR

N ur and Kaleo spent two days carefully combing over every inch of her dorm room. They pried up the floorboards, searched the desk and dresser for hidden compartments and went over the walls with a fine-toothed comb. Nothing.

The rest of the numbers in the sequence seemed to correspond to dorms, but Nur could hardly break into someone else's room and search it. Besides, it seemed frustratingly likely that she wouldn't find anything. It had been over ten years since the note was written. There was no telling what could have changed at the Academy since then.

Nur sat against a tree at the edge of the main courtyard. Students milled about, their voices filling the space with idle chatter. She tuned them out as best she could as she scanned the sequence once more. Her leg bounced up and down as she tried to decipher the hidden message. It was pointless. She had the code memorized by now, she just didn't know what it meant.

"Does that piece of paper really deserve more attention that I do?"

Nur looked up to see Talia standing over her. Her red hair was tied in a messy bun atop her head, and her green eyes gleamed with interest.

The Stormwitch opened her mouth to speak, then closed it, unable to think of anything.

Talia laughed quietly, then reached forward and plucked the paper from Nur's hand. She examined the numbers written on the back of the page and frowned. "I don't understand. What is this?"

Nur snatched it back. "It's a code."

"A code?" Talia's eyes lit up. "You found something. What's this for?"

"I'm not sure." She pocketing the note, hesitated a moment, then asked, "You've lived on this island your entire life, right?"

Talia nodded. "Never left."

"Have the dorm room numbers changed in the last ten years?"

Talia shook her head. "No. Actually, until about twenty years ago, there weren't numbers at all. Then there was some sort of incident and a large part of the Academy was destroyed. There was so much confusion about what may and may not have been lost in the aftermath that the Masters decided to number everything in the Academy. Dorms. Buildings. Even the docks." A pause. "Why? Do you think these numbers correspond to places on this island?"

"It's possible," Nur said evasively.

The other woman considered. "I think there may be a catalog in the Med Suite, in case of emergency. I suppose I could get it for you…for a price."

Nur narrowed her eyes. "What price?"

"Trust, Stormwitch. Once you find what you're looking for, you need to tell me what it is."

"It…could be dangerous."

Talia smirked. "I'm a dangerous person."

"I know that, but—"

Talia took a step forward—stopping when she and Nur were only inches apart. "If you want my help, you agree to my terms. I know more about the Academy than anyone aside from the Masters, and I'm willing to bet you're going to need help again before this is over." She took a step back and Nur suddenly felt cold. "I won't make this offer again, so choose wisely."

Nur was half tempted to refuse, if only to wipe that smug look off of Talia's face. She gripped the note tightly in her hands. She wanted answers and if this was the only way to get them, then so be it.

"Fine," Nur said, keeping her voice cool. "You have a deal."

A FEW HOURS LATER, NUR sat at a picnic table with a detailed map of the Academy spread before her.

THE STORM GATHERS

Talia hadn't lied when she'd said that the Masters had cataloged everything. There were hundreds of tiny sequences of numbers and letters written across the page. Thankfully, there weren't many sets that went above ten, which narrowed down Nur's search considerably.

The only groups that had all the numbers she was looking for were the dorms, garden beds, and Academy ships.

Nur didn't believe the dorms held the answers she was looking for. Either that, or whatever had been in her room had been removed. She decided to start her search with the garden beds, as that was the easiest. Ships would be more difficult. Not only did they come and go frequently, but it was likely that—over the course of ten years—one of the ships she was looking for sank or disappeared.

She examined the map. The garden was broken into sections A, B, C, and D. She was in A. If she followed the path, she would reach garden bed seven. Nur drummed her fingers on the table. Part of her wanted to wait for Kaleo to return from the Warehouse, but the other part of her was desperate to begin her search.

She was on the right track now. She had to be.

Unable to resist, Nur folded up the map and headed for the bed 7A.

As she walked through the garden paths, her mind became lost in the clouds. The truth was that she didn't know what she would find at the end of this treasure hunt. She wasn't even certain there was anything to find.

Why couldn't she give this up?

It wasn't because she wanted to find out what had happened to her father. At least, that wasn't the whole reason. Nur had accepted his loss long ago.

It wasn't because of Kadar. He'd made it clear that he had no expectations that she would uncover the truth. Still, part of her did relish the idea of proving to him how capable she was.

It wasn't even because Nur loved puzzles.

No, those were the reasons she'd began this quest, but they weren't why she continued. The simple truth was that once Nur had her sights set on a goal, she wasn't be able to quit until she accomplished it. It was her fatal flaw, as Eva had once said. And it was liable to get her killed one day.

Nur approached her target. Inside the bed was an assortment of small, multicolored flowers spilling over the stone sides in tangled vines. Kneeling down, she pushed aside the plants obscuring the outer wall, searching for some sort of clue.

With nothing visible, she took to trailing her fingers across the rough stone, searching for any indication of a marking that may have faded in the ten years since Nanook's disappearance.

"Normally, I would be curious as to why someone was crawling around in the dirt…but for you, Del Sue, well," Bird smirked above her, "it seems you've finally learned you place."

Snarling, Nur climbed to her feet and squared off with her classmate. The humidity in the air began to die as Bird readied himself for an attack.

"You don't want to fight me, Nur. Need I remind you what happened last time?"

Her fists clenched. "I'll take my chances."

Bird shook his head. "You overestimate your abilities. It doesn't matter how much you're beaten. It doesn't matter how many times you've failed to make an Amulet. It doesn't matter that even your damned eyes mark you as being lesser. You still think that you deserve to be here. You *don't*."

Nur screamed as a hurricane of wind slammed into Bird, sending him flying across the courtyard. The burst of power was so extreme, she had to steady herself against the rim of the garden bed to keep from collapsing. Her chest burned, and she was having trouble breathing.

Bird lay at the base of the tree he'd crashed into, dazed. She knew she had seconds before he gathered his senses and came at her.

She staggered over to him and collapsed to her knees at his side. With one hand she gripped his face, forcing him to look at her.

"Why do you hate me?" she demanded. "I never did anything to you. Is it just because of my father? I'm not him. Why doesn't anyone understand that? Why doesn't anyone understand that I am more than my blood?"

Bird didn't say anything. He just stared at her with that same hate in eyes.

"Tell me!" Nur screamed, shaking him.

Bird jerked his head away. "Everyone acts like you're special because you overcame your eastern blood. Sylvie favored you. Hettie sponsored you. Now people are saying that Kadar has taken an interest in you." He shook his head. "You don't deserve it. You say you're more than your blood, but without your father, you would be nothing. You would be just like the rest of us."

Nur turned away from him in disgust, climbing unsteadily to her feet. "That's not my fault," she snapped. "You don't get to blame me for things that aren't my fault. That's not fair."

Bird got to his feet as well, cradling his side gingerly. He opened his mouth to reply, but a shout cut him off.

"What is going on here?" Kaleo demanded, striding towards them. He looked at Nur. "Did he hurt you?"

She shook her head. "I'm okay."

"I'm fine, too. Thanks for asking," Bird grumbled.

"After everything you've done, do you really think I give a shit how you're feeling?" Kaleo snapped.

The Seawitch looked away. "No, I don't suppose you would." Rubbing at the back of his neck, Bird sidestepped around the two friends and headed back the way he'd come.

Nur brushed a stray strand of hair from her face and turned to Kaleo. His eyes still lingered in the direction Bird had gone. She tapped his shoulder. As frustrating as the Seawitch was, he was unimportant.

Ignoring the pounding in her skull, Nur dug the map out of her pocket and handed it to Kaleo. "Talia gave this to me." She ignored the look her friend shot her at the mention of the Earthwitch and tapped the numbers on the map. "I'm starting with the garden beds. Can you look over section C?"

He took the map and shook his head. "This is going to take forever."

"We can start tomorrow," Nur said. Truth be told, she was far too tired to continue the search today.

Sighing, Kaleo gave her back the map. "I'm working in the Warehouse until the sixteenth bell. You can meet me there."

Nur nodded. She'd never visited the place before, but it wasn't too far from the outer garden boundary. "It's a plan."

Kaleo smiled and wrapped a loose arm around her shoulders as they started walking. "Now then, Nunu, how about you explain to me exactly what motivated Talia to hand over this incredibly helpful map…?"

TWENTY-FIVE

A lana's stitches itched. Still, she didn't scratch them. It had been a week since the attack, and she was bored out of her mind. No one came down to the brig anymore and Sarasin didn't summon her on deck.

She wanted to pace. She didn't.

She wanted to scream. She didn't.

She wanted to *let go*. She didn't.

She was in control.

Alana watched the people around her. Maria and Penn. Johnathan and Wren. It wouldn't be long before Kaius would remove her stitches in his cabin. That was her opportunity to finally get the information that they needed to escape. To accomplish that, however, she needed to *remain* in control.

"What happens if Kaius doesn't cooperate?" Jonathan asked.

"I don't expect him to," Alana replied, not looking up from her nails. "But if five years in Jaarin have taught me anything, it's how to get information out of people who aren't willing to give it."

"Just make sure he does not scream too loudly while you are torturing him," Maria commented. "This ship is not soundproof."

"Could you *not* torture him?" Penn asked. "I mean…we have the key. Can't we just escape? There are hundreds of islands in the Western sea. Maybe we'll get lucky?"

"We can't leave without knowing where we are," Johnathan said firmly.

"I'd rather take my chances at sea than with a murderous gang of pirates," Wren argued.

Maria snorted. "Says the sailor."

"Says the royal guard who failed to protect her queen."

Maria got to her feet at that, ready to charge Wren, but Penn stepped in the way. "Now isn't the time to turn on each other."

Before either of them could say another word, Layla hopped down the stairs. "All right, Your Majesty," she announced. "Time to get those stitches removed." The quartermaster hesitated, her eyes bouncing between Maria and Wren. She grinned. "Oops, don't mind me. Keep going. Actually, do you mind if I watch whatever foreplay this is?"

"Not all of us are as depraved as you are," Wren snapped.

"Maybe not," Layla conceded. "But I have my suspicions about you." She looked him up and down. "So, how 'bout it, pretty boy? Want to have some fun?"

"Only if that fun involves me shoving a sword through you heart."

Layla made a disappointed sound and turned her attention to Alana. "Is he always this difficult?"

"Most of the time," Alana confirmed, ignoring the look Wren shot her.

Layla took a step forward and unlocked the cell. "In that case, you should be grateful I'm allowing you a reprieve."

Alana stepped outside and started up the stairs without a word. She kept her shoulders relaxed and her head high as she walked across the deck. As usual, Sarasin was at the helm, but his eyes stayed on the horizon, purposefully ignoring her.

Layla kept close as they walked to the first mate's cabin. Once outside, the quartermaster knocked twice.

Kaius opened the door, gave Alana a quick once-over, then stepped aside enough for her to slip into the room. She took a seat on a chair beside the porthole and watched as Kaius silently removed a box of medical supplies from beneath his bed.

He pulled up a chair beside her. "Roll up your sleeve."

"Is this going to take long?" Alana asked.

"Don't move."

"I didn't."

"You talked. Talking counts as moving."

"Would hitting you count as moving, too?"

"*Yes.*"

Alana stared forward as he gently took her arm and positioned it on the armrest of the chair.

Removing the stitches was a long and painful process. Alana kept her eyes trained ahead and senses as pushed down as possible as Kaius finally finished his work and re-bandaged her arm.

"Done."

She rolled her shoulder, wincing slightly at the flash of pain.

"It's going to be sore for a little while."

"It's fine."

Alana got to her feet, eyes going to the cabinet of liquor. She was supposed to be finding out the last of the information they needed today. She was supposed to be asking careful questions and playing the part of the manipulative queen. Despite Maria's comment, Alana had never developed a taste for torture. It wasn't an effective means of getting reliable information. The best method was finding a person's motivation. What did they want? What did they care about? But she knew nothing about the man standing before her.

"Are you okay?" Kaius asked. "I mean," he added quickly, "you look sort of...dazed."

That snapped her back to focus. "Where are we going?" she asked, then immediately cursed herself for the lack of tact.

"Alana." Kaius took a step towards her, his voice full of warning. "I know you're probably scared right now, and you're not thinking clearly. Whatever you and companions have been planning, it won't work. Just—"

She went for the door, but Kaius was faster. He slammed his hand against it, blocking her exit, and pushed her against the bookshelf. He stood over her, his hands braced on either side of her head.

Alana allowed her eyes to close for a brief moment. *Focus.*

"What's going on?" Kaius demanded.

"Idiot."

She went for the pocket where he kept the key to her cell. Kaius grabbed her wrist, twisting it to reveal the iron key gripped in her palm. "You shouldn't have tried that."

"And *you* should pay more attention."

Before he could react, Alana pressed the dagger she'd grabbed from Kaius's belt against his throat with her free hand.

The first mate went still, eyes widening. "How?"

He dropped her wrist, and Alana let the key fall to the floor.

"Tell me where we are."

"I don't know precisely. We've been ambling north for the past week, but we're eventually going to set a course to one of the northern islands."

Unhelpful.

He shifted slightly, and Alana dug her blade in harder. She wasn't skilled enough to hold him for much longer.

"Sarasin's going to come to check up on us in just a few minutes, so you'd better get on with this little plan of yours."

Alana's blood boiled at the mention of the captain.

"One more question, then. If you answer, I'll let you go and return to the brig without a fight."

Kaius agreed with the closest thing to a nod he could manage, considering the blade against his throat.

"Tell me why you kidnapped me."

"I can't. Not yet."

"Then I'm sorry this is how it had to end."

"Would you really kill me, *Kiydra*?"

"It would be the smart move, pirate."

Kaius searched her eyes but she kept her face impassive and watched as the first mate's expression hardened in response.

"What happened to you, Alana?" he whispered. "How did you end up this hollow?"

Hollow. Of all the words he could have chosen, she wasn't expecting that one. Hateful, heartless, cruel, insane—she'd heard those a hundred times. But not hollow. She supposed it fit her, at least as much as the others did. She was a shell. Living without caring. Living—because that was the only option.

"Who says I wasn't always this way, Kaius?" Her voice equally soft.

"No one is born like this." The first mate looked down at the knife she was holding and his jaw set. "Just get on with it."

Something about the way his eyes hardened pulled at her soul. It was familiar and she hated it. Alana wrapped her free hand around one of the bookends on the shelf behind her. "I wish I could," she whispered. "But apparently, I've gone soft."

Before he could react, she slammed the bookend against his head. Kaius crumpled to the floor.

Alana didn't let herself dwell on what she'd just done. She tucked the dagger into her belt and went to work. She ran to his dresser and ripped apart his shirts, then stuffed the rags into the bottles of amber liquor. Next, she went to the oil lamp hanging beside the door and used its flame to light the cloth. She opened the cabin door and, one by one, threw the bottles onto the deck, setting the *Fe Ressu* on fire.

TWENTY-SIX

N ur stood before the metal doors of the Warehouse. The entire building was a mismatched collection of materials ranging from drift wood to obsidian slabs. There were no windows, but the building's roof had vents cut into it to allow airflow through the massive structure.

Kaleo had showed her the schematics for a fuel-free lamp. A battery was filled with fire magic by a Flamewitch and used to power the device for a time. With a large enough battery, a lamp could remain lit for nearly a year.

"Like an Amulet?" Nur had asked, tapping the drawing.

"Not exactly," Kaleo had explained. "Amulets—for all intents and purposes—are a part of their wearer. It's just something that allows a witch to take more power from Eriysha's Current without hurting themselves. You don't draw *from* an Amulet—you just use it." He pointed to a note on the schematic. "Batteries act as a condensed form of Eriysha's Current that a source draws upon." He shrugged. "Theoretically, you could use the magic of a battery in that same way you use the Current, but it would be relatively pointless since it's far less powerful."

Everything the Warehouse made was fueled by elemental magic. The inner workings of which were for more complex than Nur had anticipated— or had the patience to understand. But it was the type of work that could engage Kaleo's mind and hands.

On their home island, he'd often complained about how dull everything was. Magic came easily to him—something that Nur had always been se- cretly jealous of—as did pretty much everything else. The Warehouse was different. It challenged him.

She paced in front of the twin doors. She'd known her friend wouldn't be on time, but by her count it had been nearly fifteen minutes past the sixteenth bell. Unable to contain her restless energy for another moment, Nur yanked open one of the doors and stepped inside.

The scent of burning metal filled her senses as Nur took in the enormous room before her. Stoves, kilns, workbenches and other devices she couldn't identify dotted the space. Students milled about wearing various forms of protective gear.

She scanned the Warehouse for Kaleo, but between the welding helmets, over-sized heat ponchos and goggles, it was impossible to identify anyone.

Cubbies filled with materials lined the entirety of one wall, at the end of which was a desk where a man Nur recognized to be Master Turic sat, bent over a large leather-bound book. She began to make her way over to the desk where the Master sat, intending to ask after Kaleo's whereabouts, but something caught her eye.

The cubbies where the materials were kept were labeled using the same system as the rest of the Academy.

"Nur?" Kaleo pulled up his welding helmet's visor, allowing a view of his soot-stained cheeks.

"It's fifteen minutes past the bell," she informed him.

"Ah, I'm sorry, I didn't hear." He pulled off one of his large gloves. "Give me a moment and I'll meet you outside."

Nur grabbed his shoulder. "Why didn't you tell me about these?" She motioned to the labeled cubbies. "The system is the same as my father's code."

"These shelves are constantly being restocked," he explained. "Nothing could be hidden here."

Nur licked her lips and scanned the wall. "What if you put them together?"

"Put what together?"

"The materials on the list. If you put them together, what would happen?"

Kaleo frowned. "I'm not sure. I would have to go over everything. Look at different schematics…"

"Would Master Turic know?"

"Probably, but—"

"Then let's ask him."

Nur dodged out of the way as Kaleo attempted to grab her arm. He chased after her. "Master Turic is a very busy man. We can't just march up to him and demand information."

"Why not? Isn't he supposed to be mentoring you?"

"I guess technically he is…"

"Please, K," Nur implored. "This could be the answer. What real harm is there in asking?"

Kaleo let out a long sigh. "None, but let me do the talking."

Grinning, Nur allowed her friend to lead her to Turic's desk.

The Master greeted his pupil warmly. "Kaleo, what can I help you with?"

"It's a little thing," he assured Turic. "We found a list of materials in the library and were wondering what you could make with them."

Kaleo quickly wrote down the sequence and handed it to the Master. Turic's eyes flickered to Nur for a moment before reading over the list.

"Interesting. The materials here are usually used to make elemental lockboxes. They can only be opened using the power of the goddess. Usually, they just need one form of magic, but from the looks of it, this one would require all four elements."

"Is there any chance we have one in storage?" Kaleo asked. "I'd like to examine it."

"I'll check the ledgers." Pushing aside the book he'd been reading, the Master pulled out a large scroll from a desk drawer.

Nur turned to Kaleo and whispered. "Is it possible my father could have made such a device? He didn't have any magic."

"Definitely," he assured her. "Something like this wouldn't require the direct use of magic. It's an interesting concept, though. It must work by having four separate batteries, all specifically made for one type of elemental magic. When filled together, they could be engineered to trigger the release of a lock."

"So, if we were to open this type of lockbox, we would need both a Sea and Earthwitch?"

THE STORM GATHERS

Kaleo nodded his confirmation, turning back to Turic as the Master cleared his throat. "There is one lockbox of this type in storage," he announced. "As far as I can make out, it has been there for over ten years. I imagine it was created by some former student practicing their craft."

"Do you mind if we check it out of storage?" Kaleo asked.

Turic hesitated. "I doubt you will be able to open it, Kaleo. Even with someone from each element, a lockbox of this make is likely tied to the blood of whoever created it. Without them, it would be a waste of time."

"Still," Kaleo pressed. "I'd like to examine it."

The Master sighed. "Well…I suppose that would be fine as long as you bring it back within the hour."

He held out a slip of paper to Kaleo, who took it carefully.

"Thank you. We will."

Her friend grabbed her arm and pulled Nur towards a doorway at the back of the Warehouse.

"An hour?" she hissed. "That's all the time we have to get this thing open?"

"Master Turic doesn't allow anything that has not been specifically commissioned to leave the Warehouse. The fact that he's letting us to take this outside is a miracle."

"What about the blood thing?" Nur pressed. "My father's dead. We won't be able to get it open."

Kaleo flicked her ear. "I thought you were supposed to be clever." They reached the door at the back of the room. "You're Nanook's daughter. You have his blood in your veins. That should be enough."

"And if it's not? Is there another way of breaking a lockbox open?"

"I doubt it."

He shoved the door open.

They entered a long, narrow room crowded with various devices, all tagged with a string of identifying numbers unlike her father's code. Taking the piece of paper Turic had given him, Kaleo searched through the room while Nur waited by the door. Her eyes ran over the room as her body hummed with anticipation. Part of her didn't care what was inside the lockbox, just as long as she had solved the puzzle.

185

"Got it!" Kaleo held up a medium-sized box, the sides of which were shorter than the bottom and lid.

Nur leaned in close to examine the metal. On each of the short sides was a circle of silver inlaid into the black steel. Inside each was an engraving that indicated a type of elemental magic.

"Those are the ports," Kaleo explained. "I'd guess they would all need to be filled at the same time to properly trigger the lock. That means we have an hour to find a Sea and Earthwitch willing to help us."

"Preferably ones that won't ask too many questions," Nur added. She nodded towards the doors of the Warehouse. "I'll meet you at the picnic table where we eat lunch in ten minutes. Don't be late."

WITHOUT MEANING TO, NUR FOUND herself in front of the Med Suite. There were only two patients today, both fast asleep. In the corner, Talia was organizing medication.

Nur cleared her throat. "I need your help."

Talia looked up, a smile blossoming across her face at the sight of the Stormwitch. "Anything."

"I found something, but I need your help to open it," Nur said. "I'll explain more on the way, but we only have an hour."

The redhead gave a pointed look around. "I'm on duty right now. Are you sure this can't wait?"

"I'm sorry, but it can't. Can you help me or not?"

Talia sighed. "This isn't playing fair, Stormwitch. You know I can't say no to you."

Nur couldn't help the grin that spread across her face as she led Talia out of the Med Suite. They hurried down the garden paths until they reached the small clearing where she and Kaleo ate lunch.

Nur froze as she took in the sight before her. "What is *he* doing here?"

"I've been asking myself the same question," Bird grumbled, ignoring the annoyed look Kaleo shot at him.

"We need a Seawitch," her friend explained. "And with less than an hour to get this done, I recommend we skip the argument."

THE STORM GATHERS

Clenching her fists, Nur stalked forward. "Why would you help me?" she demanded of Bird.

"I think the reason is fairly obvious." He gestured towards Kaleo. "I'm being extorted."

Resisting the urge to push the issue, Nur focused on the lockbox on the table. "So, what do we do?"

"Each of us needs to channel power from the goddess and direct it into the ports. The batteries all need to be finished filling at the same time, but you should be able to sense their power level. Once they're all almost full, we'll do the last bit together. Got it?"

They all nodded and organized themselves around the lockbox in accordance to which side was meant for their element.

Kaleo reached into his pocket and pulled out a small knife. He used the point to prick his thumb, which he pressed against the port before passing the knife to Talia, who did the same before handing it off to Bird. Finally, the knife came to Nur. She cut her finger and watched as liquid so dark red it was almost black beaded to the surface. For once in her life, she was grateful for her father's blood.

She pressed her thumb to the port. "Let's do this."

She began to draw power for Eriysha's Current, directing it into the port. Just as Kaleo had said, she could sense the battery's energy level as she directed her magic inside. Without an Amulet it took her longer than her companions to fill. Once she had, she nodded, then the four of them topped off their batteries together.

For a moment, nothing happened. Then, something clicked, and the lid rose a few centimeters off the sides.

The four of them exchanged looks around the table.

"That's it?" Talia asked, looking at Kaleo.

"Yep," he said.

"I thought there would be…I don't know, flames or something?"

"Apparently not," Nur said. Reaching forward, she unscrewed the lid and peered into the box. Inside were two folded pieces of paper and an Amulet with a crack running through the glass.

187

Nur took out the paper. The first was written in Terran and therefore undecipherable. But the second was in Suhryn. She took a step away to read the letter.

Nur,

If you have found this letter, then I am sorry. I have made a terrible mistake. I thought I could continue my research here without consequences, but information such as this always comes at a price.

I don't have time to explain everything, but know that this is my fault. I trusted the wrong people and now you are in danger.

I first went to Hettie, but it soon became clear she was using my knowledge for her own ends. I sought refuge with Kadar, but he, too, manipulated me. I have become a pawn in their games against one another.

Inside this box is Hettie's Amulet. I tried to destroy it, but without the power of the goddess, I was unsuccessful. Still, it appears I have managed to damage it in such a manner that she no longer poses so great a threat to me.

Whatever happens, do not let her retrieve her Amulet. Similarly, you must not let Kadar get possession of my notes. I have discovered how to find Eriysha's Compass and I shudder to think what might happen if he were to get his hands on such power.

He searches for me now. It's only a matter of time before he finds me.

I am so sorry, Nur.

I hope one day you will be able to forgive me.

—Ranook Del Su

Nur stared at the letter, rereading it one last time before tucking it and her father's page of notes into her pocket. She reached for Hettie's Amulet as well, only to discover that the lockbox was now empty. She whipped her head around to find Talia holding the broken piece of magic.

Nur held out a hand. "I need that."

Talia took a step back, shaking her head. "I'm sorry, Stormwitch, truly. But this belongs to my mother and I cannot let you take it."

Nur stared at the woman before her. "You knew?"

"That your father was the one who broke my mother's Amulet? Yes."

"So, you've been manipulating me this entire time?" Nur demanded, unable to control the hurt in her voice.

Talia lifted her shoulder in a shrug. "It's like I said—everyone here has an ulterior motive."

Nur's hands curled into fists. What had seemed like friendly acts before were now tainted as she reflected on the help Talia had given her. If she hadn't been so set on her goal, she might have noticed.

"Would someone like to explain to me what's going on?" Bird demanded.

"I second that," Kaleo added.

Nur didn't take her eyes off of Talia. "K, take the lockbox back to the Warehouse. Tell Master Turic that we couldn't get it open."

"I'm not just going to leave you—"

"Please," Nur cut in. "It's important."

Kaleo ground his teeth. "I'll be right back."

"I'm leaving," Bird announced. "Whatever this is, I want no part in it."

Neither Nur nor Talia acknowledged either man's departure as they stared each other down.

"You can't beat me, Nur," the Earthwitch said. "Walk away now and we can pretend like this never happened."

"I can't. Hettie manipulated my father into finding the answers to Eriysha's Compass. If you give her that Amulet, she'll come after me."

Talia clenched her jaw. "You want me to let my mother to continue to suffer as she has for the past *twelve years*?" She shook her head. "Maybe you do belong here, Nur. You're as heartless as the rest of us."

Nur readied herself to draw power from the goddess. Across the table, she could sense Talia doing the same.

"Don't make me do this," Talia murmured.

"Don't make *me*."

Nur had just begun to draw from Eriysha's Current when she heard someone clear their throat.

"It appears I have arrived just in time," Kadar said, stepping into view. He *tsked*. "You should know the rules, girls, no fighting on campus." He extended a hand. "Why don't you give me that Amulet, Talia? And you, Nur, empty your pockets."

"You're delusional if you think I'm giving you what rightfully belongs to my mother," Talia snapped.

Kadar sighed. "Hettie always had a penchant for the dramatic. It's a shame to see you inherited her volatility." He turned his attention to the Stormwitch. "Everything I told you was true, Nur. Your father and I worked together for years. I never betrayed him. He betrayed me. I beg of you not to make the same mistake."

"What happened to him?" Nur demanded. "What did you do?"

"What the fuck do you think he did?" Talia spat. "He killed your father."

Kadar cleared his throat. "What happened to Nanook was regrettable. But if you cooperate, we can prevent things from getting out of hand."

"I propose a truce, Nur," Talia said. "We fight together today and face each other tomorrow. What do you say?"

Nur stared at the Headmaster. There was no way she would win in a fight against Kadar. The only chance she had of making it out of this situation alive was to be smart.

"I fought my entire life to come here. If…if you promise not to expel me or hurt me, I'll give you my father's research."

"No! Don't!" Talia took a step forward, but was thrown back by a sudden burst of wind from the Headmaster. She landed on her back. Her loose, red hair tangled around her face.

"I promise," Kadar assured Nur. "Now, give it to me."

The Stormwitch reached into her pocket and pulled out the piece of paper. She handed it to Kadar.

He took a step away from her as he read Nanook's words. A frown split the Headmaster's forehead, and he turned back to Nur, mouth open in confusion.

THE STORM GATHERS

She wasted no time. She ripped power from Eriysha's current and attempted to force wind down Kadar's throat—just as she had done to Bird during their duel. Nanook's letter—not his page of notes—slipped from the Headmaster's fingers as he choked on Nur's power.

"You murdered by father," Nur told him. "You tried to use me. And now...now you will—"

A wall of air slammed into her, knocking Nur onto the ground. She jumped to her feet and tried to return Kadar's strike, but the moment the wind she commanded got within a foot of the Headmaster, it dissipated.

Beside her, Talia climbed back to her feet, using the table to steady herself. Her eyes narrowed and a nearby tree branch began to curl its way towards Kadar. It got to within a few inches of him before suddenly retreating. Talia let out a frustrated cry and the branch burst into flames.

Kadar waved his hand. The flames disappeared as quickly as they had come. "I see neither of you have faced a full Elemental before," he said casually. "Allow me to demonstrate just how far out of your depth the two of you are." He held out his hand and a circle of fire exploded around the two women.

Nur stumbled backwards, nearly knocking into the picnic table, which was now consumed in flames.

Roots broke from the earth and began to climb their way up her ankles. She managed to break free, but more came—attacking her faster than she could escape. Before long, she was trapped in place as the plants continued to climb up her legs.

Beside her, Talia wasn't faring much better—a slew of curses escaping her lips as she struggled against Kadar's power.

The Headmaster stepped forward, passing through the ring of fire as though it were simply air.

"I don't want to kill you girls," he murmured, "but I will."

Nur made another effort to pull against the roots binding her, to no avail.

"May the goddess curse you," she spat.

"And Etrim claim you," Talia added.

Kadar shook his head and Nur could feel the static of electricity skating across her skin.

191

Her hair stood on end. She closed her eyes and inhaled a shaky breath as she waited for Death to take her.

Suddenly, the electricity in the air died. The roots that had been holding her in place crumbled and the heat of the fire that surrounded them dissipated.

Confused, Nur opened her eyes to see Kadar passed out on the ground. Standing over him was Bird, holding a broken tree branch.

Talia ran forward and landed a hard kick across Kadar's head, causing his body to jerk. Bird took a step between them before Talia could attack the Headmaster for a second time.

"The two of you need to get off this island."

Nur stared at the unconscious man who had murdered her father.

"You're right," she whispered. "We need to leave." She looked at Talia. "Both of us."

"I can't abandon my mother," the Earthwitch argued.

"Kadar will come after you," Bird pointed out.

"Not if I'm able to restore my mother's Amulet. He won't risk a head-to-head against Hettie of the Flame." She turned to Nur. "But you do need to leave. I'm sorry. I didn't know this hunt would lead us to your father's research as well."

"I'll make sure the Headmaster stays unconscious long enough for you to steal a ship," Bird declared. "The other Masters may be in league with Kadar, so if you intend to make it out of here alive, you should probably take Talia with you for protection."

Nur stared at the man before her. "Why are you helping me?"

"I'm *not*," Bird snapped. "I'm sending you into the Shatter. In case you've forgotten, that's a death sentence."

"I have the answer to finding Eriysha's Compass," Nur shot back.

An answer you can't understand, she reminded herself.

"Doesn't matter." Bird turned back to the unconscious Headmaster. "You don't have an Amulet. You won't last a week."

"I'm stronger than you give me credit for."

"No, Nur, you're *exactly* as strong as I give you credit for. In fact, I may be the only person who knows the true extent of your power. I've certainly been on the receiving end of it enough. So trust me when I tell you that you don't have what it takes to survive the Shatter alone."

Nur's reply was cut off by a yank on her arm—Talia.

"We don't have time for this," the Earthwitch said. "We need to go."

Nur inhaled a shaky breath, desperately trying to cool her emotions. She couldn't let Bird's words get to her. He was wrong. He'd always been wrong about her. She had proven that today. She'd solved the puzzle and now held the secret to the Shatter in her hands.

She gave Talia a small nod before allowing the red-haired woman to drag her down the garden paths.

They passed through the Academy and down the trail to the docks without incident.

From there, Talia led Nur to a small vessel on the end.

"This should be small enough for you to sail on your own. All the ships are stocked with at least a week's worth of food and water." She swallowed. "After that, you'll be on your own."

Nur tried not to dwell on that information as she stared at the ship.

"It's written in Terran," she whispered. "My father's research. I can't read it. I'll be lost to the Shatter."

"You'll find a way to translate it," Talia said firmly. "And I expect you to return here with Eriysha's Compass, ready to kill Kadar."

"You manipulated me. Same as him," she challenged. "Maybe when I return, I'll kill you, too."

"You're certainly welcome to try, Stormwitch."

"Believe me, I will."

Grinning, Talia grabbed Nur's shirt and pulled her into a kiss. For some strange, stupid reason, Nur didn't step away. Her mouth softened against the other woman's and let herself become lost to sensation.

Finally, they broke apart.

"You'd better come back to me, Stormwitch," Talia said, slightly breathless. "We're not finished here."

Unable to think of a clever response, Nur just swallowed and said, "Protect Kaleo. He's innocent in all this."

"I will."

With a nod, Nur climbed aboard the small ship. Together, they cut the lines securing it to the docks. Then, with a last look at the island, Nur summoned some wind and sailed into the Shatter.

Bird was right.

She was definitely going to die.

TWENTY-SEVEN

Alana sprinted into the brig. "Let's move!"

"Did you get the information we need?" Johnathan asked.

"Not exactly."

"Alana!" Maria looked at her in disbelief. "What happened?"

"There's no time to explain. The ship's on fire. We need to leave." No one moved. Instead, they stared at her with incredulity. She made a wild motion with one hand. "*Now!*"

That snapped them into motion. Maria pulled the key Alana had given her from her pocket and unlocked the cell door. Swearing, the group rushed up the steps and out onto the deck.

Although evening had fallen, the world was bright with fire. Pirates ran across the deck, attempting to put it out, to no avail. The main sail was in flames, and one of the riggers fell from his perch, his body slamming into the deck with a crunch.

Wren winced as the group hurried toward one of the lifeboats.

Johnathan pulled aside the tarp and began loosening the knots securing the small vessel in place.

"Faster," Maria urged.

"You want to help? Get the other side."

Maria jumped to the task, Wren coming to aid her, leaving Alana and Penn to keep watch.

"The Queen of Darkness!" someone shouted. "She's trying to escape."

Eyes started turning away from the fire, searching the deck for her.

Alana tucked Penn behind her as a man with tattoos cover his face advanced toward her with his rapier unsheathed. She recognized him as the one who'd hit Maria.

"Hello, Your Majesty. Leaving so soon?" he purred.

"Maria!" Alana called. She gripped the dagger she'd stolen from Kaius, but it wouldn't help her much against a sword. "I could use some help."

"Coming!" Maria looked up from her work and unsheathed held out a hand for Alana to throw her the dagger. "I am going to enjoy th—"

Before the royal guard could make it a step, the pirate struck out. Not with his sword, but with a throwing blade. It flew toward the queen, aiming for her heart.

She didn't move as the metal twisted through the air, idly wondering if this was the moment that would finally claim her life.

Something came at her from the side, and she barely had time to register Penn's boyish face as he shoved her out of the way—blocking her body with his.

The blade lodged in his chest.

Alana caught his body as he fell, one hand pressing against the wound in the boy's chest as she tried to staunch the bleeding. Vaguely, she was aware of Wren's screams as he attacked the pirate.

"You're going to be okay," Alana told the boy, hardly aware of what she was saying. "It's going to be okay."

Penn sucked in a breath, tears streaming down his face. "It hurts."

"I know," Alana said. From the wetness on her cheeks, she knew she was crying too. "I know. I'm sorry. I don't know what to do." She gripped Penn's body tighter. "I don't know how to help you."

"It's okay," he whispered. "I don't think there's anything you could do, anyway. Can...can you tell Wren goodbye for me? Please."

"I will," she assured him. "I am so sorry, Payton. I should have chosen a different ship. I...I'm sorry."

Penn's gaze met hers one last time before sliding to the sky.

Alana let out a strangled sound. She closed her eyes for a moment and when she opened them again, Wren was by her side. She opened her mouth to say something, but before the words could escape, someone was pulling her away. She staggered to her feet, spinning to face her assailant, and came face-to-face with Kaius. The pirate wore a murderous expression. His temple was still bleeding.

For some strange reason, Alana couldn't help but smile. "You look good angry," she yelled over the roar of the flames. Her throat ached from crying, and she knew her cheeks were stained with tears. So why the fuck was some part of her relieved right now?

"And you look as insane as ever, *Kiydra*," Kaius returned. His gaze flicked over the ruined ship and he shook his head. "What have you done?"

From her right, there came a deafening snap as the crossing of the main mast broke. Ropes and rigging flew through the air.

Alana instinctively dropped to the ground.

Kaius wasn't as quick, and something hard slammed into the first mate, sending him over the edge of the ship.

Alana stared at the spot he'd just been standing. For some reason, her brain was having trouble coming to terms with what had just happened. First Penn and now…

Gods, why did she even care?

The man had kidnapped her and her crew. Kept them in a cage. He was an arrogant bastard who she should have killed hours ago.

Alana climbed to her feet and stared over the railing of the *Fe Ressu*. Despite the roaring fire behind her, the sea was pitch black. The most she could make out was the vague outline of the lifeboats that had been cut loose. There was no sign of him.

Either he was being hidden by the waves or whatever debris had sent him over the side was now dragging him into the depths. She couldn't help him. To do anything would risk her own life and the lives of her crew. It was better like this. At least she didn't have to watch him die.

Alana turned halfway away, and caught sight of Penn's lifeless body. She swore at the reminder and looked back at the railing.

Fuck it.

Alana took a deep breath, cursed the gods, then leaped over the side of the ship.

Dark water closed above her and she kicked her way to the surface. She looked around, frantically searching the waves for any sign of the first mate. After a few terrifying seconds, she caught sight of his body floating in the water a few yards from her.

"I really am going soft," she muttered before taking a deep breath and swimming for him.

By the time she reached him, her eyes were stinging from the saltwater and her limbs felt heavy. She grabbed *Kaius's* body and pulled him towards her, feeling for his pulse. It was difficult to tell with her own elevated heart rate, but she was fairly certain that he was still alive.

Exhaling a relieved breath, she looked around for anything she could use to keep them both afloat. There were a few floating pieces of debris from the ship scattered around but...there!

Floating not too far from them was a lifeboat. The white of the painted wood stood out against the night sky. She couldn't tell if it was occupied or not, but judging from the stationary ores, she was willing to bet it had floated away in the chaos without being claimed.

Alana swam both her and the unconscious pirate to the unoccupied vessel. Still gripping Kaius to keep his head above water, she tried to grab the lip of the boat but lacked the reach. She let out a cry of frustration and tried again, only to fail once more.

It wasn't fair. She had made it. She had *made* it.

Penn was dead. He'd died for her, and she couldn't even find the strength to get into this damned boat!

She readjusted her grip on Kaius—now only holding on to one of his wrists. It wouldn't keep him afloat, but hopefully he would be out of danger soon.

She slipped low into the water, then kicked upwards. Her free hand wrapped around the lip of the lifeboat, tipping it towards them. Alana kicked again and managed to get an elbow over the edge, then her legs, until the only part of her not in the boat was the arm still clinging to the first mate.

She leaned over the side of the lifeboat and grabbed both his arms. She pulled him upwards, only for her strength to once again fail her. A sob escaped her as tears ran across her face. She had to save him. She wasn't sure why. It would be easier to let him drown. But, for some reason, she couldn't let him go.

Alana sucked in an uneven breath and squeezed her eyes shut. She waited for a few moments, gathering her strength before pulling him towards her with everything she had. Her hands crawled down his body, gripping his underarms as she dragged him onto the lifeboat.

They landed with a thump at the bottom of the boat, and Alana rolled over onto her back. She was wet, freezing, and her entire body ached.

Above her, the stars twinkled happily. She closed her eyes, exhaustion already beckoning her into unconsciousness.

Beside her, Kaius stirred. He would probably kill her when he woke up. But somehow, at the moment, Alana couldn't find it in herself to care. She deserved a far worse death than whatever he could come up with. His would be a mercy.

You killed him, that voice inside her whispered. *You killed Penn. You should have protected him. Instead, you let him die. Why couldn't you just stay away? Why do you have to care?*

Fresh tears blossomed in her eyes and she squeezed them tight, trying to keep the moisture from running free.

Control.

She was in control. Yes, she was drowning. But Alana had been drowning for five years, so what did that matter now? She wasn't dead. Not yet. Maybe not ever. And as long no one else knew the truth, she could keep on pretending as though she was strong.

Beside her, Kaius groaned. "Alana?" His voice was raspy from seawater.

She kept her eyes closed, praying that sleep would take her before he fully woke. The edges of her mind darkened.

You killed him.

She had. And it wouldn't be long before she killed Kaius, too.

TWENTY-EIGHT

Rae watched as the storm gathered above them. The wind picked up, churning the waves into a froth. The air sizzled with electricity.

So much for finding Eriysha's Compass.

It had been two days since the ty'vairr attack. Two days on a lifeboat with barely any water and no land in sight. They wouldn't last much longer. Perhaps this storm would offer them the blessing of a quick death.

The lifeboat lurched beneath them. Aram toppled to one side and swore bitterly as his elbow collided with the side of the boat. Rae grabbed onto him, one arm wrapping around one of the benches to keep her steady.

"*Hold on!*" she screamed.

Their little boat lurched violently forward. A wave of ice-cold water rammed into Rae, stealing her breath. She choked and sputtered. Nearby, Aram was doing the same.

She tightened her grip on him as the storm grew in fury.

"We're going to die," Aram gasped.

"Possibly."

"*Definitely.*"

A massive wave hit their lifeboat, tipping them both into the sea. Rae kicked to the surface and scanned the water for Aram. She spotted a dark shape a few yards from her and swam for it. The ocean pummeled her from all sides, but Rae kept her head down and kicked with everything she had.

Thunder shook the skies, and the rain started pouring down harder. Rae dove beneath the ocean as another wave rose to drown her. It crashed over her, sending her body spinning through the water. Her legs became tangled with something hidden in the depths and images of the multi-limbed ty'vairrs flashed through her mind. Panicked, she kicked wildly towards what she hoped was the surface.

She broke through the water and was greeted by the sensation of a razor-sharp wind scraping across her face. A shape bobbed to the surface beside her—Aram. Rae grabbed onto her friend, turning him towards her. His breathing was strained, but by some miracle, he was alive.

She let out a relieved laugh. "You're not a ty'vairr."

He looked at her as though she were insane. "Rude. Besides, you're one to talk, Toma. You look like a drowned ceprra."

She clung to him tighter. "Fuck you."

"You wish."

Water slammed into them with punishing force, but neither let go of the other. Eventually, they found their way to the surface once more.

"Still alive, I see," Aram gasped.

"Can't rid of me that easily."

His grip around her tightened. "You never could take a hint."

Rae laughed, relief washing through her even as they were dragged under once more.

They clung to each other, kicking their way to the surface time and time again as wave after wave assaulted them.

Salty water stung her eyes, lips, and throat each time she broke the surface. But Rae held on. Blind, deaf, and numb from the cold, she held on to Aram, and he to her.

The rain came down in buckets, as terrible as the sea beneath them until Rae couldn't tell if she'd truly reached the surface or if her mind was playing tricks on her. All around her was blackness. No matter how hard she kicked, there came no light and no air until she wasn't even sure she was kicking at all. Wasn't sure if she was asleep or conscious. Alive or dead. The only thing she knew was that if she was dead, then Aram was, too.

So she kept fighting.

Because that was their promise.

Rae woke with land beneath her and sand on her tongue. She opened her mouth to breathe but instead vomited up a lungful of seawater and sand. Her body groaned in pain as she crouched on all fours until her stomach finally let up and she collapsed onto her back.

The sun beat down on her and she cringed at its light—familiar and yet foreign at the same time.

Memories from last night slowly trickled back to her.

The lifeboat.

The storm.

Almost dying…again. Gods, it was becoming a habit. Aram was going to kill her.

Aram!

Rae shot up, her eyes searching wildly across the stretch of sand she'd found herself. For a terrifying moment, she couldn't find him. Then she saw his body curled in a fetal position down the beach.

She got to her feet, her knees shaking each step of the way until she collapsed beside her friend. Rae shook him and Aram's body jerked upwards in a wet cough, water exploding from his lips. She turned him back onto his side as he coughed up seawater.

"So…" he said, his voice raspy. "Just to recap. Since we've been together, I have crawled through a sewer—"

"*Abandoned* sewer."

"Was chased through the streets by soldiers—"

"We escaped."

"Been pushed off a cliff—"

"*Pulled.* And it was into water."

"Was almost killed by ty'vairrs—"

"I really don't see how that's my fault."

"And nearly died in a storm."

"Also, not my fault."

Aram laughed. "You certainly make things interesting."

"We're alive, aren't we?"

"True, or we could be dying, and this is a hallucination."

THE STORM GATHERS

Rae snorted. "If this was a hallucination, this island would be full of really attractive people, all in various stages of undress."

Aram lifted his head—as if looking for said attractive people—and frowned. "What about her?"

Rae spun in the direction he was looking and froze. A ship had appeared further down the beach. It looked like a long canoe with a cabin built at the back and a large white sail. The owner, a woman wearing a gray shirt and dark purple pants, strode towards them. Her eyes were a startling blue, and her curly hair was pulled back from her face by a dark band of cloth.

Instinctively, Rae released the knives from her cuffs.

The woman stopped a few feet from them, and Rae realized she couldn't be older than seventeen.

"My name is…" The woman hesitated for a moment, then continued with new conviction. "My name is Nur Del Sue, and I need your help."

Rae forced herself to her feet and jabbed a thumb behind her where Aram still sat. "Aram Brayvare." She motioned to herself. "And my name is Rae Toma." Her gaze slid past Nur to the boat she'd arrived on. "And we could use some help ourselves."

TWENTY-NINE

AGE FIFTEEN

Alana Zaya, Princess of Okaro, shifted in her seat. Every crunch of footsteps shot a mixture of fear and excitement through her. It was a pleasant day—cloudy, but there was rarely a day in Okaro that wasn't. She didn't like the sun, anyway. She preferred the darkness. There was something easier about it. Something that was safer than the light.

Her sister, Arya, disagreed. She feared the darkness and the monsters hidden in it—waiting, lurking, ready to pounce. But she was wrong. The worst monsters didn't need to hide. They lived in the sunlight, strutting about like gods armed for battle.

"Princess."

Alana grinned as she met the gray eyes of the boy she'd been waiting for. "Landon." She stuck out her chin. "You're late."

He shrugged, taking a seat beside her. "I had a stop to make."

"What for?"

In answer, he held out a cloth stained a reddish purple. Alana took it hesitantly and pulled apart the cloth to reveal a branch heavy with a dark red berries. "You said you liked them," he murmured.

Alana smiled down at the cloth. "They're my favorite."

She plucked a berry from its stem and popped it into her mouth. The taste—both tart and sweet—flooded her tongue. Swallowing, she offered them to Landon, who pulled off two.

THE STORM GATHERS

"Thank you."

Alana smiled at him.

Landon was the apprentice to Carlo, a butcher from the city. He and Alana had met while he'd been delivering meat to the palace kitchens. He hadn't known who she was, and the princess had liked that. Although the people in the palace didn't treat her with the exaggerated fondness they showed Arya, they still acted differently towards her. But Landon didn't. Even after he knew. They met like this every few days and would sit and talk for hours.

Landon had a younger brother he was responsible for since their parents passed, but he hoped that one day he would save up enough money to buy them a house or a ship. Somewhere that was all their own.

He tucked the empty, stained cloth into his pocket. "How have you been?"

It had been three days since they'd last met. Alana glanced over the high bushes and caught a view of the top of the palace.

"The same," she said simply. "Things around here…they don't change."

"That sounds nice."

"It's boring," she countered.

"Maybe, but I hope one day my life is boring." He smiled. "But not now, though." He grabbed her hand, and Alana's heartbeat picked up at the touch. "Let's go to the cliffs," he suggested. "We can watch the sunset."

She bit her lip. "No one can see us. If my mother finds out about you…"

"She won't," Landon assured her. "I know how to sneak in and out of the palace. I've been doing it for weeks."

Alana hesitated a moment longer, then nodded her agreement, letting Landon lead the way. She'd been the one to show him the hidden passage in and out of the gardens, but she liked him holding her hand.

They slipped out of the gardens and climbed down a small ravine until they reached a formation of rock that jutted out to overlook the ocean.

They settled beside each other—shoulder to shoulder—and watched as the sun arced towards the ocean.

"We could leave, you know?" Landon said quietly. "Steal a ship and sail around the world."

"We don't have any money."

"You have jewelry. That has to be worth something. And once that runs out, we could work. There's always someone that needs help."

Alana chewed her lip. "I don't have any skills…"

Landon laughed. "That's not true! You know every language. You can read, write. You're practically the smartest person I know."

Alana raised an eyebrow. "Practically?"

"Aside from myself, of course." She punched him in the shoulder and he grinned. "Come on, princess. You hate your life in the palace. I hate mine."

"What about your brother?" Alana asked. "What about Payton?"

"Penn can come with us," Landon said. "Arya can too, if she wants to. I know you don't want to leave her."

Alana closed her eyes. It was a nice idea—sailing the world with Landon and Arya.

"I can't," she whispered. "Arya needs me. She's going to be queen, and she needs someone she can trust."

Landon watched her for a long moment, then turned back to the ocean. "I know." He sighed. "One day, Alana, we are going to be able to live for ourselves and not other people. Arya will become established in her rule, and Penn will be grown up. Then we can run away."

Alana smiled at the fantasy. It would probably never happen. But it was something for her to hold on to.

"One day," she agreed.

They watched as the sun disappeared and darkness swept in.

ALANA'S HEAD WAS IN THE clouds for the next few days, dreaming of day when she could have a life that was her own. She loved Arya, she really did, but Alana lived in the shadows, hiding from the monsters that strutted about in the sun. One day, she wouldn't have to. One day, she would be able to enjoy the light.

She looked up at the blue sky. This was not that day.

She was supposed to be meeting Landon again, but she was late. The princess hurried her way through the lackluster garden. It was more a maze of bushes than anything. Few plants were strong enough to survive the constant storms.

THE STORM GATHERS

Once, she had suggested to her mother that they plant qiras flowers to brighten the place up. Emira refused, informing her daughter that the plants the princess loved so much were nothing more than weeds. Alana had stopped giving suggestions after that.

She turned a corner into the small pocket where she and Landon met.

"Hello, daughter."

For a brief moment, Alana considered running away at the sight of Queen Emira Zaya sitting on the bench that was supposed to hold Landon. It was a foolish thought, of course, her mother would find her. At the very least, she would send guards to track her down.

"Your Majesty," Alana said formally. "How are you?"

Emira turned something over between her fingers. Alana's eyes tracked the motion. It wasn't normal for her mother to fidget. But…this didn't feel like nervousness. A flash of fear ran through her. Did she know about Landon?

"I am well," the queen answered. "However, I have been worried about you, my dear. You've been acting differently lately."

Alana forced her face to remain neutral. They were playing a game now. She recognized the challenge in her mother's eyes. It was the same look she got when they played chess.

"Have I?"

"Yes." Emira stilled her hands and Alana caught a glimpse of a carved chess piece—a bishop. "Naturally, I had my servants keep an eye on you." She smiled a false smile. "You can imagine my surprise to discover that you've been sneaking around here with the butcher's apprentice. What's his name? Landon?" Emira set the bishop on the bench beside her. "Honestly, Alana, what were you thinking? That boy is nothing. You are a *Zaya*."

"I'm not the heir," Alana pointed out. "Why does it matter?"

"It *matters* because your actions reflect on our family and I will not let you tarnish my name." She rose to her feet. "Arya will become queen, and as tempted as I am to rid myself of you permanently, I have found another use for you." Emira strode towards her daughter and it took everything Alana had not to back down. "The king of Jaarin recently reached out to me with a proposal. You and his son will be married the *moment* you come of age."

No. No, this couldn't be happening. Jaarin was across the Western sea. They worshiped sleeping gods and sewed their clothing with diamonds.

"What about Arya?" Alana demanded. "She needs me."

Emira scoffed. "Your sister doesn't need you. If anything, you hold her back. I am the one she needs. I am teaching her how to be a queen."

"You drown her in studies of topics that any scholar could advise her on. Trivia doesn't make someone a good leader."

"Oh?" Emira challenged. "Tell me, daughter, what does make someone a good leader?"

Alana didn't break eye contact. "The trust and respect of their people."

"*Wrong*. Power is what makes someone a leader. Power *forces* respect."

"Not always," Alana said simply. "You have power."

Emira's left eye twitched and, for a moment, Alana was worried her mother would strike her.

Slowly, the queen's face changed, and a small smile crept across her lips. "You are right, daughter, I do have power. And yes, sometimes people forget to show me the proper respect. For example, a boy sneaking into my palace to corrupt one of my children. Did you think I would let that go unpunished?"

"What did you do?"

Emira lifted her chin. "I used my *power*." She turned to leave, but Alana blocked her mother's path.

"What. Did. You. Do?"

The world around them seemed to darken as she focused on her mother. Emira's eyes darted around them, suddenly seeming on edge. Finally, she turned her attention back to Alana. "I did what needed to be done. The specifics of which are none of your concern." Once again, Emira tried to walk around Alana, only to have her path blocked once more. The queen gritted her teeth. "If you don't move out of my way, *daughter*, I will call for the guards and have you thrown in the cells."

Alana weighed those words for a moment. She didn't doubt that her mother would make good on the threat, but there was something odd about the way Emira was acting. She wasn't one to make such blatant threats, especially not in a situation where she held all the cards.

THE STORM GATHERS

Unsure of herself, Alana took a small step aside, giving the queen just enough room to slip through the bushes and out onto the garden's main path.

Suddenly, she was alone. Her eyes traveled back to the chess piece on the bench. It had fallen over sometime during her conversation with Emira. Alana stared at the bishop. Landon was gone. Whatever her mother had done…the princess knew she would never see him again.

"I should have gone with you," Alana said quietly. "We should have run away."

THIRTY

Nur studied the two easterners she'd found on the beach. The boy was tall and thin, but she could spot defined muscles beneath his wet clothes. The girl, Rae, looked like some sort of goddess, with golden eyes like the color of eastern coins.

She eyed their weapons. Both had at least one sword and she was willing to bet there were more hidden on their persons. They were warriors. Or something of the sort. What had they done to end up here?

Nur had met easterners before. No matter what country they came from, what language they spoke, or what their customs were, each and every one of them had been broken and desperate. It was the way of the Shatter. It destroyed the strongest of hearts and wore down the most stubborn souls. Nur had barely been sailing for a week and already she was feeling drained.

She took another step towards the two easterners. They were certainly desperate, but they weren't broken. And so, the Stormwitch decided that they might be of use.

AN HOUR LATER, THEY SAT aboard Nur's ship, which they'd dragged onto the beach. Rae was grinning, and her companion, Aram had gone utterly still as the Stormwitch summoned a rain cloud that filled two tin cups with water.

"That's amazing," Rae whispered. "And there are people who can do this with all four elements?"

"Some," she confirmed. She held out the folded piece of paper that contained her father's notes. "You can actually read Terran?"

Rae nodded and took the page. "Fluently." A pause. "As long as it's not in future tense. Then things get a little tricky."

Aram glanced at Nur. "Are you sure about this?" He gestured to his friend. "She's not exactly an easy traveling companion. I would totally understand if you wanted to just…" He made an exaggerated pushing motion with one hand.

"If she can read it, I need her."

Rae squinted at the paper. "Do you have something I can write with?"

Nur went to a hatch in the ship, pulled out a charcoal pencil, and handed it to the easterner. "How long will it take?"

"A few hours. I'll need to double-check everything after I'm done."

Aram climbed to his feet. "While you're doing that, I'll check the island for fresh water."

Nur opened her mouth, but he cut her off. "That rain thing you just did was very impressive. But we don't want you to drain your strength." He hesitated a moment, then added, "That's how it works, right?"

She nodded her confirmation and got to her feet as well. She removed four empty bottles from storage and handed two to Aram, keeping the others for herself. "I can go with you," she said. "In case you need help."

Rae let out a little sound of protest. "You're going to leave me here? With your ship and the information for finding Eriysha's Compass?" She met Nur's eyes. "For someone who was just betrayed, you need to learn to be more untrusting."

"Rae!" Aram exclaimed.

The warrior shrugged. "It's true."

"Would you leave Aram behind?" Nur questioned.

"Maybe he's leading you off to kill you," Rae suggested.

The Stormwitch raised her hand. Lightning burst across her fingertips. "I think I can handle myself."

Rae grinned. "That's more like it."

"I'm sorry," Aram muttered. "We're not going to try to kill you. Neither of us are sailors. And we're not interested in taking the Compass for ourselves."

Nur frowned. "Why not?"

"It's not for us to take," Rae answered. She glanced up at Aram, a faint smile on her lips. "We're soldiers and criminals. And considering your magic, it's clear it was meant for someone like you." She nodded to Nur. "If you'll accept our help, we'll get you there. It's preferable to dying on an island in the middle of nowhere."

"That...was actually sort of sweet," Aram said. He turned to Nur. "Appreciate that because moments like it don't happen often."

Rae rolled her eyes and made a dismissive gesture. "Both of you, go. You're distracting me, and I need to concentrate."

A FEW HOURS LATER, THEY returned from their expedition with four full containers of water. Nur had been pleasantly surprised to find that she enjoyed Aram's company. She liked Rae too, although after recent events, she was cautious about putting her trust in these strangers.

As they came into view of the ship, Rae got to her feet and held up Nanook's research.

Nur dashed forward. "You finished already?"

"It was pretty simple, actually," the warrior said. "At least his theory is. Putting it into practice, however..."

"Just tell us what it says, Rae," Aram prompted.

The Sioran girl stuck her tongue out at her friend before turning back to Nur. She passed the Stormwitch the paper and pointed to a sketch on the page. "The hand-print—" she started, "does your island have rocks with this symbol?"

Nur frowned. "There was one on my island. I didn't see any at the Academy, but I didn't explore the jungle. Why?"

"Your father believes they are what will lead us to the Compass," Rae explained. "Sail in the direction they're pointing, and you'll eventually reach the island where Eriysha's Compass is kept."

"So, we just follow these stones from island to island?" Aram asked. "That's it?"

Rae snorted. "That's it? We need to search each island we come to without getting lost. Then manage to stay sailing in that direction for days—possibly for weeks—without getting thrown off course."

"We can use the stars," Nur said. "They shift position each day, but they don't move during the night."

"First, we need to find where the hand-print is on this island," Rae said. "Apparently, on both your island and the Academy's, the stone was near the coast. So, we should probably start by hiking the perimeter."

Aram let out a long breath through his nose. "Fantastic."

"It shouldn't be too difficult," Nur assured him. "Just watch for serpents."

He stiffened. "Excuse me?"

"Oh, relax," Rae said, giving him a dismissive wave. "I'm sure we'll be fine." She turned to Nur. "Don't worry about him. He has a penchant for the dramatic, but when push comes to shove, he always makes the right decision."

"And if I don't, you push me off a cliff."

"*Pulled.*"

"Same thing."

"*Very* different."

Aram rolled his eyes. "I need to find better, less insane companions."

"That sounds boring," Nur said, heading for the railing.

"Come now, Aram," Rae said, hooking her arm in his. "How often do you get to be trapped on an island with two gorgeous people?"

"Don't get any ideas," he growled.

"How do you know I have any ideas?"

"You always have ideas. And they're rarely good ones." He turned to Nur. "You should never trust this woman."

The Stormwitch hummed. "I don't know. Bad ideas usually end up being the most fun."

Aram pinched the bridge of his nose. "Gods help us."

"Let's go, Brayvare." Rae hopped off the ship.

The others followed.

As they made their way up the beach, the Stormwitch observed her new companions. They were a strange pair. But there was a familiarity about the way they interacted that put Nur at ease.

"So," Rae asked, as they broke through the tree line, "what's the name of your ship?"

Nur glanced back the way they'd come. "It doesn't have one." She knew it was customary for easterners to name their ships, but given that so many on her island went missing, people tended to try not to get attached to their vessels.

"That won't do," Rae chided. "It needs a name. How about *The Rae Toma*?"

"Classy," Aram muttered.

Nur turned to see that he was walking beside her. Gods, he was light on his feet. Even when actively listening, she could barely hear him despite the dead leaves underfoot. She considered. "What about *The Storm Rider*? Or *Compass Seeker*?"

"How about *Les Eruse*?" Aram suggested.

Rae nodded. "That's actually not bad."

"What does it mean?" Nur asked.

"*Les Eruse* means 'our song' in the Old Tongue," Rae explained.

"How many languages does your continent have?"

"Suhryn and Fehrun are the main ones," Rae said. "But there are dozens of other dialects left over from old countries."

"Like Terran?"

Aram nodded. "Yes. But the Old Tongue is a dead language."

"We can name my ship the *Les Eruse*," Nur decided. "I like it." She glanced at Rae. "How do you know so many languages?"

"It's a gift, I suppose. I've always been good at learning different dialects."

"It probably helps that she does so many mind exercises," Aram added.

"Mind exercises?" Nur asked, frowning.

"We call it *reinta*," Rae explained. "Battle thinking. When you're fighting, you need to have a calm and focused mind. *Reinta* is an exercise in building that control."

"Control," Nur echoed. "That's what I need."

"With your magic?"

She nodded. "It's why I haven't been able to make an Amulet." At Rae and Aram's confused looks, Nur clarified. "It's something that helps to amplify my power. But to make it, you need to have a degree of control over your magic."

Rae considered for a moment, then said, "I can help you. Control starts with the mind. We'll practice some *reinta* after we find this damned rock." She kicked at a pebble that went scurrying over the path. "So, why can your people access Eriysha's—what did you call it?"

"Current of power."

"Right," Rae said, snapping her fingers. "Why can you use it and those on the continent can't?"

"I'm not sure," Nur admitted. "Maybe it has something to do with us being in the Shatter?"

"What about the other gods?" Aram asked. "Do Seoka and Orik have Currents, too?"

"I assume so," Nur said. "Sometimes I feel as though I can sense another power, but it's too faint for me to be sure."

"If Seoka has one as well, that would explain the Teratt witches," Aram said eagerly.

Rae rolled her eyes. "Those are a myth. It's been hundreds of years…"

"But wouldn't it make sense?" he pressed. "Given everything Nur just told us? It's said Oriane Asha was a Teratt witch."

"What are you talking about?" Nur asked. "What is a Teratt witch?"

Rae sighed and ran a hand through her hair. "About seven hundred years ago, there are myths of powerful beings from Teratt. Magicians with illusionist powers. Apparently, they could make people see and experience things that weren't real."

"They could also imbue their power into objects," Aram added. "But they all disappeared after the rise of Tala. Perhaps Seoka's Current died out."

Nur mumbled something incoherent. Her mind was too focused on the concept of the Teratt witches. *Illusionists.* She'd always suspected that there were additional forms of magic in their world. But to have it confirmed…

Then again—according to Rae—the illusionists were gone. What had happened to them? Was it possible that her people could befall a similar fate? Nur shuddered at the thought.

They continued walking for the next hour.

Rae took up the lead while Nur and Aram moved more carefully through the dense jungle. They were just discussing whether or not to turn back when they heard a *whoop* from Rae up ahead.

"Turns out your father wasn't an idiot!" the warrior called. "I regret all my thoughts up until now."

Nur rolled her eyes and quickened her pace through the trees as the trail turned sharply upwards. Huffing, they crested the hill and found their third standing before a tall, white rock.

Rae raised an eyebrow at the two of them. "The two of you took your sweet time, didn't you?"

"Shut up," Aram snapped. "Not all of us like to run up cliffs as a hobby."

Nur ignored them and walked to the stone. The top was slanted and flat, aside from a large hand-print pressed into its surface. She fitted her hand into the print on the stone. Nur closed her eyes and when she opened them, her gaze fixed on the horizon.

"We should mark this spot on the beach," Rae said, gesturing to the sand below them.

"And are you volunteering to climb down?" Aram asked.

Rae shrugged. "Sure." She grabbed a large, dead branch from the forest floor and tossed it to the sand beneath them, then did the same with three more. "I'll set up the marker and you two sail the ship around."

Nur glanced over the edge. It couldn't be more than a thirty-foot drop, but the rock face was smooth, providing no hand-holds that she could see.

If Rae was at all concerned, she didn't show it. "If I die," the warrior announced, "I want you to bury me with my weapons."

Nur glanced at Aram. He, too, seemed completely unbothered.

"You're really not going to leave me anything?"

"I suppose you can have my clothes, as I have every intention of being buried naked."

Aram snorted and motioned for her to continue. "Just get on with it, would you, Toma?"

Rae swung over the edge of the cliff. Nur rushed to the edge to see the warrior climbing smoothly down, her fingers and toes clinging to invisible crevices in the stone.

"Don't worry about me, Stormgirl," Rae called.

Aram laid a hand on Nur's shoulder. "Come on. She'll be fine."

Nur stared at the warrior a moment longer. "That's amazing"

Aram shook his head. "You have a strange sense of the remarkable."

THIRTY-ONE

Alana woke with a delicate breeze running through her hair. It was evident that she was still on the water, but something was different. The rocking of the boat was too great for the *Fe Ressu*. And she was outside... not in the brig with her companions. She couldn't hear Johnathan's gentle snoring or the occasional way Penn mumbled in his sleep.

Penn.

Oh...gods.

The memories came back to her.

The boy's blood coating her hands. His eyes, wide and unseeing.

Alana sat up, her eyes flying open as she took in her surroundings. She was in a lifeboat. The same lifeboat she had swum her and Kaius to the night before. Above, the pale hours of dawn painted the sky as stars began to give way to the sun. The ocean stretched around her on all sides. No sign of the *Fe Ressu* or any other lifeboat. Only her and...

"Finally."

Alana whipped her head towards the voice.

Kaius was seated on one of the benches, an oar in each hand.

A thousand thoughts, accusations, and profanities ran through her head. But, instead, the only thing that came out was. "Penn?"

Kaius's face softened. "He's gone. Alana, I'm sor—"

She cut him off. "What about the others? Maria and Johnathan? Wren?"

"I don't know. I woke up, and we were...here." There was an unspoken question there, and one she purposefully did not answer.

THE STORM GATHERS

Alana got to her feet, the boat rocking precariously beneath her.

Kaius swore. "*Please* don't stand up."

She ignored him, looking around for any sign of another lifeboat. But there was nothing. They were gone. They were all gone. And she was still here. Again.

She slumped back down into her seat and closed her eyes briefly before gazing around the rest of the lifeboat. It was big enough for a dozen people, and Kaius had built a shaded area on the opposite side using a tarp—inside she could see the food and water.

"I'm sorry for what happened to your friends," he said.

She didn't reply for a long time, then finally, "I am Alana Zaya. I don't have any friends." The words came so easily, it hurt. The lies of her life were so tangled with the truth, she could hardly tell the difference anymore. Not that it mattered. Nothing mattered. Not anymore.

"That's not true," Kaius said, and something in his voice made her look up. "I saw you with them. How can you say they weren't your friends?"

"You've had a traumatic day," she said flatly. "You should rest. And your head looks like it was bleeding a little while ago."

Indeed, dried blood matted one side of his head. Kaius reached up and touched the spot self-consciously.

"Yeah, that's from when you hit me with a bookend." He gave her a pointed look. "I'm still waiting for my apology, by the way."

She stared at him in silence. Once it became clear that no apology was forthcoming, he took up the oars and resumed his rowing. The silence continued through the day until the sky had once again turned orange—this time by the sunset.

"You're really not going to say anything?" Kaius asked as they broke into their meager supply of food.

Alana swallowed a piece of dried meat. "Is there something you want to talk about?"

The pirate shook his head. "You set Sarasin's ship on fire. Your friend died. None of that merits a discussion?"

No, it didn't. At least not with him. Still, she knew he'd keep asking if she didn't chance the subject.

"I imagine being separated from Sarasin and Layla is difficult for you. The three of you seemed...close."

Kaius blinked at her. "Is this you trying to be nice?"

"A wasted effort, I know. Can we go back to silence?"

He chuckled. "If that's what you wish, *Kiydra*."

Biting back her reply, Alana ate the rest of her dinner. Silence wrapped around them. She turned her eyes toward the sky.

"We should sleep in shifts," she said finally. "In case of a storm. I can take first watch."

Surprisingly, Kaius didn't argue when she stepped out of the shade and took a seat on the bench between the two oars. She didn't attempt to row. It had been years since she'd had any exercise, and she didn't intend to embarrass herself in front of the pirate.

Kaius settled himself in the bottom of the boat, wrapping his jacket tightly around himself against the chill. He winked at her, then closed his eyes.

Alana waited until he was asleep, then picked up the oars.

SHE HAD ONLY BEEN ROWING for about twenty minutes, but her arms were already burning. She tried to push through the pain, but by the time the stars had fully appeared, she'd given up. The only saving grace was that Kaius was soundly asleep in the corner of their lifeboat and thus unable to witness her humiliation.

She settled down on the bench and laid back, bracing her feet against the side of the boat to keep her steady as she gazed up at the stars.

It wasn't often that she thought of her father, Madoc. He had been from the Vettan state in Nuska, journeying to Okaro to seek out a new life, as so many did. He wasn't noble. Or wealthy. Or possess any remarkable skill. But Emira had married him, anyway. It was the only time in her life that Alana's mother had not followed the traditions of her ancestors.

If not for him, Alana wouldn't have thought her mother capable of love. She certainly hadn't loved her daughters. Not even Arya. No, Alana's sister had simply been a means to an end for their mother. But Emira had loved Madoc. Truly. Deeply. And without fear of the consequences.

Alana couldn't imagine what that must be like.

THUNK.

Alana spun, expecting to see Kaius rising to his feet, but he was still asleep, one of his legs now stretched out at an awkward angle. His lips moved, the words coming out slurred and indecipherable.

Without warning, his arm shot out with surprising speed and slammed against the bench beside him with a crack. She winced at the sound, expecting him to wake screaming. But the man's eyes remained closed even as his body jerked to the side and head smacked against the side of the boat.

Slowly, Alana rose to her feet, picking her way across the ship to him.

"Kaius," she said, hoping the sound of his name would wake him up. "You're having a bad dream."

He didn't even stir. His mouth continued to move, speaking words that weren't words, running too close together for her to understand.

Cursing in every language she knew—which was most of them—Alana knelt down beside him. She reached forward cautiously. "If you hit me, I'm going to kill you." She took Kaius's face in her hands, letting her fingers run under his jaw. Alana tilted his face towards her and said, "Wake up."

His eyes fluttered open a moment later, blinking as they adjusted to the dark. His gaze met hers, wild and searching. She released her fingers from his face and made to pull back, but he was faster.

With one hand, he gripped the back of her neck, holding her in place while the other pressed a blade to her throat, the cool metal digging into her skin.

Alana closed her eyes for a moment before opening them again. She held his stare. "You were dreaming," she said. "You're awake now. This is real. *I* am real."

Kaius blinked, some of the frenzy leaving his eyes.

Alana's lips twisted into a brutal smile as she gave a pointed look down at the knife. "Are you going to keep tempting me with a good time, or are you finally going to follow through?"

That seemed to do the trick. The knife fell away, and Kaius released his grip on her.

"Tease." She rolled back on her haunches, giving him an appraising look.

"Sorry," he said, rubbing a hand over his face. "I'm so sorry. I get nightmares sometimes. I didn't even think—I mean, it's been so long since..." He shook his head. "Are you all right?"

Ignoring the question, she reached forward and grabbed his arm. He made a sound of protest, but she cut him off with a look as she ran a hand down his forearm. She'd worried he might have broken it in his thrashing, but the bones were intact. She moved her examination to his wrist—to the pulse thrumming too quickly in his veins.

"Your heart is racing out of control."

"Alana—" his voice came out as a croak. "I—"

"Tell me what you dreamed about."

He shook his head. "I don't want to talk about it."

Sighing, she tipped her head to the stars. Her fingers still pressed to his wrist, counting his racing pulse.

You are the Queen of Darkness. She reminded herself. *You are a monster.*

And yet, Alana settled beside Kaius. She stretched her legs and let out a breath. "You need to relax," she said. "Talking about it helps."

"I—" He swallowed and closed his eyes against whatever memories rose. "It's not a good story, Alana. It's not a part of my life I want to remember."

She leveled him with a steady look. "We're going to die out here, Kaius," she reminded him. "Whatever you say here tonight will never leave this boat. Besides," she said, allowing some of the hardness in her voice to ebb away, "I'm in no place to judge anyone."

His gaze met hers. She watched as his mind calculated just how much to tell her. Finally, he spoke, "I was raised in the North, in the former country of Qrestall. At the time, there was a lot of unrest in that part of Nuska, so my parents sent me to live with my uncle. They died shortly after I was sent to him. I remember that when he told me...the way he said it...it was as though he didn't even care that his sister was dead. If anything, he looked relieved. I was always asking when I could go back to living with them. I think he thought that—since they were dead—I would finally give up. And he was right. I stopped caring. And my uncle took that as an opportunity to turn me into a killer. He was—is—a powerful man with a lot of enemies and he used me as a weapon against them." There was a beat of silence, then Kaius said, "In my dreams, my parents are alive, and I'm inside the house where I grew up. Except I'm not a child anymore and when my mother sees me, she starts screaming." The pirate looked down at his hands. "And then I kill them."

There was a moment of silence as he finished. Alana realized he was waiting for her to speak. Waiting for her judgment or her pity.

Instead, she just asked, "How did the three of you end up working together? You, Sarasin, and Layla, I mean."

He blinked, finally turning to face her. "*That's* what you want to ask?"

"Are you going to answer?"

Kaius rubbed a hand over his jaw. "I was on an assignment for my uncle in Teratt, bidding for one of their ancient artifacts to bring back to him. After winning the piece at auction, I caught Layla breaking into my room to steal it." He shrugged. "From there, Sarasin offered me a deal for the object and a way to escape my uncle. I took it."

"That explains *your* presence," she pressed. "How did Sarasin and Layla meet?"

Kaius narrowed his eyes—he knew she was using his current vulnerability to pry. Alana waited, half expecting him to shut her down. "Layla," he said carefully, "used to work as a member of Empress Kyrin El-Tess's elite band of warriors. She and her cadre were on some sort of mission when they were attacked by desert raiders. Layla and the others that survived were taken prisoner. Kyrin refused to send any soldiers to help, but Sarasin was working as an advisor for the empress at the time and arranged for a group of mercenaries to rescue them. After that, he and Layla began working together."

Alana considered his words. "Sarasin was an advisor to Kyrin?"

"It was a long time ago." Kaius stretched his arm with a groan before refocusing on her. "All right, now it's my turn to ask a question." He gave her a sideways smile. "Don't think I don't know what you're doing, *Kiydra*. The truths I gave you tonight come with a price."

It was fair. But Alana hated playing fair. There was a reason Tal was her favorite card game.

"Fine," she ground out. "One question, pirate."

Kaius smirked. She resisted the urge to hit him.

"Why did you save me?"

"Who says I did?"

"We're telling the truth tonight," he reminded. "Now answer the question."

Alana looked away. "I don't know," she said honestly. "Maybe I'm just tired of watching the people around me die."

She could feel Kaius staring at her.

The attention made her skin crawl.

"You should go to sleep," she told him, her voice tight. "We have a long day tomorrow."

"Alana—"

"Sleep," it was a command, and one that he at least pretended to follow as Alana moved back to her perch on the bench across the boat.

She felt raw. Aside from Maria, she never spoke openly with anyone, and it usually took each of them a bottle of wine to open up—both women were wrapped so tightly in their respective secrets that they would have suffocated without the other to confide in.

But what had transpired between her and Kaius was different.

In some worlds, it may have been natural for people to talk freely, but not in hers. She hated the vulnerability of it. But some part of her liked it too. And that was dangerous.

We're probably going to die out here anyway, she reminded herself. *It doesn't matter.*

For her sake, Alana prayed that was true.

THIRTY-TWO

Rae had been in the Shatter for six and a half weeks and had officially come to the conclusion that she was not suited for a life at sea.

The *Les Eruse* was small compared to Ydric's ship, but still comfortable with just the three of them. Rae and Aram slept on the deck while Nur kept to the cabin at the back of the vessel.

The Stormwitch had taught the two soldiers how to sail so they could keep the ship on track at night while she slept. During the day, Nur expended her energy, keeping them on course as they traveled from island to island.

It was becoming easier to find the hand-print stones that directed their path, but after weeks of travel, Rae couldn't help but wonder if they were sailing in one giant circle. Not that she was complaining. The varying geography of each island was fascinating. And while Aram despised the constant presence of serpents, she liked them. She'd seen one large, yellow and green one that could have easily swallowed her whole—something she did not mention to him.

Nur let out a relieved sigh when the sun faded from the sky above them, giving way to the stars. Sweet beaded on her brow, and the girl swayed slightly on her feet as she stretched from her perch atop the cabin.

"Careful," Aram called.

The Stormwitch made a dismissive gesture and took a step forward, teetering precariously close to the edge.

Aram got to his feet, eyes darting back to Rae, who sat at the bow of the ship, the wind whipping her loose hair into a frenzy. She shouted a warning to her friend as Nur attempted a graceless climb down and immediately lost her balance.

Aram launched forward, catching her around the shoulders before she could crash into the deck.

"Are you all right?" He offered her some water, and she took it gladly, swallowing down a few mouthfuls.

"My head hurts," Nur told him. "But other than that, I'm fine."

"Good," he said, taking back the water and settling down beside her.

"I guess I'm still learning when it comes to this whole control business," the Stormwitch grumbled.

"You'll get the hang of it," Aram said confidently. "And while Rae may have her faults—*many* faults—this is one area where she actually excels."

"I'm going to choose to ignore that middle comment and focus on the compliments," Rae said as she took a seat beside her longtime friend. "Aram has always looked up to me, you see. Seen me as a role model. A mentor. A goddess among mortals—hey!" She shifted out of the way as the man in question threw a loose punch in her direction. She grinned. "Admit it, Brayvare. You've always been in love with me."

"In your dreams, Toma."

Nur glanced between them. "Are the two of you? I mean, are you guys…?"

"Together?" Aram chuckled. "No." He stretched his back. "I have no interest in physical intimacy. With anyone." He gave Rae a pointed look. "And that's all she's interested in."

"Not true!"

Aram snapped his fingers, as if remembering something. "Ah, that's right. I'm forgetting about Illian."

Nur raised an eyebrow. "Illian?"

Rae let out a sigh, seeing there was no way out of this conversation. "It was before the war when Argos had just become king. We—" She groaned. "I don't know how to explain this…it was just fun. It was sex and companionship, no great romance or anything. Illian…he understood me." She licked her lips, unable to think of a better explanation. "He understood, and that's more than anyone else ever did."

"What happened?"

"Illian is King Argos's son. When he found out about us…let's just say that things turned ugly." Out of the corner of her eye, she saw Aram grimace. Nur looked between the two warriors in confusion. Before she could ask more questions, Rae spoke. "It's been a long day. And you look exhausted, Stormgirl. Why don't you rest in the cabin for a bit while we prepare some food?"

Nur hesitated a moment, her eyes still filled with curiosity, before finally nodding her agreement and disappearing into the cabin at the back of the ship.

Rae stretched out, tempted to leave the food preparation to Aram and take a nap herself. The impulse made little sense as she'd hardly moved today. Maybe it was the mention of Illian. The thought of him had a tendency to leave her drained.

Forcing a smile to her face, Rae got to her feet and began to help with their dinner.

THEY REACHED THE NEXT ISLAND the following afternoon.

As usual, Nur and Aram spent the first few hours on land, searching it for resources and drinkable water, while Rae staked out a campsite.

She arranged a circle of stones on the beach, near the edge of the tree line, and collected wood and kindling to use for a fire. Next, she set out the old canvas bags they'd recycled as bed rolls. They could have slept on the boat, but after days on the water, her limbs ached for dried land and a solid place to exercise.

She brought out the fish they'd caught earlier that day. They were small, but combined with the berries they'd found and dried from the last island, it wouldn't be a terrible dinner. Especially if Nur and Aram managed to come back from their venture with something useful.

Once everything was set up, she went in search of a flat piece of earth she could use for training.

She finally found a place inland. The hardened earth, packed with bits of rock, was hardly ideal, but it would serve its purpose.

She began with simple stretches, followed by core exercises, lunges, and push-ups before moving on to sword craft, first with her falcata and then with *Teruth*. Her body moved seamlessly through it all, years of practice making the work instinct. It wasn't easy, but the familiar motions calmed her.

She was halfway through the eighteen points of sword work when she heard the cracking of branches and the roar of something that was definitely not human. Fear leaped into her throat.

"Aram!"

A second roar rumbled through her bones, followed by the distant boom of thunder. One glance at the sky made it clear—Nur was in trouble.

Rae took off through the trees, her legs screaming in protest as she swerved through the dense jungle until she came across her companions facing off against...

"What the actual fuck *is* that?"

A massive figure loomed over Aram and Nur. It looked like living black stone cracked with lava. Although the figure was relatively humanoid, massive horns grew from its forehead, and its legs ended with hooves. It looked, well, it looked like a creature Rae had only heard in stories. A zeduir. A creature of fire and earth.

It towered over Rae, easily twice her height with its horns adding an extra foot. As she stared at it, something tickled that back of her mind. A strange sort of rhythm.

Across the clearing, Nur brought her hands down, and a bolt of lightning struck the earth, missing the zeduir by inches. The beast roared again and charged for Nur and Aram.

Rae pushed aside the strange feeling and ran to help. She pulled the knives from her boots and flung each at the monster, the blades piercing its...skin? She had no idea what to call whatever the creature was made of.

The zeduir swung its head towards her to reveal eyes of smoldering coals.

Rae glanced at Aram, their gazes locking. His expression was one filled with horror while hers spread into a grin as adrenaline filled her veins. *This* was what Rae lived for.

She pulled her falcata from its sheath as the zeduir reached for her. She dodged it easily, sliding between its legs and lashing out with her sword to cut open the inside of its thigh. Lava—or maybe it was blood—poured from the wound, and the monster reared back, nearly tripping over Rae as she scrambled to get clear.

The zeduir charged for her again, its head lowering to reveal the sharp points of its horns.

She dove out of the way at the last moment, her aching muscles long forgotten at the excitement of the exchange. Rae pulled a knife from its sheath and threw it at the monster's head. The blade ricocheted off its horns and embedded in a tree—buried to the hilt.

Rae swore. She'd never be able to get that out.

Aram finally launched an attack. Slicing his sword against the zeduir's calf. More lava-like blood poured freely, but the wound quickly healed.

"Now would be a good time to run away," her friend yelled.

"And surrender? I don't think so."

"We're both looking at the same fire monster, right?"

Rae ignored him and ran to where Nur huddled against a tree, her eyes wide with terror.

"Aram's right," the girl said. "We need to flee."

Rae snorted. "Why?"

"Because that thing is about to kill us."

"You're just being a pessimist. We can win this fight. And it's not like we can leave. We haven't found the hand-print yet." Rae got to her feet and offered a hand. Nur hesitated a moment, then took it. "All right, Stormgirl, here's the plan. I need you to summon a lightning bolt." The Stormwitch raised her arms. "Not now," Rae said quickly. "You'll need to hit it directly on the top of its head."

"It's moving too much—"

"Let me take care of that. Just be ready."

Nur nodded, her hands tightening into fists.

"Hey," Rae said, catching her arm. "Just breathe. It's going to be okay."

"And if it isn't? What if you die?"

Rae shrugged. "We're all going to die sometime. Might as well go out fighting a massive fire monster." She winked, then sprinted to help Aram as he narrowly missed being flattened by the zeduir's massive hooves.

"I need your sword!" Rae called.

"I'm using it at the moment!"

Rae removed the knife from her opposite thigh and threw it at the creature. It flew through the air before lodging in the beast's knee. The zeduir roared in pain at the blade in its leg. It fell to one knee. One massive hand braced against the ground while the other reached to dislodge the knife.

"Throw it now!" Rae screamed, gesturing to Aram.

The sword flew towards her, and she caught it in one hand. She sprinted forward and drove Aram's blade through the hand on the ground, pinning it to the earth. Sliding the knives from the cuffs at her wrists, she launched into the air, burying both in the zeduir's side and using the momentum to climb onto its shoulders. She wrapped her legs around its neck, holding onto one horn as it tried to shake her off. The heat of its body burned her thighs, and Rae did her best to ignore the pain as she re-sheathed her knives and grabbed the short sword braced against her back. The blade was long and thin with a metal handle. She drove it through the top of the zeduir's head. The monster went momentarily still at the shock of the blow, but she knew it wasn't dead. Not yet.

"*Now!*" she screamed to Nur.

Mercifully, the Stormwitch didn't hesitate. Lightning crackled in the air around Rae, her hair standing on end as she pushed off the zeduir's back a second before a massive lightning bolt seared the air and slammed into the monster.

Rae's world exploded as she was thrown backward onto the ground. There was a ringing in her ears, and she was fairly sure her nose was bleeding, but she was alive and, aside from a few burns, unharmed.

Rae lay on her back as her senses slowly returned to her.

A figure crouched by her side—Nur. "Gods! Are you okay?"

Rae propped herself up on one elbow and laughed. "That was the most fun I have had in a long time. And you, Stormgirl, are absolutely amazing."

The islander grinned. "It was pretty awesome, wasn't it? Imagine what

THE STORM GATHERS

I'll be able to accomplish once we get the Compass!"

"It will be pretty amazing," Rae agreed. "What do you plan to do?"

Nur shrugged, but the warrior could tell that the casual motion was forced. "I was born in the Shatter, but everyone on my islands always treated me as an outsider. They thought I was weak because of my father's eastern blood. But if I get the Compass, it will be *because* of my father." She took a deep breath. "I want justice for him and I want to prove to the world that they were wrong to doubt me."

Rae's eyes shifted over the girl across from her. She could see monsters lurking beneath the surface and how close Nur was to giving into them. She was so determined. So strong-willed.

Not for the first time, Rae wondered if it would be better if they never found the Compass—never unleashed its power upon the world.

"Take my advice, Stormgirl. Get justice, but not at the expense of yourself." She climbed to her feet. "My value in this world is based on how efficiently I can kill people. That's it. That's all I am. If you take the Compass and use it to hurt others, you'll become like me. You'll be a weapon. And one day you'll look in the mirror and the person staring back at you will be unrecognizable."

Nur was quiet for a moment, then she said, "I want you to be at my side, Rae…to make sure I don't become like them. I don't think I can do this on my own."

The warrior clasped the witch's hand. "You won't have to."

231

THIRTY-THREE

AGE SIXTEEN

Rae swung her training sword in a casual arc and smiled at the two men in the training ring across from her. "Come now, Warner—Owen. It's two against one. Don't tell me you're afraid?"

Only the latter took the bait, charging forward with his sword. Rae ducked beneath the strike and drove her elbow into his ribs, sending the man stumbling back. Warner attempted to land a blow while Owen distracted her, but she blocked his strike and rolled out of the way, putting space between her and the two men.

They both converged on her, victory in their eyes as they came at her from either side. They attacked at once, their movements so precise she couldn't help but wonder if they'd practiced this. The drawings for duels were supposed to be random, but Rae suspected Varim purposefully fixed hers to give her more difficult competition.

She dodged Owen's thrust and parried Warner's strike. She moved in on Owen, knowing him to be the weaker opponent. Rae stepped around him, putting both men on one side of her as she aimed her next attack at Owen's already bruised ribs. He attempted a clumsy block, and she used the opportunity to step closer to him and land a punch across his jaw. He stumbled backward, nearly knocking into Warner.

Rae closed in on them before either got the chance to regain their footing. She attacked in a flurry of blows, the two men struggling to keep up.

First, she disarmed Warner, his sword skittering uselessly outside the training circle. Swearing, he stepped away, his hands raised in defeat.

Rae turned her attention to her remaining opponent. "Ready?"

Owen lifted his sword halfheartedly, but they both knew it was over. She didn't bother holding back or giving the audience a show. She unleashed herself on the poor man and had him on the ground within a minute, the tip of her sword pressed against his throat.

To her left, Varim sounded the bell, signaling that the match was over.

Owen ignored her hand, scrambled to his feet, and stomped out of the ring.

Rae walked over to the container of water by the side of the ring and poured herself a small glass, downing it in a single swallow.

"Are they all that short?"

Rae glanced up to see a dark-haired man with striking hazel eyes and a gold earring standing beside Varim. He looked vaguely familiar, but she knew he couldn't be a student at the Citadel.

"Usually, it's more evenly matched," Varim replied. "But some students are more advanced than others."

Rae rolled her eyes at that and swallowed another cup of water.

"So, that's the general's daughter?" The man nodded in her direction.

"She is, Your Grace."

Rae stilled at the title. Her head snapped up, turning to meet the eyes of Illian Vedros, the Crown Prince of Siora. She'd only met him once before as children. Before she'd entered the Citadel and he'd been sent for private tutoring in the northern part of the country.

"I think I'd like to have a try," the prince said, taking a step forward.

"I must discourage this," Varim said, putting himself between Rae and the prince. "It is a threat to your health and—"

"Do you think so little of me?" the royal asked.

"It's not a question of your skill. But Rae is..." Varim trailed off.

"I won't hurt the prince," she assured her teacher.

"If you had any measure of respect for your betters, I might believe you."

Rae walked over to her training sword and addressed Illian directly, "Shall we?"

Illian held up a hand. "No weapons. And certainly not training blades."

"Your Grace," Varim hurried to say. "I must once again caution you—"

"Yes, yes," Illian said, with a wave of his hand. "Just call the match."

Varim gave Rae a look that promised death if she hurt the prince.

They stepped into the fighting ring.

"Would you like me to go easy on you?"

The prince grinned. "I could ask the same."

"I don't think I could tell the difference either way," Rae replied.

She kept her hands loose at her sides, even as the prince raised his. She took a step forward, to within striking range. He took the bait and launched forward, punching out. She spun out of the way and grinned.

She could feel Varim's eyes boring into her head, silently begging her to throw the fight.

Illian advanced, moving faster than she expected, and Rae finally raised her arms to block.

"Are you going to keep retreating, Toma?"

She lifted her shoulders in a shrug. "I didn't realize the fight had started."

The prince bared his teeth in a snarl and came for her again. Rae engaged this time, but Illian blocked each of her strikes and managed to nearly catch her shoulder with one of his punches.

They broke apart for a moment, then came back together. Rae feinted left, and the prince fell for it, allowing her to crack a hand across his jaw.

Illian spun out of the way, one hand going to his chin in surprise. He spat blood and looked at Rae with a new light in his eyes. Then he charged, ducking low. He tried to slam into her and knock her off her feet.

Rae adjusted for the attack, attempting to knee him in the stomach. But the prince caught her leg and pulled her down. She rolled out of the way and got to her feet before he could pin her.

Illian was there the next moment, slamming an elbow against her ribs.

She attempted the same and missed, but caught his chest with her left fist, knocking him back and giving her space to adjust.

He came for her again, arms raised. But he didn't attack with fists. He hooked his legs around her waist and brought her to the ground. She took him with her, flipping him onto his back. The prince tried to rise, but she drove an elbow into his stomach and caught the first punch he threw. The second slammed into her cheek, sending a flare of pain across her face. Rae returned the strike with another across his jaw and leaped to her feet.

Once again, Illian tried to rise, but she kicked him in the ribs and placed the heel of her boot against his throat.

"Yield."

He attempted to grab her leg and throw her off balance, but she dug her heel in harder. "*Yield*," she repeated.

The prince glared at her, obviously trying to think of a way out of this.

She smiled sweetly at him. "If you don't yield, I'll have to knock you out." She considered for a moment. "Or kill you. I suppose that could work, too."

Illian sighed through his teeth and looked at Varim. "I yield."

Rae stepped away and offered her hand to the prince. He took it and got to his feet. "You are what you claim to be, Toma. I respect that."

"*I* never claimed to be anything."

"You both did well." Varim strode over to them, looking nervous.

"Some of us did better than others," Illian replied smoothly, rubbing a hand across his bruised jaw.

"Come, Your Grace. I will take you to our healers."

"That won't be necessary, Varim."

"I insist."

Rae rolled her eyes at the exchange and strode away, pushing past the students crowding the outside of the arena.

She was halfway across the courtyard that circled the grand clock tower of the Citadel when she felt a prickle at the back of her neck. Rae spun to see Illian striding up to her.

"It was a good fight," he said in greeting.

"It was. Next time, I might even try."

The prince's grin was feral. "Likewise."

Rae returned to her journey toward the clock tower. Illian matching her pace seamlessly.

"You have a cut on your cheek," he said.

She frowned and brought a finger up to her cheekbone. It came away dotted with blood. "Interesting."

He chuckled. "You're a fascinating creature, Toma."

"Careful. I bite."

"As do I."

Rae grinned and paused to give the prince an appraising look. "Would you like to do something incredibly foolish and dangerous with me?"

Illian's eyes went to the building in front of them and the scaffolding surrounding the tower. It was the Day of the Gods, a holy day, and thus the clock tower lay empty and completely open.

"And if we get caught?"

"I won't get caught."

He crossed his arms. "How can you be sure?"

"Because I'll knock you down and run away."

Illian barked out a laugh. "Let's go, Toma."

"Right behind you, Vedros."

They ducked beneath the large gray tarp covering the entrance to the clock tower. The building's insides had been stripped away for the remodeling. The only structures remaining were the support columns and winding staircase that led up the many levels.

They picked their way through the debris until they reached the staircase.

"Dare I ask what you're planning?"

Rae gave him a curious look. "What's the fun in having a plan?"

Illian chuckled and stepped past her on the stairs. He looked back and smirked. "Try to keep up, Toma."

"Try to avoid the knife I'm about to shove in your back."

"Thanks for the warning."

They wound up the twisting staircase until the height became dizzying.

The prince didn't seem troubled. He glanced down and gave the slightest shrug, as if daring the world to hurt him.

Rae smiled a bit at the expression. She spent so much time with Aram it was surprising to have a companion who wasn't constantly complaining or pointing out how dangerous the situation was. Then again, without his rationale, Rae knew she would have gotten herself killed a long time ago. They needed each other. Him, to keep her from doing something stupid, and her to ensure he did stupid things.

"You're thinking," Illian said, a slight admonishment to his words. "Thinking is like planning. It takes away the fun."

"How would you know?" Rae countered. "Princes don't need to have thoughts. They only need to be pretty."

He smirked, head tilting slightly so that his golden earring caught the light. At that moment, he looked more like a pirate than a prince. "You think I'm pretty?"

Rae snorted, pushing past him, intentionally jostling his bruised shoulder.

Illian exhaled through his teeth. He reached out, catching her wrist and twisting it painfully. "You want to go for round two, Toma?"

"How about we just skip to the part where you're lying on your back?"

"I'm not strictly opposed to that idea."

She broke away from his grip and glanced pointedly at the construction equipment and the floor, which was littered with nails. "Another time."

They continued up the final levels of the tower until they reached the clock face. Bells and heavy machinery took up the majority of the space. It looked to be the only level so far that the contractors hadn't started.

"You know, I think I'm starting to figure you out, Toma." Illian focused on the large bells hanging over them and the low hum of the machines.

"I wish you luck, Vedros," Rae replied.

"I'm serious." The prince kept his gaze clear of her. "You're a warrior who can't walk away from the fight. Not because you want to win, but because you love the high of danger."

Rae kept her face as neutral as possible despite the surprising accuracy of his statement.

Illian finally glanced her way. "I know because I'm the same. That's why no one can beat us. Everyone else is always looking for a way to end the fight, while we're looking for a way to keep it going."

Rae gave him an appraising look, then smiled. "Well then, prince, what do you say the two of us have some real fun?"

THIRTY-FOUR

Alana and Kaius sat beneath a canopy of stars. Dawn was fat approaching, painting the horizon in warm colors. He'd had another nightmare, as he did most nights.

In the two weeks following her escape from the ship, the two of them had gotten into a steady routine. Kaius rowed in the mornings and late afternoons when the sun's rays weren't too high. She would row at night—only when he was asleep. If he knew, he didn't comment on it, and she was grateful for that. But the man still took every opportunity to pry into her life.

"You were sailing to Okaro for your mother's funeral, correct?"

Alana let out a dramatic sigh. "Why did you have to ruin it?"

"Ruin what?"

"The silence, it was so wonderful."

"Come now, you know how this game works. If you don't answer, I'll just keep asking."

"You'll die eventually," she pointed out.

"And if I did, you would be sad. Admit it, you like my company."

"I hate you."

"No. You don't," he countered. "You wish you did, but you don't."

Alana glared at him. "To answer, no. If I had it my way, her body would be dumped in the sea without ceremony. I was returning to claim my crown."

Kaius narrowed his eyes. "You hate your own mother that much?"

Alana shrugged. "Emira did everything in her power to destroy me and in doing so, helped make me into the thing I am today. Of course, I hate her."

Kaius watched her for a long moment, then said, "It sounds to me as though the person you really hate is yourself."

She ground her teeth. "I think that's enough conversation for today." The pirate opened his mouth to argue, but she cut him off. "*Unless* you promise to answer one of my questions with complete honesty."

He hesitated a moment before nodding his agreement. "Fine, I promise."

Her lip curled. "Why did you kidnap me?"

Kaius exhaled a long breath. "Alana…"

"You promised me an answer."

"I did…" He rubbed a hand over his face. "Gods, I don't know how to say this without sounding insane."

She crossed her arms. "That ship sailed the moment you took me captive, so suggest you forgo your worries and start talking."

"Fine." Kaius's eyes went to the water as he began. "There is a prophecy," he said. "Legend says it was spoken by the goddess Seoka and recorded by the First Empress, Oriane Asha. It speaks of an ancient power created by the gods millennia ago. Terrible and brutal, it has the ability to either unravel our world *or* preserve it." Kaius paused, glancing at her, before returning his gaze to the sea. "The prophecy speaks of one, very specific person, who has the ability to unleash this power. For good or ill. A leader of nations who will come to power a thousand years after the Great Desolation. They alone will decide the fate of the world."

Alana closed her eyes. Another prophecy. Another dictation of what her life would be. It should have been her choice. But it so clearly wasn't, and she was *tired*.

It was the kind of exhaustion that seeped into her bones and left her feeling raw. One day, she wouldn't have the energy to fight anymore. What would happen then? Would they finally find a way to kill her? Or would she kill them?

Alana opened her eyes and stared at the man across from her. "If you think I'm so dangerous, why not just kill me instead of taking me prisoner?"

"Sarasin wanted to see for himself which side of the prophecy you would fall. I'll admit that kidnapping you wasn't the best idea, but we were running out of time. There are others who know of the prophecy. I believe you met some of their men when they attacked the Jaarin palace."

The mercenaries.

A wave of anger washed through her. "Who sent them?" she demanded.

Kaius winced. "The King of Nuska. Igo Mordul."

Alana took a deep breath. "This is insane. *You* are insane."

"Quite possibly. But that doesn't change our situation. If the king learns that you are still alive, he will come after you. He believes that you possess extraordinary power. He intends to use it to conquer the rest of the world."

"Right now, I'm inclined to side with the tyrant."

Kaius's lip curled. "I would encourage you to reconsider. Because if it's a choice between you and the world…" he shrugged. "Well, I'm afraid *I'm* inclined to save myself."

Alana couldn't help the faint smile that twitched across her lips. "Then why don't you do it? Kill me. Right here. Right now. You could prevent the prophecy. You could save the world."

Kaius pulled the knife from his belt and pressed it against her throat, leaning in close. "Don't tempt me, *Kiydra*. I just might."

The blade bit into her skin and she closed her eyes.

"Do it," she urged, her body vibrating with adrenaline. "See if you can do what no else can."

Suddenly, the pressure eased.

"Not yet," Kaius whispered. "Not while there's still some goodness inside you."

She snarled and shoved the man off of her. "You should have killed me when you had the chance, pirate. One day you'll look back on this moment and wish you had."

He smirked. "I doubt that."

They surveyed each other across the charged silence.

Something caught her attention and Alana's eyes lifted to the horizon. Her breath caught in her throat.

An island. Black beaches with sheer mountains and trees that jutted from the land like towers hurtling for the sky. She nearly sobbed at the sight, but managed to gain some composer as she turned back to Kaius whose eyes were also fixed on the new landscape. *Dymoura.*

Alana cleared her throat. "We're not done with this discussion. But it can wait until my feet are on dry land."

Kaius took a seat, picked up the oars, and put them in the water. "Agreed."

IT TOOK THE BETTER PART of an hour for them to come within clear view of the island. By that time, the sun has crested the horizon to light up the world.

"There are tracks on the beach," Alana said, pointing to where footprints had marred the black sand.

Kaius halted in his rowing, one hand inching towards the sword strapped to his waist. "Do we wait?"

Alana gave him an incredulous look. "For what? Another prophecy?"

He ignored her jab and continued rowing towards the beach with a huff.

They had just reached the line between the reef and a crashing surf when two figures emerged from the trees.

Kaius tensed, his eyes trained on the two people.

Behind him, Alana got to her feet and a small sound escaped her lips as she realized who the smaller figure was. *Maria.*

"Go," she ordered Kaius. When he didn't move, she shoved him out of the way and took up the oars, pushing their lifeboat into the surf and towards her guard. They made it through the waves before the bottom of the boat became stuck on the sand. The water was only about knee high, and Alana leaped over the edge of the ship. She ran through the water—ignoring Kaius's shouts—and onto the beach.

Maria collided with her. Tears running down her face, she wrapped her arms wrapped Alana in a fierce hug. "I thought you were dead," she sobbed.

"You should know better."

Maria laughed, then pulled away, looking her over. "Are you hurt?"

She shook her head. "Are you? Who else is here? Johnathan? Wren?"

Maria nodded. "They are both here." She hesitated a moment, her eyes going back the way she'd come. "Also, Sarasin and Layla. There were a few more people with us at the beginning, but Layla killed them."

Alana frowned. "Why?"

"Because I wanted to," Layla said, striding across the beach towards them. Johnathan trailed behind her. Alana caught a glimpse of Sarasin, too, running down the beach to help Kaius.

"They were your crew," Alana argued, focusing on the woman.

"They were hired hands," Layla countered. "They had no loyalty and, in a situation, where food was scarce and water scarcer, I decided it was best to eliminate unnecessary competition. Can you really tell me you wouldn't have done the same?"

"I would have," Alana agreed, then glanced to the sea where Kaius and Sarasin were dragging the lifeboat onto the black sands. "I *should* have."

Johnathan cleared his throat, directing her attention away from the subject of her ire. "I am glad to see that you are well."

She smiled at the man. "And I you."

"It seems fate is determined to keep us in each other's lives."

"Or the tides are favorable."

"Ever the cynic."

"One of us needs to be."

"And how was your voyage?"

"Unpleasant. I assume Sarasin told you of this…*prophecy*."

Johnathan looked away. "He did."

"And?"

"And," he said carefully, "I do not believe the words of the First Empress should be so easily dismissed."

"What about the words of the pirate who took us prisoner?"

"I—"

"It is a pleasure to see you again, Alana." The company's attention shifted as Sarasin and Kaius joined them. The captain cleared his throat and continued speaking. "I know you have had a long journey," he said, "but I believe there are certain matters that must be discussed."

Alana stepped towards him and smiled. Beside his friend, Kaius tensed and opened his mouth, possibly to shout a warning, but it was too late. Alana raised her hand and slapped Sarasin—hard—across the face. "There is only one thing that needs to be made clear," she snapped. "I don't like you. I don't answer to you. I don't think I've ever met anyone so ignorant of their own stupidity." She took the tiniest step back, not a surrender but a dismissal. "So, stay out of my way, and I'll stay out of yours."

The captain's jaw tightened, his eyes sliding past her, presumably to Layla. "You certainly haven't lost your taste for the dramatic."

Alana chuckled darkly. "You have no idea how *dramatic* I can be."

Kaius stepped forward. "Alana…"

"And *you*!" She turned on him, her voice rising in fury. "Contrary to your beliefs, I am every bit the monster the world believes me to be. Destruction or salvation. Good or evil. It means nothing to me. Tayrn means nothing to me. It can burn for all I care, but *I* won't be the one to light the match."

"Then you're a coward."

"I am," she agreed. "And you should be thanking the gods for that, because if I am forced to act, you won't like which side I choose."

He opened his mouth to respond, but she was already walking away, following the trail Maria and the others had cut across the black sand.

The woods closed around her, dark green leaves, sweet-smelling sap, and the trill of birds enveloping her senses.

She followed the path of trampled earth until she reached a small clearing. The two lifeboats the crew had used to escape the ship had been stripped bare. Alana could see that the wood had been used to set up makeshift beds that were raised off the ground and away from anything that crawled in the night. The rest had been used to make benches surrounding a small fire pit.

On one of those benches sat Wren.

The sailor gaped at her like she'd just returned from the dead, which Alana supposed, she had.

"Hey there, sailor."

"You're alive."

"Unfortunately." She gave an appreciative look around. "Nice setup."

He grinned at the compliment and jabbed a thumb through the trees to where she had caught a glimpse of the beds. "Layla and I built those. I can make you one if you'd like."

She cocked her head to the side. "Layla? What happened to wanting to her dead body thrown into the sea?"

Wren swallowed. "We...came to a truce."

"I see." Alana took a seat beside him. "Good for you, sailor."

"You're not...I mean, they took us prisoner."

She shrugged. "I applaud anyone who can find even the smallest measure of happiness in this world. If you are happy with Layla, then what does that matter to me?"

Wren blushed, then did his best to steer the conversation away from him and the quartermaster. "And what would make *you* happy?"

"Right now? Beheading Kaius."

"He's alive? You didn't kill him?"

"It was a mistake."

"There's time to rectify it."

"Exactly my view." She sighed, smiling at him. "It's good to see you, Wren."

"It's good to see you too, Alana." He cleared his throat. "A few things about the island—there's a freshwater spring not too far from here. I think there might be another near the mountains on the west end, but I haven't looked yet. There's a xygrith nest near there. We've kept to the east so as not to disturb them." Wren sighed. "It's a shame, though. Storms will be coming soon and I'm fairly sure the mountain has some caves we could use as shelter."

Alana considered for a moment. "What other animals live here?"

"Not much," Wren said. "A few bird species and some smaller mammals."

"Have you caught any?"

He nodded. "Layla and Maria have set a few snares. They check them in the mornings and evenings. We've only been here for a few days, so food hasn't become an issue yet, but I worry about the future. I just wish I knew where in the Western sea we were."

"We are on the island of Dymoura."

Wren blinked. "How do you know that?"

"The black sands. They are fabled in Okaro. Dymoura is the island Extoir the Great shipwrecked on before continuing on his journey to found Okaro. Supposedly, it is the land where lost things are found."

THE STORM GATHERS

"If it's famous, do you think other people may come here?"

She shook her head. "Dymoura is not as well-known as it once was. And those who do know it, avoid it. It is considered a sacred place to Okaron sailors. A place you only come to when you are in the greatest need."

"You're saying we're screwed?"

"It would seem so." She climbed to her feet. "If you don't mind, I'd like to explore a bit."

"Go ahead." He pointed to a tree behind her. "That's the tallest tree on the island. If you get lost, just follow it back here."

Alana gave the sailor a nod, then ventured deeper into Dymoura.

ALANA WASN'T SURE HOW LONG she'd been walking when she reached a rocky section of land.

Massive boulders towered around her from some ancient avalanche, each showing signs of being warped by the storms that tore through this section of the world.

She climbed her way to the top of one of the medium-sized rocks. Behind her, she could see the tall tree that marked the camp, and ahead she could see the line of blue ocean in the distance.

She closed her eyes.

They were alive.

Maria. Johnathan. Wren.

They were *alive*, and that was all that mattered.

For the first time in a long time, she felt like she could finally breathe again. She knew that she should have never allowed herself to care about these people. It could only bring her torment and only lead them to their deaths. And if the prophecy Kaius and Sarasin spoke of was true, then that was all the more reason to cut herself off from them.

Maybe it would be better if she stayed here. On this rock. On this island. Separated from the rest of the world. If Life refused to let her die, then perhaps this was the closest she could get.

Alana closed her eyes and leaned back, letting the sun warm her skin—finally finding some measure of peace.

THIRTY-FIVE

N ight fell, and Alana walked west, her boots digging into the black sand as she made her way across the beach. She closed her eyes as the night breeze washed over her. There were times she hated being alone—when her mind was free from distraction and the punishing thoughts washed in. But tonight was not that night. Tonight, she was free. Truly and completely. Because on this island, on Dymoura, she was no one.

Besides, it wasn't as if she were actually alone. There was someone following her.

Eventually, Alana reached the mountains that ran the length of the island. She reached into her pocket and pulled out a pouch of dried meat wrapped in wax paper.

"You can come out now!" she called.

A moment passed, then Kaius emerged from the tree line.

He held up his hands. "Listen, I—"

"Stop talking," Alana said, walking over to him. "You need to do as I say. No questions until after, okay?" She fought the urge to roll her eyes when he tensed. "Go back into the trees and don't make a sound. No matter what you see. No matter what happens. Your presence will only aggravate the situation, and I would prefer not to get set on fire."

"What—"

"Agree or leave."

He pursed his lips, then nodded. "Fine."

She waited until he disappeared, then turned back to the mountains.

THE STORM GATHERS

Alana inhaled deeply, then let out two long bird trills, followed by a second shorter one. She repeated the sequence twice more before something called back from over the mountains.

A moment passed, then a chorus of high bird songs followed.

Alana waited as a flash of red emerged from over the mountains. The xygriths circled the sky above her twice, then landed in the sand before her.

They were pure flame. Birds made of living fire. The only solid parts were their claws, eyes, and beaks, all as black as coal.

The largest rested in the middle, the glow of its flames reflecting off the dark sands. Alana let out a warble and bowed her head as she pulled a piece of meat from the paper and held it out to the xygrith. She kept her eyes lowered and waited. Thirty seconds, then a minute, then two minutes passed before she felt the rush of warm air as the food was torn from her hand.

Slowly, she rose back up and removed another piece from the wax paper. She held it out again, this time without the bow.

One of the smaller xygriths moved forward cautiously, its dark eyes trained on her. As it got closer, its flames flared a bit. Alana didn't balk as the bird darted forward, faster than the eye could track, and took the meat.

She peeled another piece off the wax paper and did the same with the next fire-bird and then the one after that.

Once she was out, she folded the paper and bowed once more to the largest xygrith, a low trill rumbling through her throat.

It mimicked the sound and took a cautious step forward. Its flames dimmed slightly, and Alana lifted a tentative hand forward and ran her fingers through the fire. It didn't burn, she'd learned as a child that xygrith flames didn't always burn. Still, it felt strange—like pushing one's hand through the rippling wind.

Finally, the xygrith stepped back. Its flames flared brightly once more, and let out a high bird call before shooting into the sky—the others following close behind.

Alana watched them go, then turned her attention back to the woods.

Kaius emerged from the shadows. "How did you do that?"

"I'm not certain how to answer that question," Alana said blandly.

"*Why* did you do that?"

"This is a breeding island for the xygriths," she explained. "They need to know we mean them no harm."

"What would happen if they thought we did?" Kaius asked, giving the high cliffs an appraising look.

"They'd probably set us on fire," Alana answered, still watching the surrounding greenery. She glanced at him. "Why are you here? I thought I made myself clear earlier."

"Just because you want a conversation to be over, doesn't mean it is. I asked you once what happened to you to make you like this. I want you to answer. And I want you to tell me the truth."

Alana crossed her arms. "Why should I?"

"Because you want to."

"I don't."

"Liar. You aren't afraid the truth will scare me away. You're afraid it won't."

"Truth is relative."

"Truth is *truth*," he countered.

"It varies based on perspective. How I see the world is not the same as how you see the world."

"And thank fuck for that." Kaius narrowed his eyes. "You're evading the question, *Kiydra*. Don't think I haven't noticed." At her silence, he dared another step towards her. "You want the world to hate you. You want *me* to hate you. Why?"

Alana met his eyes. "Because you're right. I am hollow." Her mouth was suddenly dry. She licked her lips. "I...died five years ago. And I've died twice since then. I don't mean I was saved or revived. I *died*. I stood in the eternal darkness and I heard Etrim's voice." Her voice dropped to a whisper. "I heard the voice of Death."

Kaius shook his head, clearly not expecting her answer. "I don't understand."

"Have you heard the story of how I came to Jaarin. My first voyage?"

"I remember something about you jumping off the ship."

"I didn't, actually. There was a storm that appeared out of nowhere— blue skies one minute and gray the next. I could hardly see or hear anything over the rain and thunder. At some point, I got swept overboard. I didn't even feel myself hit the water, but I knew I was in the ocean because the sound of rain was muted. It was nearly pitch black and I couldn't find the surface but remember...a shadow. There was something down there with me. It..." She shrugged away the unsettling memory. "It was probably just a hallucination. I lost my breath a few seconds later and...I drowned." She closed her eyes for a moment. Remembering. *The pact remains, L'edrahlan, Etreysum is not finished with you yet.* "I heard Her voice," she murmured. "Death." She opened her eyes. "That was the first time."

"Maybe you just got lucky," he argued.

"I know what it's like to get lucky. And I know what it's like to almost drown. This was neither." She flexed her fingers, unsure of how to continue. "My life when I first came to Jaarin...I was lost. Alone. I was the strange princess from Okaro who'd just married the prince. A month later, the king died, and I became queen. Then Arya was murdered, and I had no one left besides a husband who didn't love me, and a mother who wanted me dead. And I—" She stopped her story and glanced up at Kaius.

His expression was neutral, but his eyes were fixed on her face.

She didn't want to look at him anymore, so she turned her attention back to the beach. "They don't really have cliffs in Jaarin, at least not like there are in Okaro. I went there one night. I remember standing on the edge. The waves beneath were so quiet. Too quiet. It was all wrong. My life back then was so wrong, and it didn't feel like it would get better. So, I let myself fall. And I felt my body break. And everything ended. Except it *didn't*." Alana clenched her jaw against the memory. "That night made it abundantly clear that I couldn't continue to be the lost princess from Okaro. That girl had no control over her own life. She was weak, always waiting for other people to save her. But that's not how the world works. And when people do come, they're always too late."

Kaius didn't speak for a long time as they stared at each other. Finally, he asked, "What was the third time?"

She waited a beat before responding. "My mother and Bane, a man on Erik's council, hired an assassin to kill me. He attacked me in the gardens.

We fought, but he had a dagger, and I was weaponless." Alana rubbed her chest as the memory of the blade ripping her apart flashed through her mind. "What you have to understand, Kaius, is that each time I died, I lost a part of myself. A piece of my soul. And now there is something inside of me I don't understand—broken and dangerous. It scares me, and it should scare you, too."

"It should," he agreed. "But it doesn't."

"You're an idiot."

He shrugged. "I've heard worse."

Alana rolled her eyes and turned away from him. She wrapped her arms around herself, holding tight to steady her trembling body.

Above them, the sky split with the sound of thunder as the stars, which had been visible only minutes ago, were swallowed by dark clouds.

"We should head back to camp," Kaius said.

"We won't make it before the rain." Alana turned her attention to the mountains. "Wren said there were caves on the west side of the island." She started forward, pausing when she didn't hear him behind her. "Are you coming or not?"

"I want a promise that you're not leading me into a nest of hungry xygriths."

"No."

Kaius sighed. "For the record, I didn't use to have a death wish."

"What changed?"

"You, apparently."

Alana ignored the strange feeling that washed over her at his words.

They picked their way over the jagged landscape and found an opening in the rock face just as the first fat drops of rain started to fall.

The cave wasn't particularly large, but it would keep them dry from the natural shower.

Alana brushed aside some of the loose rocks and sat with her back against the cave wall. She'd lost her red coat when Penn had died, so she tucked herself in a ball to keep off the chill.

Without prompting, Kaius took off his jacket and wrapped it around her shoulders before settling down beside her.

"What's your favorite color?"

Alana blinked. "What?"

"I've always liked gray. There's something calming about it. It reminds me of the mountains in Qrestall."

She was silent for a moment, debating whether to respond. What she had just confided in Kaius all but confirmed the prophecy—it showed that there was something about her that was damaged beyond repair. But he didn't seem to mind. And now he was…what was he doing? He was acting normal. Even though the two of them were anything but.

Finally, she answered. "My favorite color is red. There are wildflowers in Okaro called qiras that grow across the cliffs. They can survive the bitter cold. The storms. Even the ocean waves." She paused, clearing her throat. "I always thought they were beautiful."

"If I gave you a bouquet of qiras, would you marry me?"

"I'm already married."

"Ah, you'll have to get divorced first, then."

"I'm not going to marry you, Kaius."

"Why not?"

"For one, you kidnapped me."

"And you tried to kill me," Kaius countered. "But I'm willing to look past that." Reaching up, he removed something from around his neck and handed it to her. "Here," he said, "you can wear this until I find a ring."

Alana rolled her eyes. "I'm not—" She took a closer look at the necklace he'd handed her. "What is this?"

At the end of the chain was a black metal pendant shaped like a bird mid-flight. In the bird's claws was a clear, gray stone. She ran her finger over the intricate metalwork.

"Do you remember when I told you how I met Sarasin and Layla?" Kaius asked. When Alana nodded, he said, "this is the piece we were bidding for."

"You keep stolen jewelry around your neck?" Alana let out an overly dramatic sigh. "Pirate, indeed."

She handed the necklace back to him and relaxed against the cave wall, eyes closed.

"You're breaking my heart, *Kiydra*."

"You'll survive. Unfortunately."

He chuckled, the sound vibrating through the cave. He leaned towards her. "Let me tell you a secret."

"Hm?"

"I've died too. When I was young, I was in a boating accident on one of the lakes near my town. I was dead. No pulse, for over a minute before they brought me back."

"Well, then," Alana said, lifting her arm lazily. "To those of us that Death doesn't want."

"May we live forever," Kaius whispered, clasping her hand in his.

"*Valnuskata, Kiydra*."

"For all the stars, pirate."

THIRTY-SIX

Nur watched the storm churning in front of them with a careful eye. After defeating the zeduir, treating Rae for her injuries, and finding the hand-print stone, they'd set sail once again. Unfortunately, their path was currently being blocked by a wall of gray clouds.

"I don't think it's moving," she said.

"Well, it needs to," Aram grumbled. "We can't sail into a storm."

Nur cocked her head to the side. "I don't know. Maybe we should."

The easterner shot her an incredulous look. "Not all of us are magical."

"No, I mean…" She shook her head. "I didn't feel it before. But now I'm starting to and the storm…it's different. It feels like home." Nur looked to Rae. "Like I'm meant to be there. Does that make sense?"

The warrior held the other girl's gaze for a few moments, then turned to Aram. "Let's do it."

"You can't be serious."

"We're searching for a magical compass and the witch we found says we need to sail into a storm because it feels like home." Rae cocked her head to the side. "What part of that doesn't sound serious to you?"

Aram dragged a hand over his face. "I'm going to die." He jabbed a finger at the two of them. "And it's going to be both your faults."

"It was your idea to go into the Shatter in the first place," his friend pointed out. "I feel you should share some of the blame."

"I'll be *dead*!"

"You really want to put that on my conscious? I'll be mourning your death."

"That *you* caused."

"Debatable."

Aram threw up his hands and turned to Nur. "Let's go. Suddenly, I'm wishing for the peace that Etrim will bring me."

The Stormwitch looked between them, grinning. She perched on the cabin and soon their sails were once again filling with wind—carrying them towards the storm and almost certain death. Or, perhaps, Eriysha's Compass.

As they sailed nearer, Nur felt her chest growing lighter—the effort of controlling the wind easing as the power of the goddess wrapped around her like a blanket.

This was it.

It had to be.

On the other side of this storm was the Compass. She could almost see it—feel it in her hand, the magic pulsing effortlessly through her veins. She saw herself creating tornadoes with a wave of her hand. Bending water and air. Forcing seeds to push stems up through the earth and holding fire in her palm.

And slowly, the rest of the world faded away.

The two easterners.

The waves.

The water.

The ship itself.

It all became of little consequence because Nur knew if she just made it...no. No, she *would* make it. She had to. And once she did, the power of each of the elements would be hers to command.

"Slow down!"

She couldn't tear her eyes away from the storm. She knew that someone was saying something. Knew and yet didn't. It wasn't important. Or at least, it didn't feel important.

The rain was coming down now. The waves pounded their ship and traitorous winds ripped at their sails.

"Nur!"

There came that voice again. But this time she blocked it out entirely.

THE STORM GATHERS

They were close.

So close.

She pushed the wind into their sails harder. But if it made a difference, Nur couldn't tell. There were too many elements throwing off her balance.

Control.

She needed to concentrate—to clear her mind the way Rae had taught her to.

Rae.

That was the voice calling to her.

Again, Nur felt that background sense of urgency. There was something wrong. Her limbs felt heavy and there was a loss of feeling that only came when...when she was using up her power.

How had she not felt it until now?

This place. The storm. It was messing with her head. She had to stop. Had to stop. *Had to...*but couldn't. She'd fallen for the storm's trick. She'd let it take control of her power and now it would flow through her until it tore her apart.

Suddenly, there were hands wrapping around her, pulling her down from her perch atop the cabin.

Aram, she knew distantly. And Rae was there too, her golden eyes appearing in front of Nur's blue ones. She said something, but all Nur could hear was the storm.

A wave crashed over them, water washing across the deck and drenching their clothes.

Nur couldn't imagine what she must look like right now. She knew the fabric she'd been using to tie back her curls had broken, and the hair was now plastered to her head. She was shaking, but she couldn't feel her limbs. Would the magic still run through her after she was unconscious? Would she die?

She really, *really* didn't want to die.

Nur had to return to their islands. She had to get justice for her father and prove herself to everyone who had doubted her.

Aram let go of her, following some command of Rae's. Then the warrior's arms were wrapping around Nur, holding her steady as wave after wave crashed over them. Something buzzed in her ear and dimly, Nur became aware Rae was humming. She focused on the sound. The melody was simple, but something about it calmed her and the magic that had been wrapping around her mind and tearing apart her body began to ease. She could breathe again. She could *think*.

"I'm sorry," she managed, the words swallowed up by the wind.

Rae growled into her ear. "If we survive, Stormgirl, I am going to kick your ass."

Despite everything, Nur smiled.

The boat lurched beneath them, tipping violently to the right. Nur shrieked as her body flew across the deck. From the corner of her eye, she saw Rae crash into Aram, the two of them landing in a heap of limbs—unmoving. Nur prayed they were simply unconscious.

Beneath her came another surge. She crawled across the deck and wrapped her weak and ravaged body around the mast of the ship as the storm that should have been hers to command attempted to kill her.

"This is not how I die," she whispered. "This is *not* how I die."

And the words, however ridiculous, gave her strength. Warmth flooded through her limbs. It didn't stop their ache—or the hollowness—but it gave her the power to stand.

"If you can stand, that means you are alive," Rae had once told her. "And if you are alive, then you have not been beaten."

THIRTY-SEVEN

Rae Toma felt like shit. Worse, she way lying on top of Aram, who was incredibly uncomfortable.

"*Gods*, why do you weigh so much?" he demanded.

Rae rolled into a seated position. "It's called muscle, Brayvare. Something you never managed to develop."

"Very funny." He rose to sit beside her. "What happened?"

Rae shrugged. "Last I remember, we were about to die."

"Hardly a rare occurrence nowadays." He looked around. "What happened to the storm?"

The sky above them was clear and blue, with no hint of the gray clouds and endless rain that had plagued them. Rae shook her head, half convinced she was hallucinating. Or dreaming.

One moment they'd been in the center of a brutal storm—their tiny boat failing miserably against the press of rain and waves—and the next she was being thrown across the deck. Now, they were…where were they?

"The two of you look terrible."

The easterners' attention shifted to the Stormwitch striding up to them.

Nur's disheveled clothes covered her body, adorned in scrapes in bruises, but the girl was grinning.

"You don't look too good yourself," Rae returned. "What happened?"

"I'm not sure," Nur admitted. "I kept the boat from capsizing while you both were knocked out. But with the speed of those winds, I had no way of sailing us to safety. After a little while, the storm just sort of…disappeared."

Rae inhaled. "So, what now?"

"Now," the Stormwitch gestured to the prow of this ship where a massive island decorated in spiraling cliffs that rose from the sea before them, "we find the Compass."

Rae climbed clumsily to her feet, steadying herself using Aram's head, something the still-seated Sioran was less than pleased about. He slapped her hand away, standing as well. Then gave her a shove that nearly sent her crashing to the deck.

Nur watched the exchange with a raised eyebrow.

"So," Aram asked, attempting to look innocent, "do we just...get out?"

Rae raised an eyebrow. "As opposed to...what? Staying in the boat?"

"It's a magical fucking island, Rae. A little caution might serve us well. Especially since the last rash move we made nearly got us killed."

"*Nearly*," Nur emphasized.

"Not helping," Aram muttered, his eyes returning to the island.

"How are we supposed to find the Compass, anyway?" Rae asked. "Do you know where it might be?"

"Not really," Nur admitted. "Maybe we should start by climbing one of those mountains. That way, we can get a view of the rest of the island."

Aram let out a long breath. "Great, more opportunities to die."

Rae laid a hand on her friend's shoulder. "Come now, Brayvare. Almost dying is the fun part."

"Besides," Nur added as she lowered the anchor, "there are worse places to die."

Rae looked at the island. The air hummed with magic that was both reminiscent of Nur's and foreign at the same time. But there was something just slightly wrong with how it skated across her skin.

Rae adjusted the falcata at her waist. She did not want to die here.

THEY DIDN'T FIND THE COMPASS. Not on the first day. Or the second. Mercifully—at least in Aram's opinion—they hadn't been set upon by any mythical monsters. Rae, however, would prefer a zeduir to the swarms of buzzing insects that populated the island.

THE STORM GATHERS

Nur had not yet attempted to access her magic since coming to the island, and she was restless from the excess energy.

Rae tried teaching her the basics of fighting, but the Stormwitch had little interest in it. The only time she successfully stayed still was during their *reinta* sessions.

Currently, their camp was on a bluff raised above the ocean. Rae got a small fire started, which they piled with greenwood—the smoke helped to keep the insects away.

Nur's eyes were closed, lids fluttering as she slept against a tree. Aram covered her with his jacket, then took a seat beside Rae.

He let out a long sigh, then said, "This has been fun."

"What?" the warrior asked.

"This," he said, gesturing around. "The adventure. I never imagined… well, any of this. Or her," he added, nodding to Nur's sleeping form. "But I've enjoyed it. For the most part."

"There's more fun to come," she reminded him. "And we may even survive some of it."

"We may," he agreed and reached into his pant pocket to pull out a folded piece of paper. "I only joined the Citadel because my family needed the money. But as a child, I wanted to be an artist. To create things rather than destroying them." He handed her the piece of paper. "Anyway, I drew this for you."

Carefully, Rae unfolded the paper. It was a drawing of her. Her face, tilted upwards and smiling faintly. The shading he'd done with Nur's charcoal pencil gave the image a depth and realism that was shocking to behold.

"Do you like it?" her friend asked hesitantly.

"I love it." And she did. There was something almost peaceful about her expression on the paper. It reminded her of how her life had been before the war.

Gods, that felt like another lifetime ago. More than once, Rae had wished she could return to that time. Even then, she hadn't been innocent. But life had at least been easier. Simpler. Those days…when it had just been her and Aram. And later, Illian…

The last time she had looked like this, she had been when the two of them. A moment of peace before the storm of war had torn them apart.

"Do you…" She swallowed. "Do you mind if I keep this?"

Aram nodded. "If you'd like."

Rae tucked the paper into her pocket. "I—"

From across the fire, Nur sat up with a gasp. Her blue eyes were wide as she stared into the flames. Rae got to her feet, one hand going to her falcata.

"What is it?"

"I know where the Compass is," Nur whispered, eyes darting away from the two easterners to the path ahead of them. "She told me."

Rae and Aram exchanged a look. "Who?"

"Eriysha."

THIRTY-EIGHT

They followed Nur through the trees. It was too dark to see where they were going, but Rae got the sense that they were traveling inland.

She quickly lost track of their progress as all her energy went into avoiding walking into any trees. Aram—silent as ever—was faring far better.

"Watch out," he whispered, reaching out in the dark and steering her away from a protruding branch.

She let out a string of curses, earning a *hush* from the Stormwitch ahead of them.

"Does the great and powerful Eriysha say how long this hike is going to be?" Rae snapped.

Nur pointedly ignored her as they continued through the dark.

Rae was seriously considering turning back—magical goddess be damned—when a faint blue light pierced the trees. It refracted and shimmered as if reflected off a body of water.

Through their travels, they'd found some freshwater lakes and ponds, but none were particularly large. And yet, watching the eerie light, Rae knew in her bones that this was big. And strange. There was no moon in the Shatter—at least none that she had ever seen—and the stars, while bright, were still too faint to cast enough light to cause this display.

They wove through the thick forest before Nur threw her hand out. "Stop. We're here."

They stood at the edge of a cliff...or something of the sort. It was as if something had punched a perfectly-cut hole into the ground. In the darkness, she would have never noticed the drop if not for the blue light emanating from its depths.

"Please don't tell me we're supposed to jump," Aram said.

"I…" Nur frowned. "I don't know what to do." The Stormwitch looked around helplessly. "I just knew to come here."

Rae's eyes scanned the cliff edge, snagging on a podium-like rock a few yards to their left. She began walking, Nur and Aram trailing after her.

"It has a hand-print," Aram said, running a finger over the rough stone. "I think you're supposed to put your palm in."

The Stormwitch looked at him skeptically. "I've done that before, with the other ones, and nothing happened."

"I think this situation's a little different," Rae commented.

Hesitantly, Nur reached out her hand and pressed it into the grooves in the stone. It didn't fit. The print was far too large.

They waited, all three of them expecting some crack of thunder or rumble from the earth, but nothing happened.

After a few minutes, Nur removed her hand, wiping it self-consciously on her clothes. "Maybe I'm not worthy."

Rae snorted. "The goddess directed you here. I seriously doubt she would have bothered if you weren't."

"It's all getting fuzzy now," Nur said, running a hand over her face. "What if it was just a hallucination and—"

"Blood," Aram said, interrupting the Stormwitch's spiral. "You said that when you made your Amulets, you used sand washed in your blood. Maybe there's magic in it. Some key to who you are."

Nur considered, then looked down at her hand. "Maybe."

"It's worth a try," Aram encouraged.

"You're not the one about to cut your palm open," she reminded him.

"And we don't know what animals might be in these woods," Rae added. "The smell of blood could attract some magical beasty."

Silence fell as they both turned to the Stormwitch.

"It's your choice, Nur," Aram said. "We'll stand with you, no matter what you decide."

THE STORM GATHERS

Nur looked back at the hole in the ground, at the blue light that danced around them. A blue, Rae realized, that matched the Stormwitch's eyes.

"I need a knife."

Rae couldn't help but smile at the girl as she removed a small blade from her boot and handed it to Nur. She took it and pressed it into her palm. Then, closing her eyes, dragged the knife across her skin, leaving a trail of crimson. Rae winced at the sight, but Nur didn't seem to notice the pain as she pressed her bleeding palm to the rock.

Almost instantly, the dancing blue light ceased, plunging the three of them into darkness.

Rae released a breath, her wrists flexing and triggering the two blades hidden in her golden cuffs. She sensed Aram readying himself, too, as Rae quietly tried to move closer to Nur. The Stormwitch had no power right now, and if anything should attack, she'd be helpless.

What seemed like an eternity later, the blue light sparked up again, revealing an empty space where Nur had just been standing.

"So…" Rae said slowly, "I guess that means it worked?"

Aram narrowed his eyes. "What are we supposed to do now?"

She peered down into the bottomless cliff. "I guess we just…wait."

"Wait?" he repeated, incredulous.

"I suppose we could try to climb down, but if the goddess wanted us in her domain, I imagine she would have extended an invitation."

Aram paced the edge. "I don't like this. She's, what, seventeen? That's too young. She shouldn't be alone with a fucking goddess. Assuming it actually is Eriysha and not some horrific creature out of nightmares."

"I don't think the two are mutually exclusive," Rae commented, earning her a glare from Aram.

"If she's not back by sunrise—or whatever they call it here—we'll climb down to find her."

Rae nodded. "Okay."

He blinked at her. "Okay? That's it? No arguing or sarcastic comments?"

She shrugged. "I like the girl. I'm not particularly fond of the idea of her being dragged into a bottomless pit with no way out. And she has my knife."

Aram let out a huff and settled himself against a tree, sword draped across his lap. "This is insane," he whispered. "This is fucking insane."

Rae tossed her hair behind her shoulder as she settled down beside him. "Well, we are in the Shatter.

"Don't start," he grumbled. "Ty'vairrs and zeduirs are one thing. But this is a *goddess*. Eriysha created this world."

"*Helped* create," Rae corrected, her eyes going to the pitch black where Nur had disappeared. "She wasn't the only one."

THIRTY-NINE

They spent weeks trapped on Dymoura and soon everyone had settled into a steady routine. In the mornings, Layla and Wren left to set traps while Maria swam in the ocean. Johnathan—who was convinced a sea creature would attack his fellow guard—watched from the beach.

Alana spent most of her day on the west side of the island exploring the mountains—occasionally joined by Kaius or Maria—and her evenings sitting on the beach.

Layla's snares hadn't caught any creatures that evening, so they'd been forced to break into their meager supplies of dried meat, fruit, and nuts. The evening had quickly devolved into everyone comparing their worse injuries while Alana had retreated to the beach to watch the tide come in.

The soft crunch of sand sounded as someone approached. She turned, and was surprised to find that it was Sarasin standing behind her.

"Is there a problem?" she asked.

"Do you mind if we talk?"

"I would prefer we didn't."

"Please, Alana."

She sighed and got to her feet. "Let's walk."

They started down the beach, keeping a generous distance between them as they went.

"I've been thinking about you for some time," he said.

"I've had enough proposals for a lifetime, so if that's where this conversation is headed, you'd better leave now."

The captain ignored her. "I know you may not believe in the prophecy, but you cannot deny that you are in a remarkable position of power. The heir to one throne and the queen to another. With two countries behind you, you could make a real difference."

"And what would you have me do?"

"Nuska needs to be stopped," Sarasin said firmly. "With Jaarin's wealth and Okaro's navy, you might coax other countries to your side."

"Each country conquered by Nuska has attempted the same thing," Alana argued. "Creft reached out to Aaran, even before the war, and look where that got them."

"What would you do then?" Sarasin questioned. "Let Nuska take over the world?"

"Well, that's certainly an option," Alana said dryly. "In fact, I imagine that would solve a number of my problems." At the withering look Sarasin sent her, the queen sighed and made a vague motion with her hand. "Fine. There are rebels in each conquered country. If I wanted to stop Nuska, I would provide them with supplies and use the unrest to weaken them from the inside. From there, yes, I would need to recruit other kingdoms. Siora has strong ties to Nuska. Yovar may come to help if bribed with the proper amount of money. And Aaran will join if they believe the fight to be winnable."

Sarasin nodded along.

"However," Alana said, raising a hand. "The problem with attacking Nuska lies with geography. The Skyfall and Dorsal mountains prevent Okaro, Jaarin, and Aaran from launching a direct attack. The Great Divide is too treacherous for a large number of ships to navigate. So, ships from Okaro would need to sail around the continent to get access to Nuska's eastern coast. Victory would depend on the strength of the rebels. Whether they can buy enough time for aid to come from other countries. Assuming aid *can* come."

"Not a terrible idea. Although, you didn't mention Teratt."

"The Walled Country will do what it does best. *Hide*."

"Perhaps," Sarasin admitted. "Or perhaps they could be the deciding factor, as they were in the battle of Empero Bay."

Alana snorted. "Seven hundred years ago."

THE STORM GATHERS

"Never discount your potential allies. As unlikely as they might be."

"I suppose that's the mentality that led you to kidnap me."

"An error I will not be making again."

Alana was silent for a moment. "Why go to all this trouble preventing a prophecy that likely isn't true?"

He met her gaze. "Because I believe it is real. I discovered it in the back of an old book in the Aaran libraries, recorded in Vettan runes, which took me more than a month to translate. When I read it…I can't explain it—I simply knew it was true. I felt it in my bones. And since then, I have seen things that…" He exhaled, shaking his head. "Do you believe in magic? The gods? Anything?"

She shrugged. "There is magic in the world. The Shatter is proof of that. As are the xygriths. But whether that magic comes from the gods or something else, I don't know."

Sarasin straightened his jacket. "This world is worth preserving, Alana. There is beauty in it, despite the pain. If you are ever faced with the choice to either save or destroy it, please remember that."

She looked away, towards the sea. She was tired of this conversation. Tired of arguing and fighting. She was tired of losing. She squinted into the distance as a shape in the water caught her eye and frowned. "Is that…a ship?"

Sarasin followed her gaze. "It looks like it's anchored." His gaze when to the black sand of the beach. "I don't see any lifeboats."

"They could be around the bend," Alana said, motioning ahead to where a small cove was carved out.

Sarasin stopped walking, his eyes looking back the way they'd come. "We should alert the others."

"I'm afraid I can't allow that."

Alana spun to see a tall woman with light blond hair step from the trees, flanked on either side by soldiers dressed in dark armor and helmets. She sucked in a breath in recognition. These were the mercenaries that had attacked her at the palace. And this woman—her voice was the one that had echoed outside her room all those nights ago.

"Nessa," Sarasin breathed. "I thought you—"

"Were dead? I'm afraid your attempt to kill me failed miserably." She smiled at the captain. "You look terrible, Sarasin. Dymoura is supposed to help the lost find their way, but it appears even its magic cannot save you. If I were feeling generous, I would take the initiative and put you out of your misery. Unfortunately, there are others willing to pay quite handsomely for the opportunity to kill you themselves." She winked. "I think you know of whom I speak."

Sarasin drew his sword. "I'm not going anywhere with you."

Alana stepped away from the man beside her. She knew as well as anyone that he was no soldier—this would go poorly.

Nessa's eyes went to Alana. "Ah, the Queen of Darkness. We didn't get a chance to speak during our last meeting. But there are no doors to hide behind now."

Alana forced her shoulders to relax despite the swords pointed at her and examined her nails. "Apparently not."

Nessa nodded toward her men. "Bind their wrists."

Sarasin slashed his blade through the air. "Stay back."

Alana held her tongue, deciding not to point out the opposition's obvious advantage.

Nessa let out a dramatic sigh. "Please, Sarasin, we both know how this will end. Let's save some time, shall we?"

The captain didn't lower his weapon, instead electing to charge at one of the nearest mercenaries. Two others converged on him. To his credit, Sarasin blocked the first few strikes levied against him before one of the mercenaries landed a kick to his stomach, knocking him to one knee while another disarmed him. The last soldier delivered a swift crack to Sarasin's head before they got to work on binding his hands.

The remaining men circled Alana, who raised an eyebrow. "I'm flattered you consider me a threat." She held out her hands. "But I assure you, I'm not much of a fighter."

Cautiously, one man stepped towards her, a rope in hand, and quickly tied her wrists together. Across the beach, Sarasin was being searched for any further weapons. Once it has determined he had no more, Nessa stepped forward.

"Tim, Hale, guard these two." She motioned to Alana and Sarasin. "Kill the big one if he tries to escape. As for the queen, well, if she tries to flee, feel free to cut off any parts you might want to keep." Nessa grinned and motioned to the rest of her company. "We'll follow their tracks back to their camp. And remember, Kaius is mine."

The two men Alana assumed were Tim and Hale brought her and Sarasin towards the forest, setting them on opposite sides of a small parting in the trees. Grumbling to each other, the two mercenaries stationed themselves in view of the beach.

She counted the minutes, marking when five passed and their two guards were suitably bored. Then, slowly, she reached into her pocket to the slit carved there, and retrieved the thin dagger she'd stolen from Kaius all those weeks ago. She positioned the dagger between her legs and slowly began to saw through her binds.

Across from her, Sarasin's eyes widened once he realized what she was doing. He wisely stayed silent and she paid him no mind as she cut the rest of the rope.

Her gaze snapped to their captors, who were still complaining to each other about their assignment. Alana knew that if she moved, they would see her. She gripped the dagger tightly in her right hand as her left scrabbling blindly on the ground until she found a medium-sized stone. She tossed it, careful to keep her movements as unnoticeable as possible.

The stone landed on Sarasin's side of the trees with a crunch. Both Tim and Hale's eyes snapped in that direction, their hands going to their swords. Alana wasted no time. She shoved onto her feet and slipped around a tree. Taking a few breaths, she moved silently away from her captors, stopping only to crouch behind a bush as shouts sounded back from where she'd come.

"Where's the queen?"

More swearing.

"She couldn't have gotten far."

"I'll stay here. Hale, you head that way."

There was the sound of heavy footfalls as the man stomped after her. Alana adjusted her grip on Kaius's dagger and braced her feet beneath her. Her eyes tracked the enemy soldier's dark shadow as he cursed his way through the trees and underbrush. She held her breath as he moved past the bush she was hiding behind and continued through the trees.

Slowly, Alana got to her feet and headed back the way she'd come, stopping every few seconds to listen for signs that she'd been spotted. Finally, she made her way back to the small parting in the trees.

Tim paced nervously back and forth, sword gripped tightly in both hands.

Sarasin watched him with hungry eyes.

Alana slipped around the perimeter of the small clearing until she was on the other side of the tree that the captain was leaning against. Carefully, she slid the dagger beside him. Sarasin retrieved it quickly and started cutting through his own binds while Tim's eyes were fixed on the direction Alana had originally escaped.

"Hale?" he called. "See any sign of her?" Tim took a few steps toward the shadow of the trees when no response came.

There was a soft snap as Sarasin finally cut through the last of the rope tying him. The captain didn't hesitate. He charged toward the mercenary. Gripping the collar of Tim's armor, he wrenched him back and drew Kaius's dagger across the man's throat. Blood gurgled from the mercenary's mouth as he dropped to the forest floor. Sarasin quickly retrieved the sword from Tim's belt and tested the weight.

Alana stepped into view and extended her hand for the dagger.

"I didn't know you had this," Sarasin said, passing it back to her.

"Weapons are far more effective when you keep them hidden."

"Hale will be back soon," Sarasin warned. "You should take refuge in one of the caves on the west side. I'll help the others."

"Because you're such a great fighter? I think not. I have an idea."

Sarasin raised an eyebrow. "You have a plan?"

"An idea," she corrected, her eyes going to the mountains looming above them. "We're not the only ones on this island."

FORTY

Sarasin and Alana hurried through the trees, keeping off the beach in case they were spotted. Eventually, they reached a rock formation a few yards from the base of the mountains. The captain waited in the shadows while Alana called up to the xygriths—not her usual call of food, but an urgent warble she'd heard younglings use with their mothers. It didn't take long for the fire-birds to appear from behind the mountains.

Alana had taken to calling the largest one Extoir, named after the first king of Okaro. He and seven other xygriths landed in front of her, each blazing bright. She took a step back from the heat and pointed a hand towards the mercenaries' ship, still anchored off the coast. She repeated the urgent warble.

Extoir returned it with a low rumble that bordered on a growl. Then he shot into the air, followed by the other firebirds. As they flew, half split off from the pack and turned towards the camp.

"Well," Alana announced as she watched the creatures arc towards their camp. "That either went very well or very poorly."

Sarasin stepped from the shadows, his eyes traveling down the island. "I expect we're about to find out."

"So," she said as they began the trek towards their camp, "are you going to tell me how you know that woman?"

Sarasin swallowed. "Nessa is an old...acquaintance of Kaius. They worked together while he was still in Nuska. When he left, she was sent to bring him back." There was a breath of silence as he sucked in air. "The two of them destroyed an entire town in Yovar fighting each other. I thought he'd killed her...but apparently not."

Alana raised an eyebrow. "An entire town?"

Sarasin let out a huff of confirmation and they slowed their pace across the sands. "I don't know what he has told you about his past, but it is safe to say that Kaius has his fair share of monsters. More than most. In the South, we treat combat as a dance—an art form—but in the North, you're handed a weapon and if you cannot wield it, you die. The mere fact that he is still alive should tell you enough."

Ahead, fires had started across the sands, consuming the bodies of fallen mercenaries. Xygriths circled the sky above the beach, attacking anyone who ventured from the tree line.

Sarasin lowered his voice. "Since I met Kaius, I have watched him battle his monsters. But he only began to win after meeting you. There is something about you, Alana—something I cannot see—that calls to him."

She didn't say anything as they veered off the beach and into the trees. The sounds of fighting drifted towards them as they closed in on what had become the battlegrounds of Dymoura. Maria, Layla, and Wren were fighting side by side against six men. To their left, Johnathan cut a path through the mercenaries as he came to their aid.

Kaius grinned as he faced off in a vicious duel against a man twice his size. His sword flashed through the air faster than Alana's eyes could track before finally coming down on his opponent's shoulder, severing the limb. Another blow to the neck decapitated the mercenary.

With a shout, Sarasin stepped into the fray while Alana let herself sink into the shadows.

The captain joined Johnathan and together they fought their way to the others. Together, the five of them finished off their foes.

Breathing hard and covered in blood, her companions leaned on each other. Wren's leg was visibly injured, but everyone else seemed fine.

Alana waited on the border of visibility, unsure if she should join them or not. After a moment's hesitation, she decided it would be best if she simply returned to camp. She took a step back and felt something sharp pressing into her ribs. A hand landed firmly on her shoulder.

"Don't move," Nessa hissed. "Don't scream."

Alana sighed. "I knew it was too much to hope you'd been burned alive."

"Shut up." Nessa pressed the blade in harder. "Let's go."

The woman directed Alana away from her companions, back towards the beach. She could feel the mercenary's hot breath on her neck and noted the careful trail Nessa was making through the trees to prevent being heard.

Alana waited until they came across a suitably large branch and stepped down—hard. The wood split with a resounding snap that interrupted the hiss and crackle of the fires.

"Whoops."

Nessa pulled them both to a stop. "You think you're clever? Don't you?" Alana felt a prick as the blade in her back pierced the skin. "But allow me to make something clear, Your Majesty. The money I am getting for your capture is barely enough to keep from killing you. Make trouble and I will cut my losses without a second thought." She twisted the blade. "Did you know that if you position the knife just right—just like this. It will take the victim up to three minutes to die. That's enough time for some last words. I wonder what yours will be." Her voice dropped to a whisper. "Do you know what your sister's was? *Please.*" Nessa made a disgusted sound. "She was weak. Like you."

Alana's breathing grew heavy. *Please.* She could imagine the scene in her head—Arya terrified and alone with a blade in her chest. And the last face that she'd seen was Nessa's.

Her body began to vibrate with anger, and the pressure of the blade at her back eased. Alana broke free of the mercenary's hold and spun on her. She froze.

Nessa's eyes were completely black, and smoke oozed from her mouth and nose to drip down her shirt. She stood still for a moment—eyes unseeing—before crumpling to the ground like a puppet with its strings cut.

Then the darkness started spreading from Nessa's body. It crept across the forest and any living plant it touched began to wither and die. The black smoke moved gently, as though it was trying to mimic something natural, like the flow of water or wind.

Slowly, a tendril creeped toward her, and Alana watched it with sick fascination. If she let it reach her, would it kill her? No, she didn't think so. She had seen something like this once before. Back in the gardens of the Jaarin palace the night her mother's assassin had come for her. She'd died that night, but when she'd come back, the plants around her were dead, withered just as the ones on this island.

Alana crouched down and reached a hand toward the black smoke. It wrapped around her fingers, then up her arm. She couldn't feel it precisely, but some part of her sensed that it was there, as it slithered around her neck and down her body. Soon, more of the darkness spread towards her, redirecting its meandering path of destruction.

Because it's mine, she realized. That thought should have been terrifying, but for some reason, it wasn't. Not right now. In fact, she liked it. There was something so familiar and comforting about this darkness. It was like reuniting with an old friend she'd never expected to see again.

She studied it as it moved around her, slithering like one great serpent around her body. Its movements were investigative, curious, as if it were just as fascinated with her as she was of it.

From her right, Kaius broke through the trees with his sword drawn. The darkness rose around her, readying an attack.

"*No!*" She wasn't certain who she was yelling at. Kaius, the darkness, or herself.

You don't have control, that tiny voice in the back of her head reminded her. *The cage is open and the monsters are running free and. You. Don't. Have. Control.*

She sucked in a breath, trying to focus her mind. The darkness was her creation and as much as she wanted to study it, this part of herself she kept hidden and ignored, Alana knew it was too dangerous to allow into the open.

She focused on the sensation of it wrapped around her and slowly she sensed more things about it as well. It was curious and afraid and alone. It was her. A part of her, at least and so she could control it. She latched on to the connection she felt between her and the shadow, silently commanding it to obey her. It didn't want to leave. And if she were honest with herself, she didn't want it to go. But this had to be done, and so she did it.

She forced away this part of herself to a space where it could not be seen. Around her, the darkness began to fade and the feeling of it wrapped around her—protecting her—went, too.

Alana wanted to cry.

Another hand closed over hers and suddenly she was staring into Kaius's eyes. "Are you okay? Did she hurt you?"

It took Alana a moment to register who he was talking about. Nessa. Arya's murderer. Who lay dead by their feet.

"I killed her," she said quietly.

"I know," Kaius replied.

She pulled her hand from his. "I don't want to kill you, too."

He smiled. "You won't. But you have to stop running, *Kiydra*. You have to face the truth of what you are. The events of tonight prove that."

She shook her head. "I can't."

"Why not?"

"Because I loved it. I *loved* it, even though it was killing everything around me."

"Not everything. It didn't kill me. It wanted to, but you didn't let it."

"But—"

"You need to face this," he repeated. "If you don't, you'll always be afraid of it and that fear will continue to dictate your life. We'll help you if you ask for it. You are not alone."

You are not alone.

The statement was both comforting and terrifying.

She had spent her entire life in one form or isolation or another. She didn't know how to operate outside of that or what the consequences would be.

"What if you end up getting hurt?"

"Are you finally admitting that you care about me?"

"I...no."

"It's all right. I won't tell anyone. Besides Maria."

"She'll still kill you if I ask," Alana snapped.

"No, she won't. I've won her over. I'm actually very charming."

"Delusional, too."

His smile widened into a grin. "Admit it. Admit that you care about me, and I won't tell anyone that Alana Zaya has a soft side."

She glared up at the infuriating man.

You are not alone.

And she wasn't. Not anymore. Because for some, strange reason, Kaius knew her darkest truths and stayed, anyway. *So does Maria*, she reminded herself.

She let out a sigh, breaking their staring contest, as she said, "You're an arrogant bastard. I hope you know that." Before he could snap a response, she grabbed his collar and pulled him towards her, pressing her mouth to his. The kiss was slow at first, but quickly escalated as Kaius pulled her closer to him.

When they finally broke apart, the pirate raised an eyebrow. "'Arrogant bastard,' huh?"

Alana narrowed her eyes, and he chuckled. With one hand, he removed the bird pendant from his neck and fastened it around hers faster than she could stop him. He gripped both of her hands in his to prevent her from taking it off.

Alana rolled her eyes. "That kiss was not an invitation for an engagement."

"I didn't say it was. And since we're not engaged, there's no harm in you keeping that necklace. Consider it a gift. No strings attached."

"You're insane."

"So are you." She ripped herself from the pirate's grasp, but made no move to take off the necklace.

"I am not going to marry you," she repeated.

Kaius smirked. "We'll see about that."

FORTY-ONE

N ur was underwater, but she wasn't drowning. Somehow, she'd become encased in a pocket of air that kept the crushing pressure and suffocating water from killing her. She stood on a jagged piece of rock jutting from a wall of sediment behind her. She could feel the presence of small creatures and debris floating around her.

The cut on her palm stung. The blood spilled over the sides and down her fingers, landing on the ground she stood on in soft plops.

You humans are so fragile. So breakable. It's a wonder you've lasted so long in this world.

The voice slammed into Nur's skull, taking up all space for thought or action. All she could hear were the words of the goddess Eriysha. It was husky and low, almost seductive, but beneath the surface was danger. Power.

Nur squinted into the dark, knowing that she must be close. As if answering her unspoken question, the darkness in front of her deepened and then broke apart as Eriysha emerged.

Gods…

Goddess…

Eriysha was beautiful and terrible. Terrifying and graceful. A sea serpent beyond any artist's recreation. Her face was long like that of a dragon, with white whiskers and scales of silver and cream intermingling with slashes of color. Her eyes were a mixture of green and blue and seemed to change constantly, shifting in a kaleidoscope of shapes and figures. There was no pupil, no black spot to provide anchor as Nur became mesmerized.

If she had arms or fins, she couldn't be sure. The goddess was too massive to fully take in.

You are the first to see my face in a thousand years, Nur of the Storm. Eriysha's mouth didn't move, but the words thundered through the Storm-witch's brain, nonetheless. *Or is it Del Sue? Such an interesting parentage. Unfortunate, I suppose.*

"You know who I am," Nur managed. It was somewhere between a statement and a question.

I know enough. I do not have the sight of my sister or the interest of my brother. But I have tasted your blood...and power. I know where you come from. I know what you are. And I know what you seek.

"The Compass."

My *Compass*, Eriysha corrected. *You do not know its value. Or what was sacrificed in its making. I will be frank, girl. You did not pass through my storm on your skill. Your companions aided you. That girl, yes, the one that reeks of earth and metal—she saved you. That is not even to mention how your father's blood dilutes your access to my Current. With this deficiency, I wonder if you can even handle the Compass.*

Nur gritted her teeth. "Do not discount my abilities. I am the first to make it to your island. I have fought monsters, the sea—even your storm—and prevailed. Yes, I had help. But so did you when you created this world. I can handle this power..." She paused, lowering her voice to avoid offending the goddes. "If you are gracious enough to grant it to me."

If the goddess was moved by Nur's plea, she didn't show it.

I am going to tell you a story, Nur of the Storm, Eriysha said. *And when I am finished, we will see if you still wish to lay claim to what I have created.*

Nur managed a nod. Her body was trembling.

Let's see, the goddess considered, oblivious to the plight of the girl before her—or, perhaps she just didn't care. *How do your human stories begin? Ah yes, once, long ago, there were three gods who descended to this planet. They spent most of their power in the making of this world, and when that power was all but spent, they called to their brother—still living in the stars—to help them maintain it. Their brother answered the call and de-*

scended to the world you now call Tayrn. But when he saw what his siblings had created, he grew angry. He hated what they had done. Hated its power and strange magic. So, he sought to destroy it.

And thus ensued a battle that brought us all low. He was the most powerful of us, you see, and none of us could gain the upper hand over the other. Finally, after millennia of war, Rion came before us. He'd given up his power and become mortal. He cursed us and vowed that this world would bring us only pain. Angered, we killed him and put an end to the war.

Or so we thought...

Eriysha trailed off for a moment, lost in memories. She shook her head clear—whiskers bobbing in the water—and returned to the story. Before he died, Rion bound his magic to an object—a Crown—so that his power may live on. Weak as we were, we could not destroy it ourselves, so Seoka looked into the paths of the future and saw a way we might save this world.

Together, each of us, Seoka, Orik, and myself, created objects imbued with our power. These pieces siphon our magic and release it into the world as Currents. But they serve a far greater purpose than giving you power, Nur. They can also become vessels used to contain our magic. They will give you the power of the gods themselves. With this power and a representative from each of the gods, the Crown may be destroyed. But doing so would break our pieces as well—and our magic would be forever lost.

Nur frowned. "Is that the only way to destroy the Crown? By destroying magic, too?"

The goddess hesitated. There is a being. One who possesses all forms of magic. An edrahlan. Only they have the ability to unite the powers of the four gods, but they would need each of our pieces to do so.

Eriysha shifted in the water, coming closer. The Dark Crown is rising, Nur, and with it comes the end of an age. There are two paths are before you, but the future lies in three. Sooner or later, you must make a decision. Knowing all this, will you accept my gift and the responsibility that comes with it?

Nur considered her options. She could take the Compass and all the power and burdens that came with it. Or refuse it and live a life lost to the ocean and islands.

Her eyes drifted upwards to where Aram and Rae waited, probably freaking out at her disappearance. Would they help her if she accepted this task? She was fairly certain they would, even if it meant their own deaths.

Finally, she nodded. "I will take the Compass."

Eriysha rose higher in the water. *Very well.*

Something solid appeared in her hands, but the Stormwitch didn't dare take her eyes off the goddess before her.

The world around her darkened as Eriysha's voice sounded in her head one last time.

Power destroys power, Nur. It is the rule of the Universe, as unbreakable as magic itself. Whatever happens, this is something you must not forget.

FORTY-TWO

Rae and Aram sat on the edge of the Eriysha's den. The silence dragging between them as they waited for the Stormwitch to return.

"Did you ever meet my mother?" she asked, after growing suitably bored with the island's stillness.

If the question startled him, her friend didn't show it. "Once," he answered. "I remember she showed up one day during training and whisked you away."

Rae nodded at the memory. "She took me to the Evrice planes. They're about an hour outside the Capital. We just stood in the grass, and she kept telling me to listen."

"Listen for what?"

"I have no idea. We stayed out there for hours, just standing in silence. Finally, when it was time to go, she grabbed my shoulders and told me that if I was ever lost, or in need of help, all I needed to do was listen." Rae looked back at the gaping hole in front of them. "Honestly, I'm not entirely sure what the Tiskona believe. She never spoke so freely, but I know she tried to teach me things in subtle ways." The warrior shook her head. "But I'm not of the Forest. I know I have the eyes, but not much else. I'm Sioran, whether I like it or not."

Aram smiled softly. "It's a fucked-up kingdom, isn't it? But it's ours. At least you tried to make it better."

Rae snorted. "Tried and failed, mostly."

"You helped a lot of people."

"And abandoned countless more." She shrugged. "It is what it is. I did what I could while I had the chance, and I hope that someone else is able to continue what I started, at least in some way."

Aram was quiet for a long moment. Finally, he said, "I haven't thought about my family much since we left. We weren't very close, as you know, but I keep wondering about my younger brother. I made my parents promise they wouldn't send him to the Citadel. He likes to read. Last time I saw him, his room was covered in books." He glanced over at Rae. "Sometimes I wonder what he's reading now. If he *is* reading or if my father hasn't forced him into some sort of trade. I told him that when he was older, I would take him to the great libraries in Aaran." He looked at his hands. "I guess I broke that promise, didn't I?"

"Hey," Rae said, nudging his shoulder, "you don't know that. If Nur *does* get the Compass, maybe we'll make it back to Siora, avoid the axe, and take your brother to the libraries of Aaran. How does that sound?"

"Unlikely. Improbable. Borderline impossible."

She snorted. "I'm Rae Toma. I can do anything."

"Except shoot a bow."

Rae smacked him on the arm. "The bow is a coward's weapon. I have no interest in such a thing."

He chuckled. "Don't feel bad, Rae. We all fail sometimes."

"I didn't fail," she snapped. "I lost interest."

"You snapped your bow in half and threw the arrows like a spear," Aram reminded her.

"And it worked just as well."

"It was a disaster."

"Exactly."

Aram chuckled. "At least there's *something* I can best you at."

"There's a lot you can best me at." Rae removed her friend's drawing from her pocket. "I wish I could give you something like this."

"You used to compose," Aram said. "How about you write me a song?"

"I'll see what I can do."

A new, comfortable silence stretched between them and, slowly, her

THE STORM GATHERS

thoughts turned back to the Evrice planes.

Listen, her mother had said.

So Rae did.

There was a strange sound coming from the pit. Two high notes repeating over and over. Interesting, but not particularly helpful. There was something else, too. A deeper set of notes, one that seemed to come from the ground itself. The two sounds clashed together, canceling each other out when they met.

She froze. There was another sound. It was different, smaller, and it seemed to grow louder, as if moving towards her. Frowning, Rae got to her feet, head swiveling as she searched for the source.

There!

A dark shape loomed above her. She opened her mouth to cry a warning to Aram, but was abruptly cut off as something hard slammed into her.

A moment later, the world exploded.

FORTY-THREE

A lana sat on the beach, her back leaning against the smooth bark of one of the many trees lining the barrier between sand and dirt. Wren was somewhere behind her, making a racket as he failed to untangle a bird from one Maria's snares.

She turned her attention to the sea, where Nessa's ship was anchored. It was too far away to make out any details, but she knew it was now occupied by the rest of their companions. The five of them were taking stock of the damage the xygriths had done to the vessel and cataloging any usable supplies their enemy had left.

Due to his injuries, Wren had been forced to stay behind.

Alana had volunteered to stay with him.

"How much longer do you think they'll take?" she called, hoping he could hear her over his own cursing.

A few seconds later, the sailor appeared beside her, limping slightly from the wound in his leg. "Normally, I would say they should have been back by now. But given all the bickering they'll have gotten into…" His voice trailed off as if doing some complex calculation. "I would guess we have at least another few hours left to wait. Possibly days."

Alana rolled her eyes. "Helpful."

He threw her a knowing look. "If I didn't know any better, I'd say you were worried about them."

"As charming as this island is, I would prefer to get off it as soon as possible," she lied. "No offense to your company."

Wren settled down beside her. "None taken."

Alana let out a soft sigh, content to sit in silence. It was a skill she prided herself on. The art of silence was one that many dismissed, but she'd found that most people couldn't stand the quiet, especially while in the presence of another.

Still, she didn't mind when Wren spoke again. "Sometimes I wonder what Penn would think of all this," he murmured. "I taught him how to read a few years ago and he always liked adventure books the best. He got so excited every time we set sail. A new adventure. New challenges." A moment of silence. "It's not fair a boy like that should be killed, and people like you and me survive."

"He was brave."

"He was stupid."

Alana smiled faintly. "I wish there were more people like him in this world. People who are brave and foolish. It's been hundreds of years since we had a proper hero."

Wren closed his eyes briefly and when he opened them, Alana saw that they were rimmed with red. "Penn was *good*. Better than any of us on board Abin's ship. Maybe it's because he was young, but I know he was better than me at that age. He should have lived. Out of all of us, it should have been him. We've only made this world worse, but I think Penn might have been the one to make it better. I—" He sucked in a breath. "I'm sorry, Alana, I just—" He rubbed a hand over his face. "I shouldn't be dumping all of this on you."

"I knew Penn's brother," Alana whispered. "We were friends. He was the only other person I had besides Arya. I tried to keep him a secret, but my mother found out about him eventually and…" She sighed. "I honestly don't know what happened to him—whether she killed him or simply sent him away. But by the time I had the resources and influence to find out, any trace of him had been erased." A pause. "His name was Landon."

Wren sucked in a breath. "Alana—"

"I tried to help Penn," she continued. "I knew of Abin's reputation, so I sent him a letter suggesting he take him onto his crew. This trip…I just wanted make sure he was happy." She shook her head. "I should have stayed away."

"What happened wasn't your fault," Wren said.

"Yes, it was. I never should have gotten involved in Penn's life. I rushed our escape. I—" She waved a hand in the air, cutting herself off. "I don't want to argue, Wren. I am simply telling you this in order to illustrate a point I'm about to make. As terrible as it is to have people taken away from you, the only other option is to never have anyone." Alana turned her attention back to the ocean. "You need to choose which pain you are more able to handle. Loss or loneliness."

"You chose loneliness?"

"Yes," she murmured. "Or, I tried to, at least."

Wren watched her for a moment before asking. "Do you regret it?"

"No." She took a breath. "Everyone I have ever truly cared about has eventually been taken from me. Letting people get close—it only ends in death and, unfortunately, it's never my own."

"What about Maria?" Wren questioned. "The two of you are friends. I saw it the first day aboard Abin's ship."

Alana was quiet for a moment. "Our friendship is complicated. It is made even more so by the nature of our positions, but there is nothing I would not do for her." She cast Wren a sidelong look. "But you must not tell her that. If you do, I'll never hear the end of it."

The sailor smiled. "I promise."

"How's it looking?" Wren asked when the rest of their crew finally made it back to shore.

"The hull is intact," Sarasin said. "There's some damage to the mast and sails, but we think we can repair them with the supplies we found." He looked at Layla, who was grinning like a child with a secret. He nudged her slightly with an elbow. "The supplies?"

The soldier coughed. "Right, well, upon careful examination, I've decided the mercenaries had good supplies." She exchanged a look with Maria. "*Very* good supplies."

Wren threw the two older men a questioning look. "What does that mean?"

Johnathan sighed. "They found Nessa's store of wine."

"Very good wine," Maria added helpfully. She reached into one of the lifeboats and pulled out a bottle. "See?"

"It is good," Kaius agreed.

"You were supposed to be watching them," Alana said, directing the statement at Sarasin and Johnathan.

Her guard lifted his shoulders in a shrug. "They're fast. And sneaky."

"We are," Maria said, nodding emphatically. "Very sneaky." She took a step towards Alana, nearly tripping over her own feet before Sarasin reached forward and steadied her.

"Besides the wine," Wren said, "did you bring us anything to eat?"

"I take it that means you weren't able to conquer Maria's snares," Johnathan said.

Wren shrugged. "I'm a sailor, not a butcher."

Maria snorted and crossed her arms. "And what is that supposed to mean?"

"No fighting," Layla said with a lazy wave of her hand. "I'm too dizzy. Maybe later." She collapsed beside Wren.

The sailor wrapped an arm around her shoulders.

Alana glanced sideways at the couple lying beside her. "Can someone please get them away from me?"

Layla stuck out her tongue before climbing clumsily to her feet, dragging Wren along with her. The two began the return journey to the camp while Johnathan, Sarasin, and Kaius unpacked the lifeboats as Maria supervised.

"Would you like some?" the tipsy woman asked, holding out the dark green bottle of red liquid.

"Not tonight, Mari."

Maria expelled air loudly through her nose. "Where is the woman that used to drink through the nights with me?"

Johnathan's turned to face his fellow guard. "You did *what*? You were supposed to be protecting her!"

"In my defense, she can be very persuasive," Maria said.

"*You* brought the wine, Mari," Alana reminded her.

The woman made a dismissive gesture. "Semantics."

Johnathan looked ready to argue, but Sarasin laid a hand on his shoulder. "Let's take this back to camp," he said, gesturing to the supplies. He nodded to Maria. "You can take the wine."

"Will do!"

Johnathan rolled his eyes as the Yovari bounded after them, holding a crate clanking with bottles.

Alana watched them go. Neither she nor Kaius saying a word until their company was out of earshot.

"You coming?" he finally asked.

"I'd rather stay here," she replied. "It's comfortable."

"How are you…" He made a vague gesture towards her. "Faring?"

"I'm fine." Alana cocked her head to the side, noting his leaning posture and the slight glaze of his eyes. "You're drunk."

"Maybe a little." He nodded to the ground beside her. "Can I sit?"

"I think you'd better," she said, unable to contain her smile as he took a swaying step forward.

He half-sat, half-crashed into the sand beside her. "I don't usually drink," he confessed. "But Maria and Layla are very persuasive. And very good at consuming liquor." He yawned and sank into a horizontal position.

"You should sleep," Alana told him.

"Not yet. I…" he yawned, "want to show you something."

In the distance, a chorus of voices rose, forming what was probably meant to be a song.

"They're not very good," Kaius observed.

"No," Alana agreed. "They're not." She looked down at him. "What do you want to show me?"

"Oh, right." He ran a hand over his face then gesture to the spot beside him. "Lay down. I want to read your fortune in the stars."

Alana raised an eyebrow. "You're a Starreader?"

"My grandmother was," he said. "She taught my father, who taught me." When Alana didn't move, he gave her a crooked smile. "Come now, *Kiydra*, indulge me this."

"I think you've indulged enough for one night, pirate."

Kaius chuckled. "I love that sharp tongue of yours." His eyes turned imploring. "Please."

Alana settled down beside him.

"I need your hand," Kaius said. She obliged him, and he took her hand in his, raising it to the sky with her palm towards the stars. He turned her hand until the tips of each of her fingers covered the stars of Tecqal, the First Dragon. "Now, my little dragon, let us see what the stars reveal."

Alana fought the urge to roll her eyes as Kaius took her hand once more. He kept her thumb on Tecqal's star, but twisted her palm until her fingers aligned with new stars in the sky. After a moment, made a low sound in his throat, then adjusted her hand back to its original position. He did the same process with each of her fingers, holding on Tecqal's constellation and turning her hand to fit others. When he was finally finished, Alana dropped her hand and raised her eyebrow at him.

"So? What do the stars say?"

Kaius cleared his throat. "I have no idea. I've forgotten what each constellation and star means. But I'm fairly sure it shows that you're a terrifying woman with the eyes of a fallen star who can reduce her enemies to ash with a single look." There was a pause, then he added, "and you'll fall in love with a dashing pirate from the North."

Alana's lips quirked up into a wry smile.

He nudged her with his elbow. "You liked that reading, huh?"

"I find it amusing, but untrue."

"I may have taken a few creative liberties."

Shaking her head, Alana climbed to her feet. "I'll be back in a minute."

"I'll be here," he called.

"That's because you're too drunk to move," she replied over her shoulder.

She returned a few minutes later with a cup of water.

Kaius sniffed at it. "What is this?"

"Wine," she lied.

"It doesn't smell like wine."

"It's a special kind."

He gave her a suspicious look. "I'm not sure I believe you."

Alana fixed him with an angry stare, which the pirate returned with a grin before lifting the cup to his lips and draining it in one gulp. She settled down beside him.

There was a breath of silence, then Kaius said, "The air is different around you. Easier. Quieter." He looked up at her. "It terrifies me, but I'm not afraid of you. Isn't that strange?"

Alana didn't respond and instead sat in silence, listening to his drunken musings that slowly became more incoherent as sleep took him. She fidgeted with the bird pendant hanging from her neck. Despite their conversation after the attack, she still wanted to run. It hurt, and she hated it. But the pain was also familiar, and that was enough to encourage her to keep going.

What would happen if she faced her monsters?

Alana looked down at Kaius's sleeping face. "You terrify me too," she told him because she knew he couldn't hear. "In the best and the worst ways. And I wish you were truly afraid of me. Because all I can do is lead you down a road of darkness."

Kaius shifted suddenly, one eye opening a crack. He said in a groggy voice, "What makes you think that I'm not already on my own path of darkness, *Kiydra*? I've lived in the shadows as long as you." He gripped her hand clumsily, the drowsiness still in control. "Let me walk this road with you. If there is light at the end, we'll find it. And if all that's left is darkness, we'll conquer it together."

FORTY-FOUR

Nur stood over Aram.

Her sudden arrival from the goddess's lair had knocked him onto his back. He now lay dazed on the ground.

"Aram," she said, nudging him with her foot. "Get up. Look! I did it! I have the Compass." She held the golden piece before him. It was lighter than she expected and without the directional points. Where the N normally sat, there was a green gem.

Slowly, the spy pushed himself into a seated position.

Nur knelt down beside him. "Listen, there is a lot I need to explain, but first we have to find Rae. Where is she?"

At that, the easterner finally seemed to focus. "What do you mean? She was right beside me?"

Nur looked around the deserted forest. "Where?"

Realizing his friend was gone, Aram leaped to his feet. "Rae!"

Something scuttled in the wood, fleeing his call. It was too small to be a person.

She stood up as well. "What happened? Did something attack you guys?"

"No! She was just here!" He took a step towards the trees. "Toma!"

Still no response. Nur looked around, trying to pinpoint any sign of movement in the dark. "Rae!"

Nothing.

Was this some sort of test from Eriysha? No, that didn't sound right. This wasn't the work of gods. It was something else. Something strange.

Rae couldn't have just disappeared without a trace. But there were no new tracks on the ground and no indication of where the warrior had gone or what had happened.

Numbly, Nur met Aram's gaze. "She's gone."

FORTY-FIVE

I t took two weeks to finish the repairs to the ship. Alana helped where she could, but she ended up spending most days sitting on the beach, enjoying the music of the waves and chitter of birds in the trees.

"Our last day on the island," Sarasin said in lieu of greeting. "Where will you go next?"

It was a loaded question. "Okaro," she answered.

"Homesick, are we?"

"Desperately," she deadpanned, peering up at him. "Do you miss yours?"

"You set my home on fire."

She made a dismissive gesture. "The *Fe Ressu* wasn't your home. You were forced to leave your real home, weren't you?"

His expression didn't change, but she saw the way his shoulders tensed.

"I may not be from the South, Sarasin, but I have an ear for dialects. It's interesting, that of all the names you could have chosen for your ship, you chose one in the language of Old Suhrhys. But what is more interesting, is the meaning behind those words. *Fe entress e fe ressu si en vri elta'la.* Isn't that how the saying goes? 'By blood or by fate, we will see each other again.'"

"I would prefer we not speak of my past," Sarasin replied brusquely. "There are more relevant topics that need to be discussed."

"Or we could simply not speak at all."

Sarasin was all too eager to deny her request. "Do you plan to reclaim your crown?"

"Well, I *have* always liked shiny things."

The captain let out a huff. "You're impossible to talk to."

Alana smiled as Sarasin turned on his heel and strode off.

"You could try being nicer to him," Maria suggested, stepping from the trees and taking a seat beside her.

"I could also bite off my pinky finger."

Maria raised an eyebrow, but Alana could see the amusement in the tilt of her lips. "Do you really intend to take your mother's throne?"

"I don't know," Alana said simply. "I expect the world we left behind when this journey began will not be the same one we return to."

"What do you think has happened?"

Alana shrugged. "Pestilence, war, famine, death, the usual."

Maria chuckled. "You are a terrible person."

"If I only I were worse."

"Something to aspire to."

"Certainly."

The Yovari woman was quiet for a long moment, then she said. "I think Sarasin knows."

Alana tensed. "Has he said anything?"

"No, but he was one of Empress El-Tess's advisors, he would know about the Yovari Blood Season."

"That doesn't mean he'll put two and two together," Alana told her. "Even if he does, I don't think it's something you need to worry about." She leaned back. "In fact, I imagine he could help you. Sarasin knows the South better than I. He might be able to find hidden allies that could arrange passage for you in and out of the country without being noticed."

"I *want* to be noticed," Maria snapped. "I want them to know and see and be afraid because I'm coming for them. I want—" The Yovari sucked in a breath, cutting herself off, and lifted a hand to the leather collar that wrapped around her neck, rubbing at it absently. "Are you ready to leave?" she asked in a blatant attempt to change the subject.

Alana's eyes returned to the ocean. "No," she murmured. "I'm not."

Maria gave her a sympathetic look. "We do not have to go back."

THE STORM GATHERS

She let out a breath. "Yes, we do." Silence stretched between them until, finally, she said, "I've never thanked you, Maria—not properly—for standing by me all these years. For saving me. I don't deserve your loyalty, but I appreciate it all the same."

The other woman was quiet for a moment, then said, "Back in Yovar, I could never trust anyone. Not even my own family." She shook her head, a small smile creeping across her face. "Of all people, who knew I would come to trust Alana Zaya?"

"You have poor judgment."

"Obviously." Alana looked over, hesitated, then wrapped her arms around Maria, who stiffened in shock, then returned the gesture. "I love you, Mari. No matter what happens, please don't forget that."

"I will not."

Alana pulled back and smoothed the wrinkles out of her clothes. She cleared her throat. "Never tell anyone about that."

Maria chuckled. "I promise."

"Must I promise that as well?" another voice said.

Alana turned in time to see Johnathan emerge from the trees. She wrinkled her nose. "If you want to keep your head attached to your body, you will."

"And here I was worried you were going soft."

"Never."

Johnathan looked out to sea. "It seems our little adventure is coming to an end."

"And greater, more terrible ones await."

Maria sighed. "Why must you always be so pessimistic?"

"I have to balance out your relentless optimism."

"At least I am not superstitious like that one," the Yovari replied, jabbing a finger at Johnathan.

"I was right about the Shallows."

Alana snorted. "You were not."

"Our ship sunk as we passed them."

"Not by evil spirits, unless you consider Sarasin to be some sort of ghoul—which, admittedly, would explain a lot."

Jonathan shot her an exasperated look. "He's right. You are impossible to talk to."

She flashed him a sweet smile. "Talking about me, are you? I hope you mentioned my beautiful eyes and sparkling wit."

"At length," he deadpanned.

She smiled as Johnathan settled down beside her and Maria. The three of them stared into the horizon, and Alana's mind couldn't help but return to memories of days long past. Between the crushing weight of the Jaarin palace, there were light moments. Johnathan and Maria's bickering as the three of them played cards. Drinking with her Yovari guard during the nights and sitting with Johnathan as the sun rose in the morning.

Those days are long gone.

Alana knew in her bones that her trials were not over. If anything, they had just begun.

EPILOGUE

Maria watched as the island of Dymoura faded in the distance, the wind whipping at her loose hair.

No matter the season, the seas around Alana's homeland were the roughest in the world. Waves as tall as mountains would rise without warning to swallow ships like hungry ty'vairrs. The weather could turn in the blink of an eye and unexpected currents would appear without warning to throw you off course. But despite the dangers, Okaro was a sanctuary. A place the desperate flocked to when they were in need—Maria included.

Due to the nature of the island, people claimed that the Okarons were wild, but Maria didn't see them that way. They weren't wild. They were fearless. There was a difference.

To put it simply—the rules of Okaro were different from those of the rest of the world. But there were still rules. You didn't leave your homes during a storm—however, many fishermen still braved the water during the hours before. You didn't interact with the xygriths—although they were still revered by many. Most importantly, you bowed to whatever Zaya sat on the throne. Those, Maria had learned, were the three great rules of Okaro—and the people followed.

But Alana was different. She *was* wild. Or had been. She often snuck out during storms. She fed the xygriths. And not once had Maria seen the Okoron princess bow to her mother.

A figure joined Maria on the quarterdeck. He wasn't stiff like Johnathan or twitchy like Wren. No, Sarasin's posture was both relaxed and formal as he rested a hand against the wooden railing. She had seen it before. It was a noble's way of standing.

"Does she know?" the captain asked.

"Know what?"

"Does Alana know who you really are, Lady Kitza?"

Maria stiffened at the use of her last name. It had been years since she'd heard it. *Kitza*—the name of the greatest of the Yovar Royal Houses. A House that was now nothing but ash.

"Yes," she answered. "She does."

"Is that why you stay loyal to her?" he pressed. "Because she knows your secret?"

Maria bristled. "I *stay* because she is my friend. I know her secrets same as she knows mine. You may be clever, Sarasin, but you are not half as clever as you think you are. How long did it take you to figure out who I am? A month? Two? Alana knew after our first meeting. Do you know how? She said it was the *cadence* of my voice. Apparently, nobles from Yovar speak differently than the commoners."

Sarasin's lip twitched. "I take it you didn't like her at first?"

"My entire family had just been slaughtered. I was in hiding, and here was this princess who seemed to have everything. Of course, I hated her."

"What changed?"

The Yovari shrugged. "I realized I was wrong. Alana had nothing. Even her life was not her own. You could say we have that in common." She turned her attention back to the sea. "I am not naïve, Sarasin. I know what she is. I know what is coming and what will happen if we cannot stop it."

She felt his eyes on her.

"You believe in the prophecy?"

"I believe in Alana and I believe in myself. The rest does not matter. Not to me." Maria shook her head. "These monsters that live inside us. We run from them, we fight them, but what would happen if we were to walk alongside them instead?"

"That is a question for the philosophers."

"What a shame, then, that they are all dead."

THE STORM GATHERS

They stood in silence for a few moments before Sarasin finally left her side to join Layla by the rigging.

Maria's eyes focused on Alana once more. Although the fires caused by the xygriths had masked it, she recognized the damage that had befallen the area where Nessa had died. The withered, dead plants a mirror of what she had witnessed in Jaarin all those years ago.

Maria had been present the day the blackness had wrapped around Alana's body like a cocoon, killing everything it touched. No one else knew the truth of what had happened in the gardens. Not even Johnathan. But Maria would never forget.

It was the day the Okaron princess had become the Queen of Darkness, and the First Empress's words were proven true.

Alana Zaya would bring the world to ruin.

HARDCOVER EXCLUSIVE SCENE

N ekoda Juni, E'tresal to the Yovar Royal Council, sat in a tower that touched the clouds. The Tower of Saints was once the greatest piece of human engineering—a wonder to behold. With over a thousand steps and fifty floors, it was the tallest building in the world, complete with five different lifts that reached the top. Now, the jewel of his country was nothing more than a forgotten relic.

He tapped a rhythm on the table. It was the same sound the Shadow Fire gave off. He wasn't certain why he could hear it, while others couldn't, but he attributed it to his ancestry. His blood. The blood of Saint Alexis of the Salt Isles. Where there once had been two families of that line, now there was only one. And he was the only member of his family that could hear the music. The magic.

He stared up at the ceiling, where ten panels represented each of the Royal Houses. Ten sides enclosed the room with windows on every other panel. In front of him was a pentagonal table with the space for every member of the Council. A chamber of perfect geometric design.

The room represented order at its finest. Yovar was a country known for eccentricities and chaos, but their government—the heart of the country— had always been an organized system. And that was why this room—this table—should not have been empty.

It was the turn of the month. Tradition, custom, and even the gods-damned constitution—the foundation of Yovar—dictated that the five Council members were to meet at the beginning of every moon cycle.

It was the *law*. But no one cared for laws anymore. They didn't care about order. Only power.

Even Nekoda's own House had encouraged him not to come today. They were cowards. And fools. They saw danger lurking in every corner but refused to acknowledge the sword pressed against their throat. They didn't understand—*couldn't* understand—that Yovar was doomed. Their government was no longer a true government. There was no more discussion. Only letters passed in secret and shadowy alliances. It was no way to run a country. They were splitting apart, just like Jaarin was without its Queen of Darkness.

Nekoda closed his eyes as he waited. Hopeful that someone would show up. *Anyone*. No one did.

He shouldn't have been surprised. And he certainly shouldn't have been sad. Three years ago, there hadn't even been a Blood Season. He supposed there was no need for it now, anyway, as the Council no longer mattered. The ranks didn't matter. *Nothing* mattered anymore.

The destruction had begun with the fall of House Kitza. They had once been the greatest of the Yovar Royal Houses, blessed with the blood of the saint. Now, they were nothing but ash. And he, Nekoda Juni, had been the one to light the match. Had he known the consequences of his betrayal, he would have let himself burn with them.

He snorted as the thought passed through his mind. It was a lie. The kind he would tell his grandchildren or send in a letter to one of the Houses to earn sympathy. Nekoda didn't regret what he'd done. But he regretted his guilt-ridden weakness in the aftermath. He should have been a leader—he should have stood strong and demanded order. Instead, he'd let the Council dissolve.

"Well, now, isn't this a sorry sight? The E'tresal, the most powerful of the Yovar Royal Council—sitting alone in an empty room. I suppose when your greatest legacy is the betrayal of the last E'tresal, people aren't so willing to trust you."

Nekoda shot to his feet and wrapped a hand around the hilt of his sword. He blinked the light from his eyes, expecting to come face to face with a small militia. Instead, the only person standing before him was a young woman. Woman may have been a stretch as Nekoda doubted she had made it beyond her teenage years.

"How did you get in here?" he demanded. "Did one of the Houses send you?" He didn't think so. Her accent was strange. In fact, the more he looked at her, the more he realized just how strange this girl was. Her hair was yellow at the root, fading into orange, red, then black. Her eyes were a deep amber and seemed to glow.

"Which question would you like me to answer first?"

Nekoda frowned. "What?"

"You asked two questions. Do you want me to answer them in order, or is there one that should take priority?"

"I…" Nekoda couldn't even remember his questions, let alone which one he'd asked first. "Just…let me know who you are."

"I have no idea. Does anyone? Does anyone *really* know who they are?" She cocked her head to the side. "Do you? More importantly, do you *like* who you are?"

Nekoda withdrew his sword. "What is this? Are you mocking me? I am E'tresal. I am the leader of my House! Despite what you may have heard, I am not some doddering old man you can—"

The girl pressed her fingers into her ears. It was the act of a child, and the shock of seeing such a petty gesture brought Nekoda's rant to a halt.

Once she was satisfied that he was no longer speaking, the girl smiled and removed her fingers. "Are you done? Good. Since you refuse to ask the *right* questions, I will save us both some time and pretend you are intelligent." She cleared her throat. "My name is Dawn and I am here at the behest of the Aaran empress who has asked me to pass along a message."

"Kyrin sent you?" Gods, that woman certainly kept strange company.

"That is her name," Dawn confirmed. "Although I suggested she change it. I picked out my name, you know? It took me ages to decide. Do you like it?"

"Dawn? It…it is a fine name." What was wrong with this girl? And who in their right mind would trust her with a message of any importance?

"Well, obviously, it's a fine name. I wouldn't have chosen it if it weren't. But my brother—stars above—he has no creativity. I'm positive he just copied me." She waved a hand. "But that's not what I asked. I asked if you liked dawn?" She gestured to the morning light come through the windows.

Nekoda tried to rub his temple, only to realize he was still brandishing his sword. He sheathed the weapon. He couldn't kill this girl, no matter how tempting the idea was at the moment.

"Yes," he said wearily. "I do. May I have the empress's letter now?"

Dawn released a disappointed breath. "Fine. Stars, you're no fun to play with." She reached into her jacket pocket and removed a small scroll. "I wanted to fold this into a dragon, but Her Excellency gave me express directions not to. Shame, don't you think?"

Ignoring her. Nekoda took the scroll and broke the empress's seal. He unraveled the paper and read the words.

The mountains have awakened.

Nekoda's blood ran cold. He turned the paper over, searching for further explanation, but it was blank.

"What is this?" he demanded. "Why would...?" He trailed off as his eyes met an empty room. Dawn had disappeared. Stuffing the scroll into his pocket, Nekoda hobbled to the door. He threw it open and looked at his guards. "The girl who was just here. Which way did she go?"

"The girl?"

"Yes, the one with the strange hair—where did she go?"

"No one has passed by us, E'tresal."

Nekoda shook his head. No. No, they were lying. This was some sort of trick. He pulled out the scroll and waved it in the air. "She was here. She gave me this!"

His guards exchanged a look. "Apologies, My Lord, but we didn't see anyone. Perhaps they used a secret entrance?"

Nekoda hesitated. Yes, that made sense. Didn't it? The only other explanation was that he was going mad. He looked over the piece of paper. There was no signature from the empress, only her seal. And such things could be faked, couldn't they? This was some sort of joke perpetrated on him by one of the other Houses.

Nekoda walked to one of the lamps lighting the hallway and dropped the small scroll into the fire.

Straightening his robes, he made a motion to his guards and began to walk down the hall to the first of the five lifts. He would not allow himself to be the fool again. He was smarter than this—smart enough not to waste his morning in an empty room that would never again be filled.

The other Houses thought that they could manipulate him—an old man with a guilty conscience. But he was more than that. Much more. He was Nekoda Juni. He had the blood of the saints. He was E'tresal of the Yovar Royal Council. And he was finished with living by laws that no longer mattered.

They wanted to rule in chaos? *Fine.*

He would show them what true chaos was.

Acknowledgments

First and foremost, I owe a huge thank you to Zara Hoffman, my editor and the founder of Inimitable Books. You have quite literally made my dreams come true.

Thank you to Keylin Rivers, who designed this beautiful cover. And Grayson Wilde, who made the map.

Finally, thank you to my friends and family. Especially Stella. I love you.

ABOUT THE AUTHOR

Maelan Holladay was born and raised in the bay area. She likes rock music, dragons, and stories about villains who conquer the world. Currently, Maelan is pursuing a bachelor's degree in animal biology.